**Strange Beginnings**
*Vamp Squad Series, Book 1*

I0549504

**The Death of Innocence**
*Vamp Squad Series, Book 2*

**Other Books by Miriam Matthews:**

The Ghost of Port Chicago
The Good, The Bad, and the Bet

# The Secrets Of San Leyre

## Vamp Squad Series: Book 3

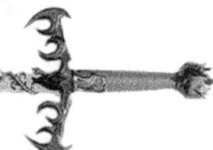

## by Miriam Matthews

# The Secrets of San Leyre
*Vamp Squad Series: Book 3*

By Miriam Matthews

Published by Miriam Matthews
Edition 1.2018.v3HC/DIG

Cover Design by Miriam Matthews

Hard Copy Production 1.2018.v3HC by CreateSpace
www.createspace.com
Digital Production 1.2018.v3DIG by Smashwords
www.smashwords.com

Published in both paperback and digital format by
Miriam Matthews, and available at most mail-order or Internet
providers.

*This book is a work of fiction. Any reference to persons, living,
dead or undead, or places, events or locales is purely for the
purpose of enhancing the story. The main characters are
productions of the author's imagination and used fictitiously.*

ISBN: 978-0-991455-8-4 (Digital)
ISBN: 978-0-991455-9-1 (Paperback)

## Dedication

To all people, alive and undead, who fight the battle of PTSD in all its hurtful and traumatizing forms – you are heroes in my book. Keep the fight alive!

As always, to my husband, Timothy. Your love and support and hours of arguing over words and semantics has made me a better (and slower!) writer. And a very frustrated, but grateful partner.

To my Cuz, Celeste, who gave me the idea of a sexy, blonde, French vampire in the first place. Your namesake lives on – undead, of course.

## Note to Readers

If foreign words are not written in English or using the English alphabet, they have been phoneticized from the text of the actual language.

# The Secrets of San Leyre
## *Vamp Squad Series:Book 3*

Author's Cheat-Sheet: Because this is the third book in my Vamp Squad Series, I have included an outline of the major people in my wonderful world of the Vamp Squad! The VS Team and Zoeltel Coven continue to grow, adding new characters and coven members along the way, so this may be helpful telling the live from the dead, and the undead. I have taken great artistic license with historical figures, events, agencies, and locations for the enhancement of the fiction I create. After all, it is fiction!

### Monique's Family

**Duke Pierre Laroque Mariquiesse Merchant**: Monique's Father
**Duchess Fabienne Eloissie Laroquess Merchant**: Monique's Mother
**Dowager Duchess Alys Marie Talondue Merchant**: Monique's Grandmother
**Duke Laurice Quessique Talondue Merchant**: Monique's Grandfather
**Phillipe LeGlaute, Duc d'Orleans**: Monique's Sire (maker)

### The Vamp Squad

**Colonel Frank Maddox**: Commander of the Vamp Squad. Human.

**Captain Robert Devlin**: Vice Commander of the Vamp Squad and Frank's best friend. Human.

**Sergeant Milo Miller**: IT NCO, Logistics NCO, Supply NCO, and all round support person. Human.

**Bear**: Vamp Squad Special V-Force Soldier. The huge Army Specialist Greg Heightner known as *the Bear,* signed up for the US Army through the buddy plan with Trevor *the Tank* Canfield. He automatically got every assignment his buddy did, including the Vamp Squad. Human.

**Tank**: Vamp Squad Special V-Force Soldier. Trevor *the Tank* Canfield earned his name by braking out three soldiers being held prisoner by the Taliban. He literally broke through the walls of the cell with his shoulders. Human.

**Lieutenant Harold Previn**: Head bean counter, hater of vampires and governmental watchdog of the Vamp Squad. He destroyed a coven of vampires that included his sister. Human and dirtball.

**Q2 (Henry Rollins):** The squad's Armorer and tech geek. Inventor and builder of extraordinary tactical equipment. He once compared himself to a second generation Q in the James Bond series. The nickname stuck. Human.

**Ted Vanderloss**: Civilian asset and basic all round great guy from the very beginning. Human.

**Doctor Helga Anderson**: Brilliant doctor recruited from the CDC to research VMD… and other things as needed along the way. Human.

**Captain Casey Calhoun**: Vamp Squad pilot and lover of Pop-tarts. Human, we think.

**Elizabetta Zoeltel**: Coven Mistress, daughter of Dracula and surrogate mother to Susannah. Vampire.

**Susannah Maddox**: Daughter of Frank Maddox and reason for the development of the Vamp Squad – see Book 2. Turned into a vampire during her first college Spring Break. Vampire.

**Natalia Vyrubova:** Russian Countess from old money, protector of the descendants of the Russian royal family, wife of Yuri Milassoviech whom she liberated from the Taliban and turned – see Book 1. Vampire.

**Yuri Milassoviech:** Russian Captain, Vamp Squad Operative and transporting machine! Husband of Natalia. Vampire.

**Monique Alys Merchant**: Vamp Squad operative liberated by the Vamp Squad from the torturous hands of the monks at the Monastery of San Salvador de Leyre. Susannah's surrogate sister and best friend. Turned by Phillipe LeGlaute, Duc d'Orleans during the French Revolution, she was almost destroyed as the monks of the monastery attempted to 'remove the Devil from her soul.' Vampire.

**MorningStar:** Vamp Squad operative and Kaw Tribal Skinwalker. She was found and recruited in the third year of the Vamp Squad's conception. Her vampiric gifts include a special connection to the elementals (earth, wind and fire). Vampire.

*******************CLASSIFIED: TOP SECRET *******************

# TOP SECRET

*******************CLASSIFIED: TOP SECRET *******************

## Center for Disease Control (CDC)
## Medical Alert (Report Date: 22 JULY 1954)

**<u>Vampticious Meticulosus Deliriotum</u>** *n*
*(Also called VMD or Vampire Virus)*

1) A contagious virus causing an individual-specific genetic mutation following a death-like comatose state. The VMD virus is transmitted through blood-to-blood transfer, the VMD T-cells retain the base genetic strain of the parent virus thus providing a genetic link to the parent and progeny virus and host.

2) A virus that causes death and then rebirth as a vampire – in European folklore; a dead person who rises from the grave to live off the blood of humans by biting the neck and sucking blood through extended fangs.

**MISCELLANEOUS INFO:** Infected individuals initially enter a coma, which imitates a death-like state while VMD begins to mutate the genetic code and physical body. As the virus grows and multiplies, more mutations occur and initial mutations become enhanced. Continued introduction of the parent virus speeds the process while increasing specific side effects including; (1) bone and joint pain, (2) muscle growth and extreme cramping, (3) development of extended canine teeth as a feeding mechanism, (4) the need for additional amounts of plasma and blood products to sustain mutations and tissue repair, (5) enhanced metabolic recovery rates, (6) increased cerebral tissue functionality (up to 98% tissue usage), (7) heightened cell replacement, (8) low body temperature accommodating hyper-metabolic rates, (9) temporary psychosis including Obsessive Compulsive Disorder, Narcissistic Personality Disorder and/or Sexual Addiction, (10) VMD specific-allergic reactions (sun, silver, some kinds of water, garlic, etc.)

**PROGNOSIS:** Genetic mutations of VMD are irreversible and continually adapt to accommodate the apparent survival instinct of the virus (unsubstantiated theory; Dr. Helga Anderson, US Services Institute of Genetic Study, Walter Reed National Military Medical Center, Bethesda, Special Projects Department). Mutated individuals seem to develop extraordinary abilities, however, individuals lack adequate melanin in the skin causing a severe allergy to ultraviolet radiation (sunlight). In reaction to this allergy, VMD initiates a sleep cycle in its host causing extreme exhaustion and weakness during daylight hours. A mutated individual's cell structure no longer contains the human genetic code, instead possessing deoxyribonucleic acid, or DNA with 3 chromosomes in a triple helix design.

\*\*\*\*\*\*\*\*\*\*\*\*\*\*\*\*\*\*\*CLASSIFIED: TOP SECRET \*\*\*\*\*\*\*\*\*\*\*\*\*\*\*\*\*\*

# TOP SECRET

\*\*\*\*\*\*\*\*\*\*\*\*\*\*\*\*\*\*\*CLASSIFIED: TOP SECRET \*\*\*\*\*\*\*\*\*\*\*\*\*\*\*\*\*\*

## Chapter 1

### Bible Babble

For from within, out of the heart of man,
Come evil thoughts, sexual immorality, theft, murder,
Adultery, coveting, wickedness, deceit, sensuality, envy, slander,
pride, and foolishness.
All these evil things come from within, and they defile a person.
*The Holy Bible, Mark 7:21-23*

So…from within, out of the heart of woman, comes…
What?

*Monique Alys Merchant, Operative*
*Vamp Squad*
*Olney, Maine 2015*

Christmas Eve, Paris, France, 1792.

"Monique, you are now a grown woman. Pay attention to your station and manner. Do not leave the side of Ansell. He is charged with protecting you, dear." She placed a light kiss on her daughter's cheek. "I shall expect a complete report on everything! I will dread missing High Mass, but grand-mère is ivre once again. I must see she does not hurt herself… or anyone else. Au revoir, chère."

"Oui maman!" Monique allowed Ansell to help her into the family carriage. She was going to High Mass at the Sainte Chapelle, all by herself.

Just like a grand lady!

In the family carriage, displaying their noble crest across each door!

With her own footman.

"Do not worry, maman. I shall recount everything, just for you when I return. And I shall pray for King Louis and for us all."

"Do so my child, for these times are pressing. I fear for us all in this time of discontent. Be safe chère. Your father has grand plans for your marriage this coming year."

Monique's hand flew to her lips.

A marriage for her?

This coming year?

Who could her father have in mind for his only daughter?

Monique sat alone on the velvet seat of the family carriage as it bumped along the cobblestone streets of Paris. Monique Alys Merchant, daughter of Duke Pierre Laroque Mariquiesse Talondue Merchant, was to be married next year! The young woman could not stifle the childish giggle that welled up inside. Like a bubbling fountain, her joyous sound filled the carriage.

Ansell kept his eyes on the floor and his face as cold as the marble floor of the Duke's luxurious home. The chit was spoiled beyond belief while his people starved in the streets. She was filled with happiness while mothers cried for their sick children and fathers died in their hovels.

Ansell allowed a touch of frown to ghost his shadow. The food she left behind on her plate at dinner would feed his brother's family, but the cursed Duke was resolute – no scraps to be shared. Every evening the housekeeper piled the leftovers in the pig pen while the Duke relieved himself over the mess. His food would not fuel the rebels who defied the government and demonstrated in the streets. The egotistical man only saw the revolution as a joke for the unclean masses, while he contemplated a politically strategic marriage for his young daughter and his coffers. Ansell sighed.

Monique was spoiled, but even Ansell had to admit she had a good heart. He'd seen her many times with her grand-mère. The loving touches. The care behind each carefully formulated sentence. The old woman lost her wits years before when her husband, the old Duke, was hung by rioters at the beginning of the revolution. The old Duke of Merchant was a mean cuss and violent as all hell could produce. He treated his workers like animals and sorely used their wives and daughters whenever the mood possessed him.

It was little wonder Alys Marie found him hanging from a peach tree in the orchard one morning. His face was bloated and blackened. Someone had cut his genitals away and stuffed them in his mouth. The maids say Alys Marie ran through the main house, scratching her eyes out and babbling about meeting the Devil hisself. After that, she was never the same. But Monique did not care. She tended her beloved grand-mère with sweet care and devotion. They spent many hours in the sunny salon, stitching and giggling about all sorts of nothings. Like two children making up games and rhymes, Monique sat patiently until Alys Marie would lapse into sleep… or simply lapse.

Ansell chanced a glance at his charge for the evening. The child was almost a woman and as delicately beautiful as the angels that graced the windows of the Sainte Chapelle. Her golden hair was styled in high fashion and perfectly powdered to a glistening pale gold. Statuesque in the gilded fashion of the day, her regal bearing rarely allowed view of the sixteen year-old girl beneath the powder and paint. Her slippers were sewn to match the pale blue satin of her skirt and were demurely tucked beneath the lace edged petticoat that peeked from beneath the hem of her gown. All together she was a very appealing package some old influential politician, or Lord would have, come spring. The dowry her father would settle on his choice would be as pretty as the daughter he will deal away. Perhaps a member of King Louis' inner circle would win the privilege of tasting her virginal delights, if, in fact, there was a King Louis come next spring.

A man such as he, a simple footman in the employ of the Duke, would never taste such a morsel. He was not considered fit to even touch the muddy hem of her dress. But a man could fantasize. Ansell licked his lips and clasped his hands over his lap to hide the results of his imagination jutting harshly against the linen of his uniform pants.

"Ansell, look!" Monique bounced in her seat. "It is a parade. Or some kind of celebration."

There were people in the streets with flags and torches.

They were singing a familiar song.

"Peatre, turn the carriage. Quickly!" Ansell shouted to the driver as he pulled the drapes together to shield Monique from view. "Peatre! Peatre! Now. Turn. We must leave this area now." The footman banged on the roof of the carriage. "Mistress, pull your cloak over your head and get down."

"But Ansell, They are…" Monique screamed as the coach rocked precariously. The song had stopped and angry shouts surrounded the carriage. "What is happening, Ansell? I am afraid. Make them stop!" The carriage was rocking and Monique grabbed for the velvet handgrip next to the door.

"Cover your head. Sit still and be quiet." Ansell ordered. All stations considered, he was charged with protecting Monique.

He would do what had to be done despite his position and her station. He opened the hatch behind the driver's seat and peeked through. "Peatre?"

There was no answer from the driver.

There was no driver.

The door to the carriage flew open and filthy hands tore at Monique's cloak.

Ansell jumped between his young charge and the angry crowd. "No, leave us in peace. There is only a child here."

His words fell on deaf ears as rough hands pulled him from the carriage.

Monique screamed as her footman disappeared beneath the feet of the enraged throng. "Ansell! Don't hurt him. He's just a footman… no!" Monique felt herself lifted and dragged from the carriage. Her cloak was ripped from her body and a melee of hands tore at her clothing.

Filthy hands.

Torn and bloody claws.

The first to disappear was her mother's diamond and pearl necklace. A woman with rotten front teeth and putrid breath clawed at Monique's throat, breaking the necklace and leaving behind long deep scratches that immediately began to leak bright red blood. Panic ensued as the rioters scrambled for each scattered piece of the necklace. A tall man behind her, buried his hands in her stylishly coiffed hair dragging her backwards. Slammed up against the carriage door, her head exploded with pain. The grimey peasant tore the christening ring from her hand and bit it sharply.

"Gold! I got me gold!" He roughly searched her hands and arms for more treasure, before he tore her grand-mère's brooch from the bodice of her gown, ripping the delicate silk and lace open to her waist.

Exposed to the eyes of the thief and the crowd, Monique froze in terror. Tears began to flow and she did not know what to do. As a lady of the estate, she had never been handled in such a manner. She turned to hug the door of the carriage and held on for dear life. The carved family crest on the door dug into her wet cheek as the crowd snatched and ripped at what was left of her clothes and shoes. Soon all that she wore was her chemise and pantaloons, but still she clung to the door of the carriage.

It was all she knew.

Two burly men carrying heavy axes smashed the door from

the carriage and Monique was lifted from the ground and hoisted above the heads of the crowd. Everywhere shouts of *off with her head,* and *kill the bourgeoisie slut* hammered in her ears. Still she clung to the shards of the broken door, pulling it ever tighter to her face. Hands grabbed at her body. Fingers ripped at her hair. Blood soaked her chemise and stuck to her skin.

What was happening?

It was Christmas Eve.

She was only going to church.

To pray.

For King Louis.

For all souls.

This could not be happening.

Monique screamed again and again. With each scream the crowd became louder and more violent, fueled by her pathetic pleas. Her body moved above the seething mass enduring all manner of insults and attacks, as her mind shut out the scene, clinging as she did, to the wooden scraps and the last vestige of her family's honor. When she thought she would surely die at the hands of these dissidents, a single gun shot rang out above the din.

Monique prayed it had pierced her heart and she would die quickly. She'd heard the house maids talk of brutal assaults against women and the torrid rapes of young innocents. The reality of her situation struck like a lightning bolt.

The crowd hushed and lowered her to her feet. Moving back in a circle, they surrounded her with empty space, but still hurling insults and vicious accusations.

Monique stumbled but stood, lowering the precious shield from her face to see where the shot came from.

In the middle of the street rode a man dressed in the uniform of the Royal Guard, complete with a huge hat of embellished fur. The horse upon which he rode was the largest, pure-white beast Monique had ever seen. More to the point, his hands held a musket, aimed directly at the burly man who'd stolen Monique's ring. Behind her savior rode six mounted guardsmen, all armed and wearing uniforms of the same style and color. Torch light bounced off the gold braid edging their red coats.

The crowd parted as the soldier rode forward, training his musket on first one rabble-rouser, then another. "Leave this one alone. Can you not see she is a child? Have the French sunk so low, that now we kill our innocent children in this civil war? Do we now hold our children responsible for their parentage?" His guardsmen fanned out behind him, intently watching the crowd with carefully aimed muskets. The man rode directly to Monique who cowered alone in the middle of the crowd, trying to cover herself as best she could.

Dismounting with practiced grace, he unbuttoned his coat and slipped it around Monique's shoulders. "Allow me, Mademoiselle."

Saved from certain death, she stared up into the man's gorgeous brown eyes. "Phillipe Le Glaute Comte d' LeEgalité, at your service."

Of all the fairytales and legends Monique and her grand-mère shared secretly together, her favorite was the one where the princess of some far away land was stolen by ugly monsters in the night. Her father searched the land day and night for her, but to no avail. The entire country mourned the loss of their fair princess until one day a knight in shining armor, riding a pure white steed, came to the village. He promised to find the princess and free her if the King would give the knight his daughter's hand in marriage. The King agreed and so off the knight went to find his future wife. He searched high and low, found the monster's lair, fought a gruesome battle and freed the princess. They were wed and lived happily ever after.

Just like in the fairytale, Monique's knight in shining armor appeared to save her from the monsters.

And she promptly fainted. Dead away.

Right into the waiting arms of Phillipe Le Glaute, Comte d' LeEgalité.

"Ah chère, you are safe within my arms for now." A gloved hand caressed Monique's wet and bloody cheek. "Yes, for now…"

"Sir, we should withdraw. These animals may come at any second." Phillipe's Second in Command drew his horse up next to his Commander who held Monique's limp body. He spoke quickly and quietly.

"Of course you are correct, Francoise. Do take this child from me before…" He handed Monique up to his Lieutenant and swallowed hard. "… and we shall depart from this dirty business before we, too become casualties."

Free of his burden, Phillipe swung into his saddle with a grace equal to that of his dismount. "Disband now and I shall not report this disturbance to his Majesty." He fired a single shot into the air and watched as the crowd drew back into the alleyways to take cover. Like specters dissolving with the sunrise, quietly they melted into the architecture of the city.

A lone body lay in the gutter, mangled and still.

"Ah, one less fanatic to deal with. Let us go." Phillipe motioned to his men and rode back the way he had come.

The Lieutenant cradled an unconscious Monique in his arms as he rode behind his Commander. The Count's contingent thundered through the midnight streets of Paris, riding hell-bent for election. At each intersection or square, a scout sent forward cleared the way or redirected the unit as needed. Christmas Eve in the Paris of 1792 was not safe for man, woman or child. Even the ghosts of long-dead poets feared the streets this night.

After being turned back several times, Phillipe drew his guard to him. "This will not do. We can ride the streets all night and not find a clear path. I know a place close by that will provide safe harbor until the morn, and a way to my estate." He pointed to an alley halfway down the street. It was a well known alley that lead to a central complex where the horses and men would be safe and concealed.

Francoise glanced at the young woman in his arms. "Sir, we cannot…"

"Desperate times require desperate measures, Lieutenant. What is the worst that will happen? A child's eyes will be opened to womanhood a little sooner than her marriage bed, no?" He sighed a little too heavily. "Let us, each one of us…" He pointed individually to each soldier at his command. "… make sure it is only her eyes that will be opened. She is gentry. Let her remain that way for as long as this insane world allows." With that statement, he rode toward the alley entrance and a concealed way to the establishment of one Madame Grace Elliott.

"But, Sir?" Francoise simply shook his head, adjusted Monique's weight on his lap and followed his leader through the elegant gates topped with a bronzed, linked G and E in flowery script.

The alley was dark with a single lamp light at the far end. It cast a soft yellow light on the two massive oak doors that closed the alley to any who ventured into its shadowy recesses. As the group rode toward the doors, small wooden panels in the sheer walls slid open revealing long shiny barrels. The decorative gates behind the last rider slid silently into place, efficiently trapping the seven men and one unconscious woman.

"Madame Elliott, it is I, your Duke, come to pay a visit. Open to me." Phillipe shouted toward a shuttered window above the massive doors.

"Aye Phillipe, stop yer yellin' man. My guards will open the doors in a moment. What 'er ya doin' out and about on Christmas Eve? Should ya not be home with that wench ye call a wife?" The barrels withdrew and each small window slid shut. The clinking of a chain could be heard behind the huge oak doors.

From the darkness into the light, the huge doors swung open to reveal a wide courtyard decorated with all manner of Christmas joy. Candles glowed around a central fountain strewn with holly branches and gold tipped lace. A Christmas crèche set majestically in one corner with life size figurines. Unlike Mary and Joseph of the Bible, these characters were dressed in French finery. The central staircase leading to the upper floors was festooned with waxed mulberry and holly twigs interspersed with gold foil stars and creamy silk strands.

"Mademoiselle Elliott is well prepared for the morrow, Sir." Francoise murmured under his breath as he handed Monique down to Phillipe. "I do hope you know what you are doing."

"Desperate times, Francoise, desperate times."

"For you Sir, most assuredly." The Lieutenant grinned secretly, then immediately sobered and sat stiffly upright.

"Phillipe, what have we here?" The most beautifully constructed woman in the world descended the marble stairs, one carefully placed gold slipper after another. Mademoiselle Grace Elliott was most probably the only woman on earth who completely embodied heaven within the satin and silk confines of her clothing. Her delicate features and crystal blue eyes could capture a man's soul, while her soft Scottish accent entranced his mind. What she could do with her body was no secret to most of the entire male population of greater France, and the British Empire. What she did for Phillipe was anyone's guess. But he kept her in style and comfort for a reason.

"Darling, we have rescued this child from the revolutionaries. Heaven only knows what she was doing alone in that carriage, on that street, at this time of night." He carefully laid her on a bench near the bubbling fountain.

Grace glanced appraisingly at the young woman who lay prostrate on her bench. "And heaven knows why you thought to bring 'er here, Phillipe." A slight tip of an eyebrow sent the appropriate message.

"The revolutionaries prowl the streets. They are everywhere. My men and I are not safe on the streets without more support tonight. I thought…"

"Quite the contrary, Phillipe. You did not think." Grace interrupted him before she bent and slapped Monique's face.

Phillipe caught the wince of his Second in Command out of the corner of his eye.

When the girl did not rouse, Grace slapped her again. "She is dead?" Grace smiled at Phillipe.

"No, only fainted from the trauma. Be nice, my love, she is only a child." Phillipe's men, still astride their horses, were moving toward the open doors.

"Of course, chére. Eitenne, see to the Duke's men. Leonie, call Mathilda and wake this *child*. Put 'er to bed upstairs and see to 'er needs. I'll see to the Duke's." Grace linked her arm with Phillipe's and pulled him toward the stairs.

"Mon chére, please do not call me Duke. I have taken the name Citoyen Phillipe d' LeEgalité. Louis' titles can be dangerous these days.

"Of course, mon trésor." She pushed the door at the top of the stairs open with her satin clad slipper. "Of course." Twirling like an exotic dancer, Grace pulled him through the doorway and into her elegant boudoir.

# Chapter 2

*Personal note: My grand-mère was fond of saying: when God closes a door, he opens a window.*
*Lately I find her naiveté so sweet, yet so disturbing.*
*I saw her pass from this world to the next, with a placid smile gracing her dead face.*
*Her demons chased back to the realms from which they had sprung, finally she was at peace.*
*There and then I knew, that was something I would never be.*

## Alpha and Omega?

The windows of her mind lay shut and locked tight,
Against the reality that prowled the night.

And still her world evolved.
To a bitter end, her life crawled.

Becoming something she did not want,
But given in lust, forever to haunt.

Her mind, her soul, for eternity,
Forbidden death's serenity.

*Monique Alys Merchant, Operative*
*Vamp Squad*
*Olney, Maine 2015*

Christmas Morning, Paris, France, 1792.

Citoyen Phillipe d'LeEgalité, or, as the location and climate would have it, Phillipe Le Glaute, Duc d'Orleans, third in line for the French throne, sat in an old rocking chair next to the bed of his latest unknown possession. Her soft hair, liberated from its smothering powder and secured coiffure, lay long and soft against the embroidered linens that covered her sleeping body.

Mathilda busied herself stoking the fire and bustling about the room, adjusting the thick drapes and surveying her patient.

18

"Monsieur, the girl will survive." Mathilda pressed her fingers against Monique's wrist feeling the pulse. "She is strong. She shall recover soon." The maid pressed a cool wet cloth to her patient's forehead and saw movement for the first time.

Monique heard voices, but her eyelids were too heavy to lift.

Where was she?

How did she get here?

Suddenly, the terrors of the night came back in one swift memory, assaulting her senses with violent scenes and hateful taunts.

*Run!* Her mind screamed.

Monique bolted from the bed and stumbled blindly toward…

What?

"Mademoiselle, calm yourself! You are safe." Completely taken by surprise, Mathilda ran after her charge. Grabbing Monique by the arm, she was met with flying fists and screams for help. "Mademoiselle, please…" Mathilda stepped back as Monique cowered in the corner by the closed door, batting hysterically at the mysterious attackers in her mind.

In a flash, Phillipe held Monique's face in his hands, crouching before the young woman he'd rescued from those she now tried to ward off. "Calm, child. Calm." He stroked her cheek. "You are safe and at peace in this house."

Monique felt his words sooth her scattered thoughts and still her body. She slumped against the floor and let the tears flow. Strong arms drew her from the cold tiles and carried her safe and secure to a chair near the fire.

Phillipe settled Monique on his lap as Mathilda draped a thick quilt across the young woman.

Monique buried her face in the satin ruffles of his shirt and let the sobs come.

Her fear was gone.

The pains of her attack, temporarily forgotten.

She was safe.

Or so this man who held her said.

She opened her eyes to a Bourbon royal emblem dangling from a thick golden chain lying against a matte of pale curly hair. The man's shirt opened to below her chin and she could smell the most exotic scent she had ever known. Monique snuggled in closer and wiped her eyes with a fingertip. Someone tucked a lace handkerchief into her hand and she murmured her thanks, seconds before sleep swept her into darkness.

"Shall I help you put her to bed, Sir?" Mathilda could not understand why Phillipe still held the woman on his lap. Her mistress would be furious if she saw this quaint picture of intimacy. Who was this woman that the Duc d'Orleans took such interest in her wellbeing? Madame did not recognize the girl. None of the house staff seemed to know her. Apparently, Madame Elliott had never seen her before and her mistress ran in the best of French society, on occasion.

"No. She is quiet here. I shall comfort her for a time." Phillipe studied the girl's features as he spoke. She was heavenly; an angel from above with hair as fine as silk, skin as smooth as a newborn baby's back side and a fine, voluptuous outline that spurred his senses and tickled his inquiring mind. It remained to be seen who this girl belonged to, and if he would return her to her family.

Grace Elliott was an extremely handsome woman, but their relationship cooled with his increased political intrigue. Grace looked after Grace and knew as much of the world as many men. She was a great friend and covered for him in some tight circumstances. In return, he saved her good friend, the Governor of Tuilleries Palace, when Louis Rene Quentin de Richebourg de Champcenetz was suspected of treason. At Grace's urging, Phillipe had come to the man's rescue. He could trust Grace... as long as he didn't push too far.

Monique stirred, wiggling deeper beneath the quilt. His manhood stirred as well. It was time to put the girl back to bed. He gazed at her tear-stained face and whispered, "Sleep child. Sleep until the morrow. Wake rested and clear of mind." A pale red glow lit his eyes as he concentrated for a time, before easily lifting the girl in his arms and laid her back on the bed. As his eyes cleared, he drew the covers over her and silently left the room.

It was almost daybreak. He and Grace would spend the day behind the curtains of her boudoir, between the silk sheets of her large and inviting bed. Down the hallway, he entered her room with less enthusiasm than in the past.

Mathilda took great care to avoid the Duc's sight as she crept back into Monique's room. Satisfied the girl slept un-molested, the maid returned to her room. Though the entire

National Convention adored their Citoyen Phillipe d' LeEgalité and his generosity for the cause, there were things Mathilda knew of the man and found abhorrent. The sun would be up soon and her duties would begin despite the evening's unexpected activities. Mathilda held her breath as she silently descended the back stairs. One of those unusual things she knew well about Phillipe d' LeEgalité, was his extraordinary hearing. It would not do to be caught checking up on him. She needed her soul intact when she passed from this world into God's great garden. As the door to her room closed behind her with an unavoidable clunk, Mathilda crossed herself. Twice.

******

"I have sent for the Captain of the Guard, Fabienne. What more can I do? The carriage has been found on the Rue de Tallassard." Pierre lowered his voice, pacing the floor. "Along with the bodies of Ansell and Peatre. Ansell was beaten to death and Peatre, it was a quick death. He took a bullet to the head. That is good."

At Fabienne's sharp intake of breath, the Duke looked up at his wife. "Do not misunderstand me, wife. I only meant that our daughter's body was not there." The Duke paused, surveying his distraught wife. "That means she may still be alive. Possibly she escaped and is hiding. Or possibly someone took her for ransom." The Duke stood before the full-length mirror in his wife's apartment speaking to Fabienne as if he were addressing the King's Council. "She could have been injured and is being treated at a hospital. She may have found harbor…"

"Stop!" Fabienne shrieked at her husband. "Do not expound upon your vast list of possibilities to my face. I am not some underling or a political opponent to be convinced. Find my Monique!" She leaned heavily against the polished doorway of her dressing room. "Find my daughter…"

"Our daughter." He calmly replied.

"Only when it benefits you." With that, Fabienne fled into her dressing room, slamming the door behind her.

The Duke turned to his footman who stood in the shadows, quietly observing the exchange. "The Duchess does not understand the world beyond her tapestried walls. Let us remove ourselves so she may calm herself."

With that grand statement, Pierre departed the room followed by his footman nodding in generous agreement.

Behind the dressing room door, the Duke's words could be heard clearly. Chelestienne expertly ducked, avoiding her mistress' fierce gesture. Chelestienne had been the Duchess' Lady in Waiting for several years and was well aware of her mistress' temper, and, the contentious relationship she had with her husband. Though gentile and reserved in public, as befitted a woman of her rank, Fabienne was a tigress when it came to her only daughter. Few were ever allowed to see the claws, but when they came out, all knew to beware.

All, but the Duke.

Chelestienne smirked to herself. Her mistress' husband was insufferable. And plain dull when it came to women. No wonder in twenty-five years of marriage they produced only one child, a daughter. And now that precious child was missing.

"Cheleste, what am I to do? My Monique is gone. Most assuredly dead in some dark, damp gutter." Fabienne was rapidly descending into the depression the Duchess often shared with her mother-in-law.

"My Lady, she will be found, safe and alive. I know this." Chelestienne placed her hand over her heart as a kind of sacred promise. "You will see. Do not borrow grief before it comes to the gate." She placed a cool washcloth on her Lady's forehead. Helping her to the divan, Chelestienne settled the Duchess comfortably with a soft down throw. "You must rest and conserve your strength. Monique will need you when she is found. I shall go below stairs and return to you as soon as there is news."

The Duchess patted Chelestienne's arm. "You are my savior, Cheleste. I do not think I can live if Monique is gone." Fabienne's eyes closed and her arm dropped to the coverlet.

"Yes, my Lady." Chelestienne tiptoed from the room. Her mistress would sleep for hours. Emotional upheaval always did that to her. It was better for the woman than hours of endless crying in helpless frustration.

In the kitchen, Chelestienne found the Dowager Duchess seated comfortably by the fire, stitching away on a small handkerchief. She was lost in her own world. The compact, concise letters of blue silk stood out against the soft pink satin. "Ah, Franchesca, these letters confound me so. Would that I should have married a man with a shorter name." Alys Marie giggled conspiratorially. "When Laurice returns he will be so proud."

"Oui, maman. Papa would be so proud." Chelestienne kissed the old woman's powdered cheek. Alys Marie was off in that peculiar world where her husband was whole and loving…where her children were still just that, children. Franchesca died fifteen years ago with the birth of her sixth child, but in Alys Marie's mind, her eldest daughter was still at home and had just kissed her cheek. At least the old woman would not despair for her missing granddaughter.

"Franchesca, do come and help with the setting." Cook called from the doorway to the dining room. A knowing wink told Chelestienne the summons was simply an excuse to escape Alys Marie's fantasy world. There was work to be done and information to be gleened.

"Of course, Cook. I must go Maman." Chelestienne kissed the old woman's other cheek. This simple conspiracy had played out many times over since the Dowager Duchess' mind departed with the violent death of her husband many years before.

"Off, off, off with you, chére. Go and have some fun with Cook." Alys Marie returned her attention to the initials she was embroidering. Laurice would never come home. Franchesca was gone. But the staff would never let on. They all loved the sweet, crazy old lady as they did Monique.

The old Duke was long hanged and dead, but Alys Marie blocked that out of her world some twenty years back. It was just as well. He gave her three children and years of heartache. She usually remembered the children, but not the cruelty and philandering of her husband.

Cook pulled Chelestienne into the dining room. "Have you heard anything more of our Monique?"

"Not a thing. But my Lady had such a row with the Duke. He is an arrogant bastard, that one. At least he doesn't take after his father in all ways. The Duke has called the Captain of the Guard to help with the search."

"Oui, as if that will help. Lady Monique is of the noble class. I hesitate to think what may have become of her, out there all alone." Cook shook her head sadly. "As well, I pray for Ansell's brother. Ansell kept his family fed and clothed with his position here, in this household. They do not even know he has been killed. Shush!" Cooked waved Chelestienne off as the Duke and the

Captain of the Guard entered the hallway off the dining room.

"So, my men have retrieved the carriage, Your Grace. It is... shall we say, in need of some repair." The Captain of the Guard placed a fist to his mouth and coughed slightly. "I would never presume to instruct you, Your Grace, but if I were you, I would not allow the Duchess to view the remnants. There is a great deal of blood. Whose, we cannot tell."

"Remnants?" The Duke rubbed his temple.

"The rioters were most generous with their hatred, Sir." The Captain paused. He did not wish to weigh in on the volatile political situation in France. Quite frankly, the Captain's sympathies lay with the revolutionaries.

"I understand, Captain. I am most concerned with finding my daughter. I can repair a carriage, but my daughter's reputation? I have contracted her to the Duke of Meldhiem and the date has been set for this coming spring. It is a strategic and very lucrative arrangement. You understand, Captain? I must find her post haste."

The Captain bit his lower lip. "And if she is not...pardon, Your Grace. If she has been compromised?" It was touchy territory. The Captain was well aware of the meaning behind his words, as was the Duke.

"She is my daughter, no matter her circumstances, Captain. I will deal with it."

"Of course, Your Grace." The Captain breathed a sigh of relief, bowed low and turned to leave.

"And Captain... I want to know who is responsible for this attack. That, I will also deal with." There was anger and a burning hatred in the Duke's eyes. His tone was deadly.

"Of course, Your Grace." At that, the Captain made a hasty retreat and left to join the search for the only daughter of a very wealthy, powerful and angry Duke... and an extremely revengeful father.

\*\*\*\*\*\*

Monique awoke to sunshine shimmering through the half drawn curtains of...

Where?

She looked around trying to remember where she was, and how she had gotten there, but all that came to mind was an angel of a man holding her tight, whispering to her that everything would

24

be alright.

An angel? Or a man? He was extremely handsome, she recalled.

His blondish good looks were clear in her memory. As was his strength and glowing chocolate eyes.

The last clear memory was of saying goodbye to her maman before starting off for Christmas Eve mass at Sainte Chapelle.

Christmas Eve?

Then today would be Christmas.

Why was she not in her own bed, awaiting her maid who would come to dress her for morning brunch with her family, before opening the many gifts strewn about the salon?

Monique heard a soft knock at the door. "Come."

"Ah, mademoiselle, you are awake and in clear health, I take it." Mathilda carried a tray covered with a white linen cloth.

"Where am I? Who are you? Is it Christmas Day? I must get…" Monique sat up and pulled the tangled covers from her legs. Immediately she flopped back against the pillows as the room spun and her stomach did a flip and roll.

"Tut, tut. Have a care, mademoiselle. You were injured." Mathilda set the tray on a bed table and moved to sit next to Monique on the bed. "Dizzy? Here, let me…"

Monique swatted Mathilda's hand away. She pressed both of her own hands to her own forehead to still the spinning. "Where am I? What day is today?"

Mathilda stood and clasped her hands in front of her apron, standing patiently. "You are enjoying the hospitality of Madame Grace Elliott. Today is the day after Christmas. You were brought here on Christmas Eve." Mathilda waited for the dizziness to abate and her patient to respond. "I have been caring for you since then."

Monique looked out from beneath her fingers. "You have?"

"Oui. You slept for two days. You must need to relieve yourself, oui?" Mathida brought a chamber pot close to the edge of the bed. "Do move slowly, mademoiselle. There is nothing in your stomach and you will become nauseous easily." Mathilda moved back to a respectful position, but close enough to lend aid if needed.

On the second try, Monique held her head and moved by inches until she was sitting upright. The room spun, but not quite as fast. Her stomach heaved but settled with the lessening

25

movement of the room. "I think I can..." She slid from the bed, landing on the floor next to the chamber pot with a giggle. "Fall on the floor all by myself." Her sixteen-year-old nature surfaced with the giggle.

This time Monique allowed the maid to help her with her personal care. When she was back on the edge of the bed with the room once again quiet in her mind, she took a deep breath and just sat for a moment.

Madame Grace Elliott ?

She was in the home of the infamous Grace Elliot? The Scottish beauty who charmed the King, bedded a Duke... and his wife, broke the heart of no less than one thousand men... in five countries?

This was not good.

"If I might now ask, who are you, mademoiselle?" Mathilda stood again at a proper distance, her hands primly clasped before her.

Monique stared at the maid. Of course Grace Elliott's staff would not know who she was. Grace would probably know her father and uncles, but a sixteen year old girl who had never been introduced into Society yet?

"I am Monique Alys Merchant, daughter of the Duke and Duchess Talondue-Merchant. I was on my way to..." The tears began. "I was on my..." Monique hid her face as memories came flooding back.

Ansell.

Peatre.

The crowd.

The rough wood of the carriage door pressed to her face.

A hand flew to her scratched and sore cheek.

She'd been in the middle of a ring of hateful people taunting and screaming insults at her.

Her clothing was ripped from her body...

A cry of anguish issued from her lips just before Monique threw herself onto the bed and curled into a ball. It did not matter that her head spun furiously and her stomach heaved and rolled like waves of a storm tossed ocean.

She remembered.

Mathilda whispered words of comfort but knew better than to touch a woman of such noble station. With nothing to do but fetch Madame Elliott, Mathilda excused herself and went to find her mistress.

Madame Grace Elliott was in her drawing room settling accounts from her Christmas spree of purchases. Mathilda wiggled her toes in the new shoes which had been one of her mistress' gifts. Madame Elliott was a generous employer. Mathilda cleared her throat and waited.

After a moment, Madame Elliott spread wood fibers across her account book to dry the wet ink and looked up. "What is it, Mathilda?"

"My Lady, the young woman is awake." Mathilda took several steps into the room in haste. "She is nobility, Madame. A Duke's daughter. And she is distraught."

"Ach, vera well. Thank ye, Mathilda. I'll see to the chit... Duke's daughter, eh?" Grace stood and moved around her desk. "Would ya bring up a tray with tea and cakes?"

"Yes ma'am, but I already have a tray in her room with juice and toast."

"For me, Mathilda. For me." Madame Elliott winked at her maid as she swished by to take the stairs to the second floor. "Do not wake Phillipe, Mathilda. He sleeps late into the day in..." she paused at the top of the stairs and pointed to her room, then pressed her finger to her lips.

Mathilda nodded her understanding. In Madame Elliott's house, it was no secret that Phillipe d' LeEgalité slept until night fall, or why. It was also no secret within which room he did that sleeping, like most men her mistress entertained.

As Mathilda dashed to do her mistress' bidding, Grace strode down the hall toward her guest room. She could already hear wails drifting toward her. Obviously, the girl was distraught.

Grace snorted. Of course the girl was distraught. The daughter of a Duke was insulated against the knowledge of the world. She would have been coddled, protected, pampered and spoiled to a degree that disgusted Grace to no end. The country, especially in these desperate times, was not a pretty place. Grace knew that better than just about everyone, but a Duke's daughter? She would live in beautiful gardens, surrounded by willing servants with sumptuous meals... and not a thought in her perfectly coiffed head.

She knocked once and entered her guest room. The sight turned her stomach. Still curled in a ball, howling to the rafters, lay the girl. Her hair was a mass of wet tangles and her snotty nose

27

dribbled across the pillow she clutched to her chest. Splotches of dried blood and dirt dotted her chemise and torn pantaloons. The souls of her feet were black with soot and filth.

"Stop yer hollerin' gel. You'll scare my household. They'll be thinkin' I torture a wee animal in here." Grace crossed the distance from the door to the bed in two wide steps and slapped Monique soundly. "Stop yeowlin' and sit up. I want to know who sleeps in my guest room." Grace stood over Monique, her hands on her hips.

Grace's slap did exactly what it was intended to do. Monique ceased her sobs and tried to sit. The room tilted back and forth and she plopped upon the mattress once again. "I can't." Her face planted in the pillow, her words were muffled and weak.

"Then stay where ye are, but talk." Grace was in no mood to be solicitous. Even as disheveled and filthy as she was, the girl was way too beautiful to remain in her home for long.

"I am Monique Alys Merchant, daughter of the Duke and Duchess Talondue-Merchant. I already told the other maid." Monique rolled onto her back and pressed both hands to her pounding head. "Get me some water. My mouth is as dry as a dessert."

Petulance was something Grace did not tolerate. "Get yer own drink. I be the lady of this house and I will not tolerate disrespect from ye, no matter yer station." Grace moved to sit in the high-backed chair next to the bed. She pointed to the tray. "My maid brought you a tray. Serve yourself."

A soft knock preceded Mathilda's entrance with a tray for her mistress. A pot of tea, a cup with sugar cubes and several cakes were placed next to Grace. "Me thanks, Mathilda. That will be all."

Dismissed, Mathilda departed but remained outside the closed door to listen in on what would be a very interesting conversation.

"I can't sit up. Every time I try, the room spins and I want to throw up." Monique wailed into the mattress.

"Sit up slowly and squeeze your head. It will pass." Grace did not make a move to help the girl. "Yer simply injured, not dead. Ye'll mend."

From the mattress, Monique's muffled words made Grace laugh. "Why are you so mean to me?"

"Mean? Do you even know the meaning of the word, young woman?" Grace had lost her Scottish accent completely and now spoke like a true noblewoman. "I cannot abide worthless women trained to be helpless, always needing to be served. You are not witless, Monique Alys Merchant, daughter of the Duke and Duchess Talondue-Merchant. Get up and deal with your infirmary. It will only make you stronger."

Apparently, this Grace Elliott was not a woman to be manipulated. Nor would she send for a maid to help Monique in any way. There was but one thing to do, and that, was to help herself. Monique pressed her hands as tightly as she could to her temples and worked her way into a sitting position.

The first time was unsuccessful and she wobbled over onto the pillows again.

Grace Elliott sat calmly without comment, munching her cakes.

The second time, Monique managed to prop herself up with one hand on the bedpost and one on her spinning head. She held her breath, squeezed her eyes shut and waited for the room to settle down. It took a few moments, but soon she chanced a single eye to open.

There sat the most elegant, voluptuous, beauty Monique had ever seen. If the gossip circle spoke true, Grace Elliott bedded half the men in the world and now Monique understood how. The woman virtually glowed with sensuality, still dressed in her day robe. Her skin was perfection, her pose regal, yet seductive.

"Vera well." Grace elegantly motioned to the tray, still covered with linen. "There be juice and something to break yer fast." The accent was back. "Dinna wait on me." Grace poured herself a cup of tea and popped a teacake into her mouth from the tray her maid had silently placed on the table next to her chair.

Monique reached for the linen cover and winced. The room heaved but stabilized more rapidly this time. After a few moments, she was able to reach a glass of juice and bring it to her lips.

"Slowly, gel. My maid'll not be wantin' to clean yer juice from the floor." Grace smiled sweetly while she demolished another teacake.

After a couple very slow sips of juice, Monique decided the sweet orange liquid would remain where she placed it. She reached for a piece of buttered toast, chancing solid food.

"So, who will I be contactin' to send ye back to yer palace, princess?" Grace spoke around what was left of the teacake in her mouth. "I be imaginin' yer folks are a touch worried about their precious little gel."

Monique eyed Madame Elliott over the toast she was biting. Why was this woman so... mean? Mean wasn't the right word. Callous? Unpleasant? Monique had never met a woman like Grace Elliott. She simply had no experience with her kind, and no word would come to mind.

"My father's estate is on the Avenue des Champs d'Élysées near the Rue Pierre Charron. If you take him a message, he will send a ... he will send for me." The tears began anew.

"Why yer tears now?" Grace sipped her tea as if Monique's heart were not breaking into a million parts.

"Our carriage was destroyed. I do not know where Ansell, my footman is. Peatre, the driver disappeared we were attacked... I have no clothes and my mother's jewels are gone. A hateful woman with rotten teeth tore them from me." Monique dabbed at her face with the linen towel from her breakfast tray.

"Phillipe told me the driver was dead. He rescued you just before the rabble was about to kill you, as well." Grace reported the news as if it were the highlights of some common news plate. "He brought you here just before midnight and here ye been a-sleepin' since." Grace ignored the sobbing girl and rose to leave. "I will send to your father for a carriage... and clothing. Do stop bawling, gel." With that, Grace left Monique alone and proceeded to the business of relieving herself of one slightly disheveled daughter of a Duke. And a possible rival for the affections of one Phillipe Le Glaute, Duc d'Orleans.

******

"Monique!" Fabienne gathered her daughter in her arms, fiercely hugging the young woman with all her might. "Thank God you are home and safe. I thought to die when I heard your carriage was over-run by that mob."

Monique squirmed from her mother's arms and kissed her on the cheek. "I am fine, maman. My ordeal is over and do not worry, I am whole." She took both of her mother's hands and stepped back. "Now you can stop worrying and rest. Father says you have been ill."

"Your father wouldn't know ill if it took him off to hell." Fabienne linked arms with her daughter and dragged her toward the morning salon. "Tell me everything, Monique. Your father said

Le Glaute, Duc d'Orleans saved you from the rioters. The message we received said you were unconscious for a time. He placed you with a doctor to treat your wounds and keep you safe until you woke and identified yourself. He is such a hero. Such an amazing man, and cousin to the King! I wonder if Louis knows of the heroic deeds of the Duke?" The Duchess settled her daughter on the divan and took her usual place at the small table where she kept her embroidery basket.

Clear of mind, Monique caught the words of her mother with complete comprehension. She'd been with a doctor, not the infamous Grace Elliot. Her wounds had been tended and she was whole. A good story for her mother's infallibal ability to only recognize what the Duchess wanted to.

The story continued.

"Tell me everything, dear. I am so glad to hear there was a doctor to help you. Your father said you did not have any serious wounds. I see there are scratches on your face. Did it hurt much? Why were you unconscious? Did you faint or was your head hurt? The doctor must have done a superb job because here you are, sitting right in front of me, healthy and happy. You are happy to be home aren't you, dear? I certainly would be after such an ordeal. I would probably take to my bed for a week after such a..."

"My Lady, pardon the interruption, but Mademoiselle Monique must be exhausted. If my Lady wishes, I shall have a bath drawn and help her to bed." Chelestienne acted the perfect humble and helpful Lady-in-Waiting. "I will take the best care of your daughter, my Lady."

"Oh, silly me. Of course you are tired after your ordeal, mon chère." Fabienne truly looked at her daughter for the first time since her arrival. "And in need of a bath. Cheleste do help Mademoiselle Monique up to her room. I can hear everything later. When you have rested, chère. I am so glad you are home." Fabienne rose and kissed her daughter's cheek. With one more fierce hug, the Duchess allowed Chelestienne to take Monique upstairs.

At the top of the stairs Monique paused and looked down toward the salon. "Does insanity effect all of the women in my family, Chelestienne?" Monique tiredly waved off any answer and stumbled toward her room with the steadying support of her mother's Lady-In-Waiting.

## Chapter 3

## Left Behind

Left behind in the world of the dead.
My childhood eradicated. Replaced instead,
With a life so hideous and repulsive to me,
That beyond the moment, I refuse to see,
What could be.
What should be.

For me, my only destiny,
Is to exist and to serve, at my Master's knee.

*Monique Alys Merchant, Operative*
*Vamp Squad*
*Olney, Maine 2015*

## December 29, Paris, France 1792.

"Maman, the Duc d' Orleans shall arrive any moment, please do get up." Monique pulled at her mother's arm, patting the Duchess' wrist with gusto. "Please, please! Maman, I cannot entertain the Duke without your presence. It would not be proper, and you know how Father is about proper."

The Duchess did not respond in the least, except for the heavy snore issuing forth from her painted lips. A small blue bottle lay uncorked by the bedside. The familiar odor of bittersweet laudanum floated on the Duchess' breath as she slept.

"Chelestienne, why did you dose maman when you knew we are entertaining tonight?" Monique rounded on the maid. "You have ruined everything."

"Mademoiselle, I did not administer anything. The Duchess has hidden many a bottle of her favorite sleeping aid throughout the castle." Chelestienne fell to her knees. "I swear on my own mother's grave, I have tried to find them all, yet..." The maid covered her face. "My Lady uses the medicine more often than is healthy. More and more, Mademoiselle." Chelestienne rose and covered her face in shame as if she were divulging some deep dark secret.

Monique sighed, knowing the maid spoke the truth. "I understand, Chelestienne. Thank you for what you have done. I know my maman well." Monique picked up the blue bottle, tipping it upside down. Not a drop fell from the opening. "She will not wake until the morning." Monique fell into the chair next to her mother's bed. "Now what shall I do?"

Aloise stood silent and unseen near the Duchess' dressing room door. "If I may, Mademoiselle, the Dowager Duchess is in high spirits this day. She may present..." Aloise let the comment drift. Not only was she familiar with the profile of the Duc d'Orleans, but she understood Monique's desire to thank the man for saving her life.

"You do joke, Aloise. Grand-mère is no more capable of being a hostess than my maman at the moment." Monique waved at her sleeping mother. "I am doomed."

"Mademoiselle, Alys Marie can be a sweet and entertaining hostess... despite her occasional lapse. From what I have been told, the Duc d'Orleans will understand. His own wife is said to be a bit touched, if you know what I mean." Aloise tapped her temple and winked at Chelestienne, who covered her giggle with a quickly placed hand. "Lady-In-Waiting to the Duchess d'Orleans just happens to be my second cousin."

"Ah. I see." Monique's youthful enthusiasm rose to the challenge. "Can grand-mère be prepared in time? What can I do to help?"

"Join your father in his study and endeavor to keep him there. We will see to your grand-mère." Chelestienne motioned Aloise toward the hall. "Do not mention this plot afoot. Quickly, Ali, we have work to do."

Always the co-conspirator when it was to her benefit, Monique hurried downstairs to her father's study and a mission to keep the Duke busy until the arrival of their honored guest.

In his study, the Duke sat reading the latest missives. Unrest in the streets was the primary topic. Several news releases indicated the governmental changes were wide sweeping. The kingdom was in peril and His Royal Highness' life hung in the balance. The opinion of the National Convention was against the frivolous Queen Marie Antionette and her careless statements. From the writings, it was clear the Duc'd'Orleans rode a precarious fence while his accounts stood staunchly on the side of the Revolution. The House of Bourbon was in trouble and a much different future faced them all. Pierre took a long drink of whiskey. As he refilled his glass, a soft knock on his door finally signaled the arrival of his wife. Her tardiness would be the death of him someday.

"Fabienne, I am glad you finally decided to join…"

"Father?" Monique did not wait for permission to enter. She was on a mission.

"Monique, where is your mother?"

"Maman is in her room, father." She strode toward her father's desk. "You have been catching up on the news?" Monique was well aware of her father's obsession with politics and the country's current predicament. It was a safe segway for her and an effective distraction for her father

"Yes, of course. A Duke of the Kingdom has many responsibilities and must …" His discourse was interrupted by the sound of gunshots. "Remain here, Monique." He opened a cherry wood box and withdrew two polished and gleaming pistols. Her father ran out of his study, slamming the door behind him.

Not one to be left out of the excitement, Monique followed her father, at a distance. Several more gunshots rang out and she heard a window shatter somewhere in the salon. Then there was silence.

Monique pressed herself against the wall at the bottom of the ornate staircase that lead to the second floor and their private rooms. She could hear her father shouting for the groomsmen to arm themselves.

A loud knock at the door caused Monique to jump. Connell appeared, immediately followed by her father. The butler opened the peephole and peered out, then moved aside for her father to look. As Monique watched with increasing interest, her grand-mère silently moved to stand close by. She felt the old woman gently take her hand and was enveloped in a cloud of jasmine and vanilla. The Dowager Duchess looked every part the grande dame of court. A high styled white wig covered her thin gray hair and heavy jewels sparkled about her neck. A gold and ruby family broach held a lacy shawl aptly disguising bare shoulders that had seen much younger days.

Alys Marie held a finger to her lips. "The natives are restless tonight, Fabienne. We shall be as quiet as church mice and they will go away."

"Grand-mère, I am Monique, your granddaughter."

"Yes. Yes, of course you are Monique, and there are no natives about. I am not daft. At least not tonight." The old woman frowned then brightened. "I shall not disappoint you, my dear. And I shall keep a smart eye. There is more to this Duc 'd'Orleans than we know."

Her father came to stand beside his daughter and his mother. "And where is my wife? Should you not be in bed, maman?" He took her arm to hand his mother off to a waiting maid.

Alys Marie pulled away from her son with a smart jerk. "Do not be so arrogant, son. It reminds me of your father, bless his soul. This is still my home, and I shall act as hostess tonight. Do leave off mauling my gown."

"Your Grace, I believe our visitor has arrived." Connell remarked.

"Yes, do show him in, Connell." There was nothing the Duke could do but take his place next to his mother and daughter. He whispered, "Behave maman, or I shall be forced to lock you in your room and send Orleans packing."

"Oh la, Pierre, I am your mother and you will do no such thing. Now present us to Monique's champion. I am interested to hear the true story from his lips." She smiled sweetly up at her son who stood ramrod stiff.

"Maman..." Monique's father began. His glare spoke volumes.

"Shush now, Pierre. Do use the good manners I taught you." With that, Alys Marie stepped forward, dragging her son to his duty.

"Ah Orleans, welcome." Pierre moved forward to take his visitor's hand as he peered around the tall Duke into the night. "Welcome to my home and again, I sincerely thank you for protecting my daughter. May I formally present the Dowager Duchess Talondue-Merchant and her granddaughter, my daughter, Lady Monique Alys Merchant. Whom I believe you have met, of course."

Both women stepped forward. Alys Marie inclined her head in grand greeting while Monique blushed and accomplished a slight curtsy.

Extremely perceptive, Phillipe Le Glaute, Duc d'Orleans,

took the old wrinkled hand of the Dowager Duchess, placed a gentle kiss on its powdered back and smiled into a set of sharp blue eyes. "I am honored, Madame. It was my pleasure to be instrumental in the safe return of your granddaughter."

"Ah, and that tale I look forward to hearing, Your Grace."

He turned to Monique, "We meet again, Lady Monique, under much better circumstances I must say." He lifted her hand to his lips. "You have recovered nicely, I see."

Was the Duke flirting with her? She smiled at the floor. "Oui, Your Grace. I am in your debt."

"Nonsense, my dear. It is the responsibility of all Frenchmen to protect our children." The point was emphasized by more gunshots. "Do not worry, my men guard this house. There is nothing to fear."

Alys Marie scrutinized the Duc' d'Orleans. "I am not so sure..." she murmured under her breath as she pulled Monique toward the drawing room. "May I offer you a libation before dinner, Your Grace... Pierre?"

The men followed. "Did you encounter trouble on your way here, Orleans?" Monique's father was desperate to keep conversation with Alys Marie to a minimum.

"Nothing my Guard could not handle. Thank you for your concern. I have an agreement..."

"So I have heard." Pierre was not in the mood to hear Citoyen Phillipe d'LeEgalité implicate himself before a loyal Duke of the realm. While it was not exactly common knowledge that Orleans sat the fence and swayed as the wind blew, the King's cousin would hear no treasonous admitions this night. "What is your position on the new proletariat proposal to redistribute government grain resources? Who will be trusted to carry out this new process?"

Alys Marie served drinks and watched the Duc' d'Orleans beneath hooded lids, while Monique sat quietly in her mother's chair. The men discussed politics, trade and hunting at length. If the Duc' d'Orleans had not been so incredibly handsome and distinguished, Monique thought she would have nodded off at the dull conversation. Instead, she took the opportunity to study the man at length. He was her savior, incredibly handsome and good at appealing to her father's somewhat large ego. Connell finally announced dinner was served and the small group retired to the dining room and the sumptuous meal that waited.

Often during their meal, a gunshot could be heard in the distance. As the fourth course was served, the shouts and gunfire were clearly closer.

Much closer.

Monique dropped her fork at the last volley.

"Father, are we safe here?" Monique's fears began to rise. Her previous experience with angry mobs sent anxious waves of tension through her body. Her head pounded and she could not make her shaking fingers pick up the fork she'd dropped. Her vision burred and the room began to spin. Monique gripped the sides of the table and held on. The sound of the Duke's men returning fire was disconcerting as her father continued to drone on about the state of the government and the royal family.

Monique glanced at her grand-mère. It was clear that the old woman was very much aware of what was going on outside... and the fact that her son continued to ignore the obvious. Monique could tell she was on the verge of loosing her wits. "Grand-mère, perhaps we should retire to the inner garden solar. I feel the need for some fresh air." Monique rapidly batted her hand back and forth in front of her face as if she were about to swoon. "Alas, I fear I am not completely recovered." She allowed her head to droop convincingly.

Another window somewhere close, shattered.

"Do as you please daughter. This house is nothing short of a fortress. The staff is armed and have taken their places to protect us. I shall not allow this degenerate misled mob to interrupt our dinner." Pierre waved off his daughter as if she were a silly child afraid of the dark.

Monique chanced a look at the Duc d'Orleans seated across from her. His quick glance toward the door told her to move. She carefully rose from the table and took her grand-mère's elbow, helping the Dowager Duchess. The old woman's eyes darted around the room and she moved with halting steps. "Then, I shall say good eve, Your Grace."

The Duc d'Orlean began to rise, but sat promptly when Monique shook her head slightly and moved her eyes toward the head of the table where her father continued his oration.

"Franchesca, I fear there is an ill wind about." Alys Marie's mind was slipping.

"Oui maman, we shall hide in the garden." Monique whispered to her grand-mère as they left the dining room.

"Someone should summon Laurice. He must control these rabble-rousers before things get out of hand, or we shall all suffer. Do find little Pierre and bring him to me. He is too small to be of help and may get in the way. Where is my Lady-in-Waiting?" On the verge of hysteria, Alys Marie whispered to her granddaughter as they entered the arboretum. Suddenly the Dowager Duchess drew in a deep breath of fragrance and, like an immediate sedative, she paused. A placid smile transformed her grave features and she wandered away to inspect the many flowers that grew in abundance in their glass hothouse, despite the cold French winter. "Franchesca, we shall have a nice little bouquet on the breakfast side in the morn." Alys Marie was off in her own world once again.

"Oui, maman." What was there to say? The old woman's wits had departed, replaced by a fantasy world of flowers, embroidery and silliness. It was a pattern Monique knew well. "Oui. I shall fetch tea and tarts while you gather a bouquet, maman. I shall be but a few minutes."

Monique locked the door to the arboretum as she left. Her grand-mère would be safe with the flowers until Monique determined the situation outside. The mansion that was home, formed a horseshoe around the arboretum which opened to the central gardens and the expansive back lawn. Beyond the lawn were the stables and housing for the footmen and Connell. The massive estate was surrounded by tall stonewalls and wrought iron gates. It would be secure against rioters. Monique said a quick prayer.

It should be secure!

The noise was getting louder and Monique could hear singing from the crowd. She recognized the song and her blood grew cold. In the hallway, she could hear horrendous banging on the front door. Why weren't the gates closed to keep the rioters away from the house?

"Lady Monique?" The Duc d'Orleans ran from the dining room, calling to her.

"I am here, Your Grace. What is happening?" She ran toward his voice. "Where is my father?"

"He has gone to collect your mother and prepare to depart. The rabble has breached the gates. You must come with me." With little ceremony, he grabbed Monique's arm and dragged her toward the servant's quarters. "We must be away quickly."

"But, grand-mère? She is in the arboretum. I locked the door." Monique shouted and tried to break free.

"The Dowager Duchess is well loved and of an age she will be spared. You, on the other hand, are a delicious little morsel that will bring a high price, dead or alive. Now, do as I say and we both shall live." He picked her up with ease and ran for the back stairs and the exit to the stable. "We may be able to escape this swarm of insanity if we ride like the Devil. You can ride, correct?"

"Ride? A horse?" Monique squeaked. Connell held two saddled horses at the entrance to the stable. Monique tightened her arms around the Duke's neck. "No. Never."

"Ah, merde!" The Duke swore under his breath. This young woman was more trouble than she was worth. "Then you ride with me and pray your stock is of a robust breed."

"Your Grace, I must see to my Master's needs." Connell threw the reigns to d'Orleans and bolted for the house. The second horse ran for the barn, startled and on the loose. The sounds of angry words and shattering glass followed Connell across the courtyard. "Good luck to you. Keep our lady safe, Your Grace."

The Duke lifted Monique into the saddle and leaped upon the horse's rump. "Hold to the strap here, my Lady." He reached around and swung her leg across the saddle to ride astride the beast. "Grip with your knees and let me do the rest." The Duke spurred the horse on and pulled it around to head in the direction of the small wooden gate nestled between huge oak trunks near a cops of fruit trees.

The gate was only as high as a man and Monique felt the horse gather strength for the jump. "Hah!" The Duke kicked the horse's rump with the strength of a man pursued by a pack of hungry wolves.

"Noooooooo…" The horse leapt then landed with a bone-jarring crunch and they were over the gate. Galloping down the boulevard and away from the commotion, Monique could smell smoke and wrenched around to see flames leaping from the stable roof. "The staff? Your Grace, my staff and the horses!" She tried to grab the reins from the Duke.

"My men liberated them hours ago. The other horse you were to ride has run wild. Do hold on, Lady Monique, or we shall both be upset." He held her arms tightly pinned, determined to keep them astride the panicking animal. She had just enough room to grasp the strap as she had been instructed.

As they exited the alley at a gallop, two hooligans stepped from the bushes. Their raised hands held burning brooms made of stitched hay and twigs.

Their horse spooked, rearing in fright at the fire. Monique felt herself fly through the air and heard the resounding crack as her skull met the cobblestones.

Then there was nothing.

The Duke deftly executed a spectacular flip, landing on his feet, still holding the reins. "You fools!" He shouted at the surprised men who lay in wait, expecting an easy loot that night. "You will have no sweet pickings from this nasty business." The Duke's eyes burned a deep red. His fangs sparkled in the firelight.

The first man turned to run but could not possibly out maneuver the Duke's preternatural speed. In a flash of light, his head was torn from his neck and rolled to the feet of his comrade. As the fellow stared at the gruesome sight, the Duke descended upon him. Fangs extended, he ripped into the man's neck, drinking deeply at the free flowing wound.

A wild growl issued from the Duke's lips. The blood was a salve to his depleted strength, but it was not the satisfaction he craved.

Monique moaned, bringing a hand delicately to her pounding head. It came away bloodied. She tried to see what had happened through her tangled hair, but twinkling stars and blurred movement was all she could make out from her position on the ground.

Stars, blurred movement… and blood.

Her shoulder was tucked beneath her at an odd angle. Her arm burned with piercing pain and she could not move her right leg. Through a tiny slit in her right eye she could see the stark white bone protruding from her wrist.

Panic rose in her throat. She tried to scream but could only manage a single whimper.

A few feet away, The Duke dropped his victim. The whimper he heard over the distant din, most assuredly came from Lady Monique. He sniffed the air. Her delectable scent drifted on the smoke. His mouth watered while his manhood leapt to attention. If the revolutionaries were as successful as he thought they may be, she would have nothing to go back to.

No home.

No family.

No status as a Duke's daughter.

He surveyed her crumpled, bloody body. His fangs nearly vibrated in anticipation. They were not the only part of his body that vibrated.

He would do her a favor if he turned her this night. The sweet young girl, not yet a woman, would be an enchanting addition to his family. She would join him in his secret chambers, forever one of his kind.

Forever his.

Bending low, the Duke pulled her from the blood soaked stones. "Shhh, my child. I can take this pain from you." He turned Monique's face to him as he held her. "I can make everything go away and give you life forever." His hand came away stained with her luscious liquid of life. "You will be eternally beautiful, young and worshiped by all." The Duke licked his fingers. Intense pleasure exploded in his brain.

Monique managed to open her eyes a bit. He was there! He'd saved her once. He would save her again. Didn't he say he could make the pain go away? She would live forever... with her savior and knight in shining armor! A slight hint of a smile overpowered the pain that tortured her body. She managed a whisper, "Oui, Your..."

Phillipe Le Glaute, Duc d'Orleans... neh, Phillipe, Comte d' LeEgalité, studied the slowing pulse at the base of Monique's neck. A craven smile crept over his lips as he gleefully sank his fangs into her pure white flesh and sucked the life from her virginal body. He embraced his natural instinct and fed with wanton gluttony. "My sweet..." Phillipe slurred his words, drunk on Monique's blood and the unbelievable lust that fired his manhood. He was so incredibly hard, it almost hurt to move.

Never had there been such a feeding frenzy and a powerful response from his body. As he drank the nectar of her life, Phillipe tried to hold back the completely encompassing need that spurred him on. His own control failed him as he felt the explosion in his mind and the tightening of his groin.

Pulse after pulse of pure ecstasy ravaged his body. Swallow after swallow fueled his orgasm until he could survive no more. Collapsing in a heap next to his dying morsel, Phillipe congratulated himself on such a spectacular addition to his little group. He brushed her blood-caked hair to the side. "Ah, my little child, soon you will be immortal. Immortally mine. Forever to have all you want… and all I can take."

The sun was still several hours from showing its face as Phillipe rode toward the country home where his *family* existed in the catacombs beneath the summer estate. He cuddled his new progeny in his arms. She would be a grand addition to his coven… and his bed.

## Chapter 4

### Secrets

The secrets of the living, beget a life of their own.
In a world of the living, one must atone.

But the secrets of the dead?
They dance in one's head.

Forever there, just beyond reason or touch.
Insanely annoying, is the life of such.

*Fiona Fabriacci, Vampire Council of Elders*
*Orsova, Romania, 2008*

**May Day, Vamp Squad Underground Base, Olney Maine, 2016.**

"Ohhhh!" Monique's scream echoed through the heads of every vampire in the facility. "Ohhhhhhh! Nooooo!" Before her nightmare could infect everyone's mind, Susannah was at Monique's bedside, pulling the beautiful French vampire from her sleep drenched horror.

"Frenchy, wake up already! You're scaring the shit out of the humans and waking every vamp within ten miles." She shook Monique soundly. "Snap out of it, girl."

Monique opened her eyes. She wasn't in the catacombs of southern France. It wasn't the eighteenth century. She was in her bed, in her quarters, at the super secret, underground military facility where she now lived... with her coven and team. Her new family. She shook her head. "Merde."

"You can say that again. Another nightmare? The same?" Susannah pushed the covers over and sat on the edge of the bed. "You gotta get this V-PTSD thing under control, sister from a different mister. It's not even sundown up-top and we're all awake. Now, anyway."

Monique sat up and rubbed her eyes. At least this time

there were no red tear stains on her face and nightgown. "Oui, do you not think I know this, Susannah? I just can't seem to make it go away. It's always the same." Now the tears flowed.

Susannah handed Monique a box of tissue from the night stand, and threw an arm around her coven sister. "I know. I know." There wasn't much to do or say. Susannah knew Monique's turning still haunted her. After more than two hundred years. The betrayal... the violence... the horror of it all. It still invaded her sleep. It invaded all of their sleep, since the coven shared each others' mental pictures and could psyche-speak. Often even if they didn't mean to. Susannah smiled to herself thinking of the many nights she lay awake, horny beyond comprehension, as the newlywed Yuri and Natalia shared their marriage bed. She sighed. "We love you anyway!" Susannah spontaneously hugged Monique.

"Oui! And I love you, ma souer." Monique hugged her back. The two vampires virtually lived in each others' back pockets, and had become closer than actual sisters while training as undercover antiterrorist operatives for the American government. "I do not understand why I continue to be tortured so." Monique wiped away more tears to keep from staining the linens and her satin nighty. "Will there never be peace for me?"

It was a prophetic question needing no answer from either Susannah, or their Coven Mistress who had just come through the door, disheveled and yawning. "Another nightmare, daughter?" Another prophetic question! Both girls nodded.

Elizabetta joined the group hug, cooing motherly nothings.

It took a few seconds for Susannah to wiggle free. The physical touch was so comforting, she wanted to remain in the arms of her covenmates forever, but there was an issue to attack. "Maybe you should talk to Dr. Anderson. She deals with her own demons every day." It was a gentle suggestion. Dr. Anderson's entire family had been killed in a horendous house fire a few years back, before she'd joined Vamp Squad. The human doctor was recruited out of a Jim Bean bottle and it saved her life. It wasn't until she became a working part of the Vamp Squad, that she started to live again. It was a common story with many of the operatives and human team members.

"It might help." Elizabetta agreed, releasing Monique. "And we would all sleep better in our beds." She yawned again. "And that's where I am going." With one last hug and a kiss for

44

Monique's clean cheek, the Coven Mistress left as quietly as she had come.

"I hate my brain!" Monique flounced onto the edge of the mattress, tossing red stained tissues into the waste basket beneath her night stand.

"You have a great brain… when you decide to use it, kiddo. But you always use…" Susannah motioned to Monique's voluptous figure. "… *that*."

"It is what I know. Susannah, you did not have to survive being sireless on your own. When the Duc d'Orleans was captured and killed by the revolutionaries, Mathilda and I were the only survivors of the coven. Everyone else was burned or guillotined. We ran so deep into the caverns, the bravest of the rabble would not follow. But then there was survival. We had nothing but each other, until the hateful monks captured us. Then we had pain." Monique stared at the floor as she recounted her early history. "And then there was only me." A single red tear hit the polished wooden floor of her room. Monique smeared it into oblivion with her bare foot. Looking up with a slight smile, "And then there was this magnificient man with very big muscles, who carried me to freedom… and this place…and you. Now I have a real home… and a brain that tortures me in my sleep. Pooh!"

"So let's work on that part. Talk to Dr. Anderson. She might be able to help." Susannah sat on the end of Monique's bed. "It can't hurt. Who's hungry?" She popped up and headed for the door. "Me, that's who."

"Oui. It is always you! If you were human, you would be in that big store with all of the other humans, riding a scooter because you are too fat to walk!" Monique finally giggled. "let us attack the refrigerator."

"That's *raid* the frig, Frenchy. And I vote yes! Let's go." She dragged Monique's robe from the vanity bench and threw it to her sister vampire. "Make like a bread truck and move those buns."

"Buns? We do not eat food, Susannah." Monique was puzzled.

"It's a saying. It means get moving." Susannah shook her head as she exited Monique's room.

Mumbling under her breath, Monique followed. "But we have no truck and no bread. I will never understand this language."

It was close to four thirty in the afternoon and the sun would soon be down. "I have a night flight scheduled. Wanna go with me?" Susannah had earned her pilot's license a few months back. Her vampiric gifts did not include the ability to v-port or fly like many vampires including Monique, so she took up flying aircraft. It was not as efficient and much more dangerous, but it got her where she wanted to go.

"Of course I will go. It is fun to watch you. You are so serious and...I do not know the word..." Monique moved her hands as if she were holding a yoke and flying a plane.

Susannah supplied her own word. "Talented! Yes." She grinned. Susannah knew it was not the word Monique was looking for, but it was how she felt in the cockpit of the little Cessna 172 when she was flying.

"No. Looking hard. Focus? Not like before Jordi. Oui?" Monique loved to kid Susannah about her long distance relationship with the young vampire from Florida. Jordan Burke had been instrumental in shutting down the Proctor coven and had taken his place in the research department of Proctor Pharmaceuticals after the Vamp Squad jumped in to get rid of the naturist coven and its maniacal Coven Master, a very old and powerful vampire. Proctor was using his own company to develop dangerous drugs to enslave vampires.

"Well, I did almost get him killed, which taught me a good lesson. I needed to get serious about my training and our team. I'm an operative, not a silly teen with no responsibility anymore." Susannah's tone turned serious for a moment. "Dad made this place because of me. Now it's no longer a *me*, it's an *us*. I may not ever be able to v-port, but I can get around."

Colonel Frank Maddox, Susannah's human father came up with the idea of the Vamp Squad after learning his daughter had joined the undead, well, a new species anyway. Vampires were simply mutated humans who lived with sun allergies and needed infusions of blood to survive. Simply was an understatement, but the Colonel couldn't destroy his daughter, undead or alive, so he built the Vamp Squad, convinced the Joint Chiefs of their usefulness and now they were a functioning undercover, anti-terrorist squad with several successful missions under their belts.

The galley was empty of humans and vampires alike. Susannah took two bags of synth-blood from the black refrigerator. She handed one to Monique as they sat at a small table. "When Uncle Rob got hurt on our second mission because of my screw-up, I was devastated, but I didn't know why. All I wanted was to get away."

"From the frying pan into the oven." Monique lisped as she placed her fangs into the two nipples on the plastic bag, designed for just that purpose.

"Into the fire, Frenchy. And yes, I jumped in with both feet. Then Proctor captured Jordi and he almost got destroyed. All because of me. I knew I needed to change my life. Figure things out. So I did." She popped the other bag on her fangs. "Not that I'm per-thect, or anthin'," she lisped as she drank.

Monique finished her bag of synthetic blood and nutrient drink. The pact they'd all signed to become members of the Vamp Squad included no warm blood, only synth-blood. The sustaining liquid was designed especially for the techno-modern vampire. "I do love a good two-thousand," she glanced at the label, "fifteen AB positive."

Both girls laughed at that. Susannah crossed her legs and affected a *spoiled-teen* pose. "Oh la, I prefer the O negative myself." Seriousness was over as they laughed at each other. "I'll be ready to go about six-ish. It's supposed to be a beautiful spring night."

"You will not fly in your Strange Bob pajamas?" Monique grinned.

"Sponge Bob. And no, I don't fly in nightware." Susannah danced off toward the vampire quarters. "Six-ish, okay?"

"Oui." Monique was left to herself in the galley with an empty bag of AB positive and some serious thoughts. Would talking to the doctor of humans help? Monique contemplated what she would say. After all, Doctor Helga Anderson was a human. She could never understand the agony of being turned, the betrayal of the one she thought to be her savior. Her angel of deliverance turned out to be a demon in Duke's clothing and her innocence was not the only thing he took from her.

## Chapter 5

### Fear

"The oldest and strongest emotion of mankind is fear,
and the oldest and strongest kind of fear is fear of the unknown."
H. P Lovecraft

Now there was a man who knew his business!
But never in a thousand years, or more, did he realize,
the horrors of his mental abhorritions lived right next door.

*Emilliano Fabriacci, Musings of a Librarian*
*Vampire Council of Elders*
*Orsova, Romania, 2010*

"Suuuuuuuusaaaannaaaaaah! Noooooo!" Fiona screamed at the top of her faerie lungs as the Cessna 172 slid into another Dutch roll. "Oh my Gods, no. Stop."

Monique watched Susannah laugh and leveled the wings. She sat, silently, for once, belted tightly into the right seat, her fists clenched around the door handle, knuckles white in fear.

"Okay. This is so much fun, don't ya think?" Susannah snickered as she spoke through her mic.

The unanimous answer was a squeaked "No."

"Chére, when you said you wanted to learn to fly, I thought you meant, you know, fly." Monique released her death grip on the door's hand-hold and spread her arms level and straight. "Like a real plane is supposed to fly. Not in this… this machine folle! If we were not already mort, mon ami, we soon will be with you at the controls. Please land thisssssss - aughhhhhhhhhh!" Monique screamed as Susannah pushed the nose over in a steep dive, and headed for the giant painted numbers on the end of the runway. All the while laughing at her two mortified friends.

"Fiona, please get your claws out of Susannah's neck." Monique commented with a smirk.

Susannah leveled the wings and set up for a straight-in approach. "November five-five-four-one zulu on long final. Full stop." She unkeyed the mic. "Fiona, please. I have to concentrate. The claws!"

"I can not watch. I must not watch!" The tiny vampire covered her eyes with her small delicate hands and slid down in the seat.

Monique glanced over her shoulder. Fiona resembled a frightened ten year-old rather than an extremely strong and skilled vampire. A Celtic bond ring glowed on the forth finger of her left hand.

"Fiona, we are not going to crash. I've done this a million times. Well, not a million, but probably several hundred anyway. Relax." Susannah had confidence in her landing ability on the private, mile long strip. She truly enjoyed flying her little plane. She might not have the vampiric gift of flight, but she sure as heck had the FAA certification and the piloting skills to accomplish the task with efficiency.

"I fear I am to be ill." Fiona brought both hands to her petite mouth and disappeared in a blink of bright light.

"Chicken." Susannah mumbled as she pulled on the carb heat and reduced the plane's power. She then turned all focus to executing a perfect landing. A slight updraft caught the plane as the Cessna 172 flew over the cool green grass, then the warm black asphalt of the runway. They were less than 100 feet above the ground and gliding evenly over the numbers in near perfect attitude.

"Eek! This is not the way I wish to end my existence, little sister." Monique pressed against her seat as if to distance herself from the oncoming white stripes down the middle of the runway.

"You're such a baby about some things, Monique." Two wheels touched the pavement with a slight screech as Susannah held the nose of the plane off the ground, bleeding off excess speed. She spoke into the mic of her headset as she carefully let the nose settle to the ground and slowed to turn off onto the taxiway. "November five-five-four-one zulu clear of the active. Taxi to Executive Hangar 5."

As the small plane bounced along toward its oversized garage, Monique breathed a sigh of relief. "Susannah, do you not think it is safer to soar or v-port? Why do you want to fly in a machine? Especially a machine that has only one form of power?"

"Come on, Frenchy, this is really cool. I love flying this way and Elizabetta said I might never v-port. We all get different gifts with VMD. I just didn't get the fly one. This is the next best thing. Dad thinks it's cool, too. He actually went up with me last week." Susannah's smile was brilliant in the early evening twilight. "He was about as white as you are now, but I have to give him credit. He didn't scream like you and Fiona do. Speaking of which..."

The little faerie vampire appeared in the back seat at the mention of her name. "Do not speak of *which* if you know what is good for you, little fledgling. I am feeling a mite better here on the ground. I do believe I shall stay to my v-porting. What color I do have, should not be green as the hills of my ancient home."

Monique and Susannah laughed. "Dad actually told me he was proud of my accomplishment and that I was coming along as an operative. Blew my socks off."

"Why would your father's praise make your stockings blow off? I do not understand. Do humans have some power I do not know of?" Fiona wrinkled her cute little nose.

"It's a saying. Means I was super surprised. Unless you haven't noticed, my father is a little tight with praise. It's a military thing, I hope." Susannah shrugged and quickly went through the shut down procedure, flipping off the master switch last. "Let's get this baby put to bed before the sun rears its ugly head."

"Yes, and I must return to the Council Chambers. Emilliano will be missing me. He complains that I am spending too much time here, these days. I believe he is a bit jealous, since we have become man and wife in the official eyes of the Council. So much has changed in such a short time." Fiona continued her musings as she pretended to help without actually lifting a finger. "Angellique continues to hate me with a passion I do not comprehend, but the others, they are considerate. Thanks to your Doctor Anderson and Petra, Emilliano no longer fears for my safety. To the Doctor of Humans, I shall forever be indebted." Fiona paused and covered her mouth as if she'd revealed a deep dark secret, then giggled like a child. "But to you, I shall bid farewell."

The tiny vampire levitated. Hovering at head height, she placed a sweet kiss on the cheeks of both Monique and Susannah. "Slán agus beannacht leat." Fiona smiled with the radiance of a happy child, then disappeared, slowly this time, a hand full of twinkling stars fading away with her bright smile. Monique felt a wave of joy infuse her entire body as Fiona's twinkling stars tickled her mind. Monique's vampirc gift was in full swing.

"Why does she do that? Say something weird, then just woosh – fade away?" Susannah unlocked the mandoor of the hangar and pushed the button to raise the bi-fold door.

"I believe, chére, it is her own language, Gaelic, or maybe something older I think. It means goodbye and good luck." Monique shrugged as she watched the massive door rise. Doctor Anderson had helped Fiona? Possibly she could also help Monique.

Just as her words were out, an eerie echoing voice twittered in the cavernous hangar, "Good bye and blessings be with you."

Monique laughed. The little vampire had somehow adopted the Vamp Squad and seemed to pop in and out at will these days. Whatever the Doc did for, or gave to the Librarian, his *official* wife was now their *official* protector and friend. It wasn't such a bad thing. Monique really liked Fiona. The faerie vampire had been invaluable in protecting Olney Farm when the Proctor coven's thugs came after Susannah the previous year.

"Chére, I do stand corrected." Monique waved a hand in the empty air as if Fiona watched from somewhere… or nowhere.

"Just let me get hooked up and you can help push." Susannah slid the front forks into place attaching the front wheel into the tow bar and waved Monique to the tail of the plane. "Just push on the back of the fuselage at the junction of the horizontal stabilizer."

"Susannah, mon ami, what is junction stabilizer? I do not understand your technical words." Monique stood behind the plane with her hands up in the air looking completely frustrated.

"The ass end where the little wings connects. The solid part, Monique." Susannah ran around the plane and pointed to the safe area on which to push.

"Ah ha! Why did you not say that in the first place." The two women worked together and soon the aircraft was safely buttoned up and tucked securely away within the hangar. Susannah could have simply pulled the plane with one hand, but Monique knew they had to maintain their human cover and do what normal humans do in public.

One never knew what eyes watched.

Soon the two ladies, in Monique's little Genesis Coupe, sped along the back roads toward Olney Farm and their first meal of the evening, or day in vampire life. The sun was down and both

Monique and Susannah were feeling the refreshment of day-sleep. Relaxed after her flight time, Susannah yawned, "I hate this sleep thing, Monique. You are a lot older than me and still you need it too. When does it ease up?"

"Chére, I was made a vampire over two hundred years ago. That is still very young for one of our kind. I was only sixteen when the Duc d'Orleans, saved me from the revolutionaries and turned me into what I am today. I guess *saved* is not the correct word to use, since he did end up killing me, ending my human life, anyway. But still, here I am, Monique Alys Merchant, Vamp Squad operative and still not much more than seventeen. Well, I guess I am really about nineteen, but I do not think I look a day over eighteen. Que pensez-vous ?" Monique glanced in the rear-view mirror at her perfect features

"Frenchy, you worry way too much about your looks! And no, you don't look a day over nineteen. Stop worrying. There's the turn off."

As they drove down the well-kept gravel road toward the farm and their secret underground facility, Monique continued to share little secrets of her life with her sister vampire. "It was Christmas Eve and I was going to High Mass at the Sainte Chapelle in the Palais de Justice. I loved the upper chapel. I used to sit with my parents and wonder how the ceiling floated above the stained glass windows so peacefully. The twelve apostles were there, watching over us in their flowing robes, their faces so fabuleusement beau. I thought always they were the holy embodiment of my faith. My faith? I lost that, as well as my human life. Phew!" Monique frowned. "The Revolutionaries attacked my carriage and tore me from my seat. I was thrown to the crowd and would have been murdered on the spot, or worse, if the Duc d'Orleans had not come to my rescue. Pah! Délivrance! I think not. He rescued me from one death to deliver me to another, only days later. He was my maker, my sire. I was so young, so scared. I went with him out of trust. He was a Duke, a gentleman… and a vampire!"

"At least you were young and innocent. I was drunk and stupid." Susannah looked out the window wistfully.

"Oui, ma soeur. And I do not need to paruse old memories." She could feel the deep regret in Susannah's memories. Her brain manifested flashes of Susannah's awakening. The cold. The fear. The loneliness and isolation. "What d'Orleans did was nothing compared to the devils of San Leyre." Monique's fingers gripped the wheel so tightly, her knuckles turned whiter than usual. "Let us think of pretty things, not the dark past."

"Whoa! Slow down, Frenchy. We have company. Looks like State Department pukes. I wonder what's up." Susannah peered out of the tinted windows as they drove by three black SUVs with their respective guards standing watch.

Monique slowed, then steered the car around to the back of the old, decrepit looking barn and through the large open doors. Stopping over what appeared to be a cement drain pad, she depressed the bright red button on the garage door opener and relaxed as the doors creaked behind them enveloping the inside of the barn in darkness. As soon as the doors had completely closed and locked, the car, pad, and women, descended below the floor and stopped on the first-level parking garage.

As the car descended, Monique hugged herself closely. "I hate big black cars. They are effrayant et intimidant. Always they bring bad things…"

"Ah come on, Frenchy. It's probably some high ranking official who never learned to drive." Susannah snickered. She'd met way too many 'high ranking officials' who thought driving themselves was beneath their station. "Besides, they're not *down-under* so Dad can't know them that well." The team and staff at Olney Fram had taken to calling the secret facility below the old farmhouse, *down-under*. It made public discussions easier and kept the secrets, well… secret.

Only those who were trusted and known individuals were allowed into the secret Vamp Squad, or 'VS' facility beneath the quaint Olney Farmhouse in upstate Maine. Colonel Maddox, approved each and every visitor who had access to the facility, himself. Their specially designed subterranean home, with its Operational Command Center, Research Lab and Operations Workshop was top/top secret. It was so well protected, even the neighboring farm, six miles down the road, had no idea what truly lay beneath the well tended fields. So an occasional helicopter landed there in the cover of darkness. And every once in a while, a few large black cars sped down the gravel road. Everything had an explanation and no one in the small community was the wiser.

Although, once a couple years back, a group of drunken high school boys found their way into the farm's pump house for a liquid party. Unfortunately for the kids, Q2 had been testing a new armored vehicle design that particular evening. The flickering lights and loud noises caught the attention of the intoxicated teens who decided to check it out. Caught on the security monitors when they crossed the field, Sgt. Miller down-under tossed a little synth-blood from the V-fridge on his t-shirt, and bounded across the field. Close to the teens, he screamed, "They tried to kidnap me!" At the same time, Major Devlin hit the external speaker button and played a portion of the sound track from *The Day the Earth Stood Still.* Good fun was had by all... except the high-schoolers. They ran for their lives, and didn't stop until they hit town. And then only because the siren and red flashing lights behind their truck were familiar. Since then, kids pretty much stayed away from the *alien farm.* No one really believed the kids' story, so the facility remained isolated and fairly well insulated.

"Monique I'm not sure what's going on. Do you have any clue? "

"No **chére**, I have no idea. We are not expecting anyone. There is no mission on the board." The French vampire surveyed the large metal door connecting the underground parking facility at Olney farm. The secret facility had been expanded in the last year and a half, to include a research department headed up by Dr. Helga Anderson. An armory, presided over by their newest recruit who called himself Q2 after the James Bond character Q, had just been completed the previous month.

"Well I guess we just have to storm the Bastille and see what's going on behind door number one." Susannah swiped her identification card and stood back as a huge heavy metal door swung open. "Here goes nothing."

"Oui, **chére**." Monique did a little flounce and followed Susannah through the door. "Here we go nothing,"

Susannah laughed and dragged her sister down the hallway. "Frenchy, you got to get this slang thing right. Otherwise you sound like you don't know how to speak English."

"**Chér**, I do not know how to speak English. And I have so much fun with the... sayings you make. You have no idea how difficult it is for a French woman to learn your American language, with all of its unique words and..."

Monique froze.

"Frenchy? Frenchy..." Susanna jerked to a stop as Monique anchored her in place. "What's wrong, Monique?"

"Susannah, do you hear that voice?" Monique remained in

place and began to shake. "It is French voice."

Monique clutched at Suzanne's arm squeezing her hand as tight she could, which for a vampire was very tight. "Susannah, do not let them take me! Please, you must not let them take me back. I could not endure…"

"Frenchy? Monique? Let go of my hand. You're breaking my fingers. I know they'll heal, but really, would you let go…"

"No, Susannah, I know they have come for me. Do not let them take me." Every part of Monique's body was shaking. Her eyes began to turn the characteristic red of a vampire who is excited or afraid.

"Monique, come on. You don't know anyone has come for you. Besides, Dad wouldn't let anyone take you anywhere. You're part of the Vamp Squad. He would never let anyone break up our team, our family. Come on, let's go see what's going on." She dragged Monique through the second security door and into the Operations Command Center, known as the OCC. In the farmhouse above, three men could be seen on the computer screen talking with Captain Devlin and Colonel Maddox. The ladies pressed their backs against the steel wall and stood quietly, eavesdropping via the surveillance cameras in the house above them. Safe, tucked below the farmhouse, they focused intently on the conversation.

"So why did General **Pantterdyck** send you to us, again?" Colonel Maddox frowned at the three-piece-suit standing a few feet away in the tiny kitchen above the OCC of the facility.

*Uh-oh. If dickhead's involved, it must be serious, Monique.* Susannah psyche-spoke to her sister vampire with raised eyebrows.

*Oui, souer.* Monique inched closer. *I do not recognize the French one.* There was relief in the emotional attachment to the message.

"Maybe I can shed a little more light on this problem, Sir. Donald Smythe, State Department."

"Yes, yes. I got the name during the very long introductions. Light… shed it." Maddox had little patience with protocol.

"Yes, Sir." Smythe stepped back so he could talk with his hands. "The Academia de Santo Domingo de Silos houses several American students from a variety of families stationed or assigned overseas. The kids are from military, as well as State Department, and government contractor's families. It is a fairly expensive school so the families are well off and of good quality."

At that comment, Monique used her little pinky finger to push her nose into the air. She sent her coven sister a psyche-giggle.

Captain Devlin cocked his head at the little man who obviously didn't understand the implications of what he had just said. Good quality? Well off families translated to spoiled rich kids in Devlin's book.

Smythe caught the body language immediately "What I mean to say is…" He stammered. "Well, the academy has very high standards. It also has very good security because of the clientele, clearly…"

"And…" Smythe had exhausted what little patience Maddox had left.

"Well, Sir. Something is going on at the Academy. It's some kind of drug issue. Kids who have never been involved in that kind of thing are ending up in the infirmary with some very strange symptoms. Two have died. One son of a very important politician, and one son of a diplomat. And, Sir, Thomas Pantterdyck and his girlfriend, Lucy Redmont are at Walter Reed. They were medevac'd in last Friday. Both are in some kind of coma."

"Tommy's in a coma? From drug use at his private school?" That immediately caught the attention of Captain Devlin. Monique was amazed at the intensity of the Captain's reaction. It made her bones rattle and sent shivers up her spine. "That's impossible. Tommy hates drugs. He would never use. He would never, *ever* give drugs to his girlfriend. Now I get it. Pantterdyck has a stake in this thing. A seventeen year old stake." Devlin shook his head in disbelief. "Frank, we need to take this mission. I mean, ya know…look into this situation."

Who was this child, other than the son of an American Army General? Monique was confused. And why was he attending a private school in Europe? In Spain?

Mr. Smythe stepped forward to hand Colonel Maddox a secure folder. The big capital letters plastered across the front read, TOP SECRET. It was about an inch thick. "Sir, intel on this… situation."

"Hold up there a minute." Maddox was playing for time. He knew Sgt. Miller would be down-under on a secure line to General Pantterdyck, as the little gathering in the kitchen of the quaint farmhouse continued to chat. "So let me get this straight. Kids in some French foo-foo school are doing drugs and that is a matter of national security?"

"Spanish... now. Perhaps I can be of assistance." A tall redheaded man behind Smythe spoke with a calm quiet voice adjusting his clerical collar. He was a priest? A Catholic priest? Monique mentally snorted catching Susannah's attention. "The drug is something we cannot identify. Even the European Centre for Disease Prevention and Control, the EDCD, has taken a look at blood samples, and is unable to provide more information than what we have, which is virtually nothing." He indicated the file with a slim, pale index finger. "The Abbott at San Leyre contacted the Vatican to request help. Now that an American child of an important person has been afflicted, there seems to be an urgency in solving this puzzle." His ginger characteristics lent a feminine mystique to his body language. His face was slightly freckled with smooth soft skin.

At the mention of San Leyre, Monique blanched, as if that was possible for a vampire. A squeak issued forth just prior to a strangling sound. "San Leyre? Mon Dieu, aide-moi!" She braced herself against the wall, panting. Spain? At the monastery where she was held prisoner and tortured? For years?

"Drugs are nasty business. Apparently, now they are an international nasty business. With, of course, the affliction of these two American students." The priest continued. Monique could feel his attitude as if he'd taken careful aim and slugged her right in the stomach.

Susannah eyed her sister. Vampires did not pant. Nor did they have the need to breathe air! This was bad. She peered at the monitor trying to read the body language of the humans.

The priest's attitude was apparent to everyone. Even Smythe looked apologetically at Devlin. Susannah could tell the redheaded priest firmly believed the privileged American kids partied a little too hard and were paying the price.

"Father Song..." Apparently Devlin could not remember the rest of his name.

"Songoria, The Very Reverend Father Disjagio von Songoria." He smiled down his long patrician nose at Devlin. "It is a simple title." He adjusted his clerical collar once again.

Hate welled up inside Monique. The priest was completely enveloped in his title and the collar he wore. Like the monks who terrorized her for so long. Her eyes turned a deep wine red and she came very close to growling at the figure on the monitor. He was a priest. A member of the Devil's band of hideous monsters.

*Italian and ginger? It doesn't fit.* Susannah psyched her coven sister.

*But the collar does. He shall die!* Monique's fingers curled leaving long scratch marks in the metal wall behind the two women.

*Down, Frenchy. He doesn't know we listen, or you are here. Let's hear him out.* Susannah took her sister's hand. *Calm down. The eyes...*

The conversation above continued.

"Right. Ah, Father..." Devlin waved off the rest of the priest's name. "I know this boy. He would never do drugs, I tell you."

"I completely understand." There was that placating smile again, firmly in place on the priest's freckled face. "But you must understand when children leave the control of their parents, they often change. These changes may lead them on a course..." The priest opened his arms wide. "Even their parents do not understand. Children will be children. They need a strong hand of discipline. The Lord's discipline."

"You mean to tell me, you think the Lord is punishing Tommy..."

"Rob, I think we've talked enough." Colonel Maddox took the file from Smythe. "We'll take a look at this and let you know if we're interested. I assume your contact information is in here." Maddox tapped the brown cover of the file.

"Yes, Sir. Thank you, Sir." Smythe turned to the last member of the group. "Franco, do you have anything to add?"

In heavily accented English, the third man in the visiting party responded, "No, I believe you have covered everything. I wish only to add..." He stopped, searching for the right word. "...help is needed to find the beginning place of this new drug dangereux. We are confondu. He bowed slightly to Maddox and Devlin. "All children are not safe now."

Smythe reinforced what the French/Spanish Liaison officer stated. "Lt. Etxebarria is correct. So far we have only seen this drug at the Academy. Its effects are devastating and we do not even know what it is. We cannot fight what we do not know. But if it goes beyond the academy..."

Lt. Etxebarria again commented in halting English. "If this thing, this drug dangereux comes out of the Académie, children in the country will die. It is bad. Très mal."

Devlin extended his hand to the officer. "Merci, Lt. Etxebarria. Nous ferons de notre mieux pour aider. Nous parlerons bientôt."

Below the farmhouse, Monique squeaked. *I did not know Captain Devlin spoke French. We will have to talk of this!* Her psyched comment came with a mental blow. *We will do our best? We shall talk soon? Hmmm. Our Captain may never talk again. I shall cut his tongue out!*

Susannah snickered. How many times had Monique murmured something in French thinking no one near understood? The cat was out of the bag now. She did not envy Uncle Rob the coming chat. Monique was constantly occupied with sexuality, but the French vampire had a temper as well.

They stood against the wall watching the three visitors depart the farmhouse above.

"Ladies, what do you think is in envelope number one?" Sgt. Miller spun his chair, as he pointed to Colonel Maddox entering the back stairs off the kitchen. Miller had a sixth sense and was aware of everyone's movements at any one time. It was almost preternatural. Miller's command center was his home-away-from-home and he could monitor everything in and around the farm from his hi-tech post. And he did.

Still uncomfortable and a little scared about the visitors above, Monique jumped.

"Beggin' your pardon, Ma'am. Ms. Maddox, what do ya think's up?" Miller tended to keep his distance from Monique as she teased him outrageously. While he had become a little more comfortable working with her, he still did not trust the sexy French vamp. He lightly touched the plastic collar he wore beneath his uniform blouse…just for personal security.

"Good question, Milo. Dr. Anderson will have to take a look at the scientific stuff. Probably way over my head, and yours too. But a new drug? Only at the private school? Sounds like experimentation to me. I thought monastery schools were like prisons. How's the stuff getting in?"

The metal door slid open with a woosh. "Children will be children, according to that swishy priest." Devlin snorted, then placed a quick kiss on Susannah's cheek. "How was the flight, kiddo?"

"Uneventful." Susannah waved to her Dad.

"Just the way I like it." Three voices combined to recite the often-repeated phrase. Susannah giggled and did a little finger explosion in the air. "Fiona joined us until final. She doesn't trust machines and didn't want to stay for the end though."

Miller mumbled across the room. "She terrifies half the people in the world, but she is afraid of machines? Really?"

Colonel Maddox had to smile at that comment. Truth be told, Fiona scared the living daylights out of him. "Miller, could you reach General Pantterdyck?"

"Sir, no Sir. His aide said he was on medical leave. Probably at the hospital with his son, Sir." Sgt. Miller kept his eyes on his computer screen.

Monique remained silent in her position against the wall. She eyed Captain Devlin suspeciously as he walked by. It didn't take long for Miller's tension to slide into her mind from his position in the OCC.

"Well, get him. I need the skinny on this situation. I'd also like to know how Tommy is doing." It was a clear order.

"Sir, with all due respect, how do you…"

Maddox cut him off with the *Colonel* look. "Miller, I've read your file, remember? Get him on the horn. Buzz me when you do." Maddox turned to his daughter.

"Good flight, huh? Fiona, huh?" Maddox patted Susannah's shoulder on the way out the door.

Monique watched as Susannah broke into a bright smile. Things sure changed in the last year. She'd gone from an irresponsible, rebellious teen, to a talented and competent operative. And a pilot. Her father had gone from an overbearing, controlling colonel, to a proud dad.

Susannah shook her head.

Monique remained against the wall, quietly eyeing the retreating Captain Devlin, her arms clenched tightly across her chest. There was fire behind her pretty chocolate eyes. The wheels were obviously churning and the target was clearly the Captain.

## Chapter 6

### Truths

"Truth be told" is a saying so bold,
But wherein lies the actual hold?
Of a person's way, a lie deftly sold,
A flittering thought, an act so cold.

*Angellique Treich-Laplène, Vampire Council of Elders*
*Mistress of the Spider People*
*Côte d'Ivoire, Africa, 2014*

"Milo, what the hell does that mean? I read your file? What does that have to do with the General and Tommy in the hospital?" Susannah moved to stand behind the Sergeant at his comm desk. Monique knew Milo had come to them under duress, but was now an integral part of the team. He was the ultimate wheeler and dealer and could be depended upon to find just about anything.

And procure it.

But personally contact a General? Monique wondered...

"Long story." Milo turned to his computer. A bunched fist hit the edge of the desk. "Can I have a minute, ladies?"

Susanna nodded quietly and moved back to Monique. They stood against the sterile steel wall, watching the comm screens.

Milo fished a small cell phone out of his pocket and moved a finger across the screen. Placing the phone to his ear, he waited patiently.

Nothing.

The usually chipper Sergeant sighed heavily. "Well it was a good try, Miller."

His thumbs raced across the screen with a message intended for someone, but Monique wondered who that someone might be. How would a sergeant be connected to a general?

In less than a minute the cell phone vibrated, twirling in a circle on the desk.

Milo watched the little telephone spin in a circle.

Elizabeth quietly joined the growing crowd watching the

Sergeant. *What is he doing?* Elizabeth psyche-spoke to her two operatives.

Susannah responded first. *I'm not really sure. Dad gave him an order to get ahold of General Pantterdyck. I have no idea how my father expects a sergeant, to call a general out of the blue. This should be interesting. I asked him about it just a moment ago. He said it was a long story. Whatever that means.*

*General Pantterdyck? The one you call dickhead? This should be interesting.* The coven mistress gently kissed Monique on the cheek. *Calm the eyes, dear. You will scare the humans.*

Monique responded. *Did you know Captain Devlin spoke very good French?*

*Calm, dear. And yes, didn't you?* Elizabetta winked at Susannah.

The phone on the desk stopped buzzing and lay still as a headstone on some long forgotten grave. Miller punched the desk again. Just as he reached for it, the phone began its dance once again.

"Ah, shit." Miller picked up the cell phone. "Jackie? Don't hang up. Please!"

With their enhanced hearing, the vamps in the room could follow the conversation as if they were all on a conference call. Monique could feel every twang of guilt, every twinge of excitement, every... well every emotion the Sergeant felt as he spoke to the mysterious person on the other end of the phone. It was her vampiric gift.

"Sergeant, why would *I* call you to hang up?" The woman on the other end of the phone had a strangely mixed American/French accent. "Oh, that's right. I'm not supposed to talk to you. And you are not supposed to have any kind of contact with me, right?" There was a very pregnant pause. "So why the call after all this time, Milo?"

"Sweet cheeks..."

"Don't call me that. You have no right to call me that any more." Monique felt the hot flash of anger in the woman at the other end of the line. Her vampiric gift of emotional empathy was certainly in good form... and growing stronger.

"Okay, Jackie. Jacquiline. Okay. Um... I ah..."

"Spit it out, Milo. You never had trouble with those lips before." The conversation was getting ugly and all signs of a French accent were gone.

"Honey. I mean, Jackie... I need to get ahold of your father." Sergeant Miller winced as he waited for a response.

"Whyyyy...?" The mystery Jacquiline drew out the word like a verse in a song. It curled around Miller's gut like a rattlesnake preparing to strike. Monique actually felt for the Sergeant as she fanned away the heat of the woman's words.

"Ah, business. Military stuff." He wondered how much she knew, and if she would cooperate.

Then it came.

The strike.

"After all these years. Let me see. Four years seven days, six hours and... fourteen minutes. You decide to call me out of the blue. TO ASK ME ABOUT MY FATHER?"

Miller could hear someone in the background shushing Jackie. He spoke quickly. "Please, Jacks. It's important. About Tommy's... condition. You know?"

The line was silent. But the message and it's intended pain blazed across Monique's mind and heart. She was beginning to understand the part this Jacks played in Miller's life.

"Jackie? Jackie? Jackie, please. I need to talk to the General." Monique had never seen Milo beg. It was not pretty. He was usually the one in control, all cocky and smart. But Monique could also feel Milo's heart begin to break into a million pieces. Obviously the good Sergeant had a serious emotional attachment to the mystery woman.

"Then speak, Miller." General Pantterdyck's voice was clear and low.

Stunned for a moment, Miller instantaneously morphed into the model soldier. "Sir, my Commander has asked that I contact you concerning the issue at San Leyre. Our unit has been engaged to investigate the situation and we were given to understand you have pertinent information. Sir." Milo hit the button that automatically buzzed Colonel Maddox's cell phone with a 'report immediately' message.

"That would be an understatement, Miller." He didn't have to be Monique to feel the deep sorrow in that simple statement, Miller could almost empathize with the General.

Almost.

There was too much baggage between them for empathy.

Monique, on the other hand, did feel the deep sadness in the General's statement. She could also feel a sense of abandonment in the man's voice. It was clear to her he'd already given up on his son's life. The man's grief was palatable and left a sour taste in her mouth.

"Yes, Sir. Please extend my…" Miller paused. Condolences? That wasn't right. "…my prayers to your family, Sir. Tommy was such…"

Such a what?

Monique could tell Miller was at a loss for words and distinctly uncomfortable.

"Not was, Miller. Is. He still is, so far." The General's voice cracked on the last word. Like a sucker punch to the gut, Monique winced.

"Milo? Is that you, chére?"

The phone had changed hands again.

Miller immediately recognized the voice of Jackie's mother. "Harold has stepped out for a moment. It is a difficult time for him."

"Of course, Ma'am. Maybe we can do something about that. I'm with a special unit now. We've been asked to look into the problem. I don't mean to sound so formal. We're gonna figure out what happened with the kids and fix it, Mrs. Pantterdyck."

Her voice could barely be heard over the cell phone. "I'm sure you will, Milo." There was another pause, then she seemed to rally on the other end of the phone. "And, Milo, it's Ceauchene now. Mrs. Ceauchene."

Maddox burst through the door on the run. "Miller?"

"Of course, Ma'am. Sorry, Ma'am. If the General is ready to talk, Colonel Maddox is here." Miller waved to Maddox to wait just a minute, not something he would generally do to a superior officer, but this was the Vamp Squad and things were a bit different, considering…

"And Ma'am, please tell Jackie… I don't know. Please tell her that I hope her brother will be okay. We'll do everything we can. And Ma'am, this unit has some pretty extensive and capable resources, if you can read between the lines."

"Sergeant Miller, that was my main job as Harold's wife. I shall tell her for you. Here is the General."

"Thank you, Ma'am." Miller pointed to Maddox then to the phone.

"Sir, please hold for Colonel Maddox." Miller handed the phone to the Colonel and offered Maddox his chair.

Devlin moved in to listen to the conversation, now on speaker.

They all listened.

Except Sergeant Miller who tried to leave the room unnoticed.

It didn't work.

"Miller, you little horndog. A General's daughter? A little above your pay grade, buddy." Susannah followed Miller through the security door, smacking him softly on the back of his head. She pulled Monique with her. Not to be left out of the gossip and intrigue, Monique followed along quietly. Many a time, following along quietly had saved her and Mathilda's lives. And often gained more than that.

Miller spun on Susannah. "Let it go, Susannah."

"Oh no, no, no my infamous Sergeant Casanova. Now I understand Dad's comment about your file. She was the one, huh? Dickhead caught you? Wow." She linked arms with Miller and strolled down the hallway connecting the Operation Command Center and the combination lounge/chow hall in the central hub of the complex. Monique followed quietly.

"Better you than me. Dickhead's hell on wheels. Everybody knows that. How could you hook up with his daughter?" Susannah began the verbal interrogation. Monique just let the feelings flow through her.

Miller shook his head with a smile. "Fake ID. Loud music. Too much booze. A quaint little bar on Sixteenth Street. A very low-cut mini dress and some very bad judgment." He continued to shake his head as he strolled arm in arm with the one person on the Vamp Squad he had come to see as a sister. "Ya know, Suze, I still think she was the one." Miller sighed again. "Turns out she was the one all right. The wrong one, according to her father."

"Ah, the memories. Buck up Milo. This might be a new beginning, a chance to renew old…"

"Oh, hell no. You've got to be kidding, right?" Miller slid his ID badge across the panel on the wall and the door to the lounge slipped silently open. The lounge was empty of humans and vamps. "Snack?"

"Yeah - good idea. Sun's down but I'm a little tanked. Flying always makes me hungry." Susannah took two bags of synth-blood from the black fridge as Miller removed a Coke from the white one. Food in the facility was stored separately for humans and vamps, for obvious reasons. She handed one bag to the silent Monique, with a wink.

The facility designers had gone to great lengths to make the habitat as comfortable as possible for the two species that lived together. They'd done a fabulous job. The center of the underground complex was a big hexagon with halls off each of the six sides. Every door was secure and required an ID pass card. One hallway led to the vamp quarters, completely adapted for their style of living. The human quarters were off a hallway directly across the lounge, behind the kitchen area. The Operation Command Center was at the end of a short hall connected to the parking garage across from the Research Lab and the recreation and training center. It was a massive complex, secure, underground and perfect.

It was home.

Homey was yet to come, but Elizabetta and Dr. Anderson were working on that. If the installation could be viewed from the air, it would resemble a kind of snowflake with six arms. Each arm having multiple rooms off the main arms. Several exits to the ground level above were built into the facility. The parking garage was beneath the old 'distressed' barn on the surface. The main lounge and kitchen were below the cozy farmhouse with an elevator to the basement washroom of the house. The research labs and training center connected to the detached garage above, with emergency exits from the vamp quarters to the farm pump house. The human quarters exited to the horse stalls across the field from the main house. Stairs came up in the tack room behind a secret wall. A retired Major and his wife were the official residents of Olney Farm and actually worked the farm while on the government payroll as a 'specialized' security detail. Mr. and Mrs. Burnside, better known as Uncle Roger and Aunt Mandy, kept the place fit and trim... and cozy looking to the outside world. No one suspected that Uncle Roger plowed some very expensive fields and *down-under* didn't mean Australia.

Susannah slurped the last of her snack, licked the red from her lips and shot Miller a goofy smile. "Hmm... Fake ID. Loud music. Too much booze. A quaint little bar. A very low-cut evening dress and some very bad judgment. Sounds just like me." She punched Miller on the shoulder.

"They both didn't end so great, did they?" Miller slumped on the couch. Susannah could see the longing in Millers face. He must have really cared for this gal.

Monique could feel the same longing for the past, but in a more visceral way. Once, when? But it was clear, once, the Sergeant had very strong feelings for this mystery woman who she now knew was a general's daughter. She waited patiently for the rest of the story.

"So, what really went down with... Jackie? Is that her name? Wait...are you talking about Jackie Pantterdyck? Oh My God! Jackie P?" The name finally connected in her mind. Susannah suppressed her excitement. Her old friend Jackie P? Milo's secret end-of-career-girlfriend-mistake was an old friend she'd lost contact with? Susannah psyched to Monique, *I know this girl! We were friends when our families were stationed together almost... well it was a bit ago.*

"Jacquiline. Yep. I call her Jackie. Her dad hates that. We met up at a bar. She had fake ID and told me she was twenty-one. She looked twenty-one. She acted more mature than most twenty-one year olds. We hit it off." Miller shifted nervously. "One thing led to another. You know how it is."

"Yeah, I know how it is. Why didn't you tell her you were an NCO?" Susannah continued her interrogation.

"I did! She told me her dad was a college professor and wasn't home very often. He supposedly worked at a university upstate. Right. Some university; Military U!" Miller sipped his can of soda. "She was so beautiful. So smart. It was weeks before I figured out something was up. Then, BAM! Up was down. Dad was on my tail, and I had a choice; 10 years at Leavenworth for rape and contributing to the delinquency of a minor, or an unusual assignment with the promise that I never see his daughter again. Never see. Never talk. Never correspond. Never touch... in any way, shape or form."

Regret swirled around the galley and landed on the table in front of Monique. Disappointment, remorse, guilt and intense heartache lay there, pulsing with life.

"So you bailed and never looked back." Susannah tossed her empty bag into the trashcan a few feet away.

"Come on, Suze. It's not like I wanted to. You know how it can be in the military. General Pantterdyck had my balls in his hands. Think about your own upbringing. Can you imagine what your dad would have done, if I tried to date you, let alone... ya know."

Wringing his hands, Miller looked pleadingly at Susannah. He needed someone on his side and she'd already decided then and there, it would be her. Monique nodded her complicity as she felt Susannah's decision.

"Nuff said, brother from a different mother. I get the point." She giggled and bounced onto the couch next to him. She encircled the Sergeant in a big sisterly hug. "My dad wouldn't have sent you down-under. He would have stripped the flesh from your bones, hung it up to dry and made a lamp shade out of it for the living room."

"I saw that once, in the World War II. The Nazi's did it to Jews. It was not joli. " Monique commented in a whisper. She was trying to rid herself of Miller's depressing emotional baggage that inundated her thoughts. Recalling Nazi torture was not the way.

"That's gross, Monique. Where do you get that stuff from?" Miller was smiling, finally.

Monique shrugged with a bit of a wince. She'd seen a lot over the years and vampires were the least of the violent species that inhabited the world.

"That's my dad. Milo, why don't you see about getting together with Jacquiline to mend fences? She's probably worried to death over her brother and you could be a convenient shoulder." She did the *Magnum PI* eyebrow thing at him. "It could work... maybe. Course, I don't know how pissed she was when you walked away, nay, got blackmailed and carted away by her father."

"Pissed? On a scale of one to ten... um, about four hundred. She called me just before I changed assignments and headed for Maine. I could hear her through the phone. From across the room." He squirmed again. "She didn't understand why I didn't stand up to her father. I didn't understand why she didn't stand up to him. I was a grown up NCO, but she was his daughter. It wasn't until later that I found out we had about the same amount of influence with him. The same amount of blackmail going on, as well." He groaned. "Jackie got carted off to private school in North Dakota. North Dakota for God's sake. I got sentenced to down-under. She got sentenced to Frozen jail time."

"Oh Milo. It's past. Let it go. And make up for it. Girls love that. Penance. We love penance. Precious stones, shoes, a good manicure and a man who understands guilt and penance. Get the drift?" She kissed his cheek and pulled him off the couch. "To work with you. Go."

"How did your nineteen year old brain get so smart, young lady?" Milo gave Susannah a quick hug. He nodded to Monique who still sat quietly, observing… feeling.

"You mean nineteen again, and again, and again, etc. Maybe, blame it on Jordan. Since we've been… ya know." Susannah made quote marks in the air with her fingers, "I've been thinking a lot about relationships."

The central intercom beeped and a mechanical sounding voice spoke from a panel on the wall. "Sergeant Miller, report."

"Gotta go, Suze. Thanks for being…you." Another quick hug and Miller was off down the hall on the run.

"Wow. That's a first." Susannah yawned and ambled toward her quarters with Monique. "Thanks for being me? Sweet! What'd you get out of that?"

"The Sergeant is very disturbed. This woman, you called her Jackie? She and the Sergeant were very close. He has big regrets. I could feel so much confusion. But also much love still. Both have it. Should I tell Sergeant Miller?"

"Nah. I've found it's best to let them work things out. Never, I mean *never*, get in between two friends when things go south." Susannah shook her head.

"Why would they go south if they are unhappy? I would go somewhere like Disneyland, or someplace very happy if I felt sad. Monique wrinkled her forehead in thought. "Or possibly shopping in Paris! That would make me happy. I do not understand this south going."

"No kidding, Frenchy." Susannah slung an arm across her coven sister's shoulder. "Let's go watch something funny. Maybe Caddy Shack. I love that movie. Whack those gophers!" She popped Monique on the head.

Chapter 7

Being Me

Grow up. It's what he would always say.
Grow up, and stop this childish play.

Well, there comes a time, when 'up' has no meaning,
And childish play, is simply demeaning.

We all see the world, through our own perspective,
But without love, nothing is reflective.

*Susannah Maddox, Operative*
*Vamp Squad*
*Olney, Maine 2015*

"Miller, set up an evening airlift to Walter Reed tonight. The General and I need to talk. Alert Dr. Anderson. I want her with us. Include Ms. Merchant and my daughter. Susannah knew Tommy well as a child. She may be able to do that head thing that Miss… I mean Mrs. Milassoviech is teaching her. Captain Devlin will arrange security." Maddox shouted through the open door of his office in the OCC. "Ms. Merchant, may be able to shed some light on the San Leyre part of this thing."

Miller peeked through the doorway. "Us?" It came out as a high-pitched squeak.

"Yes." The Colonel paused, looking up from his enormous monitor. "Us… Now."

"Sir, I'm not sure my presence would be the best, um… thing right now, Sir." Miller stood at attention as if he were briefing the Colonel on some important piece of intel.

"Grow a pair, Sergeant. She's only a girl. She can't be that bad. I know her mother."

Miller tiptoed into the Colonel's office and sat down in a leather chair facing Maddox's massive desk. Everything in the office was bigger than life, including the Colonel. "Sir, in that respect she is more like her father, than Mrs. Pantterdyck, I mean, Ceauchene. Sir, I really don't think…"

70

Maddox cut the Sergeant off with a growl. "I don't care what you think, Miller. You can get us a flight or I'll feed you to Monique." The Colonel bit the side of his cheek to keep from laughing out loud.

After a few seconds of staring at the floor, Miller glanced up. "That was a joke... wasn't it, Sir?" The whisper came out sort of strangled and low.

Maddox got up and came around his desk to perch on the edge in a fatherly fashion. "Miller, when I said I read your file, I meant I *read* your file. All of it. Pantterdyck's statement and order of discipline. Your statement. Jacquiline's statement. The JAG's comments. Everything." He rubbed his chin and lowered his voice. "My daughter calls Pantterdyck a dickhead, and she is right most of the time. He is a dickhead. Most of the time. But what I know for sure about the General is, he loves his children. All of them. By all the various wives and women in his life." Maddox shook his head and moved to the chair beside Miller. "I lost count a few years back, but that's irrelevant. Tommy's a great kid. I watched him play lacrosse last year in the EU International Challenge. He was a dynamo on the field. He's not a kid who would do drugs." Colonel Maddox paused, gazing at the picture of his family next to the monitor on his desk.

"Like your Tommy, Sir." Miller commented softly.

Male bonding time was over. Maddox stood and adjusted his uniform blouse. "No. Not like my Tommy, Miller. My Tommy never got the chance to grow up and be anything." After a short pause, the Colonel continued. "But maybe we can make sure General Pantterdyck's Tommy can." He moved back to his command seat behind the monitor. "The flight, Miller. Now. And yes, you will be with us. Devlin will make sure you have protection." The smug smirk was back under a thin veil of rank and command.

"Sir, if I may, Sir. Your daughter..."

"You may not, Sergeant. The flight."

"Yes, Sir." Miller popped a crisp salute, spun on his heel and left the office, only to come face to face with Lieutenant Previn just beyond the door.

"That was bizarre, Miller." It was clear the Lieutenant had been eves dropping just outside the office.

"Roger that, Sir." Miller headed for his own station in the corner of the OCC. Like everyone at the facility, he detested the sneaky Previn, who was assigned to the Vamp Squad as their official bean counter. In reality, everyone knew he was actually the 'eyes' of the Joint Chiefs. While his rank demanded a certain amount of protocol, respect was not something associated with Previn. No one forgot the fact that just a few years back, he destroyed a coven of vampires. One that included his own sister.

"So, Miller, what's up with the fatherly thing?" Previn followed the Sergeant back to his station.

"I'm not sure I understand what you are talking about, Sir. Colonel Maddox gave me an order to set up a night flight. Clear and simple." Miller fixed Previn with a cold stare. "Clear and simple, Sir.

"Yeah, yeah, I got it, Miller. Just make sure you do the paperwork right and get it to me on time." Previn waved off the stare and disappeared into his own office.

Ted sat at a console across the room watching the latest Oriole's game. He never took his eyes off the game, but shot Miller a 'thumbs up'. He murmured under his breath, just loud enough for the Sergeant to hear. "The little rat wants a crumb."

"No can do." Miller's response came with a big smile. "How long you staying at the funny farm this time?" Miller's fingers were flying over the keyboard as he spoke. Multi-tasking was Milo's middle name.

"Til the play-offs are over. My team's got a good chance. Maybe I'll stay through Halloween. That oughta be a gas around here." Ted was one of those fringe civilians involved with the initial conception of the Vamp Squad. Truth be told, he actually saved Maddox from his own daughter after her turning. When Susannah popped out of her coffin in the back of the ice cream truck and went for her dad's jugular, Ted was right there to slam the lid on that one. With Maddox shaken to the core and trying to figure out the universe according to Dracula, Ted was also there to help transport the baby vamp to the Olney Farm safe house. Learning about vampires was quite a challenge to his version of reality, too. However, in the beginning, he'd rallied well and had been a civilian asset ever since. His real name was Johnny Michael Hasskiss, but nobody wanted to call a six foot five inch, three hundred pound African American tackle anything that had kiss and ass in it. So Ted it was. He seemed to like it, and everyone down-under kept their body parts intact.

"You got a side bet goin', my man?" Miller always had

little bets and scams running simultaneously. He knew Ted liked the betting life as well.

"No more of that in my life, Milo. Almost lost mama last year. She told me some stuff that made sense. She said I got to clean up my life. Wish I could have told her about this." His arms spread wide. "Course, a good Christian woman would never have believed I actually live with vamps. Sometimes, I still don't." Ted returned to his game and shouted. "Oh no, man! How could you?"

"Know what ya mean. Sometimes I still don't believe it. I just do what I'm told." Miller hit a key with a little more gusto than necessary. "There. Done. Done and done. Flight, paperwork and orders."

Miller forwarded the information to the necessary people and joined Ted in front of the game. "But I don't mind the duty, ya know."

"Nice toys. Eye candy all around…"

Miller cut Ted off. "Eye candy? More like killer candy. Nice to look at, as long as you avoid the eyes. Don't forget the dead part. Oh, and then there's the blood sucking…" Miller gave an exaggerated shiver. "Burrrrr."

"Come on, Milo. You know the gals ain't dead. They just got a virus. They got changed. You know, like zombies, only pretty and sexy as hell." Ted jumped in his seat. "Damn, see that boy run. Someone tackle that son of a bitch. Jeeze." Ted smacked his palm with his fist.

"Watch the language, Ted." Milo nodded toward the Colonel's office.

"Yeah, yeah. I'll watch my language and you watch your dick." Ted grabbed his crotch and moved it up and down. "I heard."

"Crap, Ted. Could you be more crass?" Milo hit the intercom buttons for Dr. Anderson and Elizabetta. He lowered his mouth to the mic. "Ladies, your ride will be here just before sundown. We plan to over-day at Bethesda. Accomodations have been arranged."

"Got it, Sergeant Miller." Dr. Anderson was obviously in her lab. Milo could hear some kind of mechanical buzz in the background.

"Thank you, Milo." Elizabetta mumbled her response. The Coven Mistress was clearly close to day sleep.

"So, you wanna talk about the annoyed woman on the other

end of the phone?" Ted was digging for answers and some fun at Milo's expense. "After all, us human guys have to stick together."

"Negatory. I want to finish the paperwork and hit the rack for a while. Obviously I've got the night shift, again."

"So, you gonna leave me hangin' bro?" A commercial flashed across the TV.

"Yep. It's classified. If I tell ya, I gotta kill ya." Milo smirked.

"Whoa, bro. That shit don't work here. I got me a top secret, double top secret thing goin'. You know that." Ted got out of his chair and stood in front of Milo's computer screens.

"You don't have my clearance. No digging into my life here. Your file is a lot bigger than mine."

With that, Ted returned to his game and Milo headed towards the human quarters.

"Night, sweet thang." Ted's girly voice followed the Sergeant down the hall.

## Chapter 8

### Family

As a child, you are with family
Surrounded by love and happily
You reach for the knowledge of life,
To find a role in the worldly strife.

It seems to be egregiously unfair
Yet still you haphazardly dare
To test the Guardian Angel of Fate
Only to find, it is too late!

Too late to go back, reverse, return,
To that which only you did discern,
Would be your life, your family and fate.
Child of the Night, it is way too late!

*Monique Alys Merchant, Operative*
*Vamp Squad*
*Olney, Maine 2015*


The CH47 helicopter landed on the PT field behind the Uniformed Services University of the Health Sciences at Bethesda. The new title for the base that combined Walter Reed and Bethesda hospitals was too long to remember and had gone through so many changes in the last few years, Sergeant Miller just referred to it as Bethesda. The new landing field near the front of the remodeled Walter Reed National Military Medical Center (WRNMMC) was not yet completed, so a caravan of black Suburbans ferried the group to the hospital entrance not even half a mile away. Milo sat fidgeting next to Elizabetta. He was not looking forward to the reunion that awaited on the fifth floor, room 516. He was curious to a point. But like passing a horrific accident on the freeway; you didn't want to look, but couldn't look away either. He didn't want to face Jackie, but couldn't resist seeing her again. Just one more time.

He chewed a hangnail until it bled.

"Milo, please sit still and refrain from producing fresh blood. I am old enough to resist your leaking finger, but I am not sure of the rest of my coven. Susannah is but a baby still.

"Ma'am, she would never..." Milo looked startled.

"Forewarned is forearmed, Sergeant. I prefer protecting my coven against any little transgressions. You are worried seeing this young woman of your past, once again?" Elizabetta took the hem of her black skirt and pressed it to Milo's finger.

"We did not part under such good circumstances, Ma'am. I was..." Another finger came to his mouth and Elizabetta promptly lowered it to his lap, placing her cool hand over his. "It is complicated."

"So I am given to understand. The Colonel shared some of your story with me." The Coven Mistress smiled at the nervous Sergeant in a motherly fashion. She patted the hand she already held down. "You will survive, dear."

"I certainly hope so." He grimaced.

The caravan pulled up to the Emergency department drive-through and the passengers began to disembark. It was past sunset but still early for some of the team to be out and about so the transition was rapidly accomplished. The General's Adjunct met them in the receiving area and escorted them to the fifth floor as quickly and quietly as possible.

Milo hung back, but kept the group in sight. Walter Reed was a maze of corridors, ramps, elevators and doorways. He would never have found his way to Tommy Pantterdyck's room on his own. Half of the new hospital was completed several years before, but the construction continued to date. It was an expansive complex with a mixture of old, new, traditional and modern.

From his position in the rear, Milo watched the Colonel and General Pantterdyck's friendly greeting. At the commotion, Chantal Pantterdyck-Ceauchene poked her head out of Tommy's room and flew into the arms of the Colonel, then crushed Susannah to her. Captain Devlin was next to receive Chantal's warm greeting. He blushed appropriately and Milo had to snicker. Captain Devlin was not used to beautiful women smearing red lipstick across his face.

After hugs and kisses all around, Colonel Maddox introduced the other members of the team, leaving Milo for last. "Milo, my dear, I was so happy to hear from you. Especially now…" Milo felt a little faint. He could smell Chantal's perfume and it began to overwhelm his senses. Or maybe it was the vicious glare of the General's daughter who stood her ground at the end of the hallway.

"If looks could kill…" Susannah whispered to Monique before she ran to greet her old friend Jacquiline. "Jackie, how the hell are you?" Susannah hugged the stiff young woman.

"What's *he* doing here?" The question was loud enough for all to hear.

On purpose.

"Come on Jacks. He wants to help. He's part of our team." Susannah took the girl by both arms and shook her lightly.

Monique winced at the level of emotional tension the young woman broadcast. It was like a punch to the kidney followed by several blows to the head. Her legs almost buckled beneath her and she had to steady herself against the hospital wall.

"Part of *our* team? When did you join the grand military tradition? Last I heard you were on your way to the beach for Spring Break. I heard a rumor that you were…"

"Ah, you can never trust the rumor mill, Jacks." Susannah waved off any further speculation about her nefarious spring break in Daytona Beach. "I've done a lot of growing up, Jacks, and I have developed a certain respect for what my dad does. I just decided to help out in any way that I can. So I have a civilian position with his team. I'm an operative now."

Milo appeared behind Susannah. "And a damn good one, Jackie. Susannah has also learned to fly." He was searching for common ground that was not mined or booby-trapped. "This is Monique Merchant, another operative. She's French."

"Ah chante." Monique's greeting went unacknowledged, but she could feel the tension in the moment, like a heavy, cold wet blanket. Hate was often a hot emotion, but what emanated from this young woman was frigid cold… and something else. Monique could not quite put her finger on it, but this gal was very special. There was power in the woman's every move.

"Really…" Jacquiline crossed her arms and stood her ground. The dry comment was aimed at Milo and it struck home. "And just how did fate put the three of you together?"

"We've got to go listen to the medical briefing on your brother." She pulled Monique with her toward Tommy's room. "You two probably want to catch up on…stuff." Susannah hugged

Jacquiline one more time. "Chin up, kiddo. We will figure this out and help Tommy."

"Uh, Suze...Monique..." Milo watched Susannah and Monique disappear into Tommy's room with the rest of the team.

"Oh, no you don't, Milo Miller." Jacquiline took Milo's arm, dragging him to a private corner. "You're not getting away this time, you little rat."

Captured and contained by a strong hand, Milo followed, his head hung low. He knew what was coming. He was dead meat.

Jacquiline rounded on him with a hiss. At that moment, Milo was more afraid of this one human girl than all of the vamps in the world.

"So?"

There was silence.

Milo squirmed.

"I'm waiting." Jacquiline stood ramrod stiff, her arms crossed in boiling anger. Milo didn't need vamp skill to feel the anger and hurt. It emanated from every pore in her entire body.

He tried to form a word, but nothing came out.

"Where's that gift of gab now, Miller? Huh?" She glared at him.

"I..."

"You what?" Her words cut him to the bone.

"I am so...Jacks, I am..."

"Don't call me that! You don't have the right to call me that any more." She punched his shoulder.

It was a direct hit to his heart.

"Jacquiline. I was such a shithead. I never..."

He tried to think of the words he could use.

It shouldn't be so hard to apologize to one girl... no. He corrected himself. Woman. She stood there all gorgeous, and seriously furiously... sexy mad. His gut twisted. "...never have left it like that."

"That's your way of saying what?" Her lips split in a feral grin. "Oh, Jacquiline, I'm so sorry I ran out and left you high and dry. To face my father? By myself? While you just transferred to another job? I got two years in boarding school in some God-forsaken hellhole. You got a new job?" She was pacing back and forth.

At every turn Milo flinched.

"Do you have any idea what North-fucking-Dakota is like?

No, of course not! You went to play undercover ops guy in some super secret location. Do you know what they do for fun in Purgatory, North Dakota, Miller?" Jacquiline stopped pacing and shoved her face into Milo's. "They break the ice on puddles in the road. It's oh so much fun! They tip over sleeping cows. They drink beer and practice burping the alphabet. They use words that I don't even consider part of the English language. Stuff that starts with yee and ends with hah!" She was winding up for the smack down. Her voice rose with her anger. "On Saturday night, they sneak into Canada. For God's sake... Canada!"

"Jacquiline, darling, keep your voice down. This is a hospital." Chantal's soft voice floated down the hall on a waft of perfume. "Sergeant Miller, please join us for a moment?"

He had his out.

And he took it.

"That's right, Miller. Run, run away. That's what you're good at." Jacquiline knew how to hit low and hard.

Milo paused at the door to Tommy's room to look back at the woman who taught him the meaning of the word 'love.' He sadly shook his head. For him, realization had dawned too late.

But maybe not for Tommy. He entered the room with a quick smile of thanks to Mrs. Pantterdyck-Ceauchene. Still, he couldn't miss Jacquiline's furious stomps down the hall outside Tommy's room.

A whisper tickled his ear.

"She will get over it, Milo. I know my daughter. She is angry because she still cares." Chantal's soft comment was a welcome salve for his wounded soul. His gut twisted again. For a very different reason.

Monique stood quietly in one corner of the room observing the exchange and sensing the tumultuous feelings ebb and flow with amazing ferocity.

"Miller? Sergeant, are you with us?" Colonel Maddox addressed him stiffly.

"Sir, yes Sir." He stared blankly at the Colonel.

Maddox tried to hide the snicker. But it didn't work.

"We've been considering some of the more unique talents of our team." Susannah came to his rescue. "The Colonel was considering bringing Ms. Vyr...Mrs. Milassoviech in as a consultant." Susannah motioned toward the unconscious Tommy, then to her head. "She's been teaching me some of her methods, but this is way past my abilities." Susannah frowned at her lack of skill.

"Got it." He turned to the Colonel. "Sir, that may be a good idea. In fact an excellent idea. Mrs. M. could do that thing…and maybe it would help Tommy reconnect. Sorta like rebooting a hard drive."

Dr. Anderson nodded at Susannah who brightened immediately. "This will take Natalia's expert hand, General. I can vouch for that."

"This Mrs. Milassoviech…what? Anyway, what can she do? The doctors said Tommy is in a coma. He can't hear or see…or anything." General Pantterdyck covered the emotional moment with a cough. "They don't know why."

Monique immediately recognized the anguish in the General's heart. Susannah called him a dickhead, but the man held tremendous love for his son… and ex-wife! Monique smiled to herself. What things humans spend endless energy hiding from the world. She drew on her own energy and sent calming, warm feelings toward the General and his ex-wife. She didn't know if it would help, but it couldn't hurt.

"Milo, who is this woman? What can she do that the doctors here cannot?" Chantal did not share the closed military mind-set of her ex-husband, or the need to cover her emotions. "She is part of this 'special' team you speak of? No?"

"She…" Milo was at a loss as to how to proceed. "She has a unique talent. She was a…" Milo was searching for words. "…a healer in her own country. Before… well, before she came to work with us. Consider it a kind of holistic medical approach." His gift of gab was back in place and rolling.

"Colonel, I will not have some nut case fooling around with my son. We have the best doctors in the world, right here. If anyone can save my son… bring him back to us…" Another cough ended the General's discourse.

Ever the queen of diplomacy, Chantal interjected. "Harold, he is my son as well. I should like to meet this Mrs… darling, what did you say her name was again?" She turned to Milo with a warm smile.

"Mrs. Milassoviech. She just got married to a guy… never mind. Ma'am, I believe she can help. I wouldn't recommend her, if I wasn't sure. Tommy is a great kid. He doesn't deserve this." Miller motioned toward the boy in the bed with a host of tubes and machines hooked to his body. "She's at… the base and could probably make it here by tomorrow night. If it's okay with you… and the General." Miller kept his eyes on Chantal's hopeful face. Her velvet covered iron fist would probably make the decision.

As the General began to object, his ex-wife cut him off. "Oh hush, Harold. Let this woman try whatever it is that she does. For once, step outside your military rules and regulations. Our son's life hangs in the balance and you…" Chantal seemed to melt into Milo's arms as the tears began to flow.

"Chantal, I do not… oh hell. Fine." General Pantterdyck stormed out of the room and down the hall.

Chantal immediately straightened. "Why is it men always give in to tears?" She wiped the tiny single tear from her cheek. "Thank you, Milo."

Susannah laughed and hugged Tommy's mother. "I believe we have just seen the sinking of the USS Pantterdyck. We'll be back tomorrow night. With Natalia. You'll like her. She's Russian, old Russian."

"If she can help my son, I will worship her, my dear. And Milo," she turned to the departing Sergeant, "do not let my daughter's temper chase you away. She is so like her father at times, I worry for her happiness."

"Yes, Ma'am." Milo saluted Chantal stiffly as he departed behind Colonel Maddox and Captain Devlin.

"Things will be fine." Even though they'd just met, Monique quickly hugged Chantal. "Just wait and see. L'équipe est incroyable." With a quick smile and a kiss blown in Tommy's direction, Susannah chased after her father and his contingent, leaving the two French women to speak in their native language.

※※※※※※

In their secure quarters later that evening, Sergeant Miller set up an impromptu comm link to the base at Olney Farm. Ted, Natalia and Yuri sat in the conference room, Ted in one chair, Natalia on Yuri's lap in another. Previn was nowhere to be seen. As usual.

"I keep tellin' 'em to get a room, but they have one." Ted joked with Miller. The newly married couple's happiness infected the entire team. It had nothing to do with the fact that Natalia was one of the strongest compellers in the vampire world. They just exuded a happiness everyone could feel.

"Communications established, Sergeant?" Maddox asked from the kitchen of their small apartment that members of the team used as a Command Center at one of the Fisher Houses a couple blocks from the hopsital. By special arrangement, they had been offered one wing for their unique team's needs.

"Yes, Sir." Miller responded in immediate military mode.

"Good." Maddox stood staring at the microwave on the kitchenette counter. "Would you…"

"Push time, then 50, then high, Sir." Miller hit the mute button on the keyboard just before Ted dissolved into laughter. The Colonel was not good with modern conveniences.

"Miller!"

"Sorry, Sir. Comm established, Sir. I have buzzed the others. They should be here any minute." Miller turned his attention back to the group on the screen. "So who won the game, Ted?"

The glower on Ted's face answered the question as Susannah, Monique and Doctor Anderson came through the door, followed by Captain Devlin munching on an apple. Monique recognized frustration immediately and calmly removed the bag of food from the Colonel's hands, placed it in the microwave and pressed the correct buttons. She'd mastered the machine from the seventies and loved to watch the little round plate revolve as food was cooked. She didn't like the food, just the magic show.

"Red Sox. Sixty-eight to twelve. It wasn't a game, it was a massacre."

Susannah shot a thumbs up toward the screen. "You owe me, Ted."

Ted responded with a raspberry and a double thumbs down with both hands.

The microwave beeped and the Colonel joined the cast with his dinner-in-a-bag.

"Dad, really? Even as a human, that stuff smelled terrible. How can you eat it?" Susannah pinched her nose.

"Beef teriyaki. Yum. My favorite." The Colonel smiled at his daughter with a mouth full.

"If I could vomit, I would." Susannah turned her face away. "Could we please get down to business?"

Monique was amazed the relationship between the Colonel and his daughter had changed so drastically in the last year. She watched Doctor Anderson bite her tongue to keep from laughing out loud at the good natured teasing between the two.

"Good enough. Miller, update please." The Colonel sat back to enjoy his beef teriyaki as the Sergeant updated the team.

"Tommy's condition remains unchanged. So, the Colonel thought…"

Susannah continued with his thought. "I tried a mind probe, but I'm not strong enough yet, Natalia. You've been a great teacher, but I'm just not strong enough yet." Susannah was back to frowning.

"Do not fret, daughter," Elizabetta smiled at her surrogate daughter from the easy chair. She had just entered the room moments before, "It will come soon enough. And you have time."

"We can be there tomorrow evening, or tomorrow day, if need be." Yuri sat his wife in the chair next to him.

"We?" Natalia shot him a quick glance.

"Da. We." There was no question he would accompany his wife. Since their nuptuals, neither liked to be apart from each other for very long.

"Tommy's girlfriend, her name is Lucy Redmont, is in the same condition. Apparently they were together on a date and… either did the drug themselves, which I seriously doubt, or were slipped the drug somehow. The record is not clear."

Beef teriyaki demolished, the Colonel added his comments. "The only reason she said 'slipped' is because we know Tommy. He's not the kind of kid that does drugs. In fact, he doesn't even drink alcohol, unless it's some fancy-dancy French wine. The influence of his mother, I gather." He paused. "What do you think, Susannah?"

"He doesn't do drugs, Dad. I'm sure of that. So that leaves us with the question of how the drug got into his system and who put it there. And why?" She held up a brochure detailing the diplomatic school on the grounds of the monastery. "Tommy's mom gave me this. It talks about the school and the connection to the monastery, tuition, classes, etc. Sergeant Miller and I have been burning the circuits at both ends to research the school and the monastery."

"Anything useful?" Captain Devlin tossed his apple core in the trash.

"Absolutely nada. The tuition is rather pricey. The kids are all from military or diplomatic families all over the world. There are very few disciplinary problems. The monastery has a major benefactor that supports the actual monastery and the religious endeavors of the monks. The books are clean. The staff are well vetted and the monks...are monks." Susannah shook her head. "The grounds are even perfect. The place looks like a giant park with a castle in the middle."

"I could feel no emotion at all from the child. It was as if he was completely without feelings. I have never felt that from a sick child... there is always..." Monique rubbed her forehead, "...something. I spoke to Chantal, lovely woman. She assured me her son has much distaste for drugs. I believe her. There was no untruth beneath her words."

Miller continued, "We have very little information about Tommy and his girlfriend. We don't know where they went, who they met, or anything like that. Both kids were found unconscious near the parking lot of the school. Police assume they caught the bus at the entrance to the grounds, had a nice evening out, which by the way, is against the rules, but fairly harmless, then came back. Whatever was in their system didn't cause unconsciousness until they arrived back at the school."

"The thing that sticks out, after researching the kids' records, is how many have become ill at the school." Captain Devlin was flipping pages. "Three kids on the soccer team went home with illnesses during the last winter semester. Until I did a follow-up, I didn't realize that two of them never came back. So I contacted their parents. Both boys died. Two boys, besides the two that we were told about." Devlin went on. "When the one girl, also on a soccer team, went home and recovered, her parents chose to remove her from the school permanently. I have not been able to contact her parents or her."

"Sir, how many of the kids who became 'ill' or ended up in the infirmary, have soccer in common?" Miller was putting the pieces together.

"Well, that's the thing, there is no one thread to tie them all together. Except the kids that died. Which might, or might not, be a coincidence. At this stage of the investigation, I have a lot of questions and not so many answers."

Doctor Anderson interjected a question. "Were there any toxicology reports, Captain? You'd think the infirmary would try to find out why the kids were sick."

"According to the limited records we have, the answer is a resounding no. The monastery houses the kids and the school is separate. Run by civilians, but staffed by a lot of monks as well as a few regular teachers from the community. It's a convoluted picture and very French. Even though it is actually located in Spain. The area is kind of a mess. They are autonomous with their own police force and government, but still Spanish, or Basque I guess."

"Before we get too far into this thing, let's see if Mrs. Milassoviech can pull something out of Tommy's head." The Colonel was pondering the possibilities.

"Dad! Really…"

"Oh, sorry honey. Mrs. M., do you think you can help him wake up as well?"

Natalia leaned forward. "I cannot promise anything, but I will try my best, Colonel. We will be there tomorrow evening. Sergeant Miller, can you set up our accommodations?"

"Will do, Mrs. M. For Two?" He looked at the Colonel for a nod.

At the mention of monks, Susannah could see Monique perched on the back of the couch. The sexy French vamp looked anything but sexy. She sat frigidly still but looked ready to rabbit at any minute. "Best we try to maintain our human covers as we can. Both Tommy and Lucy are stable; comatose, but stable so time is not a problem. Yet."

That was good enough for Miller. "Transport, since Yuri's never been here before, accommodations, meals, etc. On it. I'll email you with the particulars."

"That's all for now, folks." Maddox gave a slicing motion across his neck with his finger and Miller shut down the satellite link. "I think I'll get some more beef teriyaki."

Chapter 9

Hope

Hope springs eternal, say some.
Eternity is a very long time.
I should know.

*Quote: Unknown Vampire*

Almost exactly 24 hours later, Jacquiline sat next to her brother's bed holding his inert hand. Tears rolled down her cheeks, as she smeared snot across the cuff of her sleeve. "Shit." She reached for a tissue. It came to her in the hand of one Sergeant Milo Miller.

"What are you doing here? Can't you just leave me alone? Please?" She put her head down on the edge of the pillow next to her brother and sobbed.

Miller couldn't stand to see her cry. He pulled her into his arms and held her until the sobs subsided. He wore civilian attire and the shoulder of his shirt was wet and sticky. And stained with her make-up.

After a few moments, Jacquiline pulled away and swatted at the hand that brushed tears from her cheeks. "Get away from me. I don't even like you."

"I know, Jacks. I know you hate me because I left you without saying anything. But the least you can do is hear me out. We have an expert coming. I know she can help Tommy. She has this thing she does. I can't explain it, but, well, it works."

"Right. If the doctors here can't help him, and don't even know why he is in a coma, what can this mysterious friend do?" Jacquiline fell into sobs again, landing against Milo's chest.

"Shhhh, Jacks. Just trust me." He held her close and rubbed her neck.

That was the most incredibly wrong thing Miller possibly could have said. Like taunting the school bully. Or waving a red flag in front of a bull.

"Trust you?" Her anger spewed forth, squelching the tears.

"Trust you? Are you insane? I trusted you once before and look what it got me? Hell, that's what. Loneliness. Heartbreak. Did I mention two years in hell?" She backed away from Miller enough to stare into his eyes. "You see this face? It looked like this for about three months. Because I cried for *you*. Three months. People thought I was crazy. Then one morning I woke up and looked in the mirror. I told myself I was too good for this." She pointed to her swollen eyes and puffy red cheeks. "I told myself you didn't care, never cared, so why should I. Then life went on. I was still living in hell, but at least I didn't look like it anymore."

"Jacks, please listen…"

"You call me that one more time and I will show you some of the things I learned while I was there. Like how to get a stinking drunk cowboy, with shit for brains, to lay on the floor with a bloody nose."

"Fine. Ms. Pantterdyck, if you can spare a minute of your precious time hating me and just listen, I can explain a few things." Miller was pleading.

The steady beeping from Tommy's heart monitor became erratic and a piercing alarm sounded.

"Oh my God. Oh my God. Tommy?" Jacquiline screamed.

Miller hit the hallway at a dead run. "Nurse! Come quick. Tommy's room." He grabbed the floor nurse and dragged her to room 516.

Nurse Galloway hit the emergency all-call and the room went crazy. Orderlies with machines and syringes appeared out of nowhere. A doctor slid through the door, out of breath, and set to work.

The heart monitor beeping stopped.

A crash cart rammed through the doorway.

Miller pulled Jacquiline from the room and into a chair at the end of the hall. He stood for a while before sitting next to her. They both watched the flurry of activity.

Various medical staff rushed in and out.

Various machines rolled into the room.

Another doctor showed up.

When the Chaplain appeared, Jacquiline broke.

And Miller was there to gather the pieces into his lap and do the only thing he could; hold her together as one enormous missing piece of her heart lay dying in room 516.

****** 

In their temporary quarters a few blocks from the hospital, Monique sat up with a strangled hiss. "We must go! Susannah, there is trouble with Sergeant Miller. I think there..." She shook her head and clasped arms around her middle tightly. "...is trouble with Thomas. He is dying! Quickly, we must go." Her connection to both the Sergeant and Tommy was a living breathing thing, and one was no longer breathing on his own.

Susannah caught Monique as she began to fade. "Hang on there, Frenchy. Take some strength from me." Susannah concentrated, sending strength and will power to her sister vampire as she screamed for the team.

****** 

Hours later, Miller's phone buzzed.

He saw the call and the time.

Was it really only thirty minutes?

He inched the phone from his thigh pocket, careful not to dislodge the sleeping Jacquiline. Hospital personnel still bustled in and out of Tommy's room, but the Chaplain remained.

That was not a good sign.

"Miller, Yuri and I have just arrived. How do we find you?"

He unceremoniously dumped Jacquiline onto her own chair and ran for the ER entrance. "I'll find you. Stay where you are."

In a few seconds, an out of breath and panting Miller grabbed Natalia. "We gotta go. Tommy's dying. Hurry."

Yuri intervened. "Whoa. Sergeant, this will be easier. Where to?" He grabbed the Sergeant as Natalia searched Miller's mind for the location of the sick boy.

The three disappeared in a blink and reappeared right in front of a gapping Jacquiline.

Miller rushed into the room where doctors and nurses were feverishly trying to keep a young man alive. "Out. Now." Miller began strong arming the staff, pushing them out the door.

"Milo," Natalia stood behind him. "Let me." She closed her eyes and the staff lined up against the gray walls. Their faces were blank with unfocused eyes.

"This is the boy? He is very near death." Yuri moved to

stand beside his wife. "But then I was much closer, if I remember correctly." He kissed Natalia's cheek.

Jacquiline stood at the door, staring at the hospital staff standing against the walls, doing absolutely nothing, while Tommy's heart monitor continued to slow its beep. "Milo, what's going on?" She was on the verge of hysteria and marching rapidly toward the precipice.

"Jacks, you can't be here right now."

"No Milo, we can use her!" Natalia beckoned to the young woman. "Come child. Lend me your strength and we may just save your brother." Natalia had immediately recognized a power emanating from the boy's sister. What Natalia could see was a kind of frothy blue aurora emanating from the girl's hands. Natalia had no idea what kind of power the girl possessed, but if it was power, she could use it. From the looks of the tanking monitors, she would need it.

Much to Milo's surprise, Jacquiline rushed to Natalia's side. "What can I do?"

"We shall all join hands and you must clear your mind. Milo, you have done this before. Yuri, my love, join us." They joined hands surrounding Tommy's bed and Natalia closed her eyes.

Jacquiline's eyes remained open, her fear clear in those lovely dark orbs. She stared at Milo, not understanding.

Miller closed his eyes and mouthed the words, "Trust her."

Deep into the troubled brain Natalia dove, winding through millions of networked neurons, looking for the cause of the boy's physical ailment. From the people around her, she pulled strength and endurance as her own resources began to wane. She could tell there was no physical damage to the body, but the brain... it seemed to close doors as she approached. Each door she broke through was followed by a myriad of passageways.

Which to follow?

Where was the intruder? The interloper that threatened this boy's life?

She sped down each pathway finding dead end, after dead end, until...

Her world spun into a pink haze and she stumbled.

It was here.

The invader.

Natalia's hand tightened around Yuri's as she drew from

him in a way that she had never experienced before. The incredible strength of their love combined to intensify her ability to resist the pink menace. It tugged at her racing feet and tore at her skin.

What was this thing?

Then she was there, facing the monster. A gigantic pulsing pink fiend, its tendrils entwining every neuron, loomed menacingly in front of her.

What was this evil monster that grew in Tommy's brain?

Natalia stood, feeling the malevolent creature's draw. It smelled enticing and was such a beautiful shade of pink. She inched forward wondering what it would taste like. She drew in great lungful's of the scent.

A memory stung her thoughts. Cinnamon crepes with pink cherry frosting, a favorite delicacy of her childhood as a human! She bent to sample a handful of the stuff.

Human?

Childhood?

Before her hand could touch the stuff, fear struck her heart and set her mind ablaze.

She was a vampire. Not a human.

She was hundreds of years old. Not a child.

A jeweled sword appeared in her hands as she swung at the thing that tempted her so.

She cut.

It slunk away.

She cut again.

It retreated.

She slashed again and again.

It retreated.

Outside her mind she could hear Yuri cheering her battle. "Again my love. Again."

On she continued, on and on until the only part of the entity that remained was a fading glow that dimmed as she approached. "Go you devil. Leave this boy and never return. I banish you unto nothingness where you belong."

As Natalia retreated from Tommy's mind, she soothed the hurts and healed the open wounds in each neuron. Retying broken axions and reconnecting separated tissue. She was tired of doing battle and healing wounds, but she continued until she was sure what little damage remained would knit on its own. Finally, when she was sure of her work, she withdrew completely.

Tommy's heart monitor beat strong and even. His color returned and now his freckles almost sparkled against his peach complexion. He moved slightly in deep sleep.

He would sleep for a while yet.

At least until his tissue was completely healed and whole again.

Natalia stumbled. Yuri caught her and carried her to the sofa against the wall.

Sergeant Miller shook his head to clear the joining, but continued to hold Jacquiline's hand as she bent in exhaustion.

"What just happened?" Gasping for air, she whispered to Milo. "I feel like I ran twenty miles in pink cotton candy." She was close to collapsing.

Milo took her arm and steered her out of Tommy's room to the chairs they'd occupied earlier. "Sit. I'll get us something to drink." He was drained and hungry. Sugar would help. He stumbled down the hallway to the vending machines and bought two sodas. On his way back to Jacquiline, he noticed the hospital staff quietly congratulating each other on a job well done as they exited Tommy's room. Natalia might be a vampire, but she could also work miracles. Maybe that was why Yuri called her his Dark Angel.

"Here Jacks, drink this slowly or you'll get the hiccups."

She took the open soda from his hand. "Thanks, Milo, and I know I get the hiccups when I gulp carbonated drinks."

She wasn't too tired to reject his concern.

"Sorry, I'm just trying to wrap my head around what just happened. Did you really run off, then, like, appear right back here? How'd you do that?" The sugar was taking effect. "And what did that woman do to us. And to Tommy?" She jumped from her seat, remembering her brother's imminent death, only to sway in exhaustion and collapse back into the chair. "What…"

"Sit Jacks. Tommy is fine. He's sleeping. Natalia healed him… with our help. She sort of channeled us, all of us, and healed him." Milo took a long drink, belching long and loud. He smiled sheepishly. "I thought you might be missing Purgatory."

That brought a weary smile to her face. She tried to slug his shoulder but missed and fell across his lap. "He's going to be okay? Really?" Jacquiline pulled herself upright.

"Yep. And so will we after about 36 hours of sleep and five Big Macs."

"With fries and chocolate milk shakes." Jacquiline closed her eyes.

Milo took the can of pop before it slid from her limp fingers. "Super-sized." He pulled her into his arms and promptly closed his eyes to join her.

But sleep was not to be had for the Sergeant.

General Pantterdyck exited the elevator like he'd been shot from a cannon, dragging his ex-wife behind him. At the sight of Milo and Jacquiline, heads together, eyes closed, he froze. There was no commotion near his son's room and the hallway was as quiet as a morgue.

Tommy was dead then.

He met his worst fear head on, and it decimated him. He punched the wall as hard as he could. Anything was better than the pain in his heart.

At the noise, Milo startled awake. Standing to attention, Jacquiline slid from his lap to the floor and woke.

"Dad! Mom! Tommy is…" She tried to stand after brushing Milo's helping hand away.

"Gone." The General's statement rang through the hallway.

Jacquiline looked up at her father from the floor, as she struggled to her knees and held onto the chair. "Gone where? He was sleeping just a minute ago. I think it was a minute ago." She searched for her phone to check the time.

"Sleeping?" Chantal rushed into her son's room, then rushed back into the arms of the man who gave her so much joy, two children… and so much more pain. "He's alive, Harold. Tommy is alive."

It didn't dawn on the General, until Chantal rushed to pull her daughter from the floor, hugging her in a tight embrace.

"Ah, Sir?" Milo stood wavering at attention. His legs were about to give out from under him.

"Miller?" The General was confused. The hospital had called him at his home, to tell him the Chaplain was with his son who was critical. Doctors were working on Tommy to see if they could keep him alive but the odds were not good. Could he and Tommy's mother come to the hospital as quickly as possible?

"How is this possible? They told me on the phone…" General Pantterdyck could not say the words. His son was alive? And… apparently sleeping? From almost dead to sleeping peacefully in, he glanced at his watch, twenty minutes? How was that possible?

"Sir, I can explain…" Miller collapsed into the chair. He slumped catching his head in his hands. "Tired, Sir. Explain later." Miller was panting.

"Son, what the…"

"Possibly, I can shed some light on the situation, Harold." Colonel Maddox stood behind the General, somewhat out of breath. Elizabetta, Monique and Susannah closely followed the Colonel. "I see the rest of my team has arrived and done their job admirably. Monique, can you see to Natalia and Yuri." He motioned to Tommy's room. "In there. Susannah?"

"Of course. I'll take care of Jackie and Milo, Dad."

Maddox took General Pantterdyck by the arm and dragged him down the hall aways. The two men could be seen, heads together, talking softly. Every once in a while, Pantterdyck would glance toward his son's room, or toward Susannah who was taking protein bars from a bag she carried and stuffing them down Jacquiline and Milo. Chantal had gone into Tommy's room.

After a few minutes, Chantal wandered out of Tommy's room. Her expression seemed dreamy and totally content. "My son has recovered and all is well. They told me that."

"Who, Chantal? Who told you that?" General Pantterdyck took her by the hand, speaking softly.

"The angels. They healed Tommy, dear. He woke and said he loved me." Her smile widened. "We can go home now." Chantal pulled her hand from his and strolled toward the elevator. "Come dear. I think I'll bake stuffed cannoli for dinner. It's Tommy's favorite."

"Go with her, Harold. We can talk more later. I know this is alot to swallow. Mull it around in your head. Tommy's going to be fine." Frank smiled at his old frien-e-mey.

"Yeah, okay, Frank." The General took a quick peek into Tommy's room just to verify his son's condition. "Frank, where'd they all go?"

Yuri had just v-ported his wife and Monique to the building where their quarters were set up for some libation and rest. The room was empty of all but the young man.

Chantal was waiting, her arm holding the elevator door open. "Come along, Harold."

As the General passed Maddox, the Colonel patted the General on his back. "Later, Harold. Everything will be fine. Trust me on that one."

"Ah, yeah. Okay. Ah…I guess. Later Frank." Pantterdyck followed his ex-wife into the elevator.

"Dad, we have a problem. Jackie saw everything, actually more than everything. She helped Natalia heal Tommy. Like in Afghanistan with Yuri. Her and Milo. That's why they are so tired. But Jackie is asking all kinds of questions, in between snores that is." Susannah smiled back at the dozing couple, now sitting sort of upright in their chairs. Milo was holding Jackie's hand.

"Can you wipe her memory?" Maddox knew his daughter had been training hard in the past few months. He was very proud of the progress she'd made. He was even beginning to think of Jordan, her vamp-boyfriend, as family.

"Not on my own. Not yet." Susannah was apologetic.

"No problem. We'll take her back to quarters, let her sleep off the exhaustion, then figure this all out." He kissed Susannah on the cheek. "I'm going to check on Tommy, the staff… see if we need to do any cleanup here. I'll meet you at the car."

"Right." Susannah kissed her father on the cheek. "Back at ya, Dad."

Maddox shook his head and smiled, mumbling, "Kids." as he headed for Tommy's room.

\*\*\*\*\*\*

"Slow down, my dear, save some for the rest of us." Yuri watched as Natalia finished her fifth bag of synth-blood.

"I was so hungry, Yuri, I seriously thought about biting that idiot at the entrance. Why did he question your carrying me?" Natalia was still mad about the receptionist. Apparently the staff was used to soldiers and sailors bringing their drunken girlfriends home with them late at night. There was a strict 'no alcohol' policy at the guest quarters they were occupying.

"I told him you were exhausted from a twenty-four hour flight. He did kind of sniff alot as we passed by." Yuri was laughing as he finished his third bag. "I wouldn't mind you being my drunk girlfriend." He reached to tickle his bride of less than a year.

"Both of you need rest. We have these rooms for two more days so feel free to sleep in. The windows have UV protectant on them. Great planning on someone's part." Elizabetta was checking out the huge TV screen on the living room wall.

Monique ushered them into a small bedroom behind the kitchen. "Sleep well." As she pulled the door closed, she heard Yuri mutter some sexual retort. The man was insatiable. And so was his wife.

They made a good pair. Monique giggled, the couple's love and adoration wrapping her in fluffy billows of happiness.

Elizabetta settled on the overstuffed sofa with the channel surfer. She seldom had free time any more, and catching up on her favorite cop show was a treat. Day sleep was hours away yet. She punched a series of buttons then gave up and mentally manipulated the channels as Monique came to join her.

"Ah. There we go." The familiar trio of characters appeared surrounding a mutilated body in some undergrowth. Elizabetta pulled a red, white and blue comforter over her legs and settled in. "They need a vampire on their forensic team. It'd make things a lot easier." Elizabetta chortled.

"Yes, easier and more fun. I love the snooping all around to find the answers." Monique cuddled beneath the edge of the comforter. "But I think I will not like snooping around monks. My dreams are torture enough."

By the second set of commercials, Susannah arrived dragging Sergeant Miller who carried his ex-girlfriend like a precious china doll. The pages of his discipline file flipped through Elizabetta's mind. So this woman was the huge mistake that took down the infallible Milo Miller. Elizabetta rose silently, motioning Miller into her own bedroom.

Miller stumbled after the Coven Mistress. "Thanks, Ma'am." His mumbled words betrayed his own state of mind and body. "I'll just put her…" Miller closed his eyes and lay Jacquiline on the bed "…and…" He hung, bent over the woman on the bed, not enough strength to rise.

"And you, my lovely Sergeant…" Elizabetta guided Miller to the other side of the bed. "Shall collapse right here." She settled the young man next to his sleeping beauty and covered them both with a blanket from the closet. "Right here, Milo."

A soft snore issued forth from the Sergeant's lips almost before his head hit the pillow. "Sleep well children." Elizabetta tiptoed from the room to join Monique and Susannah in front of the television.

"I'm surprised he made it that far, Elizabetta. He wouldn't

let me carry her." Susannah smirked. "I do believe we have all met Sergeant Miller's Waterloo. You should have seen him. He was so..."

"Susannah, do not make fun of the poor Sergeant. Keep in mind, young lady, your Waterloo works for a pharmaceutical company. I do believe you would have moved heaven and hell for Jordan." Monique admonished Susannah and tossed a soft pillow at her sister.

A dreamy smile replaced Susannah's smirk. "Speaking of Jordan, I have a call to make." She winked and bounced into her father's room, closing the door firmly behind her.

"Ah," A wistful sigh punctuated the end of a commercial for breakfast cereal. "Young love. How sweet."

"Elizabetta, I do not believe my sister understands how deep is Jordan's feelings for her. I worry for his heart and..." Monique touched her head. "There is more on one side..." She used her hands to make an old fashioned scale, "than the other, I fear. He is so sweet and Susannah is... like a butterfly." Monique looked at the closed door. "I hope..."

"As do we all. Do not worry that beautiful head of yours, my dear. Susannah is growing into her own at a remarkable rate. My worry is for you, and those pesky daymares." Elizabetta opened a touchy door.

"I think I will talk to Doctor Anderson. Susannah said she has demons in her head too. Maybe she can help me conquer mine." Monique stood, tossing aside the comforter and brandishing an invisible sword. "But now is time to see this story."

Once more settled on the couch with the comforter firmly in place, Elizabetta and Monique relaxed into the program, rooting for their favorite forensic team of investigators and the case of the mutilated body in the woods.

Dozing during commercials, it was close to the end of the case when Colonel Maddox returned. Elizabetta could tell he was tired but content. "Natalia did a great job on Tommy. Before she left, he opened his eyes and recognized his mom." The Colonel closed his eyes for a moment. "Tommy is recovering. Harold is flabbergasted. Chantal is going home to cook... in the middle of the night! The hospital staff thinks they pulled off a miracle. Sergeant Miller has faced the dragon and come away alive." He paused and looked around. "Where is everybody?"

"The dragon and the Sergeant are sleeping in my room.

Your daughter is on the phone with Jordi in your room. Captain Devlin is meeting with an old friend at some pub. Natalia and Yuri have retired to the spare room with full tummies, and I am here with Monique."

Monique gave a sleepy wave and cuddled deeper into the couch.

The Colonel stretched, yawned and placed his booted feet on the coffee table in front of the recliner he'd just claimed. "So I guess, all's well that ends well." Maddox closed his eyes.

"I fear this is only the beginning, Frank."

He opened one eye to look at his Coven Mistress. "Me thinks you are so right, Mistress" He closed his eye. "There is still one young girl in a coma and the mystery of the drug that put her there. Maybe Tommy can shed some light on this sordid story when he wakes in the morning. In the mean time, I think I will watch someone else solve the problems of the world." He pulled a comforter from beneath the table, and yanked it over his lap. Within minutes he was asleep.

Elizabetta smiled and turned up the volume to cover his snores. Monique closed her eyes and her gentle purring joined Franks loud snorts.

Chapter 10

Thoughts of the Past

Where there are showers, bloom great flowers.
And so it is with childhood and misspent youth.
We spring from happy to sad, elated to mad,
In the split of a second, a flash of the moment.
Yet with all we endure, we capture and mature,
Into the person we are meant to be.
As we look back on the tale, on into life we sail,
Only to wish for that which we left behind.
Such a beautiful thing, of the past we sing,
So precious and good was our humanhood.

*Phillipe Le Glaute*
*CEO, Elégance Produits deBbeauté,*
*Paris, France 2016*

Susannah saw the two nurses huddled outside room 516 before she heard the shouts inside. Obviously General Dickhead was debriefing his son. She hoped Tommy had the strength.

"This could be a problem, Frenchy. Dickhead's on the warpath."

Monique giggled.

Susannah explained the world according to Army Regulation 101; Families and Their Place, as they'd walked over to the hospital. Monique found it a little like the life of a royal child; an asset to be seen, used, but not heard. Apparently, the Maddox and Pantterdyck families met early on in their military careers, when both men were in Officer Training School. Later, their paths met, tangled, crossed and separated, only to meet again, many times over in the ultimate quest for rank and title. The men became competitive comrades, the wives, fast friends. The kids... kids didn't matter. They made their own way through life carefully bonding with those who could stand the test of world-wide childhood and remain close. Military life had its perks, Susannah was the first to admit to Monique. But it also had some pretty hefty drawbacks for a sweet little blonde girl who wanted a sister to share secrets with and giggle at silly boys. She'd found that with Jacquiline… for a few years in Texas, and treasured the moments. They'd stayed in touch and in and out of each others' lives. Looking back, Susannah told Monique, she had obviously missed the Milo years while she tried to figure out her own changed life after Daytona Beach.

Susannah bounced through the door of Tommy's room with a smile, on purpose. "Surprise. Welcome back, TP."

She waited for a response… from a flabbergasted General and a startled and confused young man.

"Su…Susannah?" Tommy squinted at the gorgeous blonde who used to chase him through the garden with a baseball bat.

Monique watched from the doorway. There wasn't enough space in the room for Monique with Tommy, Susannah, the General, and his ego.

"In the flesh, and dress. Of Course." Susannah inserted herself between the fuming General and Tommy's hospital bed. It was a daring move. She bent and plastered a noisy kiss on the freckled forehead of the somewhat larger and definitely more handsome man than Susannah had described to Monique during their evening stroll to the Hospital. The freckle-faced boy she'd talked about was definitely a man.

"Miss Maddox, we are in the middle of…"

Susannah cut him off. "Helping your son recover from a near death experience. Right?" She glared at the General. It took vampire strength.

At the last minute Monique psyched her sister vamp, *remember to keep the red glow out of your eyes.*

"I'll bet you can use a cup of Joe right now." She reached down and turned his chair toward the door. With him in it. "Go, go, go General. I'll babysit. Just like old times." She plopped down on the side of Tommy's bed and smiled at the sputtering General.

As General Pantterdyck rose to leave, he paused at the door. "Miss Maddox…"

"Au revoir…Sir." She waved him off, deftly imitating his ex-wife. French accent and all.

"You have a death wish or something?" Tommy wiped a hand across his sweating forehead.

"Been there. Done that." She reached up and placed her palm above his eyes. "You're warm." She took his wrist and felt

99

for his pulse. "Increased pulse rate. Any nausea? Pain?"

"What? Are you a nurse now? It's because of my father, not… this." He squirmed to the far side of the bed and pointed around the room. "I woke up to interrogation and this…I don't even know how I got here." Tears formed near the corners of his eyes. "Please stop yelling at me and somebody please tell me what's going on…"

Susannah slid off the bed and into the chair recently vacated by one very angry father. "Yep. That's why we're here." She motioned Monique into the room. "This is my BFF, Monique. She's French."

On cue, Monique smiled her ever glowing smile! "Bonjour."

"I'm in a hospital and my sister's girlfriend, whom I haven't seen in what? Eight years? Shows up with Marilyn Monroe to brush off my dad and explain everything?" He scrutinized her out from under bushy eyebrows that used to be pale and thin. "I must be crazy."

"Exactly…" Susannah smiled brightly. She hunched over and whispered, "While in a coma, you were transported to a parallel universe."

"Now, that I can believe." Tommy relaxed and lay back, obviously tired, but relieved to slip back into a comfortable childhood relationship with his sister's old friend… his friend, sort of.

"So here's the intel, kiddo, as far as I know, which I will also explain. But later." She crossed her legs and sat back. "You apparently took, or were slipped, some kind of drug. You and the young woman whom you are suspected of having nookied with."

"Whoa! Wow, wait. Lucy and I are not…" Tommy sat up too quickly and grabbed his head while the room spun around him.

Immediately, Monique was at his side, fluffing his pillow and easing him back toward stability, both physically and mentally.

And Tommy let her. Jaw hanging open and everything. Her beautific smile was overwhelming for most men, but to a teenage boy it was a wet dream come to life. She was tending to him and he felt like the most cherished man in the world. How…

Monique straightened the blankets and smoothed his wiry hair, then pointed to Susannah with a giggle.

"Ah, ah ahhh. Just listen. You get to report later. This is my intel. Right or wrong, TP." Wagging her finger at the young man, Susannah motioned him to lay back and relax.

"Stop calling me that. I haven't wet the bed since I was four and slept with you and Jacks up in that tree fort." Tommy frowned. "And that was your stupid fault... Spawn of Satan."

"I'll cop to that one, but past is past. Let's worry about the present. So..." She sat back again. "Apparently, you and the young woman in question were out doing the dirty with a little support from some chemical substance that did not go well with life and the pursuit of sex. You were both found unconscious in the parking lot at your school, in said clench. Sort of tangled around each other. Like comatose hugging of a sort."

It was a weird variation of Good Cop-Bad Cop as Monique tisked and wagged a finger back and forth with a wide smile.

Tommy snorted. His face was becoming more and more red as his anger grew. "I...

Susannah cut him off. She was becoming good at that with the Pantterdyck men. "Nope. My turn, then your turn. That's the rules. So... fast forward to the day before yesterday. Your dad called out the forces. *My* dad got the word. We all rushed down here and saved your bacon." She bounced in the chair. "There. Done. That was easy, wasn't it?"

Tommy's head finally turned toward Susannah. "My bacon? What about Lucy?" The question came out through clenched teeth.

"Oh, yeah. She's down the hall. Still a bit under the weather, but I assure you, she will be fine. After our expert has treated her." Susannah had to avert her eyes at the word 'expert'. She was afraid something would show in her expression.

"Expert? Are you a nurse, or studying to be a doctor? I don't get it." Tommy looked confused.

Which Susannah could completely understand, since she'd left a bunch of information out of her little tale of parallel universes. "No. Tommy, what I am now... we are..." she indicated herself and Monique, "is a little hard to explain. And classified. You'll just have to do your best with that. After all, you should be used to it. We all got used to it." Her smile gleamed con-spiratorially. "What I can tell you is, I am glad we got the call and could help. I mean, look at you! You've grown up, got some guns goin' on there." She squeezed his bicep. "What'd you do? Join the International Miracle Gym?" She tried for light and airy territory.

"Nah, my stepdad is a health freak. We used to work out together and go climbing. He's a pretty neat guy, all things considered. I can actually talk to him. And he treats mom like she's gold. Not like the General."

"Speaking of which, I need your side of the tale. Care to enlighten me?" Susannah slipped a small notebook out of her purse.

"For the record? Are you a cop?" Immediately suspicious, Tommy paused.

"Nope, not a cop! How could you think that of me?" Susannah wiggled her pen in the air. "Really… I just want to remember everything, so we can help."

"Who's we? You in league with the dark side now?"

"Not the dark side. My team."

"Time is running. We must speak quickly before your father returns." Monique sent a burst of warm, trusting feelings his way.

"Frenchy, that's time is flying! Anyway, spill the beans before the General storms the castle walls." Susannah urged.

"First of all, Lucy and I are not, I repeat NOT a couple. Lucy doesn't like guys, if you know what I mean. I like women, which is normal. Lucy likes women, which is… very European. So I'm told. She's the captain of the girls soccer team. I'm the captain of the boys team. We had a league meeting so we went together." Tommy paused and looked at Susannah's notebook. "Getting all this?"

"Continue. Faster. I hear footsteps. Angry boots."

"We stopped at the Un Beau Goût for crepes. It's a foo-foo joint but Lucy loves their food. Go figure. She has bigger muscles than me and she eats everything in sight. Then we went back to the campus. Next thing I know, I wake up here."

"Ahhh… crepes? I should love…" Monique mused.

"That's it? What about the other kids at the school? I was told some other kids got sick. Everyone thinks there is drug use on the campus. What do you know about that?" She looked speculatively at the young man who appeared to be open and truthful.

"Kids use. You know. Pot. A little coke. It's available. But not me. And certainly not Lucy. She beat the shit out of a girl on the team who just got drunk after a tough game. They lost. It was Carmella's fault. She drank away the guilt, and believe me, Lucy's good with guilt. Carm ended up in the Infirmary with a broken nose. Lucy's got a hell of a right hook."

"So between the restaurant and the parking lot, there was nothing? Think. Was the food any different than usual at the restaurant? Taste funny, maybe a little off? Like someone could have slipped something in it? Maybe your drink?"

"Food was great. I drank bottled water. Lucy had milk. Out of a carton." Tommy frowned. "We rode the bus back up to the campus. Nothing different about that. Walked up the drive." He closed his eyes recreating their walk. "Lucy kept complaining about this one ref that makes calls partial to his daughter's team. She wants to find a way to get the guy fired."

Monique nodded to Susannah. "He is truthful, Susannah."

"So you walked up the driveway..." Susannah was leading him on before their private time ran out.

"Yeah. It's a bit of a walk. Gave Lucy time to blow off some steam. Ran into Brother Berthold in the parking lot..." Tommy's eyes slammed open. "He gave us one of his weird supplement drinks. But that's not unusual. He's always trying some new health drink. But he's our coach. He wouldn't give us any kind of drug, or anything. He's cool."

"Some kind of health drink? Maybe spiked and he didn't know? Anyway, what happened next?"

"Well, we sipped the pink stuff." As soon as the words were out of Tommy's mouth, Monique took a quick breath. Tommy didn't notice and continued, "It tasted like lemonade actually. Supposed to have all kinds of electrolytes in it. We chatted with Brother Berthold. Lucy told him about the meeting and the new plans for a soccer field in Rhotta on the American base. Her dad's the contractor for the project. We went on our way and Brother Berthold headed for the gym behind the academic wing."

"Then what?" Susannah was prodding. "Talk faster. Company's off the elevator."

"What? How do you..."

"Your words are very important, Thomas, do go on. Quickly." Monique patted Tommy's hand.

"Talk." Susannah swung circles with her pen to emphasize the need to spin it up a notch.

"Lucy finished her lemonade. I don't care for sweet drinks so I tossed mine in the trashcan with her empty bottle. We started across the parking lot and... she doubled over! I remember!"

Tommy sat bolt upright. "I caught her!"

Monique caught him as he swayed toward the edge of the bed.

"Then it hit me. I felt like my stomach tried to tie itself in a knot! It was horrible. Lucy passed out and I… guess I did as well." Tommy was feeling his stomach. "There was this immediate dizziness that just took my legs out."

"Stomach cramps and dizzy. Okay. Then what?"

"Then here. How long have I been here? What's today? Will Lucy be okay? I mean…"

"Okay, hold up. One question at a time. One answer at a time." Susannah sat her pen and notebook down next to her purse and stood, pushing Tommy back against the pillows. "You collapsed nine days ago. You and Lucy. They medevac'd both of you here since there seems to be a mystery around whatever caused your illness. Lucy will be okay. I promise." Susannah pressed a finger to her lips to quiet the young man. "Shhhh for now. Let me deal with your dad."

"Better you than me." Tommy relaxed against the pillows and closed his eyes.

"What is that supposed to mean, young man?" General Pantterdyck stormed through the door followed by a teary eyed Chantal.

Susannah turned, locked her arm around the Generals waist and forcefully guided the man back out the door. "Let's let Tommy have a few moments with my friend, Sir. I'd like to have a word with you."

"Miss Maddox, you *are* aware of who and what I am, correct?"

"More than aware, General. But the real question is, do you know who and what I am?" She glared up at the General, letting just enough red glow tint the edge of her crystal blue eyes.

General Pantterdyck took a step back. He eyed the woman suspiciously. "Well now, things are beginning to make sense. So Frank not only has his own army of fanged fighters, his cute little daughter is one of 'em. I'll be damned. I'm gonna have to look into what kind of party he's throwin' up north." It was a lousy attempt to intimidate which fell immediately flat.

Susannah hated arrogance in officers, especially when they used their rank to bully people. She'd seen way too much of it to be intimidated any more. "I'd think twice about that, Sir. What you are looking for, might find you first." She allowed her fangs to grow a tad as she smiled up at the large man.

That did the trick.

The General choked and stumbled back against the wall. "That ain't right!"

"It is, what it is. And the government... your government, the folks you answer to, have sanctioned my father's work and our team. We just saved your son, by the way. And, in case you haven't noticed, we are on the trail of what caused Tommy's illness, probably killed a couple kids who dropped out of the Academia de Santos Domingo de Silos, and remains a threat to the families of service men and women who trust their children to the school." Susannah placed both hands on her hips and affected the 'Maddox' stance. Heaven knows she'd seen it enough times with her father.

"A chip off the old block, huh? Well, Miss Maddox, here's the deal. My son takes after his mother. He got mixed up with drugs, with his girlfriend. Did a little too much and almost killed himself... and the girl." He turned to leave. "You don't need a..." The General didn't know what to call the Vamp Squad, "a special team to follow that trail."

Before he could take one more step, Susannah moved to stand in front of him.

With vamp speed.

"Holy shit! What the fu..." Harold Pantterdyck stood speechless.

It was a first.

"You couldn't be any more wrong if your name was Custer." Susannah didn't wait for the sarcasm to settle in. "Lucy Redmont is not Tommy's girlfriend, unless Tommy has changed his taste in women from heterosexual to homosexual. Your son is not mixed up in drugs, nor is Lucy. They were not on a date the night they became ill. They were attending a soccer league meeting, representing their teams. Tommy tried to catch Lucy as she passed out which is why they were found unconscious on the ground, seemingly holding each other."

"How do you know that?" The General was actually surprised.

"I listened to Tommy. You might want to try that some time." Susannah turned and strode down the hall to meet her father who had just exited the elevator with Natalia and Yuri. Elizabetta followed the group a few paces behind, holding the hands of Jacquiline Pantterdyck and Milo Miller. They were talking quietly. Devlin limped behind the group. Doctor Anderson had gone over to the CDC's field office at NIH earlier in the afternoon.

Susannah shook her head solemnly as she faced her approaching dad. "He's so much worse than you ever were. I need some air."

Frank chuckled at his daughter's comment. "Thanks, kiddo. That's high praise coming from you."

"Monique's with Tommy on guard duty." Captain Devlin offered a fist bump as Susannah passed by on her way to fresh air, which she didn't need, and an open space to calm her temper, which she did need. In a bad way.

Elizabetta placed Milo's hand in Jacquiline's and followed her surrogate daughter toward the solarium down the hall. The small rooftop garden offered a touch of home to the gray and cement world of Walter Reed. The sky was clear for a change and stars twinkled above them. The air hung heavy in the aftermath of an earlier shower. "He is a very stalwart individual, is he not, Susannah?"

"My dad?" Susannah turned her face toward the garden.

"General Pantterdyck, of course. Chantal and I had a nice visit earlier. She wanted us to know she is grateful for our help with her son. She's a lovely woman. And very unique."

"I bet. She was always so nice to me. Never a harsh word. God only knows how she hooked up with Dickhead." Susannah began following the small sidewalk that wound around the tiny garden space. "Tommy told me earlier that her new husband is a real keeper. She deserves it." Her pacing led her in a small circle but helped burn off the anger in her mind.

"What else did Tommy have to say? Anything useful?" Elizabetta joined Susannah making the rounds of the garden.

"He told me Lucy is not his girlfriend. Neither one do drugs, although the usual drugs are available at the school. Monique said he was telling the truth."

"Do you believe him?" Elizabetta was not the least bit skeptical, but sought Susannah's confirmation since she was familiar with the boy. In the last year, since becoming involved with Jordan and his coven, the young vampire was developing into a crack operative. Elizabetta was witness to the many hours Susannah spent learning to fly an airplane and honing her research skills with Sergeant Miller. At times, Elizabetta thought Susannah was actually picking up a few too many skills with Milo; like picking locks and counterfeiting identification papers. But still, Elizabetta was proud of the youngest member of the team.

"He told me Lucy was a lesbian, so that puts the lid on any speculation about a relationship. I believe him about the drugs too. He's always been anti-drugs. He's an athlete and a health nut. Apparently his stepfather has been a very good influence on him. The one thing I did pick up on, was the school coach." She slid her purse off her shoulder and produced the notebook. "A Brother Berthold is their soccer coach. Apparently he concocts health drinks. Tommy and Lucy drank something the coach made just before collapsing."

"Very suspicious." Elizabetta glanced over Susannah's shoulder at the notes.

"Exactly." Susannah tapped the coach's name with her finger. "Bears looking into, I think."

"Certainly. But why would a coach poison his students?"

"Tommy was adamant that the coach would never harm his players. Especially his team captains. I would like to talk to this Brother Berthold. Think Dad'll approve a night flight? I could use the stick time." Susannah's smile lit the dim garden.

"I am beginning to worry about you, young lady." Elizabetta hugged her surrogate daughter. "You have been spending too much time with our good Sergeant these days."

"There will never be enough time in the universe to learn everything Milo has in his devious mind, Elizabetta. But I intend to try. Let's go see how the family feud plays. And when we get back, I swear Milo is going to tell me everything about what he did to Jackie. Details! I want details."

"Are you sufficiently calm to leave this beautiful place?" Elizabetta bent to smell a rose bloom near a cement bench.

"Oh, I was never that mad. I just wanted Dickhead to know who he was trying to bully. You know… the eyes!" Susannah took Elizabetta by the hand dragging her toward the glass door. "And how foolish it was to try using those tactics on one of us."

"Incorrigible." Elizabetta followed Susannah back into the hospital hallway. "Simply incorrigible."

"You love me, and you know it." Susannah placed a quick kiss on her Mistress' cheek.

Elizabetta shook her head with a smile and followed a

skipping Susannah back toward room 516.

As they passed the elevators, Elizabetta immediately sensed tension in a small group outside Tommy's room. Susannah slowed to a stop and observed the congregation.

A tall, slender middle-aged man and a fit, muscular woman in jeans, stood confrontationally in front of the General. Their body language screamed furious. The woman was talking at the speed of light and flapping her arms wildly about. The man wore khaki slacks and a polo shirt. He loomed over General Pantterdyck and spoke with an intimidating baritone voice. The name 'Lurch' immediately popped into Susannah's mind. He would have been perfect to play the character from the old television show about a very strange family. Chantal stood in the doorway blocking the couple from entering her son's room. Two obviously frightened nurses stood, pressed against the wall and three MPs stood behind the General.

It was classic circus city, military style.

"Mrs. Redmont, I can assure you the doctors are doing everything possible for your daughter. I am not sure why my son has recovered faster but…"

Mrs. Redmont burst into tears and collapsed into the conveniently waiting arms of her husband. "I want to speak with the doctor in charge immediately! This is unheard of. Why can't we see our daughter? You're a General. Order it."

Mr. Redmont held his weeping wife close. "This is your son's fault!"

The level of noise was increasing with every demand. Mrs. Redmont cried hysterically and Mr. Redmont continued to make loud demands to anyone who might possibly listen.

*Natalia, it may be appropriate for you to do something before this gets out of hand.* Elizabetta sent a tight psyche message to the strongest compeller on the team.

*Already on it, Elizabetta.* Natalia, dragging Monique, approached the loud group. Monique sent waves of calm serenity to Lucy's parents while Natalia implanted ideas in the minds of the small group. *We should see what can be done for Lucy as soon as these people can be sent off somewhere.* Monique psyched Natalia.

*You are so right, sister. Can you help me? I should be fine with Milo, Yuri and Jackie, but I can always use the extra strength. Then I won't come out of it quite so exhausted. Whatever that stuff is, I had a little trouble last time.*

*Of course I will be of help. You do not need to ask. Possibly I can help the girl feel more comfortable as she awakens.* Monique was ready to lend a hand… or mind.

Mr. and Mrs. Redmont were consoling each other more quietly now and the General had retreated to talk with Susannah's father.

*I shall assist all I can. Susannah can lend her essence as well. She should be able to see what this drug is and does to humans.* Monique sent one last burst of calm to the group of humans.

Natalia nodded her head toward Elizabetta and concentrated on sending hungry thoughts to the Redmonts, General Panterdyck and Colonel Maddox.

"Darling, you will feel better after having something to eat. Shall we get you a little something?" Mr. Redmont rubbed his wife's arms.

"The doctor won't be around for another hour or so. We have time." Colonel Maddox was feeling an unusual tug towards food and coffee. Recognizing the familiar work of his compeller, he winked at Natalia. "If he shows up early, Susannah can text me."

"I certainly can, but it's a toss up as to whether my father can figure out how to read it or not." Susannah blew a fond kiss to the Colonel. "Dad, can you show them where Main Street is? I'll stay here and hold down the fort. I'll call or text when anything changes, and wait to see the whites of the doc's eyes." She nudged her father toward Mrs. Redmont. "Can you two get Mrs. Redmont down there on your own?"

It was the perfect question. Colonel Maddox took one arm and Mr. Redmont took the other as they escorted Mrs. Redmont toward the elevator.

"I think we'll be fine, Miss Maddox. Thanks. Do you need anything?" Mr. Redmont rose to the occasion.

"Nope, but thanks. I just had dinner. Take your time. I've got this watch." She patted her dad and Mr. Redmont on the back as they passed by. "I promise."

As soon as the elevator doors closed behind the threesome, Natalia moved down the hall toward Lucy's room. Yuri, Milo, Jackie, Monique, Elizabetta and Susannah followed. Elizabetta knew they would have enough time. The Colonel mentioned an hour, but Natalia had already faced this challenge once before. She would be faster and more efficient this time. The extra strength would also help.

In room 526, Lucy Redmont lay unconscious, as white as the sheets that covered her body. An intubation tube was taped in place across her mouth while the hiss and thump of the ventilator machine was the only noise to be heard in the room. IVs fed Lucy liquid, nutrition and medication. However, even in a coma, the girl seemed fit and muscular.

"I can not sense any thought at all." Natalia frowned. "There is…nothing in her mind. This will not be as easy as Tommy, I fear."

Monique reinforced Natalia's assessment in her own quiet way. "I too, feel nothing. This is very bad."

"We will be with you, moya zheena." Yuri kissed his wife. "And we have more help if we need it. I believe Chantal knows…"

"Alright. Everyone…" Natalia spoke out loud for the benefit of the humans involved. "Join hands around Lucy's bed and try to clear your minds of anything that draws your attention from the girl. Focus on her and her alone. It will help me channel your energy."

"Wait," Susannah interrupted, "Yuri, when Natalia finds the pink stuff, can you v-port it out here. Like into a bowl or something? Just a little so we can send it back to our doc for testing?" Susannah shrugged, not knowing if it was a possibility for Yuri.

"Da, I can try. If Natalia's okay with it. I don't want to jeopardize this process by trying something risky. What do you say, darling?" Yuri's vampiric gifts were growing stronger by the day and his attachment to his wife only multiplied both of their abilities. It was something that had to do with their bonding as a mated pair. No one understood it, but everyone on the team recognized the changes in the couple.

"When I was inside Tommy's mind, the stuff seemed tangible, a pink throbbing mass. If I can take you there, maybe you can collect a specimen. But have a care, it is incredibly dangerous. I wanted it so badly, I could have easily succumbed to the attraction. It almost talked to me." Natalia shook her head as if to drive the memory away. "It was very enticing."

"If I falter, or you are in trouble, I'll v-port us both out. I know everyone wants this girl to get well, but her life is not worth yours, my love." He pulled Natalia close and kissed her forehead.

"Da?"

"Da. Alright, let's start. You all know what to do." Natalia took Yuri's hand to begin the circle. As each member took the hand of the other, power built within Natalia's psychic sense.

In she dove, knowing where to go and focusing on the target this time. No searching was necessary. She sped to the neural network brightly tinged with pink. She sent a mental message to each of the group. *This is much brighter, much stronger in Lucy.*

Then it was there, a huge mass of seething, throbbing neon pink. It filled most of Lucy's right brain, twisted and entwined with her own neural network, like a boa encircling its victim with deadly pressure.

The same ceremonial sword appeared in Natalia's hands and she began to cut. Swinging and slicing, freeing each strand, one at a time. It was exhausting work and the large mass began to glow brighter at its center. The tendrils vibrated and began to disengage themselves, retreating into the body of the thing.

Natalia smelled the perfume and again felt the irresistible draw toward the mass. At once, Yuri was at her side. In his hands he held a crystal vial. As his wife cut a tendril, he reached to place it in the jar.

*No!* Natalia's fear was fuel for the thing that held Lucy in trance. *Do not touch this. It wants our kind. It has an evil purpose.*

The mass once again began to move and grow. *It feeds on my fear.* Natalia brought the sword tip to Yuri. It held a thin slice of the thing's body. *Cap this tightly and do not let anyone touch it until Doctor Anderson has seen it.*

Yuri simply nodded as the vial disappeared along with his image.

Natalia drew power from her circle and reengaged the fight for Lucy's mind. As she continued to swing her mighty sword, chopping and slicing, the pink monster seemed to recede. Pieces lay scattered and slowly disappearing. A thin slimy tendril snaked forth to curl around her foot before she could step out of the way.

Immediately a powerful feeling of euphoria enveloped her. Natalia's sword dropped from her hand as she breathed in great lungful's of the sweetest fragrance she had ever smelled. Her mouth watered and she licked her lips; lips that tasted of the nectar of the Gods. Her body tightened and a lovely warm tingling began at her core, rising rapidly to engulf all of her senses. A dreamy smile played across her lips.

*Ahhh! Let me go.*

Yuri appeared next to Natalia, took one hand and v-ported them both back to the hospital room. The circle dropped hands to stare at Natalia, slumped in Yuri's arms.

"What the hell was that?" Susannah was the first to recover. "I saw it. That's not a drug. It's some kind of living thing! In Lucy!"

Milo caught Jackie as she stumbled toward the chair in the corner of Lucy's room. "You're okay Jacks. It just drains humans a little more than...the..." He sunk to the floor. "Wow! Head rush."

Susannah grabbed the wilting Sergeant and placed him safely on the short divan next to the window. "Easy there, cowboy. I'll get some sugar for these guys." She motioned to Milo and Jackie. "And something from our cooler for Natalia."

Monique, not quite as taxed as the rest of the group, examined the pink goo in the tightly sealed vial. She reached to pick up the vial for a closer look and the stuff inside reached back. Startled, she stepped away. "This is very strange indeed. It moves toward me. Watch." Monique once again reached for the vial. Again it flowed toward her within the confines of the vial. "Fascinating."

Natalia raised her head. "Monique, stay away from that stuff. All vamps, it is much more dangerous than I originally thought. But what is it doing inside Lucy's body?" Natalia hugged her husband tightly. "You saved me. It would have..."

"Would have what, my dear?" Elizabetta came around the bed to lend a supportive hand, as Yuri sat Natalia on the opposite end of the divan next to Milo.

"Absorbed her." Jackie's words startled both Natalia and Elizabetta. "I saw it all. I was there with you... somehow." She raised her head to look at Natalia. "Is that what was in my brother's head too?"

Natalia shook her head, yes. "How were you there? What did you see?"

Milo was dead tired, but intrigued and raised his drooping head to observe. He knew Jacks was brilliant and talented and all that, but psychic ability? Or something like that?

"I don't know. I was just there. You had a fantastic sword and you fought the thing. Until it got you. Then you stood there staring off into nowhere. You dropped the sword... in Lucy's head?" Jackie slumped against the back of the chair, but remained upright. It was clear she was recovering faster than Milo.

Susannah returned, her arms laden with snacks and blood bags. "Food's here." The vial moved toward her on the table. "Eweeee. What is that?" The pink stuff pressed against the wall of the vial. She moved away to pass out the food and blood bags.

"Good question, Suze." Milo gratefully took a handful of candy bars and read a label. "Good choice, by the way." He took a Snickers candy bar and pointed it at the pink slime. "It got Natalia. She left her sword in Lucy's head."

"Sergeant, it wasn't a real sword, just a visual representation of what I was doing to this thing." She lisped, her fangs stuck to a bag of synth-blood. The pink ooze lurched in its vial.

"It seems sentient, alive. How can that be?" Jackie had recovered enough to get up and move toward the vial. It did not react. "It only reacts to you guys." She waved at Susannah.

Reaching out, Jackie touched the top of the vial lip with one fingertip. "Nothing."

"A mystery, indeed." Elizabetta moved to stand across the room from the unknown substance. "Now what? Can you go back in? Do you want to, or should we leave well enough alone?"

Natalia turned toward Jackie. "You saw everything? You were with me? That's a first, but maybe we can use your new found talent."

"Hold on. Wait a minute. I don't want Jackie in harms way." Milo stood too fast and caught the arm of the divan. "Tommy almost died because of this stuff. No way is Jacks getting anywhere near it." He moved to stand in front of his ex-girlfriend.

Jackie gently pushed Milo out of the way. "I'll do what I can. I don't think this stuff effects me like it does you all. Milo, try touching the vial."

"No! No way. No fucking chance." He stood his ground shaking his head. "I don't need pink slime and swords in my head. Not this fellow."

"My hero!" Jackie was making fun of him but he didn't care. She took his hand and before he could pull away, they were both touching the vial.

Nothing happened.

"Well, I'll be damned. No offense, ladies and Yuri." Milo bent to look more carefully.

"None taken." Three voices responded in unison.

Jackie's hand slid around Milo's back and she pinched him on the right butt cheek. adding a loud squawk. Milo jumped back upsetting the garbage can. "Don't do that! God, Jacks!"

Suppressed chuckles were heard around the room, but Jackie laughed outright. "Fine. Who's no fun now, Milo Miller? I thought you were the ultimate trickster? Shoe on the other foot?" She couldn't help teasing the Sergeant.

"Fun is one thing. This? This is…this is…" He turned to Natalia for help.

"I don't know. What I do know, is we have to get it out of Lucy. She is so much more infected, or… exposed… or whatever. Her life signs are dropping." Natalia indicated the life monitor with several declining lines of data.

"Then lets go. Tell me what to do, Natalia." Jackie stepped back up to the edge of the bed. "Since this is a first for me, I need some guidance."

"No, Jacks. You can't do this." Milo turned to his girlfriend. "I lost you once. Don't make me go through that again." He was pleading.

"Then help. Give us all your strength. Help me help Natalia. And Lucy." Jackie held out her hand for Milo to join the circle again.

"Oh man… really?" Milo completed the circle, taking Jackie's hand. "I hate pink."

"Same as before everyone. Yuri, any problems and you v-port us out, okay? When we're done, Monique, keep Lucy calm and feeling good. It's so big and entwined, I don't know what will happen when the girl is released from this thing. Let's do this." Natalia closed her eyes and dove as fast and hard as she could. She could sense Jackie keeping up and the loving push of her husband. *We're here.* Once again the ornate sword appeared in her hand. This time Jackie stood on her left, a bazooka strapped to her chest, ready to shoot. *Nice choice.*

*It's the only big weapon I could think of.* Jackie grinned at Natalia. *When things get tough, who ya gonna call?* The Ghostbuster's line was lost on Natalia.

So Jackie fired.

Natalia swung.

Jackie fired again, and again as Natalia surgically removed tendrils with her sword.

Though time virtually made no sense, the cleanup was accomplished in what seemed like minutes. Disintegrating pink fragments lay everywhere. The large body of the thing was withering. One last blast of Jackie's virtual bazooka ended the fight.

*I'm going to have to be more creative with my mental weapons. Thanks for the backup.*

Natalia took Jackie's hand and mentally withdrew them both from Lucy's body. The circle disconnected and Milo sunk back into his chair, exhausted.

"That's weird. I'm not tired at all. I could do this forever." Jackie was excited.

Elizabetta was tired… and intrigued.

Natalia was glad it was over.

And exhausted.

Monique stayed next to Lucy sending waves of calm emotion and security to the girl.

The life monitor began to alarm as Lucy's sudden recovery wrought havoc with the machine. "Let's go. We don't need to explain how this happened." Milo waved everyone toward the door.

Jackie grabbed the vial at the last minute, passing nurses, orderlies and doctors who came running with the alarm's high pitched screech.

"Doctor Guillium, report to 526, stat!" The loud speaker announced as the little group snuck by the melee.

"Hold on tight!" Milo wrapped his hands around Jackie's hands, clamped around the vial, as they hurried on down the hall toward the elevators. "Let's get this stuff out of here." Milo whispered as they passed a dashing set of parents obviously headed for Lucy's room.

Susannah, having texted her father minutes before, waved them on as Mr. and Mrs. Redmont rushed toward the growing group of medical professionals outside their daughter's room. Sirens blasted and machines beeped, as the worried parents ducked between orderlies, doctors and nurses, and disappeared in the crowd.

The elevator doors opened as Jackie and Milo made their escape, the vial securely trapped in their hands.

## Chapter 11

## Consequences

Sometimes, the consequences of life take a heavy toll.
Often with that toll, comes a heavy soul.
Willing to repent, to reach out and come clean,
In the aftermath of destruction, in the killing of a dream.

We all face the mirror, at least once in our lives,
A view so profane, we promise to strive,
For a way to atone, a price to pay,
To relieve our conscience, so on we pray.

*Brother Berthold*
*The Personal Journal of a Monk*
*Athletic Department, Academia de Santos Domingo de Silos, Leyre, France*
*Published posthumously*

"Please, do go on, Father Christobal." The Very Reverend Father Disjagio von Songoria motioned for the Headmaster and Abbott to continue. "You found Brother Berthold in the old cemetery behind the monastery. He had apparently hanged himself. By himself?"

"I did not find him. One of the students did. I was working with Father François d'Gaton in the library. He is the Keeper of the Archives at the monastery. He heard the girl cry out and went to see what was wrong."

"And…" Songoria was not letting the Abbott off the hook. The facts about this suicide did not add up.

"The young woman fainted."

"And…"

"At the foot of the tree where Brother Berthold… hung." Father Christobal crossed himself, then folded his hands calmly on his desk.

"Then what happened?"

"Well, Father François went to fetch the girl and we called the Policia Floral, of course."

"How long did it take for the police to arrive?" The Vatican investigator pushed on.

"I am not sure. I suppose an hour or possibly less. Once Maria Pallermo was taken to the infirmary, there was nothing else to be done. Until the police arrived, that is." The Abbott spoke with his hands, then relaxed again, placing them on his desk with a shrug. "Things like this do not happen here, Your Eminence. I have given you a copy of the police report." The Abbott picked up a pen to address the work on his desk, summarily dismissing the Vatican's official representative.

It was a mistake.

"Abbot, I represent the Pope himself in this investigation. I would suggest you consider your position if you wish to remain at San Leyre." The Very Reverend Father Disjagio von Songoria glared at the Abbott. "If you get my meaning?"

"There is nothing here that cannot be handled within our own walls. Do not threaten me. I have been Abbott here for more years than you have been on this earth, son. I will not stand for your insolence. Brother Berthold was a very unhappy man. He sought solace in this monastery, but we failed him. Obviously. Now, only God can help his poor tortured soul. And I leave it in His hands." The Abbott rose, folding his hands before him. "We are finished."

"No, Father, we are not. I interviewed Maria Pallermo. Funny thing about her…" the investigator remained seated. "She mentioned seeing writing on the headstone near the tree. In blood. She also mentioned Brother Berthold used to meet someone under that tree. Where he hanged himself."

"I am sure I do not know what you are talking about, Sir. There was no writing on any of the stones. We keep a tidy graveyard. The grounds are well tended to. Surely someone would have noticed the defacement."

"It was not defacement in the usual way, Abbott. It was a message from Brother Berthold. In blood, according to Maria Pallermo." The investigator pointed to his notes.

"I can assure you I never saw any writing on any head-stones in our cemetery." He looked calm and studied, serious but unconcerned. He looked the Very Reverend Father Disjagio von Songoria in the eye. "I can swear on a Bible if it will make you feel better. I have several around here." Father Christobal's smile was a bit smug. "Maria may have seen Brother Berthold and Father

François together in the cemetery. They often spoke there. Father François counseled our tormented Brother there, at Berthold's favorite place."

"Brother Berthold's favorite place was a cemetery?" Songoria was a little surprised.

"He found solace in prayer at the small shrine by the same tree where he chose to break with God's Commandments. The shrine is just inside the cemetery. It is a quiet place." The Abbott began to wring his hands in an outward show of concern for the priest's soul. "I will never understand why someone would take their own life, especially a man committed to God and the Church. He has committed a mortal sin. He cannot be buried here, his home." The Abbott crossed himself and sat with an uncharacteristic plop. "For the life of me, I cannot understand this." He laid his head in his hands as if to shed tears.

The Very Reverend Father Disjagio von Songoria wasn't buying it. "A shrine? What shrine?"

Father Christobal's muffled words slipped from beneath his fingers. "Shrine of the Ange d'Extase. He prayed there almost every day, as do other parishioners and our major benefactor. It is common." The Abbott withdrew his hands and eyed the Vatican's investigator. "You should try it. Possibly seek your answers there."

The Very Reverend Father Disjagio von Songoria was getting nowhere with the Abbott. And knew it. "I am sure Brother Berthold rests in the arms of God, who will judge him appropriately. Thank you for your...time, Abbott. I shall leave you to your work." He rose to depart.

The Abbott also rose. "You are most welcome, Father. If you have any more questions, please do not hesitate to knock on my door." In deference to the powerful emissary from the Pope, Father Christobal bent in an almost unnoticeable bow. "And... if in the future you wish to question another of our students, please see me first. While I do not doubt or question your intentions Father, I am responsible to their parents. It would not look good..."

The Abbott's door softly clicked behind the departing Songoria. Father Christobal sat back down, his soft smile in place once again.

Through the open door to the Abbott's small reception connecting to the cloister walk, a thin voice floated. "He will be trouble. I do not like him."

"François, do not trouble yourself. There is nothing to find.

You yourself said the child... Maria... was hysterical. I am sure she would claim the Vision of Mother Mary herself, if it would gain her the 15 minutes of fame teenagers so desperately seek these days. She is calm now?"

Father François d'Gaton, Keeper of the Archives and Head Librarian of the monastery slipped back into the Abbot's office. No footsteps were heard. No ancient board creaked. The man always moved that way. "This Songoria comes from Rome. He is trouble."

"Then it is your duty to see to his needs, François. Do follow the man and see what he is up to. I have maintained this chair for many years. I know what is best for my Brothers and the children in our care. Go with this investigator and provide what service he may require." The Abbot glanced at the door through which the Very Reverend Father Disjagio von Songoria had departed. "And I shall pray for us all. Go now."

Father François retreated the way he had come. Silently. Actually, there was something to find, and it was Father François' job to make sure that something was never discovered. It would mean more than the Abbott's job, it would mean the life of the monastery and the school. Their treasured position and financial stability set them apart from the Vatican, a position François cherished. Their benefactor was most generous and François, in return, stretched his beliefs to accommodate both the monastery and it's benefactor. Should the secrets of San Leyre be revealed, the world would quake in terror.

Songoria was snooping around the graveyard and the shrine that stood nearby. This man would be trouble. Father François watched from his concealed position. Something would need to be done... and soon.

******

Doctor Helga Anderson and Colonel Frank Maddox sat across from each other at the kitchen table of their quarters near the hospital. "It looks like Pepto-Bismol, only translucent." Helga picked up the vial and shook it. Pink slime coated the glass walls but eventually slid away. "Natalia and Susannah were very specific about not opening this stuff."

"They said it moved. On it's own." Frank raised his eyebrows. "Two years ago I would have thought my daughter was being her usual delusional self... but today. I trust her observations and judgment."

"As I live and breathe..." Helga's hand slapped the table.

"Don't be so impressed. Suze has worked her ass off and I acknowledge that. Even if she is my little baby girl...grown up a bit... and a vamp." It was amazing how easily he now talked about the more unique aspects of his daughter's life. He had to smile at the last part.

They both did.

When first approached by Captain Devlin, Dr. Anderson thought the 'deep undercover research position' he offered had to do with the latest biological weapons on the market, and ways to eliminate them safely. A position she was more than happy to accept. In fact, she was elated they selected her, after having been out of the field for over a year. Her life had gone to hell in one fiery burned out mess of a home and family. She was eating Oreo cookies by the case and drinking her depression into desolation by the bottle. In a million years, she could not have figured out that the newest biological weapon had fangs and a Hollywood history to rock her world and scientific brain. A few short years later, she sat across from her boss, a Colonel, whose job was to lead a team of fanged operatives. The daughter of said Colonel, a teen-baby vampire had recently become an effective and experienced operative.

"She has come a long way. You can be a proud papa, Frank." Helga's smile faded, remembering the promising future that belonged to her own daughter, before the fire. With a sigh she placed a finger on the cap of the vial and shook it slightly. The contents behaved as any thick liquid would. "Tell me again, how we came to posses this specimen."

"If I understand it correctly, our lovely Mrs. Milassoviech entered Lucy's body and recovered it." Frank shook his head. "Our vamp group seems to be developing more and more as they remain in close proximity to each other. She somehow used Yuri's ability to v-port... stuff, and grabbed this. Ya know, I'm just human. I don't get all this v-stuff."

At that comment they both laughed. Just human? When did that become a mental and physical handicap?

"Well, I should get back to the lab and see what this pink stuff is all about. You say it moves toward vampires on its own? Could I see it do that before I leave?"

"Not sure. None of them want to be in the room with it. Elizabetta explained it was like chocolate to a choc-a-holic. She said it kinda calls to them. Irresistible, I guess." Frank poked at his phone with one clumsy finger.

"When did you start texting, Frank?" Helga was a little surprised as she watched the Colonel struggle to create a message.

"If Suze can conquer the wild blue yonder, I can figure out the little tiny word thingy." He completed the text message to his Coven Mistress with care, re-read the words and hit send. "I'll get Elizabetta in here to show you."

"I can understand that. I wonder what effect it has on a vampire?" Helga was studying the pink liquid as Elizabetta came through the door between their rooms. A bit disheveled, she'd obviously been resting.

The sludgy pink liquid flowed in the direction of the Coven Mistress. "That, Doctor, I do not wish to find out." Elizabetta visibly shivered and kept her distance. "You wished to see me, Frank?"

"Yep. And I think that did it. Helga wanted to see what this stuff does in close proximity to a vampire. I think this is an adequate demonstration. Thanks."

Elizabetta turned and left without another word.

"Wow." It was about all Helga could think of to say.

Frank watched the closing door. "Double wow. Ah… when you get this stuff back to the lab, maybe lock it up in the Haz-Mat Vault would you? I don't need my team going crazy around this stuff. Not that I don't trust them implicitly… but I've seen reactions like that before. In recovering meth addicts."

Doctor Anderson studied her boss, who was studying the door through which Elizabetta had departed…quickly and without a word. "Got that picture."

"Natalia and Jacquiline Pantterdyck were closest to the stuff. Maybe you should check them out as well. After you get rid of the spooky Pepto-Bismal." Frank poured himself a cup of coffee. "Want a cup?"

"No thanks. How did Tommy's sister get involved? Did she touch this?" Helga was intrigued as well as concerned.

"Not sure about that part of the story." He gulped the black coffee. "Natalia was exhausted but Jackie was hopping around like she was hardwired to a nuclear fuel cell. Halfway back here she crashed. They've all been sleeping off the side effects of v-healing, or, whatever it was they did to bring Lucy Redmont out of her coma. By the way, her parents are ecstatic and FaceBooking the world about the efficiency of the military docs at Walter Reed." Frank rejoined Helga at the table with his cup. "They still think she got slipped some drug on a date with her boyfriend though."

"I hope they are not blaming Tommy! His father will not be happy." Helga sat back with a chuckle.

"That guy's been such a dickhead since this whole thing started, he deserves it. But we sure don't need this…" he pointed to the vial and its contents that once again resembled regular liquid, "stuff on the Internet. Are you heading back to the farm today?"

"I plan to, if that is alright. After seeing the effects on Elizabetta, I think it would be prudent if I traveled with only humans. Did Ms. Pantterdyck react to this, or did it react to her?"

"Not sure. She and Miller are still asleep."

As if he'd been summoned by magic, Sergeant Miller came through the door and stumbled toward the coffee pot. Wearing rumpled sweats and an open shirt, he poured a full cup and drank half before he opened his eyes. "Ah, sorry, Sir. Ma'am." Miller turned around and pulled his shirt closed then gulped the other half-cup of coffee.

"Milo, that's kind of hot." Helga was chuckling again.

"Yep." He poured another cup and buttoned his shirt. It was off by one buttonhole. His hair was a mess of short spikes sticking out in every direction and his whiskers were black against a tanned face. Thick dark hair stuck out the neckline of his shirt.

"Sergeant, please join us. Doctor Anderson has a couple questions for you." Colonel Maddox motioned to a chair at their table.

"Thank you, Sir, but I may not be of any use. I'm shot." He continued to gulp the coffee but sat down.

"Milo, do you know if Ms. Pantterdyck touched the specimen she collected from Lucy?" Helga jumped into researcher mode.

"Man, I don't know. She was doing that thing Natalia does. They were…" The Sergeant rubbed his unshaven face. "I don't know where they were. Or what they were doing. Or how they did it. But all of a sudden this… what is this?" He paused, raised his drooping head and pointed to the vial.

"We don't know yet." The liquid remained still. "What we do know is that it has an affinity towards vampires. I just wonder if

Ms. Pantterdyck was effected. If we need to keep it away from her, too." Helga picked up the vial and twirled the liquid.

Sergeant Miller sat back with a start. He raised his hand to ward off... he didn't really know what he was warding off. "All I remember is that stuff was crawling all over the glass and the three vampires in the room looked like me when I see a sixteen ounce medium rare steak. Somehow Jacks knew...something. She ran out the door with the vial and everyone went back to normal. Is that what is, I mean was, in Tommy and Lucy? Is it alive or something?" Miller was full of questions, just like everyone else.

"Miller, we know very little at this point. One; Tommy and Lucy will be okay. We think. Two; this stuff has an effect on vampires." Colonel Maddox took the vial from Doctor Anderson and swiped it past the Sergeant. "But not humans, so far." He set the vial down in the middle of the table. It remained still. "And three; if this is what has poisoned the kids at their hoity-toity school, then we have a big problem on our hands. What we don't know is how these two kids got it in their systems and why." The Colonel was shaking his head.

"I'm going to take this specimen back to my lab at the farm. I was wondering if you and Ms. Pantterdyck would like to accompany me. I could run a few tests. Just to make sure you are both clean. And since Ms. Pantterdyck has seen this substance in action, she could be invaluable with my research." Helga was phrasing the request as diplomatically as she could. However it had to happen, Jacquiline Pantterdyck was needed for testing. She sweetened the pot. "You two could have some private time at the farm. Maybe she would enjoy that, now that the drama surrounding her brother is drawing to a close. And just possibly, you will have a second chance at gaining her confidence, once again." Helga patted the Sergeant's arm in a motherly fashion.

The last sentence did it. Milo needed time with Jackie and he could have it at the farm, before everyone got back and the place went crazy. "Good idea Doc. I'm sure she will be happy to know she has no residual effects from doing... that thing with Natalia." He turned to the Colonel. "Sir, does the General and Mrs. Ceauchene know about, you know, our team members? Obviously Jacks does. She and Susannah have been friends for...forever, I'm figuring *that* out." The Sergeant was a little chagrined.

"The General is aware, on some level, that the team members have special talents. His ex-wife has not been read in.

She is currently under the impression that our doctor and the doctors at Walter Reed have perfected an antidote for the poison these children were accidentally exposed to. Same with Mr. and Mrs. Redmont. Angelina is presently cooking a million cookies for everyone on the hospital floor who took care of her daughter. She's into nuts and twigs, health nut stuff. You should see the muscles on that woman. She could join the WWF. Nice woman all around." The Colonel shrugged. "Not sure about her husband."

"So you gonna have Natalia wipe the General's mind? Sir. Sorry, Sir, if it's above my pay grade." Milo slipped out of rank for just a second, but made a quick recovery. "Sorry, sir. I'm bushed." Miller gulped the rest of his coffee and went for a third cup.

"Not sure, Sergeant. We'll have to see how this all turns out. There is more to the story than just these two kids. I've never seen anything like this stuff." Again, the Colonel reached to pick up the specimen.

"Sir, do you really think you should?" Forgetting himself, Miller stayed the Colonel's hand as he moved toward the coffee pot for another cup of Joe.

"You're probably right, Miller." Maddox lifted his cup instead. "Would you mind?"

"Not at all, Sir." Miller filled both cups and sat back down at the table. "Ma'am, when do you plan to leave? Taking the plane?"

"As soon as possible, Milo. Can you and Jacquiline be ready in an hour? I want to be out of here way before any of our non-human team members rise from their day sleep."

"Good idea. I'm on it." Miller slurped what little coffee remained in the bottom of the cup and jumped up. Apparently the caffeine had kicked in. "Meet you back here at..." He checked his ever present watch."...zero nine hundred."

The doctor looked up to agree and Miller was gone. "Where? Frank, that boy never ceases to amaze me."

Colonel Maddox chuckled. "He does that to you too, huh?"

She smiled and shook her head. "I spent the afternoon with an old friend at the CDC. You know everyone there thinks I'm dead?" She shook her head again. "Guess I sort of left abruptly after... the accident. I wasn't in the best... in the best of shape to continue my research."

The silence made both uncomfortable.

"So... long story short, Pamela, my friend over there,

already knew everything about the Vamp Squad, my job... everything."

"Really? Now that's news to me." Maddox was intrigued.

"Apparently she was read in by someone from the Joint Chiefs. No-name someone. In any event, we talked openly, which was really refreshing for a change. She is willing to lend me a fellow I introduced to the CDC a long time ago. Doctor Seizemore is probably one of the most engaging and complex minds I have ever encountered. All I have to do is convince him to come up to the farm for a little while. I grabbed him as an intern and kept ahold when I found out how good he was as a chemical engineer, genet- icist and pharmacological specialist. He's amazing but... a little... well, Frank, he's weird. You know, socially awkward."

"You think that will be a problem with our little family group?"

At that question they both laughed.

****** 

Lucy Redmont sat up in bed, a paper cup of juice in her slightly shaking hand. "Mom, I swear I didn't take anything. And I know Tom doesn't do drugs. We had dinner together. And no, Dad, before you even ask, not that kind of dinner!"

Angelina smiled at her daughter, knowing full well her husband would give anything to have a heterosexual daughter. He'd always been uncomfortable with Lucy's lifestyle choice, but supportive.

Supportive as a Roman Catholic man could be with a lesbian daughter.

Angelina was simply proud of them both. Proud of her daughter for being who she was. Her husband for loving their daughter, no matter what. She took the cup from Lucy's hand. "I trust you, young lady. You should know that by now, honey. Tom is recovering down the hall. When you are a little stronger, I'll roll you down there and you guys can chat. Maybe figure out what happened."

"That I would love to know." Wesley Redmont inserted, as his fist smacked his hand.

"Dad, Tom is the captain of the boy's team. I'm captain of the girl's team. We do a lot of stuff together, that's all. Tom knows I'm not into boys. In fact, he treats me like any other girl and I like that. He's a true athlete. He doesn't even do sugar or caffeine." Lucy took a bite of the bagel on her plate. It was smothered in cream cheese and brown sugar. Just the way she loved it. "He might as well become a monk." She mumbled with a mouthful of bagel.

"Monk…okay. Messing with my daughter… definitely not okay!" Lucy's father stood just inside the doorway to her room, leaning against the wall. The chairs in the room were too small to accommodate the towering man.

"Dad." Lucy stopped chewing and glared at her father.

"Okay, okay. I get it. I'm just… concerned."

Lucy almost choked on the bagel mush in her mouth.

Angelina replied, "Like when that kid down the block threw mud at her. You were what, about four years old, Punkin? Wes, you hung the kid on the fence by his suspenders. You and the kid's dad went at it like two bulls in a pen, while our lovely innocent daughter threw rocks at the poor kid. Now that's Redmont concern." Though Angelina was proud of her small family, she sometimes needed to intervene in the amount of 'family concern' that was shown. "Alright, one Redmont needs to rest, one needs to eat, and one needs to settle down."

The commands were given. Wesley Redmont kissed his daughter's forehead and ducked through the doorway into the hall.

Angelina removed her daughter's empty tray, pushed the rolling table closer with its juice and water, then pulled the covers up a touch. "We'll be back for lunch. Can we bring you something, Punkin?"

"A Big Mac, fries and a chocolate shake would be fantastic. I feel like I haven't eaten in ages." Lucy smiled brightly at her mother.

Angelina returned the same bright smile. "I'll warn the nurses to stay out of reach. Mickey D's it is. Try to get some sleep."

"Sure, mom. Love you Dad!" She hollered after the retreating couple.

Waiting the required five minutes to be sure her parents were off the floor and on their way, Lucy threw back the covers and sat on the edge of the bed. Gingerly placing one foot, then the other on the floor, she tested her legs. They wobbled at any amount of weight. "Sheeze, how long have I been out?"

Tommy stood in her doorway. "About ten days. Take it

slow. I could barely walk at first. It comes back fast." He sat down in the chair next to her bed. "I was waiting for your folks to leave. How do you feel?"

"Like I was starved for a year, then got run over by a Mac truck. You?" She finger combed her short red hair.

"Same. But better every day. You get breakfast?" Tommy indicated the empty tray.

"Yeah but I could eat three more." Lucy bounced her feet on the floor and stretched her arms. She felt weak but whole.

"I've been grazing." He withdrew two wrapped apple pies from his pocket. He handed one to Lucy and unwrapped one for himself. "The vending machine doesn't offer much in the way of healthy snacks, but I can forego the healthy side for now. I'm recovering, right?"

Both kids chuckled as they demolished the sweet snack.

Lucy finished hers first. "My parents are really pissed. They think you did something to me."

Tommy licked his fingertips. "Yeah, I know. My father was so mad, I thought his head would blow off his shoulders. He had that red vein poking out of his forehead."

Again, both kids laughed. Recovering and out of danger, the youngsters were back to normal, mocking their parents and joking. Two apple pies down, and life was good.

"So what happened?" Lucy paused to take a breath. "I can't remember much after we got off the bus."

Tommy sobered. "Me either. We walked up the road, said hi to Berthy... then it's just blank." The pre-arranged lie rolled easily off Tommy's lips. He felt a little crappy about it, but he also knew the seriousness of the situation and what would happen if he divulged classified information. His father had made that clear before anything else. So it was easier to claim ignorance, sorta like pleading the Fifth. "How about you?"

"We saw Berthy? I don't even remember that. After the meeting we went to Un Beau Goût. I remember that much. Man, I could go for a plate of crepes right now."

At her last comment, Tommy knew Lucy was on the mend. The woman ate like a horse. How she remained trim and fit was a miracle. "Whatever happened, we seem to have been cured by the good doctors here. Any residual after effects, other than the normal weakness?"

Tommy had his orders; pump Lucy for information and

report back, asap. The General had been very clear earlier that morning. Do not divulge *anything* under threat of grounding for life. For Tommy, that was worse than death.

"Not really. Everything is blank. I did have this incredible dream about your sister chasing bad guys with a bazooka, but I can't remember if that was after I came out of the coma, or before. You have any weird dreams?" Lucy wiped the traces of apple pie off her chin with her hospital gown.

"Nope. I'm blank as a newborn. You don't remember seeing Berthy before we went down for the count?" Tommy dug around for more information.

"No. Not at all. Where'd we see him?"

"Ya know, now I'm not sure if we really saw him, or if I imagined it. I can't seem to trust my brain right now. I try to think about what happened and I get fuzzy flashbacks. The doctors say it will pass. I sure didn't see my sister with any guns! She's such a sissy, she'd never pick up a bazooka. Might break a nail!"

Both kids laughed at that comment. Tommy was successful in creating a companionable segway out of the interrogation. Lucy laughed because she couldn't imagine caring if a nail broke or not.

Tommy yawned. "I think I hear a bed calling. I've been awake for about two hours and I can't seem to stay that way for long. I'll see you later." Tommy tossed the wrapper from his apple pie in the garbage can.

"I get that." Lucy yawned and snuggled down in her bed. "See ya, Tom."

Back in his own room, Tommy called his father. "Dad? Tom. I just talked to Lucy. She's awake and her parents have gone for awhile. She can't even remember seeing Brother Berthold. I don't think she will be much help."

"Well, thanks for trying, Tommy. Get some rest. Your mom will be in to see you this afternoon." After a pause, the General continued, "Son, I'm glad you are doing better. Need anything?"

"Nah, I'm good. But thanks… for caring, dad."

"Always have, son. Just a little hard saying it. But we almost lost you. Puts the fear of God in this old heart. See you tonight." The line went dead.

Wow! His old man cared and he actually said it.

Out loud…Holy crap!

Tommy hung up the phone as his sister breezed through the

door dragging a civilian attired ex-boyfriend. "Hey, bro." She kissed her brother with a loud smack. "How ya doin"?"

"Fine but tired. Just hung up on Dad. He said he cared. Blew my mind. Is he sick or something?"

Jacquiline laughed and hugged her brother soundly. "Nope, just scared of losing his star athlete. He's proud of you, but has a hard time expressing himself. Has something to do with those stars on his shoulders."

Tommy looked past his sister at Milo. "Women… they always make excuses."

Milo punched Tommy on the shoulder, softly. "I got no dog in this fight, Tom. I've learned to keep the lips sealed."

"Except when they're on my sister's!"

Milo Miller had the good grace to blush as he shook his head almost imperceptibly behind his girlfriend's back.

"All right, you two! Tom, I gotta go up to a medical facility in Maine with Milo and his team to see if I was exposed to anything. You know as well as I do, Walter Reed docs had very little to do with fixing you and Lucy. Have you talked to Lucy yet?"

"Yeah, but she doesn't remember anything. Actually less than I do. I told Dad that."

"Well, that's actually in our favor. Dad won't have Intel crawling all over her. Her folks are happy right now and we need to keep them that way."

"Who's this 'we', Jacks? Have you joined the enemy?" Tommy eyed his sister.

"Nah, but Milo's team thinks I might be able to contribute, so I'm off for a few days." She took Miller's hand. "Maybe a little longer, depending on the business at hand." She smiled at the quiet Sergeant.

"Oh, of course. Monkey business, you mean, sis." Tommy smacked his lips in a kissy face.

"You're still weak. Better watch yourself, little brother." Jacquiline looked stern at her brother then bent and kissed his forehead. "Get better, Tommy. I love you. And I don't mind telling you. Every day if I have to!"

Tommy closed his eyes. "Back at ya, sis."

As they headed for the elevators, Milo softly said, "We have about 15 minutes until the chopper will pick us up on the field. The plane is waiting at Andrews. Everything packed?"

"Yes. Does this installation of yours have a BX just in case I need something?" Jackie was curious about the place Milo worked. She had an idea of the makeup of the team, but no idea about their home base.

"No, but the town nearby certainly does. We are deep cover, so we go civilian when we are out of pocket."

"Oooh baby, talk that secret talk. It's so sexy." The dry comment made Milo chuckle. He wanted to take her in his arms and plaster kisses all over her face. But all he did was stand there, holding the hand of the most wonderful woman on the face of the earth.

And trying to breathe normally.

Chapter 12

All Things New

Change is hard for some,
And causes the mind to numb,
To the new, the strange, the challenge of old.
All things considered, we still reach for the bold.

The unknown and mysterious,
Mis-steps can be furious,
Or simply a mistake, to be resolved with time,
Putting to test, all those in their prime.

We chase our fear,
As all things become clear.
Acceptance is, for all who see,
The truth in change, will set you free.

*Dr. Helga Anderson*
*Medical Journal of Research*
*Medical Element, Vamp Squad*
*Olney, Maine 2014*

Doctor Helga Anderson sat belted into the luxurious seats in the back of the team's private jet headed for Olney, Maine. Next to her, sat Jacquiline Pantterdyck. They'd been talking since takeoff from Joint Base Andrews in Maryland. It would be a short flight and Helga was trying to fill Jacquiline in on the teams 'special and unique' talents as well as her own research. She was amazed at the young woman's easy acceptance of everything the doctor was telling her. Maybe it was the generation. Maybe it was Jacquiline's own unusual abilities that had recently surfaced. After all, she'd jumped right in to help Natalia fight the pink monster in Lucy's brain, without a second thought. And was a true asset, according to Natalia.

"Yo, ex, how'd you get hooked up with this amazing group of people? Do you call them people? I mean… I don't have the right vocabulary. Sorry." Jackie grimaced. "I'm not exactly PC all the time."

"No apology necessary. We call ourselves humans and the vampires are vamps. Believe me, they won't take offense at anything except garlic breath and open bleeding. And please don't call me ex." Milo's look was direct and serious.

"Yeah, well... sorry, Milo James Miller." Jackie was easing up, but still maintained an edge to their redeveloping relationship. Now that everyone was fairly recovered and she was taking in so much information about the team, she was back to mildly unforgiving. Milo had a little more penance to do.

"Can you tell me a little more about this stuff?" Helga pointed to the acrylic containment box strapped to the floor near the door. The vial of pink liquid sat securely in the middle, braced by foam and a metal frame.

"Well, I can tell you it doesn't have the same effect on me, that it has on the...vamps." Jackie watched the vial. "When we were... helping Lucy... which I still don't know how or what we did, sort of...Natalia was fighting two fronts. I could feel her attraction to the stuff, but she never lost track of the fact that it had to be destroyed. She seemed to know how to kill it, or get rid of it... or whatever... It's hard to talk about because I've never been exposed to anything like this. It was like alive, but not. I know that doesn't make any sense." Jackie was struggling.

"Were you afraid of it? Did you feel a pull?" Helga probed.

"No, not really. I just had this urge to do a job. Like when you have a difficult task ahead and you know it has to be done. I didn't go in thinking that, it just popped into my head. It's not the first time something weird, extra-ordinary... has happened to me. I hate to even mention it though. My dad calls it woo-woo voodoo. Apparently mom has some kind of ESP, or something, too. When dad was in Iraq and got wounded, she knew before the call came in. We've never talked about it outright, but we both just know and understand things." Jackie looked up at Milo. "You probably think I'm nuts, huh?"

Again, Milo's look was serious and studied. "My idea of reality was significantly changed a few years back, Jackie. I don't laugh at anything anymore. You could tell me our pilot was a werewolf and I'd be prone to believe you." Milo shook his head.

"There are werewolves, too?" Jackie asked with a start.

"No dear." Helga patted Jackie's arm with a chuckle. "As

far as I know, there are only vampires in our world. They are mutated humans, not Satanic, soulless, blood-suckers. You'll have to rethink everything you thought you ever knew about vampires. Our vamps live on synth-blood, not warm, live blood. We all live under a Pact of Cohabitation. It works well for us." Helga sighed. "There is so much to tell you. When I first joined the team, my science side engaged in World War V with my fantasy side. I remember Dark Shadows and the incredibly sexy Jonathan, the family vampire." The doctor's secret sensual smile said a lot about her teen fantasy.

"Dark Shadows?" Jackie was intrigued.

"A 1960s TV show. About a family living in some castle on the east coast. It was a really messed up family with vampires, witches and weird kids." Milo chuckled. "I watched reruns on the Oldies channel when I first took this job. Before we found Elizabetta, we had to keep Susannah locked up. I had very little to do except try to find anything to block out the screams." Milo caught the look on Jackie's face and shifted uncomfortably in his chair. "Sorry. It seems cruel but we didn't know anything about vampires. Imagine your dad trying to accept you as a vamp? Long story short; Susannah got turned and abandoned by her sire. We found Elizabetta to teach her how to live. She's still a baby vamp, by vamp standards. But maturing rapidly."

"So the rumors about her little spring break boo-boo were true. She died but… didn't. Right?"

"You're catching on a little faster than her father did. Actually a lot faster than the Colonel did. But when he did, he couldn't just 'off' his daughter. So, voile! The Vamp Squad was born." Milo opened his arms wide. "Colonel Maddox offered me the top secret, undercover job and I ran for my life. More like your dad sentenced me, but it worked out okay, I guess. How do you like our transport?"

"So you couldn't even call? Text? Email?" Jackie accused in three quick questions.

Helga pretended she was part of the upholstery.

"Under sentence of death from the General if I ever even breathed your name let alone contact you? He promised a fate worse than death, castration! No, I did not contact you." Milo studied his hands in his lap. "Why didn't you tell me who your father was? Or that you just happened to be jail bait?"

The real rub finally surfaced as the two ex-lovers squared

off.

"Would it have made a difference?" She eyed him suspiciously.

The pregnant silence was thick with heartache and doubt.

"Well, I for one could use a drink. How about you two?" Helga could not allow it to drag on. The pain in both young people was too apparent. "I do believe we have a complete bar. Soda? Juice? A variety of wines…Bud Lite? Something harder?"

"I'll go for puppy piss, Doctor Anderson. He'll have crow on the rocks." Jackie tried for a joke to lighten the mood. Her thoughts were running deep and she needed time to figure out the last few minutes of conversation… or the lack there of.

"Please, Jacquiline, call me Helga. The team is very casual, but, more close than anything else. You'll see. My guess is, you've been adopted." She handed Jackie a beer. "Whether you like it or not!" The doctor clinked cans with the newest Vamp Squad recruit, who didn't know it yet.

"I think I may like it, more than not." She raised her beer can to Miller who had just grabbed his own drink.

With a shy smile, the Sergeant raised his can back.

"Doc…sorry, Helga, I've always been different." Jackie felt a huge weight lifted from her shoulders as she self-disclosed. "I've never known what to call it. But I have an idea the Vamp Squad will not only not care, but accept it. Being different among some really different folks just means I'm normal. Feels kinda good." She gulped a mouthful of beer, swallowed and promptly burped. "'Scuze me!"

"Hah! You did learn something in Pergatory, North Dakota!" Milo burped back but did not excuse himself.

Helga followed suit and laughed as she took her seat once again.

A voice came over the speaker. "Landing in thirty minutes. Vehicles standing by to transport to the Farm. Finish burping and buckle up."

Obviously the flight crew had been eves dropping! Casey, the pilot, had a great sense of humor.

\*\*\*\*\*\*

Back at Olney Farm, mystery and drama were running high. The place was abuzz with titillating gossip. "So, this

Jacquiline is the mysterious woman in Sergeant Miller's past. Oo la la! This will be so much divertissement. And they will be here tonight. How lovely!" Monique was overcome with glee on the phone. Yuri had v-ported her to the farm when the team began to close up shop, leaving Susannah and her father to the clean up. It was good to be home!

Monique giggled to herself. Home? Olney Farm and the Vamp Squad had become home, the only home she'd known since her turning and the horrors of the French Revolution.

"Be nice, Frenchy. He's been through the ringer these past couple days." Susannah actually felt for the Sergeant whose entire background was laid open for all to see. Like a fresh wound, it was raw and painful. "The planets must be in line because what are the chances, one of my old friends from military family life turns out to be the reason Milo ends up with me and the Vamp Squad. It sure is a small world."

"I cannot comprehend. What is the chance this sick child came from San Leyre? It is tres unnerving. I have been... ete tres angoisse, very unhappy, lately." Monique spoke quietly.

"Not to worry, sister. We *will* figure this out. And if there is something going on at that horrible place, I will make sure you do not have to go there. Ever. Promise!"

"This, I will hang you to. Come home soon. I have no one to watch old movies with. Au revoir." Monique hung up before Susannah could correct her slang. Monique was upset and worried. Not only for Tommy and Lucy, but about the whole involvement with San Leyre. A place she would never willingly return to. The place that sent fear through her entire body and mind.

\*\*\*\*\*\*

"Dad, when do we bug out?" Susannah turned to her father who sat at the kitchen table consuming some form of disgusting caloric combination in a brown bag.

"Probably tomorrow night. Got a few things to wrap up with the General. And I'd like to keep tabs on Tommy's recovery for a few more hours. It'd be nice to visit with Chantal as well. Haven't seen the woman since..." He stopped chewing and stared at the mess on his paper plate.

"Yeah, I know. Since mom and our Tommy died." Both Maddoxs' worst nightmare flashed across the silent pause.

"Be nice to catch up." Frank slid his plate into the garbage and got up. "Think I'll shower and catch a few winks, kiddo." He kissed his daughter's forehead. "Shouldn't you be asleep?"

It was mid afternoon and Susannah yawned.

"Guess so. I just had so much to do." She leaned against the fridge. "Think I'll grab a snack before I turn in."

"We used to call that an 'all nighter'. Guess for you, it's an 'all dayer'." He tosseled her hair on the way to his room, all of six feet away.

"Dad!"

"Come on, honey. Let an old man pretend he still has a little girl." Frank chuckled as he closed the door behind him.

"Your father has found himself, I think." Elizabetta reclined on the sofa unnoticed by the Colonel. "He seems to enjoy your company…and respects you as an operative now."

Susannah plopped down next to her surrogate mother to drain a bag of synth-blood. "Go figure. I had to become a vampire to get my father's attention and a little respect." She laid her head on the Coven Mistress' shoulder like the tired young girl she was.

"Oh no, you always had his attention. He just did not know how to show you. Fear blocked his vision and froze his heart." Elizabetta held the youngest of her coven in a warm embrace. "Finish your dinner and off to bed with you, my dear."

"Yes, mommy." Susannah giggled. Elizabetta had become the mom she hardly remembered and so needed. "Can you make sure I'm up by eight? I want to spend some time with Tommy and Lucy. Kid time. Maybe I can glean some more info. I think I can get Tommy to recall some more stuff. I'm right on the verge of being able to feel and hear things. Natalia has been a great help. She's so good at explaining how it feels and how she gets into the mind. I'm almost there." Susannah frowned in frustration. "I may not ever be able to v-port, but I think I will be a good compeller."

"Slow down, child. There is time for everything. You are still so young, but I sense great potential in you. To sleep for now. You need your strength." Elizabetta released Susannah with a gentle shove.

"Good night, Elizabetta…and thanks. For everything." She kissed the Coven Mistress and flounced off to her room.

Left to her own devices and not necessarily in need of day-sleep, Elizabetta found the channel surfer and tuned into the last rerun of her favorite TV show.

Alone at last.

She snuggled under a beautifully knitted afghan and exchanged the cares of the day for the intrigue of a newly found body at the Navy Yard.

"Gibbs, Gibbs, Gibbs! I have something…" Her favorite forensic scientist was on the trail.

\*\*\*\*\*\*

Monique sat in the main lounge of the team's underground facility flipping through the latest copy of her favorite gossip rag. Another monotonous sports program played on the wide screen TV as Ted hooted and hollered. Monique detested football but chose companionship over her own silent quarters this afternoon. So troubled she could not sleep, Monique jumped as Ted slapped the side of his chair and swore out loud.

"Damn! For Pete's sake, take him down, brother."

Frustrated from lack of day-sleep and thoughts of San Leyre, Monique asked irritably, "Who is Pete and why is he damned?"

"It's a saying, Monique. Like 'heck', or 'come on'. Like that." Ted smiled in a brotherly fashion. Unlike Sergeant Miller, Ted was completely comfortable around the lady vamps. He actually found Monique to be very attractive, in a bit of a scary way. But he was comfortable in her presence.

"I shall never master this language difficile, I fear." She tossed the magazine on the coffee table and stood. "When I was a child, I watched horse races. But it was no obsession like this…King Louis would never have allowed his entertainment to be more important than he, himself." She pointed to the TV. "However, I do like the little suits they wear… and the muscles. It is very provocateur. Don't you think?" Monique could find a bit of sex in just about anything.

"Ever see a player after a hard game? You wouldn't think so. Black and blue, face like hamburger. But the money's good. Worth it I guess. Ah man, come on…" He was glued to the TV while he talked.

"That would be intrigant…" Monique licked her lips.

Ted shivered. Everyone who worked at Olney Farm had signed the Pact of Cohabitation. Vamps kept to vamps and humans kept to humans. It worked well. Still, he found Monique sexy as hell, and as scary as the witching hour on Halloween night. It was a strange yet seductive combination. Still, he could fantasize... "Nah, they all do 'roids. You know..." His fingers measured about three inches apart just above his crotch.

"Oh so... tellement gaspilleur." Her English tended to fail her when she contemplated the opposite sex. "Such excellent possibilities, pahhh..." Monique shook her head in mock sadness. "Doctor Helga, Milo and his lady shall arrive this evening. I think I will make sure the guest quarters are ready. It is something to pass the time."

"Ah, his Lady?" Now she had Ted's undivided attention. "Miller's ex-girlfriend? The ONE?"

"I do believe so. Her name is Jacquiline. I will be happy to have another French woman to speak my own language with. Although, recently I have found Captain Devlin also speaks French." She scowled at the last statement.

"Really? Miller's Waterloo? The downfall of the maestro himself? The executioner of the Father of Philandering? Wow! And coming with him? Which one is in chains?" Ted was out of his chair and holding Monique by her shoulders. "When? This I gotta see!" The game was forgotten in lieu of this new information.

"Someone is in chains? Why? What have they done?" The fear in Monique's eyes set Ted back a step.

"No, no, no, baby girl. No one is in chains. I didn't mean it that way. It's just... a way of saying... well...Miller got into a lot of trouble over this woman. He's kind of afraid of her. He didn't want to go to Bethesda because she's Tommy's sister. The General's daughter. And... well, let's just say it was a bad break-up."

Monique's eyes opened wide and she licked her lips. "Oui, oui! General Dickhead's daughter. Ooh, this could be precieux! I shall make sure this woman is very comfortable here. I cannot wait to get to know our Sergeant Miller's lady." With that, Monique danced off to check Jacquiline's quarters, place some sweet flowers near the bed and leave a small gift for the woman who intrigued them all. Day-sleep was all but forgotten.

\*\*\*\*\*\*

In an office the size of a postage stamp, Donald Smythe sat across the desk from the disheveled Doctor Percy Millford

138

Seizemore. The desk was piled high with folders, and reports. Several instruments the State Department representative could only guess at, lay strewn about the room. One corner was occupied with carefully labeled cardboard boxes stacked to the ceiling.

"Doctor Seizemore, we think we have obtained a sample of this new substance from one of the users. She has survived with the extraordinary help of an incredible group of doctors at Walter Reed." Donald Smythe wondered if the man was even listening. Seizemore had not taken his eyes off the report he was reading.

When Percy heard 'incredible group of doctors at Walter Reed' he pushed his glasses up off his nose and eyed the State Department rep sitting in front of him. As soon as Smythe contacted him for a face-to-face, Percy requested the doctor's report on Thomas Pantterdyck and Lucinda Redmont. It read like the Sunday comic section of a local newspaper. Cute pictures. Little information. "You're kidding, right?" He shoved the report toward Smythe. "Might as well be toilet paper. Don't waste my time."

Pamela Langston sighed. She knew Percy would not want to leave his projects at the CDC, but Helga clearly needed his brain and they had worked together so well before Helga's dis-appearance. But how to break the news of the interim assignment? And the fact that Helga was alive and researching at some very Top Secret facility. Hmmm… Percy was as dedicated to his research projects as a fanatical terrorist was to his bombs.

Smythe picked up the report as Doctor Seizemore got up and abruptly left the room. Smythe dropped the report on the desk and chased after the doctor. "Wait! Seizemore, we need your help."

"Then don't waltz in here with crap. I don't like it when bureaucrats think scientists are mushrooms to be kept in the dark and fed government excrement." He continued to walk toward his lab at a rapid pace. The slender man had a long stride.

"Okay, look. Would you please stop?" Smythe realized his mistake a minute too late.

"Unless you want to come clean, Mr. Smythe, State Department Representative, I have better things to do." He halted abruptly and turned on Smythe. "Well?"

"Okay, okay. This drug… substance is completely un-known. Its effects on the user are unparalleled and mostly deadly. We can't seem to separate it from the users with normal tests. We, ah... this is difficult without the proper security clearances, Doctor Seizemore." Smythe stumbled along.

"Go on, Smythe." It was obvious Seizemore's patience was wearing thin.

"General Pantterdyck told me his team, some special doctor and... others, somehow procured a sample from one of the users... who survived."

"That was not in the report, Smythe. Which one?" Percy's interest was peaking.

"Which one what?"

"Follow man... which user? The sample came from which user?" Percy did an about face and strode toward his office and the report on his desk.

"Ah, Ms. Redmont. And she is doing fine." Smythe chased after the doctor.

Percy had the report in his hands and was flipping pages, rapidly scanning for any mention of a sample and how it had been procured. "It's not here. No mention. Why did I get an incomplete report?" Percy threw the report in the overflowing bin labeled 'SHRED'.

"Percy..." Pamela thought it was time to intervene. She'd worked with Percy for a few years and knew his mind as well as his quirky personality.

Percy was not about to let his boss pass this fellow off as legit, in his mind. He turned to her with a cold stare.

"Ah, it's highly classified." Smythe hedged from the door-way.

"I have an Ultra Top Secret clearance, Smythe. Not swallowing it." Percy perched on the edge of his desk and crossed his arms waiting for a response.

"Well..." Smythe sat down a little harder than he meant to. "Because... actually..."

"Spit it out, man. I'm a busy scientist."

"Because Pantterdyck's special team got the sample." Smythe looked helplessly at the stern scientist. "And don't ask me how. They have some crack doctor and a group of unique individuals working this case. But the docs at Walter Reed have no idea what happened. One minute Thomas Pantterdyck was crashing. The next he was fine and sleeping soundly. The doctors swear they just stood there and it happened. So they say. One doc called it bewildering medicine."

"No such animal. Everything has a reason. Things just don't happen. I do not believe in miracles, Smythe. Hard science is always at the bottom of everything. You just have to have the brains to see it." Percy pulled the report out of the trash bin and started at the beginning, reading at warp speed.

Smythe sat quietly… waiting.

Pamela stood her corner, patiently waiting.

"This crack doctor you refer to. His name is not listed. Who was he?"

"She. He's a she, Doctor Seizemore." Smythe saw a glimmer of hope. Maybe if he played the scene carefully…

"Okay, who is she? Smythe?"

"Um…" Smythe pulled a small notebook from his breast pocket. "Name's Anderson. Doctor Anderson. She used to work for the CDC. Maybe you know her." He looked up innocently.

Percy grabbed the notebook out of Smythe's hands. "Anderson? Helga Anderson?" The excitement on Percy's face was clearly apparent.

"I think so. Yes, Helga was her first name. Know her?" Smythe had no idea of what the connection was, but he was willing to exploit it.

Percy glared at Pamela.

Pamela nodded her head just enough to acknowledge Smythe's information.

"Well, I'll be. Doctor Helga Anderson, where have you been? Pam, you knew about this?" Percy was in his own world talking to the report. "I thought you were dead. Seems I was in possession of incorrect information." He looked over at the seemingly calm Smythe. "This may bear looking into. Why wasn't Helga Anderson's name on the medical report?"

"No idea." Smythe spread his hands wide and shrugged. "Above my pay grade, I guess."

Pamela Langston tried to effect a confused look. It almost worked.

"Not a mushroom, Smythe."

"Her name was excluded because she is assigned to an undercover operative group. She no longer exists in the civilian world, Doctor Seizemore. No footprint. No mention."

"I see. I must admit, you now have my attention." He carefully placed the file back into the trash bin. "And I am mildly interested in this case. I can clear my schedule by the end of the month, if that works for Doctor Anderson." He was thumbing through his fat, well-abused day planner.

"This is more of an emergency-type case. We need help now. I can have you at the facility by tomorrow evening." Smythe took out his phone and began to scroll. "By tonight, with your permission."

"Emergency, huh? Where is this facility? Traffic's a nightmare right now. The President is doing some meet and greet thing. Beltway is all stacked up."

"Olney, Maine. Sir." Smythe's thumbs were flying over the tiny touch pad.

"I do not fly, Smythe. Feet stay glued to Mother Earth. It'll have to be wheels on pavement. How long a drive is it?" Seizemore was adamant that he remain grounded.

Smythe hit the send button on his phone and handed it to Doctor Seizemore.

"Hello, Percy? This is Helga. How are you?"

"Helga? You're alive. By all that lives and breathes…" Percy smiled at the familiar voice.

"Yes, I am. And I sure could use your help. Any chance you can take a few days and see what we have here?" Helga's laugh was invigorating and enticing. Of all the surprises, this day was proving to be something very special for Percy.

The elated memories flashed back as Percy recalled the day he got the letter extending him an offer to intern with the CDC and the famous researchist. Doctor Anderson had just published a paper on the human genome and our future with genetic research. She was the talk of the scientific world. And he was going to be the lucky guy who would be working with her for the next eighteen months of his world.

Like back then, he just couldn't say no. "I'd be honored. It'll take about a couple days to reschedule some of my activities here and shuffle the staff to cover some of my ongoing experiments, but I think I can give you a few days, at least. Or maybe a year! It's so good to hear your voice. Everyone thought you, um… sorry Doctor A, but really, everyone thought you were dead."

Pamela stood and waved Percy off, pointing to his day-planner. She mouthed the words, *I can take care of it.*

Helga laughed again. "Well, to quote a very famous individual; the rumors of my death are a bit exaggerated. In any event, Percy, I have a real puzzle on my hands, and as I remember, you were my most promising intern. I have a great deal of respect for the gray matter between your Spock ears."

Percy unconsciously rubbed his left pointy ear. She was the only one who he'd ever let tease him about his rather pointed and large ears. In return, he teased her about her size eleven feet. They'd had a very comfortable professional relationship and his eighteen months turned into ten years before Helga disappeared from the scientific community. "So you're in Maine? At a military base?"

"Well, kinda of. I have an incredible lab, doing top-secret research on some very interesting items. If you come, I'll brief you on it all. And Percy, this place is your free e-ticket ride."

That was the last straw for Percy. The free e-ticket ride simply meant, to the science world, anything and everything at your fingertips with no money issues.

No financial worries?

When had any government scientist had that kind of resources?

She had him.

And she knew it.

And he knew she knew it!

"So if this Smythe guy will give me directions, I'll head up there tomorrow afternoon. Do I need some kind of special authorization to get on base?" Percy was familiar with the protocols needed to deal with national medical intelligence issues and base access.

"No need. I'll meet you at your office tomorrow. Say around four? We'll travel together and catch up." It was a little harmless lie, but Helga remembered Percy's aversion to flying. Not so much an aversion, as the three-days-in-bed after effects. They couldn't afford the down time and Yuri was perfectly capable of v-porting two extra people. His power had grown substantially since his nuptials.

"Sounds good, Doctor A. What equipment should I prepare?" Percy was up off the desk and almost dancing in his miniscule office.

"Got it all. This is my lux-lab, Percy. Just pack a few personal things. For a few days, if possible. We have guest quarters, chow hall, everything right here. Anything extra we may need we can get overnight. You'll think you are in heaven."

"Enticing, Doctor A. I'll be ready… with a list of questions a mile long. Then you can tell me what happened to those size elevens and why you dropped off the face of the earth for five years." Percy felt like the five years had never happened and he was solidly back to their comfortable teasing relationship.

"Deal, Percy. See you tomorrow. Four-ish?" Helga was known for her 'ish-ness'. Being on time was something she'd recently learned, working with Colonel Maddox and the Vamp Squad.

"Deal. And Doctor A, thanks for thinking of me. I must admit, I am totally intrigued." Percy was pacing the three steps allowed in his office.

"Thanks for coming to the rescue, Percy. Bye now."

Percy handed the cell phone back to Smythe who'd remained seated during the short conversation. His smile stretched from one side of his face to the other.

"So? Going, I take it?" Pamela shook her head. "She has quite the carrot, huh! You'll love Olney Farm. And I can handle your lab schedule and the team research projects."

"It's a farm? I thought she said a military base." Percy looked startled.

"No, that's just what they call it. The place is… surrounded by farms. It's a nickname of sorts. To tell you the truth, I've never been 'inside' the facility. Only to it. If you know what I mean." Smythe jumped in after Pamela's little slip.

With that comment, Percy was feeling about as special as he'd ever felt in his entire life. He could hardly contain the excitement. He shivered.

"So, Doctor Seizemore, until tomorrow. Four-ish then?" Smythe stood and extended his hand.

Percy mumbled something unintelligible and rushed from the room. "Too much to do…"

"Well, I guess that ends this little meeting." Smythe looked at Pamela, shook his head and headed for the parking lot and his hot car.

Pamela slipped from the room and disappeared down the hall. Disaster averted, she was no longer needed. Somehow the State Department rep had saved his own ass.

As Smythe navigated the clogged Beltway, he thought to himself, *Scientists…weird lot.* At least he didn't have to suffer the strange man's company all the way to Maine…in a car. For hours!

\*\*\*\*\*\*

Helga hung up the phone in her lab with a huge smile. While Percy Seizemore's personality was a little dry and 'focused' on science, she knew he had a brilliant mind and an incredible ability to build structural relationships from the smallest traces of data. He truly was her most promising intern, then colleague, at the Center for Disease Control. With no real family of his own, Helga's daughter Sarah, adopted the quirky young scientist as the big brother she never had, as soon as they met. He'd been to their home for dinners, birthdays, holidays, and for swimming on hot summer evenings. He'd also been there for the late night research projects neither of them could let go of. Sarah loved Percy, and, as much as he could, Percy loved her daughter. After the fire, Helga never went back to the CDC. She just faded out of life for a time, until she woke up from one hell of a drunk... at Olney Farm. She wondered how Percy would handle his 'waking up at Olney Farm'.

Helga chuckled and returned to her work.

A sample of the pink goo lay, inert on a slide in the containment microniscope. As an afterthought, she sent a quick text message to Yuri requesting his transport assistance for tomorrow. It was daytime and the guy would be cuddled up to his mate, fast asleep... she hoped. Tonight would be soon enough to discuss the particulars.

She focused on the large screen monitor next to the scope. From her computer console, she zoomed down to the molecular level and scanned the specimen. A slight movement caught her eye and she startled.

It moved?

On its own?

An inert material moved?

Helga squeezed her eyes shut for a second then returned her attention to the monitor. "Come on. Do it again."

"Do what again, doctor of humans?"

Helga jumped in her seat. "Fiona, please don't do that to me!" She turned and hugged the faerie vampire who'd just appeared behind her. "I'm working on this really interesting sample. You startled me."

"Ach, doctor of humans, I'm ever sorry to be scarin' ya. Susannah was just tellin' me to make a sound when I visit. In the future, I shall make a chime, like the bell of a door from now on. I'll not be scarin' me friends so." Fiona pointed her finger toward the ceiling and a soft set of chimes that resembled church bells echoed through the lab."

"Very nice, my dear." Helga clapped. "That will help my nerves."

Fiona peered around the doctor at the image on the screen. The sample surged toward the tiny vampire, its movement replicated on the screen. The pink material slid toward the petite vampire with an almost hungry move. Fiona's eyes glazed over and she licked her lips. Her feet shuffled forward as if the vampire walked in a trance, called by the ooze.

"Fiona? Fiona, no!" Helga hit the panic button under her lab counter.

Fiona continued to move forward, completely unaware of Helga's restraining arm… which did absolutely no good.

Sergeant Miller hit the doorway with a huff followed by Tank and Bear. "Doc?"

"Help me. She can't touch this stuff." Helga screamed in a panic.

Tank wrapped his enormous arms around Fiona but she dragged him along with her. For a very tiny vampire, she had incredible strength.

The pink liquid in the vial, held fast in the containment chamber, slapped against the glass and pushed at the cap. The cap began to bulge precariously.

"Get her out of here! I have no idea what will happen if it touches her."

"Doc, I'm doin' my best." Bear had joined the effort and both men were able to slow Fiona's movement… but not stop her. She hissed at them and bared her fangs. Her eyes were deep red and glowing. Then she simply disappeared as Bear and Tank collapsed on each other.

Reappearing next to the containment chamber, Fiona cooed and rubbed her hands across the surface of the chamber. "I'm believin' I'm in love!" She murmured. "Come ta me, sweetness." She laid her cheek against the glass and purred.

Miller froze, his hands holding tight around his neck. His thick plastic collar was not there!

Helga screamed in total panic. "Elizabetta!"

Many miles away, in front of a wide screen TV, the Coven

Mistress heard the call. Within the blink of an eye, she appeared near the door to the crowded lab. Before the stuff could have an effect on her, she grabbed the faerie vamp and v-ported them both to the dark barn above the facility. It was the only place she could think of, that was far enough away from the lab. And far enough away from the pink monster, where Fiona might recover in darkness.

Immediately, the little vamp's eyes cleared and she swayed as if dizzy. Elizabetta caught Fiona and settled her on a bale of hay. "Take it easy for a moment and let your head clear, Fiona."

"Mistress Zoeltel, I be a bit rattled. What happened? I was talkin' to the doctor of humans, then I be here." Fiona was rattled!

"You don't remember anything? Bear and Tank trying to stop you?"

"And just pray tell why the vera big, vera handsome humans wanted ta' be stoppin' me? From doin' what?" The little vamp's eyes began to tear. She was truly confused.

Elizabetta tipped Fiona's chin up and surveyed her face and eyes. "You are clear now?"

"Clear of what, Mistress? I be... just me."

Elizabetta sat on the bale next to her small friend. "Fiona, Doctor Anderson is researching an unusual substance that we found in a human's brain. Everyone thought the girl overdosed on some kind of drug. Turns out it was much, much more. Natalia got a sample when healing this girl. The stuff you saw in the lab was the sample we recovered. It is dangerous to our kind."

"I only saw the doctor of humans. She told me to be ringin' a bell when I visit because I scared her. Then I was here. I do not understand, Mistress." A big tear rolled down Fiona's face and dropped onto her gossamer blouse. "Now look what I be doin'."

A tissue appeared in Elizabetta's hand and she offered it to Fiona. "Well, don't worry about it now, Fiona." She hugged the little vamp. "I believe I will contact the Council and put our facility off limits for a time. Until we can figure out what this stuff is and why it has such an effect on vampires. It doesn't effect humans at all."

"Ach... Emilliano will want to know about this, I fear. He is so nosy these days. Your coven has sparked such interest, it seems." Fiona brightened. "And I've been gettin' me new friends." Then she frowned and another tear threatened her cheek. "I cannot come here a' more?"

"Just for a while, sweet. I react to the stuff, but not like you did. I have a theory that the more powerful the vampire, the stronger the reaction. Or possibly because we do not drink warm blood. It barely moves around Susannah and she does not feel the draw so much. She is still a fledgling and developing her powers." Elizabetta stared at the straw covered floor for a few minutes while Fiona dabbed at her cheeks and blouse. "I shall contact your husband and the Council as soon as I can."

Recovered and exuberant as ever, Fiona fiercly hugged the Coven Mistress. "Ach, say it again, Mistress. Tis' my love to hear tha' word."

Elizabetta smiled at Fiona's resilience. "What word, dear?"

"Why, husband, of course! Husband, husband, husband. Mine Husband." Fiona tittered and giggled. She bounced on the hay.

"Of course, I shall contact your *husband*. There. Now you should probably go away for a while. Just until we figure this thing out. Back to your lovely *husband*." Elizabetta emphasized the word 'husband' each time she said it.

After another fierce hug, Fiona twinkled away with her usual parting, "Slán agus beannacht leat."

Elizabetta shook her head with a smile. Fiona was off to her husband and now the work would begin. And the careful communication with Emilliano and the Council. The Vamp Squad and the facility did not need a horde of enormously powerful vampires popping in to see what the pink stuff was all about… and losing their minds in the process. Fiona's uncontrollable response to the stuff, and the stuff's response to her, truly frightened the Coven Mistress.

Elizabetta v-ported back to the Fischer House and their temporary quarters in Maryland. Colonel Maddox and Doctor Anderson were already in deep conversation on the speaker phone. Captain Devlin lounged close at hand. "Excuse me. May I intrude?"

"You will never intrude, Elizabetta. Helga was just describing that weird little vampire's reaction to our new sub-stance. And how it reacted to her. I'd like to hear your thoughts on the subject as well. Is what's-her-name okay?"

"Yes, Frank, Fiona is fine and returning to her husband. I intend to contact the Council and let them know the farm is off limits for a while. Just until we get a handle on this stuff. We really need to give it a name. Pink stuff sounds so innocent. The stuff is not the least bit innocent." Elizabetta took the chair Captain Devlin offered her. "Are Tank and Bear okay?"

"Our stalwart soldiers are just fine. Little embarrassed to be hugging each other after the little thing disappeared, though." Helga responded.

The Colonel smiled at his team's embarrassment.

"I agree with our Coven Mistress, Frank. You should have seen Fiona. She was totally out of control. She almost bit Tank. And he really likes her. She was like some Zombie vampire. It was one of the most frightening things I've seen since coming to work with the Squad." Helga spoke to the Colonel emphatically. "I want to rush order silver plating for the containment chamber. And a special surveillance camera set up to watch the stuff twenty-four/seven. This may be the most dangerous thing the vampire world has ever seen."

"Whatever you need. Get Miller on it ASAP." Maddox was concerned as well. He had a facility full of vampires and humans. Out of control vampires would be a very, very bad thing.

"I can design it for you, Helga. I used to make furniture as a hobby. I once made a huge box for a kid who had Autism. It was his escape mechanism when things got too rough in the real world. I'll have a schematic and supply list to you in an hour or so. I'll get Q2 to check it for me."

"Great, Rob. Just no leaks… and strong. I figure a quarter inch thick should do the trick."

"It's not like we don't have the capital." Captain Devlin smirked as he headed for his room. He loved having unlimited resources for his team. Thanks to the Afghanistan mission.

"I have another scientist coming to help me out, Frank. A guy I used to work with at the CDC. Actually I hired him when I worked there. He has a great mind and will be fresh eyes on the pink stuff. He's got all kinds of clearances so there should be no problem with him coming here." Helga paused. "I haven't figured out the story yet, but Yuri and I will fetch him, v-style. It's the fastest way since he doesn't fly."

"Whatever you need, Doc. Just keep me in the loop." Maddox's cell phone rang and the conversation on the speaker phone ended. "Gotta go. We should be back at the farm tomorrow."

Elizabetta motioned to the Colonel, mouthing, "I'm going

back for a bit. Helga and I need to talk."

The Colonel's response was a simple nod in her direction. "Hello, Harold."

Elizabetta disappeared.

Chapter 13

"We've arranged a society on science and technology in which nobody understands anything about science and technology, and this combustible mixture of ignorance and power sooner or later is going to blow up in our faces. I mean, who is running the science and technology in a democracy if the people don't know anything about it."

*Carl Sagan*
*Astronomer, Astrophysicist, Cosmologist, Skeptic and Critical Thinker*

"You amaze me, Jackie. There you sit, all calm and accepting. When I first got assigned here, I didn't believe what the Colonel told me. Then I saw Susannah pop out her fangs and claw the glass of her cell. If I could have, I would have crawled all the way back to DC on my hands and knees to get away from this place." Milo sat comfortably on one end of the sofa. Jackie sat on the other.

Close enough to talk softly.

Far enough away to prevent physical contact.

"Well, you didn't grow up… different. Milo, you have no idea what it's like having to live a lie. All the time. I knew things growing up, that other kids didn't. I knew when someone was sad, or happy, or hungry, or without hope. When I was in the second grade, there was this little girl." She shifted uncomfortably. "I knew she was being abused at home. She covered her bruises, but I could feel them every time we touched." Jackie curled her feet beneath her and hugged her arms around herself, remembering. "One day she didn't come to school. I knew she was dead. It was horrible. I told mom. She said to keep it to myself because no one would believe me. She explained that people would think I was strange, or lying. She said that so many times. But she knew too."

"I didn't know you had ESP." Miller squirmed, wondering what she 'knew' about him.

"I'm not sure what to call it. But I've lived with it. Covered it up, forever. Do you have any idea how refreshing it is to be around people who know and value me, and my unusual *abilities*?"

Jackie took a deep breath and let it out in a rush. "I mean, none of you are normal either! I mean...It's like starting a new life. Really."

"What happened to the girl in your class?" Miller shivered.

"They found her body a few months later. I told my teacher that her father killed her. She slapped my face and told me not to tell lies, or I would go to hell." Jackie shook her head. "Maybe I could have done something to help Sandy. That was her name. I'll never forget her face, or her name. It's burned into my brain."

Milo wanted to take Jackie in his arms and make the pain he could see in her eyes, go away forever. But he stayed where he was. "As a kid, there was probably nothing you could have done. If I've learned anything, here at the Farm, it's that ninety-nine point nine percent of the people in the world only believe what they can see and touch. And there is so much more, beyond that. Most people are pretty blind. The sad part is, they want to stay that way." He stood and grabbed a Snickers candy bar from the snack tray. "Want anything?"

"No thanks. When we were dating... whatever... I had no idea you were such a good listener." Jackie unwrapped herself and put her feet on the floor. "Want to go for a walk? This place is so quiet."

"Listening was something I had to learn. We've both grown... changed. I've been so used to living 'down under' I forgot what walking around in the sunshine is like. Let's go." He pocketed another candy bar for the road. "Let me sign us out and we can take the barn elevator. It beats the four flights of stairs! It's only noon. I'll introduce you to the Burnsides. They're our farmers above. You'll love them. They're pretty cool."

"I'll grab some shoes and meet you in your comm center." Jackie's smile brightened with the passing of childhood memories.

"Roger that." Both headed their separate ways, to meet a few minutes later in the comm center.

As Miller entered the comm center, he noticed the Colonel in his office. "Sergeant, a moment." Maddox had papers spread across his desk. The last of the team had arrived back home a few hours earlier.

"Sir?" Miller stood in the Colonel's doorway.

"How goes the penance? Is Ms. Pantterdyck comfortable here?"

"Actually Sir, she is doing very well. I had no idea she had

152

ESP when we were dating. Kinda gives me pause to think."

"Yes, well Sergeant, think on it. I'm considering offering her a position. Mrs. Milassoviech recounted her assistance with Lucy Redmont. I believe Ms. Pantterdyck may be an asset to our team. And I understand she's going to be a bean counter with a few more university credits under her belt. It would solve a lot of problems since she knows so much about our operation and the Vamp Squad."

Miller gulped at the Colonel's statement. How could last night's dream come true? "Yes, Sir. We are going for a walk up top. I'll introduce Jackie to the Burnsides. She'll love Mandy. Jackie is a runner and loves to shoot skeet."

"Really?" The Colonel looked up from his papers. "Good. Do what you can to involve Ms. Pantterdyck. Sweeten the pot, Miller. I know you can figure that one out." There was a hidden smile behind the Colonel's words.

"My pleasure, Sir." Miller straightened and threw a crisp, formal salute.

The Colonel shook his head and went back to the papers he was studying. "Dismissed."

\*\*\*\*\*\*

Monique tossed and turned in her day-sleep. Horrible dreams of her first days as a vampire haunted her, twisting her mind the way her sire had twisted her life. She remembered the days of first wakening. The hunger. The mind numbing pain that racked her body and the torrid sex which provided relief. In the throws of turning, Monique cared less that the Comte d' LeEgalité's coven watched and participated. She'd been a naive teen, sheltered and pampered. A virgin. Never in a million years would she have thought herself an eager and willing participant in the orgies that stilled the pain and grew her abilities with every encounter.

When her turning was complete, the Comte d' LeEgalité owned her mind and body. She learned that lesson well the first time she attempted to run away. Before she could leave the catacombs beneath the estate grounds, he compelled her to return and made her a lesson before all in his small coven. He locked her in a cell and withheld feeding for a week. At the end of her sentence she was a raving maniac, insane and craving blood the way crack addicts of the modern day crave their drug fix. Then LeEgalité brought a child of one of the servants to her cell. The coven watched through barred windows as she slaughtered the child and consumed every drop of blood, licking the dirt floor for every last taste. She had become an animal and she knew it. He had complete power over her. She knew that as well.

Monique woke with a small scream.

Immediately Elizabetta appeared next to Monique's bed. "Hush daughter. You are safe and your sire is long gone. Do not fear so." Elizabetta held the sobbing vampire in a tight hug."

"Elizabetta, I can't make the nightmares stop. Ever since this thing with Tommy Pantterdyck began, my mind is revolting. I cannot control the feelings. It is like I am back there, with him. He cannot still exist, can he?"

"No child. He was destroyed in the Revolution. As was all in his coven, but you and Mathilda. And you tell me she was destroyed by the monks of San Leyre. I suspect these dreams have begun because of your fear of that hideous place. I believe it is a form of PTSD, post traumatic stress disorder. Like soldiers get after serving in horrible places. Their minds cannot let go of the horrible things they saw and it haunts them. Like your dreams, dear." Elizabetta stroked Monique's hair as she held her coven daughter. "Maybe we should talk to Doctor Anderson. She may have some ideas to help you stop the dreams."

Monique pulled away a little. "You think she can vraiment aider?" Monique blew her nose and wiped away the tears with a clean tissue.

"It is a possibility. Doctor Anderson is a very intelligent woman. She deals with her own nightmares so maybe she can suggest something to help you with yours." Elizabetta shrugged. "It is three in the afternoon. Since neither of us can sleep, shall we see what the good doctor is up to?"

"Oui. I shall dress and meet you in the lounge." Monique was wide-awake and she would not be sleeping more this day.

Unfortunately, so was most of the Vamp Squad.

*Thanks, Elizabetta.* Natalia psyched her Coven Mistress.

*My pleasure, dear. Go back to sleep and I will help our troubled child.* Elizabetta immediately felt Natalia slip back into day-sleep.

After Monique changed her red-stained nighty, she and Elizabetta strolled toward Helga's lab. "Please remember, dear, the good doctor is working with an outsider today, some other doctor she has called on for help with the TPS sample."

"Oui. TPS? Qu'est-ce que c'est?"

"That's our new name for the pink stuff. Get it? The Pink Stuff, TPS."

"Oh so tres cute." Monique shook her head. "That stuff, TPS is more like a demon. You should have named it PD! Pink Demon."

Near the huge glass window of the lab, they paused, watching the two doctors in deep conversation. As Doctor Seizemore turned to view the TPS on the monitor, Monique squeaked.

"The doctor is an elf!" She covered her mouth with a delicate hand. "Look, Elizabetta, he has the ears!"

"No, no, daughter. I assure you Doctor Seizemore is just a regular human with somewhat interesting ears. Keep in mind he is an outsider. The entire facility has been warned to keep socializing to a minimum. We do not need the scientific world descending upon us."

"Oui, oui. But I must not be near the TPS. It comes to me."

"For whatever reason, it comes to all vampires. The older and stronger the vamp, the more it moves. Doctor Anderson and I have put this facility off limits for all vampires of the Council. Fiona popped in for a visit and went a little crazy near the stuff. She almost bit Tank when he tried to hold her back. She was completely out of control."

"Fiona is always crazy and a little out of control." The two women chuckled at the statement's truth. "But she adores Tank. She bared her fangs? How dégoûtant!"

"Yes, and Jordan came in last night to spend the weekend with Susannah, but left again after a few minutes. As much as our little sister loves her Jordan, she did not want him exposed to TPS." Elizabetta was shaking her head. This was the first time in all her long life that she found something she could not conquer or somehow control. It controlled her when she was in close proximity to the stuff, and that was unacceptable for an old and powerful vampire, let alone the daughter of Dracula.

"The elf is very cute, no?" Monique smiled as she watched the new doctor.

Elizabetta shook her head. There were very few men Monique did not find 'cute' in some way. She pressed the speaker button. "Doctor Anderson, could I have a minute? If you are not too busy?"

Doctor Anderson turned and waved through the window.

Doctor Seizemore turned to view the visitors and froze, his mouth half open.

"Of course, Elizabetta, be right there." Doctor Anderson's voice sounded a bit tinny through the speaker.

Outside the window, both vamps could hear without the need for a speaker, but this new doctor was an outsider, so everyone was under orders to act like humans at all times. Elizabetta and Monique smiled at Doctor Anderson's response to Doctor Seizemore's stunned behavior.

"Percy, I'll be right back." Helga touched her colleague's arms. "Percy? Percy!!!"

She shook his arm.

"Ah, what, Helga?" Percy shook his head as if in a daze and trying to clear the fog. "Who are they? Who is the pretty one? I've never seen..." He stopped in mid sentence. "Sorry, I didn't mean offense in that totally incorrect statement." Used to working in a government job where 'Politically Correct' was the name of the game at all times, he was appalled at his own reaction. The blush began at his neck and worked its way up.

Helga laughed. "Monique has that effect on men. Do not concern yourself. We are all used to it."

Percy turned his back on the window and whispered. "It seems I am not myself this afternoon. I do apologize. I did not mean any offense." His dreamy expression turned toward the window and the gorgeous blonde beyond.

"And none taken. I'll be right back. Can you see if the DNA results are in yet?"

"Of course, Helga." He glanced at the window one more time and blushed more deeply, before passing through the connecting door to the extended lab.

Through the window, Monique smiled shyly and gave the doctor a tiny, childish wave.

He stumbled and smacked the doorframe with his shoulder as he exited.

Monique giggled.

Elizabetta laughed as Doctor Anderson came through the double air-lock security doors.

"What can I help you with, Elizabetta?" Helga was smiling at Monique's little flirt with her fellow doctor. He had come to her

CDC lab so very naïve and shy. It seems not much had changed with him in all the years since.

"First of all, have you made any progress on TPS? How is your new colleague working out?"

Helga looked toward the DNA Lab. "Very well. It is as if we never stopped working together. Doctor Seizemore had a little scare at our travel arrangements, but he is handling the cloak and dagger research project amazingly well. Unfortunately, we haven't made much progress on TPS. This DNA test was Percy's idea. Don't ask me where it came from, but his mind is something very different than the usual stuffy scientist's."

"Doctor Anderson, how did you explain v-porting to him?" Monique was very interested in the new guy.

"I just said, *remember Star Trek? We're where no man has gone before, right now.* And he accepted it like a champ." Helga shrugged. "He is a different kind of fellow. Of course, Natalia then wiped his mind and implanted the memory of a high speed trip here in some James Bond car!"

"Oui, are there many scientists in the elf world?" Monique asked.

Helga looked confused until Elizabetta pointed to her ears with a chuckle.

"Oh dear, Percy is not an elf. At least I don't think so." Helga looked a little startled. "But then again, I never thought vampires were real either."

"Trust me, Doctor Anderson, in all my years and travels, I have never heard of a true elf in this world."

Helga swallowed and eyed Elizabetta suspiciously. "In this world? There are others?" Before learning of the truth of vampires, Helga enjoyed science fiction as much as the next. Entertainment was one thing. The clash of reality and Bella Lagosi's world of horror movies was something else.

"Do not concern yourself with such things, Doctor. We have a puzzle to solve. A very dangerous puzzle. The sooner, the better." Elizabetta peered through the glass. The TPS vibrated in its container. The Coven Mistress shuddered and stepped between the window and Monique.

The intercom buzzed. "Helga, you need to see this." Percy's voice conveyed excitement and impatience. "Right now."

"On my way." Helga responded in keeping with the Star Trek theme. She turned to Elizabetta, "What was it you needed?"

Her hand held her id card, ready to re-enter the lab.

"Sounds like your colleague may have something. Better go. We'll catch you later."

"Later then." The doctor was already passing through the first set of doors.

"But…" Monique was at a loss.

"Obviously, the new fellow has found something. Let's just listen for a minute. I am very interested in what he may have found. " Elizabetta held Monique behind her. "We can ask Doctor Anderson about the dreams later."

As if they stood next to the two doctors, Monique and Elizabetta listened to the conversation in the contained room.

"Look, Helga. Look at these results. This is not just a substance. It's alive. I ran a DNA scan and look!" Percy was almost hopping up and down as he showed Helga the printout. "I have no idea what this may be, but it behaves like a virus, a very strange virus. See this allele pair, it's the same one I see in the AIDS virus that insinuates itself into T-cells to mutate cell replication. But it's a triple helix. Triple! How can a triple helix exist?"

Helga scrutinized the data. The only living thing on earth with a triple helix design in genetic tissue was a vampire. She gasped.

"Didn't you tell me this was a drug?" Percy asked.

"Why, yes. Yes I did. That is what we thought. In light of this new evidence, I believe we should bring the team together and discuss this data. Someone may have additional information that would be helpful." Helga was hedging until she could talk to Colonel Maddox and Elizabetta. "We've been at this for a while. Why don't we take a break? Have something to eat? Give this some thought."

Percy rubbed a hand across his eyes and then peered at the papers in his hands. "That may be a good idea." He shook his head. "Triple helix. Can you believe it!" His entire body vibrated with excitement. "This could be a new life form!"

His excitement would have been catching, had it not been for the inside information Helga held close to her vest.

"So do we go out, or order in?"

"We have a full meal service, and it does not include MREs. You still prefer veggies to real food?" Helga knew Percy was a vegetarian and had been ever since his orphanage days.

Once, during one of his frequent visits to her home, he told her about how the children at the orphanage were expected to pitch in raising and preparing their own food. Wringing a chicken's neck was something Percy could never stomach.

"Still like my nuts and twigs. You think the kitchen can handle that?"

"It'd be my pleasure. We sort of fix our own here. I still make a mean veggie lasagna. Interested?"

Percy's stomach answered for him and he laughed. "Apparently."

"Good. Let me get things started then set the team meeting for the command center for after dinner. We can eat in the command center conference room, review the data once more, then put together a briefing for the team." That was a good way to keep Doctor Seizemore out of view of the vamp's unique breakfast habits, while the two humans had dinner.

Percy grabbed his laptop and the newest data printouts. "Lead the way, Madame."

Elizabetta and Monique cleared the corner just as Percy and Helga exited the lab and prepared to leave the research wing of the facility.

"Let's hide out in our lounge. I need to think about this new information." Elizabetta dragged Monique through the lounge and mess hall. "I've got some nice synth-blood on ice. My treat." It was a silly statement since all of the needs of the team were supplied upon request, but it lightened the mood.

"I think I shall enjoy that, Madame. Lead the way." Monique was imitating Doctor Seizemore. "Why does the elf doctor like nuts and twigs?"

Elizabetta laughed at Monique's confusion. "That simply means he does not eat meat. He is a vegetarian."

Monique shuddered. "Then he would not taste good. I once bit a man who lived on rice and fruit. It was etre desagreable. But the elf doctor is a little cute." The French vampire giggled then placed several fingers over her lips, a la Marilyn Monroe.

"Well, that is good because we do not bite humans anymore, not even elf doctors." They had reached the vamp lounge and Elizabetta was pouring them both a glass of synth-blood. "What do you think about the new information about TPS?"

"I believe this data explains why TPS responds to us." Monique sipped her drink. "We are triple helix. It is triple helix, non? Obviously a vampire has developed TPS."

Out of the mouths of babes... and Monique was quite the babe... often comes pearls of wisdom. Elizabetta had not yet made the leap between species, but to Monique, everything was simple.

"Monique, you are so much more than a pretty face!" Elizabetta was amazed at her coven daughter's simple conclusion.

Which was probably correct.

"But how does a vampire infuse vamp DNA in... pink stuff? And how does it get into a human without turning them? Tommy's blood was human. This is very strange indeed. The two should not be able to co-exist."

"That is not so complicated, cheri. He shares his blood and it lives on within the pink stuff, but changes the person in the partie principale du cerveau, the brain only." She waved her hand mixing the air. "But it didn't have time to work. And how was it changing the person if Tommy and Lucy were dying? This I do not understand."

"Susannah said it was growing in Lucy's brain much faster than Tommy's. When I talked at length with Jacquiline, she indicated it was a living thing and responded to Natalia's attack with a kind of attack of it's own." Elizabetta finished her glass and refilled it.

"Possibly that is why it responds to our kind. Like a sire to his progéniture, you know, baby. He... or it, has control. It compels, like Nat can." Monique held her glass out for a refill. "It probably came from a very strong compeller. But why? What is it for?"

"I have no idea. I believe we may need to investigate the school and what is going on at the monastery."

Monique dropped her full glass. "No. No. NO! I will not return to that horrible place. I cannot." She stood and moved back against the wall. "No, Elizabetta. I will not go there. Ever!" She slithered down the wall and crouched, covering her head. The tears began.

Elizabetta transported the mess to the small sink in the kitchenette in the vamp lounge, then rose to comfort her coven daughter. "Be calm, daughter. You will not need to go back to the place of your nightmares. I will not allow it. The Colonel will not allow it either." She held the crying woman in her arms, wiping the bloody tears from her sleeves.

Through the sobs, Monique squeaked out, "Je ne peux pas

aller. I cannot."

Natalia appeared next to Elizabetta. "Monique, do not fear. We shall all protect you with our lives. We are a coven. We will not let anything happen to you. Now stop the tears before you bloody the entire lounge." She pulled her sister vamp from the floor and wiped away her tears. "Such a mess on such a pretty face."

That was all it took. Monique grabbed the napkins offered and began cleaning the red tears from her face and clothes. "I hate to cry so much. It ruins my face and clothing. And such a waste of time. Phew!"

Calm had returned to the vamp world and Monique was recovering rapidly.

"Nat, Monique has had a revelation about TPS. She believes it was created by a vampire and infused... somehow... with his, or her, blood. The new Doctor working with Helga has found a triple helix genetic trace. He does not know about vamps yet and has no idea what he has found, or how it may relate to our team. Monique believes that is why it moves toward us... compels like you do. What do you think?"

"There are many vamps in the world that can compel. I am only one, and not the most powerful, that is for sure. Have you queried the Council?"

"No, in fact, we have put the facility off limits. It seems the stronger the vamp, the stronger the reaction to TPS."

"Monique may have a point. Since you have shuffled through the old Nazi research, we know what the genetic design of our physical system is like and how it relates to the human genetic design. It is a possibility. Didn't one German doctor keep vamp blood alive outside the body for a long time in one of the tests?" Natalia scrunched up her eyebrows in concentration. "It was the guy at Bergan Bellson, wasn't it?"

Elizabetta stood quickly. "I do believe you are correct. I must check that before our meeting tonight." She ran from the room toward her own research lab.

"What meeting?" Natalia looked blankly at Monique, who was dabbing red stains from her cheeks.

\*\*\*\*\*\*

In the OCC conference room, Percy scarfed his veggie

lasagna and talked over the Colonel. "This information is fascinating. There is no life form I know of on earth that has a triple helix genetic design." He spoke with a full mouth and the confidence of a scientist renowned in the field of molecular biology and genetic design. "This should not exist."

"Well it does and is very dangerous." The Colonel banged on the table. "Can you separate the genetic material and the rest of the…stuff? I don't even know what I'm talking about." Maddox shook his head in frustration. "With all due respect doctors, I'm in way over my head."

"It's fine, Frank. We are all in over our heads at the moment. The sample we obtained has never-before-seen characteristics. Everything I have learned in medical school and during my career, says TPS cannot be. But yet it is, and we retrieved it from a patient who survived its exposure." Helga patted Frank's hand. "Percy and I'll figure it out. I assure you."

"So you think the rest of the team may have some ideas? Ideas that won't breach our security here at the facility?' Frank raised an eyebrow as he addressed Doctor Anderson. It was becoming harder and harder to talk *around* the facts and Percy was picking up on the discomfort and purposefully short sentences.

Percy interrupted, still chewing his dinner. "I have an SAP, Colonel. That is the highest clearance one can obtain. But then you know that as well as I do." Doctor Seizemore's condescending attitude was lost on the Colonel as the doctor licked a bit of sauce from his bottom lip and picked at a wet noodle on his chest. "I think I can handle any sensitive information this facility may come up with." Finally loosening the sticky noodle, he slurped it down with a florish.

The famous Maddox eyebrow shot up one more time. "Really? Special Authorization Program? Hmm." He smiled at the new doctor. "We'll see."

"The rest of the team should be here in about twenty minutes. I gave them time to eat before we meet." Doctor Anderson thought a segway was in order. Frank was working up to a challenge and Percy was rising to the occasion. "I'll get Sergeant Miller to put these images up on the big screen." Helga excused herself. "Percy, let me show you the technological wonders of the place. Sergeant Miller is simply a wizard. And he has almost everything at his fingertips."

In the OCC, Monique sat next to Sergeant Miller pointing

at a graphic on the screen. "No, that was not there a few years ago. It looks old, but I am sure it is new construction, Sergeant." She spoke softly.

"You would know. So this crypt beneath the main building… here. That is where we rescued you. We went through the well outside the main cemetery." He touched a line-drawn map and dragged it over top the aerial photo of the grounds of San Leyre. "The school is here. It is not connected, as far as we know, but the catacombs down there are a maze. There are some natural caverns and caves that have been connected with man-made tunnels. I lost count of the monk mummies down there. Ah… sorry, ma'am. The entombed clergy."

"Sergeant, do not worry about my sensitivities. I hate those devils. They deserve to spend their false eternity wrapped in dirty rags in the dark cold caves. I would banish them to the depths of Satan's Hell if I could."

"Such strong words for such a nice girl." Percy whispered to Helga as they stood behind Monique and Miller. "Especially for men of the cloth."

To a vampire, a whisper was the same as a shout. Monique rounded on the doctor. "The only cloth they know is made of leather and silver." She glowered at Percy. "You do not under-stand, elf."

Percy looked questioningly at his colleague who stood silent beside him. "Did she call me an elf?"

"Oui! You have the ears of an elf. Has no one ever told you?" Monique rose and walked around Percy looking him up and down.

"Doctor Seizemore, I'd like you to meet one of our team, Monique Merchant. She is French… and a little unusual." Doctor Anderson murmured.

"That's an understatement," remarked the Sergeant under his breath, as he closed the windows that showed a topographical map of San Leyre on his computer screen.

Monique stopped in front of the doctor and stared at his ears. "I have never liked elves. Ils ne sont pas dignes de confiance. No trust!" She swung her finger back and forth in front of Percy's nose.

His slight frame flinched at her closeness. He was all too aware that his reaction was that of a young boy who had been chastised both verbally and physically too many times. It was muscle memory mixed with a little CTSD; Catholic traumatic stress disorder.

"That is enough, young lady." Elizabetta came through the security door dragging a sleepy Susannah, already aware of the conversation thanks to her vamp-hearing. "Doctor Seizemore is here to help with the TPS mystery. Please afford him the respect he deserves."

"Puh." Monique took Susannah's hand and pulled her into the conference room where she proceeded to whisper in her sister's ear and point at Percy's ears.

"Doctor Seizemore, I am Elizabetta Zoeltel, Civilian-side Manager of the team… and responsible for the behavior of my charges. I do apologize for Ms. Merchant's comments. She had an unfortunate experience at the Monastery of San Leyre. Quite unfortunate. I'm afraid it has colored her opinion of monks and priests."

"And elves? No one has called me that since I left the home." Percy actually chuckled. "Actually it was a Catholic orphanage, so I kind of understand the lady's comment. I had a couple unfortunate experiences myself… when I was growing up."

"Not like her." Again the Sergeant interjected under his breath. Elizabetta and Helga chose to ignore the Sergeant's comments.

As the rest of the team began to assemble in the conference room, Doctor Anderson showed Percy around the OCC and Miller demonstrated some of its capabilities. He also loaded the data from Percy's thumb drive and added Doctor Anderson's notes.

Last to join the group in the conference room was Lieutenant Previn, as usual. Jackie sat next to Miller's station and the Colonel took his place at the head of the table.

"We've assembled to see some new information on the TPS research. Without delay, I'll turn this meeting over to Doctor Anderson and Doctor Seizemore. Ma'am?" The Colonel was in clear leader form.

"First, I'd like to introduce my colleague and friend from my CDC days, Doctor Percy Seizemore. He is a biologist, pharmacologist, geneticist among other things, and an extremely gifted researchist. Percy and I have a long history." She patted his shoulder as she spoke. "If anyone can help with the TPS problem, he can. Now… Miller, if you please."

Three pictures appeared on the Smartboard behind the

164

Colonel's head.

"These are the pictures we have of the molecular construction of TPS. If you notice, the material is a composite, the *live* part is based on a triple helix genetic design and not a human double helix." Doctor Anderson paused to let the information sink in. Only Susannah let out a tight gasp. "The *live* element of this substance is as unique as its developer, of which, or who, we know nothing... so far."

Doctor Seizemore broke in. "This substance should not be able to exist unless someone has developed genetic manipulation far beyond anything science has seen to date. Of course, after my... ride here, which is still quite fuzzy, it may be a possibility." He smiled at Yuri who simply shrugged.

"Where no man... you know! We have some cutting edge technology here, but not this advanced." Yuri smiled back. "Really."

"How does...this genetic stuff... survive in a chemical... without, I mean..." Susannah was having trouble talking around the fact that vamp cells existed in the TPS.

"That is a good question. It is like a virus. It can exist in all kinds of environments before it is introduced to a host... a person. Obviously, the students were exposed to this substance through an environment in which the live material could remain viable."

"So the elf knows no more than we do. Puh." Monique was out of sorts and proving it well.

"Frenchy! He's not an elf." Susannah punched her sister vamp on the shoulder.

Monique stuck her tongue out at Susannah and grabbed the tops of her ears then pointed to Doctor Seizemore.

"Be nice, or be gone, girl." Susannah quietly repeated the orders she had often received as a young girl in her father's house.

"D'accord!" Monique rose with obvious purpose, and left.

"Okay then," Doctor Anderson continued. "The environment Doctor Seizemore referred to may have been a health drink Tommy Pantterdyck referred to in his recollection of the period before he collapsed. Both he and Lucy Redmont tried a health drink from their coach in the parking lot." Doctor Anderson was thumbing through a small book of notes. "He said they met a Brother Berthold their soccer coach, who gave them some kind of concoction he was developing. The kids did not suspect anything since it was not unusual. Apparently Brother Berthold is working

165

on perfecting an athletic enhancing supplement for his team."

"That's right!" Susannah was remembering their conversation. "Tommy said he only took a sip because he doesn't like tart drinks. Lucy drank all of hers. Maybe that's why she had more…TPS than he did."

"I'm not clear on how our sample was obtained from Lucy Redmont." Doctor Seizemore was peering over at Doctor Anderson's notebook.

"Um…" She thumbed through several pages. "We'll have to contact Walter Reed for that information."

Miller dutifully typed the question on his computer, which simultaneously showed on the Smartboard. "Will do."

"So the question is; where do we go from here?" Doctor Anderson closed her notebook and folded her hands.

Captain Devlin was the first to respond. "I think we need to find this Brother Berthold and get some information about what he's feeding the kids. Then talk to some of the team members and see who else drank the stuff."

"I believe this monastery may hide some very strange goings on." Natalia's direct look told the Colonel there was vampire involvement.

As soon as hearing the 'triple helix' bit of intel, he already suspected as much.

"Miller, contact Smythe at State and that French guy, Lieutenant Extra…whatever."

"Lieutenant Etxebarria, Sir." Miller filled in the Liaison's name.

"Right. That guy. Set up a trip to the monastery and the school. Put together a review file for the team." The Colonel nodded at Miller who got the message. Maps from the last mission, special entry points, school layout, staff and monastery personnel, etc. should be on everyone's computer within the hour. Everyone except the new doctor. "And, Miller, get General Pantterdyck on the horn. Ms. Pantterdyck, will you and Elizabetta join me in my office?" The Colonel rose adjourning the meeting. "Check your terminals for further information. Doctors, please send updates if you should have further breakthroughs. Good Evening."

The Colonel left the conference room followed by Elizabetta and Jackie. As she left the room, Jackie shot Miller a 'thumbs up' with a huge smile.

Entering his office, he motioned both women to take seats.

Behind his desk, he sat comfortably then addressed Jackie first. "Ms. Pantterdyck, I understand you were invaluable in assisting Mrs. Milassoviech in procuring the TPS specimen. I wish to express our appreciation for your willingness to jump in and help in a very unusual circumstance, without questions or suspicions. Not many young… women… ah folks, would do that in such strange… um, circumstances. To your credit, it demonstrates an… an accepting individual with an open mind. Which we desperately need, by the way. Elizabetta, you can jump in at any point." The Colonel was at odd ends with offering the young woman the Squad's thanks. It wasn't something he did well.

He gave orders well.

"What Colonel Maddox is trying to do is offer you a job, Jackie." Elizabetta laughed. "We both think you would be an asset to the team and when you finish your degree, you can take an active roll in our financial arrangements. You only have a few more credits to complete, right? Can you finish them online? From here?"

"That is, if you want to." The Colonel added quickly. "You're not being held hostage or anything."

Jackie wanted to jump up and do a happy dance, right in the Colonel's office. "Hostage? Are you kidding? This is the only place I have ever felt like I belong. With all due respect, Sir." Jackie's smile was huge. "I already know more than I should, and I am not sure Natalia can wipe my mind. We've been messing around with that stuff and I've figured out how to block her. Oops. Maybe I shouldn't have told you that!"

"Can you finish your degree from here?" The Colonel's phone was blinking red. "I have your father on the line. How about a conference call?"

"Yes, and yes!" Jackie was virtually vibrating and wanted to jump out of her skin.

"Here we go." Colonel Maddox hit the button. "Harold, Frank here. I have you on speaker phone with my… with Elizabetta Zoeltel and your daughter." Before the Colonel could continue, the General broke in.

"What's wrong? What happened?"

"Nothing, Harold. Nothing is wrong."

The General broke in again. "Have you figured out what happened to my son yet?'

Colonel Maddox took a deep breath. Before he could respond, the other Pantterdyck took over.

"Dad, calm down and listen. Colonel Maddox has offered me a job, here with the Squad. I've decided to take it."

"It's that Sergeant, isn't it? You're going to throw your life away for that pedophile. What about your school? I thought I raised you better than that, young…"

"Dad! Stop. I'm a grown woman, surprise, surprise. And here's a news flash for you, dear old pop. You had very little to do with raising me. You abdicated that to mom and a pack of textbook toting cowboys in some wasteland out west. So just listen for a change."

All three waited for some retort.

It didn't come.

"I can finish my degree online through the Distance Delivery program while working here. Sergeant Miller has nothing to do with my decision. Well, maybe a little, but he's not the main reason I decided to accept the Colonel's offer. I belong here, Dad. I fit in for once in my life."

"No doubt you are referring to your mother's rather unique ideas. She always had some weird mental thing going on. I had high hopes you were not afflicted." General Pantterdyck expressed his disappointment in both his words and his tone.

It was time to intervene. "Harold, you have a very talented, intelligent and brave girl. I would be proud to call her my daughter. Think on that. In the mean time, we can use her skills and education. This is simply a courtesy call, not a request for approval."

At that, Jackie's frown turned into a huge smile and she shot a double thumbs up to Colonel Maddox. "Dad, I'll call mom so she doesn't worry. I can handle the tuition if the GI Bill doesn't cover Distance Delivery since I'll be working too. I only have two terms to go and my GPA is three point eight five. No worries. I'll finish. It's always been my goal. You know that. Later, Dad."

She drew a finger across her throat and Colonel Maddox hung up the hand set. He wiped a hand across his face. "That went well," he apologized to the young woman.

"No worries, Sir. That wasn't so bad… all things considered." She smiled brightly at the Colonel. "Thanks so much. I won't let you down."

Jackie impulsively stood, hugged a still sitting Elizabetta, and headed out of the office. "I have to tell Susannah and Milo.

They'll shit." She stopped. "Sorry, Sir. They'll…"

"I have a sneaking suspicion the Sergeant may shit. Go!" He motioned her on her way.

As soon as Jackie was down the hall, Elizabetta broke into the laughter she'd been resisting since following the young woman into Colonel Maddox's office.

"Frank, I think you just made that young lady's day… no… life. She will be a great addition to the squad."

"I hope so." He wiped his hand across his face, again.

Happy hoots and cheers could be heard down the hall. Obviously Susannah and the rest of the team had learned the news.

"Frank, you look tired." Elizabetta's comment was just a touch smug.

Chapter 14

Sisters

Sisters, sisters!
There were never such devoted sisters.
In all kinds of weather we stick together.
Never had to have a chaperone, no sir.
I'm there to keep an eye on her.

*From Sisters, Sisters,*
*Lyrics and music by Irving Berlin*
*White Christmas (musical)*

Monique sat on the end of her bed, a heap of bloody tissues littered the floor and comforter. Her nose was red and her eyes puffed almost closed. It was an awful look for a female vampire!

Susannah had never seen Monique in such a dither.

Jackie had never seen a vampire crying jag. She was mildly disgusted, but more sympathetic than repulsed. "Sweetie, you really must stop losing blood. You will get too hungry." It was the best she could do at the moment. Consoling a weeping vampire was a new thing for her!

"Come on, Monique. Dad will never make you go to San Leyre. We need you here with the elf doctor."

At that point Monique actually laughed through her tears. "He's not really an elf. In fact I've never even seen a real elf." She hiccupped in between words.

"There are elves as well as vampires?" Jackie was serious.

"Oh la, I do not know. Fiona is so like a faerie I sometimes wonder." The tears had ended and Monique was considering asking Fiona the next time the little vamp popped in... when the little vamp did pop in.

"Another human? Hmm. This place be gettin' a might busy for me."

Monique and Susannah jumped. "Fiona, you aren't supposed to be here. We're quarantined!"

"Aye, but I am under the covers, no! Emilliano wants to

know if ye be figurin' out the stuff. He is beside hisself and pacin' a back and fer. I worry for him, Suze, me gel." Fiona did look worried. It didn't go with her childish features. She resembled a three-year-old spying a puzzle for the first time.

"Well, there is new data, but it doesn't mean anything yet. The squad is going to San Leyre to talk to a monk and some of the kids. This one guy is experimenting with sport drinks and that may be the stuff. We won't know until we talk to some of the people involved."

"Fiona, this is Jacquiline Pantterdyck. She has joined our squad." Monique made the formal introduction. She knew Fiona liked that kind of thing.

"Ach, the gel who holds our silly Sergeant's heart. Tis nice to be meetin' ya." Fiona hesitantly held out her hand.

It was a strange move for the faerie vampire.

When had Fiona begun shaking hands with humans?

Monique wondered.

Jackie took the little faerie vampire's hand in a firm grip. "Nice to meet you, Fiona."

"Ooh…" Fiona dropped Jackie's hand and stepped back. "I be mistakin' ye fer human. Me apologies Braughtenin." Fiona attempted a courtesy. A tiny crystal bell appeared in her petite hand. "When ye have news, ring fer me." She curtsied toward Jackie again. A little better this time, then disappeared with the usual parting hoopla and farewell.

"Wait, Fiona!" Monique fanned her arms in the air as the twinkling stars disappeared around the three women. "What did you call her?"

It was no use.

Fiona was gone.

Monique rang the bell.

Nothing.

She rang the bell again. A little louder.

From out of nowhere, a tiny sing-song voice sounded. "Only fer news."

Monique looked at Jackie.

Jackie looked at Susannah.

They all shrugged at once.

"Do you remember the word she used when she took your hand? She has never shaken anyone's hand that I can remember. She doesn't touch humans much. I think she did that on purpose.

171

She knew something." Susannah was thinking.

"Oui. Fiona does nothing without reason. I do believe you are correct, cheré." Monique began collecting used tissues. "I do not recall. It was a shock on me as well."

"It sounded like brighten, but with an accent. Why would she courtesy to me? I don't get it." Jackie frowned and studied her reflection in the mirror, then noticed Monique's reflection. "Hey, I can see you in the mirror!"

"Yeah, you have a lot to learn about vamps, kiddo." Susannah laughed as she helped Monique gather tissues. "And we obviously have a lot to learn about you." She patted Jackie on the back.

"I'm hungry. How about you two? My biological clock is all screwed up. It's almost midnight and I feel like it's noon."

"That happens down-under. Most of the humans adjust to one of two schedules and stick with it. Milo doesn't seem to need a circadian rhythm. He's around all the time. When you least expect it." At that statement, all three girls laughed.

"Let's attack the mess hall. I'm ready for lunch."

******

"She used this weird name that sounded like 'brighten' as best we can remember. It was very strange. Then she curtsied... even weirder. What do you think it means, Elizabetta?" Susannah sat with her Coven Mistress, Jackie, and Monique who was sipping synth-blood. Jackie chowed down on a large pepperoni pizza.

"Fiona is very strange, you are correct. But she is also very old and knowledgeable, despite her looks and, at times, behavior. I doubt we will know until she wants us to." Elizabetta waved through the air as if she thought Fiona might be listening.

"Let me get this straight, please... Fiona is the wife of some librarian, somewhere... who keeps the history of vampires? And vampires, in general, have a sort of government?" Jackie pulled a stringy piece of cheese off the crust. "There's a whole world out there most people know nothing about. Wow!"

"There are many worlds of which most people are woefully ignorant, miss." Percy Seizemore wandered out of the kitchen with an energy drink in each hand.

Jackie calmly slid her pizza into the middle of the table as Monique and Susannah hid their synth-blood containers beneath the tablecloth.

"Pizza, Doctor?" Jackie smiled sweetly.

"Why would I pollute caffeine, sugar, vitamin B twelve..." he peered over his glasses at the label on the can, "and a bunch of other chemicals with real food? I'm on my way back to the lab. Thanks anyway." He smiled directly at Monique, who did a wonderful job of totally snubbing the scientist.

Adequately rebuked, Percy strolled down the hall that led to Doctor Anderson's research lab.

"That elf doctor is scandaleux." Monique growled. "If we did not need him..."

"What? You'd send him packing? Bury him in the cornfield? He's not an elf, Frenchy. He's a world renowned scientist who has given up his work on three grant based projects that total about six million dollars, to help Doc Anderson. Cut him a little slack." Susannah had reviewed Percy's history online earlier in the evening.

"I shall not cut his slack... possibly his skinny neck. What is a slack?" Monique finished her bag of synth-blood and tossed it in the garbage bin behind her. "I do not know this word, slack."

"Never mind, Frenchy. It's a saying that means give him some credit for being really smart and helpful. He didn't have to come here, you know."

"Oui, oui. And now we all must pretend to be human. How inconvenient." Monique stood. "I must see Sergeant Miller. We have work to do." With that, she promptly disappeared down the hall opposite the research lab.

"Well! What did he ever do to her?" Jackie watched the voluptuous vamp depart, as she grabbed the pizza box and dragged it back toward her plate.

******

"This! It's the entry we used when we came for you. I found this guy who was with the Resistance in World War II. He used to hide in the catacombs. He drank a few to many with the Colonel and told us way more than he should have. He's still alive at ninety-eight. And still drinking." Milo was pointing to an old well down the hillside from the main monastery. It was overgrown with weeds and partially covered by old grape vines. The satellite picture showed detail.

Not for the first time, Monique was amazed at the Sergeant's technical skills.

"Oui. I recognize this. When Tank carried me out, I could see, but not speak very well. I was very close to being destroyed. I would not have lasted another year in the hands of those monsters." Monique shuddered then brightened. Ever the exuberant young woman, she hugged a stiff Miller. "Then you saved me!" She kissed his cheek with a loud smack.

"Please, Ms. Merchant. It was a team effort." Miller blushed and adjusted the plastic collar he always wore.

"Of course, but any opportunity to kiss a handsome man is assez bon pour moi - for me." She giggled, then settled back in her chair. "See this well, there is a cell beneath it. The opening allows a tiny ray of light to reach the bottom. My torturers would chain me there and listen to my screams while I burned. Over and over. That is where Mathilda was finally destroyed." Her voice dropped to a whisper. "She was burned so badly, she could not recover." A tiny red tear balanced on her thick eyelashes. "She turned to ash in my arms. Then there was only me."

Miller pulled a tissue from the box near his computer station and handed it to Monique.

"Merci, Sergeant." She dabbed at the tear.

"How could they do such horrible things and still claim to be saintly men living in the light of God?" Miller shook his head in disgust. "I hate organized religion."

"Ah, still discussing Catholicism, I see." Doctor Seizemore came through the door twirling a keychain of thumb drives.

"Cease this sneaking after me, elf. Go back to… wherever you came from." Monique jumped up, pointing a finger at the scientist.

Miller grabbed her finger and lowered her hand, something he would not have done in any other circumstance. "Ms. Merchant!" Partially surprised, partially tickled, Miller gently restrained the vamp. "Doctor Seizemore is here to help."

"Oui, Oui! That is what everyone says to me. He was raised by *them*!" She pointed to the monastery. "I do not trust him."

"Ms. Merchant, I assure you, had I any other option, I would not have chosen St. Agatha's Orphanage in which to spend my youth." He calmly lifted his t-shirt, which sported some chemical equation in lime-green block letters. "I might have grown into a swimming career instead of becoming a research scientist."

He turned around.

Both Monique and Miller gasped at the scars on the slight man's back.

"Unfortunately, I never quite lost my desire for rebelliousness."

Monique could not stop her own hands. She reached to him and traced the longest thick scar from his shoulder to the center of his back. "Did they chain you too?"

He turned to face her, slid the shirt back down and hunched his arms to straighten the thin material. "When you're a kid, they just grab your hair and hold you down. I think I would have preferred the typical sexual abuse most of the boys got, to this." He motioned to his back. "At least you can hide that kind of torture."

"I am sorry you had to endure that, Doctor. I thought my childhood was screwed up. Guess it can always be worse." Milo wanted to leave the secrets of childhood behind and move to safer territory.

"Oui, Doctor. I am so sorry. I did not mean to … make the fun of you." Monique stared at his bright athletic shoes. They clashed with his curly wedgewood hair.

"Maybe the priests thought I *was* an elf and they needed to beat it out of me. I don't know. But it's the past. I've moved on, and now I torture microscopic cells in hopes of improving mankind. Go figure."

Monique couldn't resist the sigh that escaped her luscious lips. "Oui. I know exactly what you say."

Percy felt his heart leap. Did she really? That would be a first. "Ah," he coughed, "we seem to have something in common." He cleared his throat nervously.

"Oui, oui." Her breathy whisper seemed to confound Percy's senses. Monique looked shyly at his bright neon shoes. She'd felt his emotional reaction to her statement. Why would it have such an impact on the scientist to understand how he felt? Even humans should understood emotion on some level.

Only Miller knew how close the two very different individuals actually were. He wondered if Doctor Seizemore's youth at the orphanage haunted him, like Monique's years at San Leyre haunted her.

After an awkward moment in which Miller studied his computer screen very carefully, Percy found his tongue. "Ah, Sergeant Miller, I have some more data to upload. I've broken down the molecular recipe for the containment environment, the solution the cells live in. Amazingly enough, it's based on a drug I once came across, a few years back. This pharmaceutical company was trying to develop an additive to increase blood production. Like self-blood doping, only a little more complex." He handed a thumb drive to Miller. "Files six through fourteen. If you could load them for me for the morning briefing, I'd appreciate it. I need to turn in for some rest or I won't be worth my shoes." He bumped his heels together with a squeak. "There's no place like home. Or any available bed, if you have no home."

Monique giggled. "That is from Oz Wizard movie! I saw it once with Susannah. The singing girl had chaussures rouge magique, the red shoes!"

"Good night all." Percy wandered off down the hall toward the human quarters.

Monique took her seat next to Sergeant Miller once more. "He is the nicest elf I think I've ever met." She whispered. From outrageous dislike to adoration in two short minutes! That was Monique.

Miller just shook his head. "You've met many elves in your lifetime?"

Monique giggled and shook her blonde mane.

"Back to work. I need to get some shut-eye before the morning meeting too. Back to the map. It's almost done."

Putting their heads together, two hours later the comprehensive schematic of the area was complete and posted to everyone's computer stations. Travel arrangements were posted and team assignments were in place. Colonel Maddox's station listed the names and contact information of the State Department rep, the Spanish Policia Floral contact and French Liaison Officer he'd met earlier.

Miller was headed for bed.

Monique met Jackie and Susannah in the lounge, to watch Gone With The Wind.

The old version.

\*\*\*\*\*\*

"He is not so bad as I believed in the beginning." Monique subconsciously rubbed the back of her neck. She giggled. "For an elf."

"Okay, Frenchy. No more elf stuff. You know he's not an elf. He's a very good scientist. And he's temporary, so watch the flirting." Susannah lectured her sister.

"Oui, maman." Monique, affecting a snooty teen voice, pulled a face at Susannah. "Ah, she is so beautiful, look!" She pointed at the TV screen. "I so love those clothes. They are almost as nice as what I used to wear. My maid would dress me for the day and I felt so wonderful to be alive and … ah pooh. No more." She pulled on her leggings, stretching the bright tie-dyed material.

Jackie stuffed her mouth with popcorn and mumbled. "You wouldn't want to wear those clothes in the south, if you've ever spent a summer there." She chuckled and pointed. "A corset and tons of velvet. Sweat factory for sure." She grabbed the can of soda on the end table and downed the contents.

"Women weren't allowed to lift a finger." Susannah laughed. "That would be the day."

"Only the rich, honey. My luck, I'd be a slave in rags, pickin' cotton with da rest o' da pickanninies." Jackie burped long and loud to the merriment of her two friends. "Sorry. Habit I picked up in Purgatory."

"Jordan thinks it's disgusting when women burp. He's such an elitist. Not in a bad way, just sweet and well mannered. I'm not sure where he was during the women's lib movement, but he seems to have missed some pretty important parts of our social evolution. I sure miss him."

The facility was off limits to all other vampires until the team had figured out the TPS mystery.

Jordan included.

"Young love. Nothing but trouble." Jackie burped again.

As Vivian Lee danced through the ballroom, Monique recalled part of her conversation with Percy. "The elf doctor mentioned a drug he heard about from a company in the south. He said… oh, I cannot remember. TPS had composition similar, same things inside, you know."

"Really? Hmmm." Susannah slumped into the overstuffed couch and concentrated on critiquing the old favorite. "Oh Brett, don't leave me!" She fanned her face and spoke with a thick southern accent. "That man is not even sweating! And he's smoking a cigar… in a suit and tie. Ya gotta love Hollywood."

\*\*\*\*\*\*

Across the compound, Percy lay atop his bed thinking about the chemical formula for the solution in which the triple helix DNA was found. "Impossible," he mumbled. His mind spun in fifteen different directions, then settled on a visual of a gorgeous blonde who kept smiling and saying she understood. It was distracting and each time he forcefully brought his thinking back to the puzzle at hand. "When you eliminate the impossible, whatever remains, no matter how improbable, is the truth. Ah yes, Sherlock, we do have a mystery on our hands." His arms lay above his head and he unconsciously pulled at the top of his ears with both hands. "What I need is some deductive reasoning," he mused out loud. It was a habit. Both pulling on his ears, and talking to himself.

No doubt the life long ear habit resulted in his elfin ears, but he didn't care. It helped him concentrate. "Reverse engineering. That's what I need. Take it apart PJ, disassemble that damn stuff."

He sat upright. "That's it! Data, data, data. I can't make bricks without clay!" He quoted his favorite detective. He hit the space bar on his computer and brought the machine to life. "That which is out of common is usually a guide, rather than a hindrance." He went back to the original sample and read through the data once again. Kicking the startling discovery of the DNA out of his mind, he looked at the total picture, and began a meticulous reverse engineering of the specimen.

"Holmes, you're are a genius! PJ, you are dull as dirt." He always called himself PJ. The only connection to his parentage he'd ever found, was a hand written letter from his biological mother referring to him as *her little PJ*. The priest who found him in a laundry basket in the confessional of St. Agatha's Church, named him Percy James Seizemore, after the priest's own brother. Unfortunately, his namesake died of a drug overdose in the sixties.

"Ha, ha, ha. Lookie here." He pointed to the chemical link between the viable cells and their home solution. "I wonder…" In a simulation, he targeted the link and deleted it. The cells dissolved and the original molecules realigned themselves with three unlinked chemical compounds that precipitated out. The molecular substance left was familiar. "Mr. Watson, I do believe I've found it!" Percy clapped his hands in glee.

"Now all I have to do is find the…" He sped through several files to no avail. "Damn. Must be back at the lab." Percy glanced at the time signature on his screen. Three forty-five AM. "Double damn."

He returned to his bed and lay with his arms linked behind his head. Tugging on his ears, Percy recited the Periodic Table backwards until he fell into a dreamless sleep.

******

"Where's Lieutenant Previn?" The Colonel checked his watch. It was zero-six-oh-two. "Why is the insufferable man always late?"

No one looked at the Colonel. Previn was the least popular man in the facility. He had vampire blood on his hands.

"Sir, if we can start. Doctor Seizemore has had an epiphany." Doctor Anderson yawned but motioned toward her colleague.

"Alright. Go ahead, Doctors." Colonel Maddox sat back.

"Last night I reverse engineered a simulation of the construction of the TPS. I actually targeted the molecular link between the solution in which the cells live, and their viability. I deleted the link and the cells became unviable."

Monique texted Susannah on her little sparkly phone: What is viable mean?

The answer came immediately.

Alive.

*Text? Why?* Susannah psyched Monique. She knew Monique could very easily psyche-speak to any and all of the vamps in her coven.

*Learning.* Monique smiled her thanks. *If you can fly a machine, I can write with one.*

It was definitely Merchant logic.

Percy continued. "The precipitate was an enzyme typically used in stem cell replacement therapy to suppress the immune system in recipients." He punched a series of keys and the simulation showed on the SmartBoard. "As you can see, the cells die almost immediately. The remaining components realigned themselves into this." He punched another series of keys.

The chemical formula displayed beneath a picture of the molecule it represented. "I saw this somewhere before. I tried to find my file, but it must be on the server at my lab." Doctor Seizemore apologized.

"I know this." Yuri almost jumped out of his seat. "We have dealt with this before."

Natalia cut her husband off. "Not exactly, but similar, dear. I believe it was called CE." She placed a restraining hand on her husband's thigh beneath the table. "I thought it had all been destroyed." Natalia looked knowingly at the Colonel.

"I was under the same impression, Mrs. Milassoviech." The Colonel looked toward Doctor Anderson.

"Sir, I worked with the team at Proctor to destroy all of the CE due to its dangerous nature." Doctor Anderson responded immediately. "I am sure we did not overlook any of the drug. Jordan was tasked with supervising. We could speak with him, but I believe he will tell you the same."

"Proctor Pharmaceuticals?" Now she had Percy's attention.

"Why, yes, of course. Have you worked with them?"

Everyone at the table was putting two and two together and coming up with Crysillus Extract, the Proctor Coven and the horrible practices of the naturist vampires in Daytona Beach.

Everyone except Doctor Seizemore. He was putting two and two together and figuring out everyone but he himself, knew what was going on. "I'm missing something here. Anyone care to read me in?"

If ever there was a pregnant silence, this one was carrying quintuplets.

Finally, Monique came to Percy's rescue. "Peut-être, we should check with Mr. Burke. See what he may add. That will give Doctor Seizemore time to fetch his computer…thingy." She smiled sweetly at the Colonel who peered back suspiciously.

"Good idea, Ms. Merchant." The Colonel surprised even himself. "Susannah, would you check with Mr. Burke. Doctor Anderson, please assist Doctor Seizemore in retrieving whatever he needs. We will reconvene at seventeen hundred."

Commands given, Colonel Maddox rose and left.

Percy looked around the table. He knew he was still missing something, but it seemed it would remain that way. No one volunteered anything.

He shrugged.

Even Monique would not make eye contact with the frustrated scientist.

"It will take a couple days to get down to DC and back with the data. No one on my staff has the password to my private archives, Helga." Percy apologized.

"Tell you what, my esteemed colleague, lets retire to my lab and I'll share some more of our 'specialized technology' with you. Maybe we can speed up the process."

Monique giggled.

Yuri followed the two doctors.

\*\*\*\*\*\*

"What! I don't think so!" Percy was not so happy about the 'specialized technology' Doctor Anderson was trying to explain. "You will not convince me that transporters are real, Helga. I grew up with Star Trek. It's a TV program, not reality. I will not get in that thing with your Russian bodyguard. No. Nope. Not this elf. Not doing it. Oh hell no!"

"Percy, it is real and perfectly safe. You came here that way but you don't remember." Helga bit her tongue to keep from laughing at her colleague who detested flying and fought his motion sickness even in a car.

"And why is that? Hmm… Helga? Why don't I remember? Possibly because my neurons were scrambled? Is that it?" He was peering at the glass chamber in complete objection.

The ever-helpful Q2 came up with the brilliant idea. He had assembled the phony chamber just the night before incase the team required Percy to get around. His last v-port had been wiped from his mind. It could always be done again, but convincing him that this transporter really worked was easier and didn't require Natalia's presence. In reality, it was four glass walls with a storm door from Home Depot.

"Let me show you. Yuri, take my hand. We will transport to the lab across the hall. Watch." Helga tapped some lit numbers on a numerical keypad by the door. She and Yuri immediately disappeared and reappeared in the lab. She waved to an astonished Percy, then reappeared inside the glass chamber. "See. I'm altogether. No ill effects. Yuri, how do you feel?"

"Horoshaw. Goot." He smiled with his hands out. "Just fine, doctor. You will be, too. We go now." Yuri grasped Percy's hand, pulled him into the phony chamber and immediately v-ported them to the CDC.

The three appeared in Percy's office. Yuri moved into the shadows of the bright office. The wide window faced the rising sun. "See! Not even a tiny bit wheezy. No side effects at all."

Percy patted his legs and arms, touched his chest then grabbed his head. "I'm all here! Amazing!" He tripped over the garbage can in front of his desk. "Well, my coordination hasn't changed." With a bit of a chagrined smile, he rounded the desk and proceeded to fire up his huge system. Placing a finger on the small pad next to the keyboard, three screens came to life and an automated voice offered morning salutations.

"Good morning, please enter your password."

Percy tapped a series of keys and the computer responded. "Good morning Doctor Seizemore, what can I do for you today?"

"Open secure remote access setup." The middle screen displayed a setup form. "Enter IP address signa dot three, three, seven, niner, five, two, three, N, P, Q. Name this address PINK Helga."

Helga chuckled. She never considered herself a pink kind of woman.

"Establish secure link alpha, alpha, november." Percy sat down at his desk. "Display archive folder; drug tests. Open commercial folder. Search file name EPO.HORMONE."

After a few seconds the third screen showed an open folder with several files listed.

"Transfer to desktop. Send copy to PINK Helga." Percy got up and ran his finger through a stack of boxes. "Here! Got it." He pulled a bank box labeled *Hormone – Proctor* from the stack and plopped it on his desk. "Log out. Shut down."

The computer automatically followed the doctor's commands. "Done." He looked at Helga. "How do we get back?"

"Already set to return. Do you need this box?" Helga was watching Yuri's shadowy haven shrink with the brightening sun.

"It will be handy. Can it…transport with us?" He placed a hand on top of the box.

"Of course. Yuri?"

Yuri moved to the edge of the shadowed area. Helga reached for his hand, taking Percy's free hand at the same time.

Yuri, Helga, Percy and the box appeared inside the glass chamber back at Olney Farm. Helga caught Percy as he stumbled. "Dizzy?"

"No, but you might want to give a guy some warning." He looked around. "This will take a little getting used to. How come the rest of the scientific world does not know about this?"

Yuri stepped through the door and headed down the hall.

"Doesn't talk much, does he?" Percy picked up his box and followed Helga into her lab.

"He's the strong, silent type. Makes a perfect bodyguard." She was getting better at subterfuge.

"I guess." He settled down behind the lab computer station.

It only had two monitors.

It would do.

"I guess I will leave you to your box then." Helga knew Percy was already in scientist mode. It would only irritate the man if she continued to talk to him. Peering over his shoulder, she noticed the open file on the computer's desktop. It was labeled *Proctor Trials*.

"Did you work with Proctor Pharmaceuticals, Percy?"

"No... yes... I guess you could say that. I consulted on a drug trial for a new EPO hormone therapy. They were also working on a depression inhibitor, but I was too busy to take a close look at that." He was mumbling as his fingers flew over the keys.

"Interesting." Helga murmured as she left the lab. She would see it all at the evening briefing.

She caught up to Yuri in the lounge. He sat with Natalia slurping a bag of synth-blood. "Thanks for the lift, Yuri. Sorry about the little white lies."

"No problema, Doc. Eta moyu davostnea. Now I'm off to bed with my charming wife." He finished his snack, pulled his wife from the sofa and the couple walked down the hall holding hands.

Helga's heart did a little flip in her chest. To be in love and young...to be in love at any age...the memories came flooding back. She pulled a package of Double Stuffed Oreos from the cupboard and left the lounge for her own quarters and a little trip down memory lane.

Chapter 15

Mushroom Life

So you think I should live as a mushroom,
Which is often the life of a government goon,

Kept in the dark and fed nothing but crap?
Danced out in light of some horrible mishap?

We do our best to manipulate and change,
Only to find someone else has the range.

The grasp, the intel, the facts so real,
Our fate flies in the wind, while others do deal.

*From Death of an Agent*
*Anonymous Author, 1978*

Two black Suburbans turned off the main road and sped toward the quaint farmhouse nestled in a cops of ancient chestnut trees. They carried one very unhappy Detective from Interpol, Mr. Smythe from the State Department, a Very Reverend Father Disjagio von Songoria, an unnamed DEA agent, and a Policia Detectivo de Policia Floral, a detective from the local police in the autonomous province of Navarre, Spain.

It was mid-morning. Mandy and Roger Burnside, the sweet old couple who kept the farm in farm shape and practiced tactical strategies on the side, buzzed the command center beneath their kitchen.

"Hello, Milo dear. We have company. Would you let our relatives know." Mandy always called Sergeant Miller, 'Milo dear' in keeping with their cover. As good as their security was, one never knew who watched and listened from afar.

"Of course, Aunt Mandy. Are you baking today? I sure love those chocolate drop and raisin cookies you made last week."

"Chocolate drop cookies it is. And yes, I think today is a good day for baking. Don't you?"

"I sure do, ma'am. My tummy'll be waitin'. I'll get my cousin up."

The short conversation identified unscheduled visitors in black cars with smoked windows. The chocolate 'drop cookies with raisins' was Mandy's code idea after a recipe that was a childhood favorite. She actually did bake them on occasion. They really were Milo's favorite. But more than that, it identified the approaching cars as black with unidentified visitors.

"Thank you, dear." She let go of the star button on the old style desk telephone.

"I'll go meet the company, hon. See what's up." Roger got up from the small table, put his coffee cup in the sink and went out the kitchen door.

"Thanks, Rog. I'll just clean up a bit." She reached under the sink for her M-16 in its special holder, checked the magazine and returned the weapon to its place. She then opened a drawer, removed a vicious looking knife and placed it in the sheath attached to her thigh beneath a lovely print skirt. She touched the pistol holstered beneath their kitchen table to verify its placement. The kitchen was ready. She did not need to check the four other guns, stashed behind the stove, fridge and cutting board. The butcher block held four very sharp and well balanced butcher knives, and an especially destructive meat cleaver.

Mandy fluffed her hair and checked her lipstick.

She was ready.

So was Roger. He stood passively, leaning against the pole at the end of the porch. An arsenal of weapons lay hidden, but at his fingertips. As the first suburban pulled up, he effected a lazy, comfortable stance. "Howdy. Lost?"

The first Suburban's window lowered and the uniformed driver responded with the specific prearranged response. "No, sir. Just looking for a good glass of lemonade."

"My wife's kitchen is a great place for that. Why don't you park your fancy vehicle in the barn over yonder and come on in." He motioned to the dilapidated barn. Its door stood wide open in the morning sun.

"Yes, Sir." The driver led the convoy of two toward the old barn that concealed a very large garage.

Roger followed on foot. Once inside the barn, the visitors would be covered by the facility's security detail. In jeans and flannel shirts, the farm hands were all qualified sharp shooters, highly trained in hand-to-hand combat.

"Right this way, gentlemen." Roger motioned the small group toward the kitchen door where Mandy stood with a sweet smile on her face and a loaded FNX-P45 behind her back. Behind Mandy stood Frank Maddox in his civilian tan Dockers and black polo shirt. Rob Devlin lounged at the table sipping black coffee. He looked like Frank's twin in his own tan and black.

"Welcome, gentlemen. Please come in." Mandy moved out of the way allowing the contingent inside. She slipped her weapon into a drawer behind her. "Coffee, lemonade, water?"

"My Aunt makes the best coffee north of the Mason Dixon Line." Devlin toasted the group with his flowered mug.

Smythe grabbed a mug off the hook on the wall and proceeded to pour himself a cup and join Devlin. "Let's get down to business. It was a long drive way up here and it'll be a long way back."

"Please," Mandy smiled at the presumptuous Smythe, "make yourself at home." She and Roger moved to the living room, apparently to do something important, leaving the group to talk alone in the kitchen.

"Maddox, you remember Father Disjagio von Songoria." He then pointed to an impeccably dressed, short dark-complected man. "Pauolo de Navarre de Colasion de Policia Floral. For us Americans, he's a detective from the Basque police. They have their own..." He waved for effect. "police force separate from the Spanish police. Kind of."

Maddox leaned forward in the cramped kitchen and extended his hand. "Mucho gusto, Señor Dectectivo."

The detective smiled and took the offered hand. "Gracias, Colonel. I speak English, if that will make things easier for all."

"Bien, gracias, Señor. Por favor, siéntese." He offered the detective a chair.

"Detective from Interpol, Francois Bonaventure." Smythe continued the introductions. "And Jack, DEA."

Devlin chuckled, "Jack?"

"Just Jack, to this group, Devlin." Obviously the DEA agent had been read into the situation. "Working with Interpol... as a consultant." The man poured himself a cup of coffee and took a chair, leaving the Vatican representative standing.

"Father?" Devlin was not about to let *Just Jack* insult the priest.

Father Songoria sent Devlin a tight nod and remained where he was.

"Good enough. So?" Smythe took a gulp of his coffee, setting the cup down a little too hard as a kind of punctuation mark to his question.

"So…what?" Maddox was not comfortable in the tight confines of the small kitchen.

"Come on Maddox, what do you have for us?" Smythe sat back as if he were in complete control of the situation.

"Not much more than we had before. Science takes time. As you know, the doctors at Walter Reed procured a specimen of the agent we believe the children ingested. How, we still do not know. We suspect it was mixed into a drink provided by the soccer, sorry, football coach."

"Brother Berthold?" Francois Bonaventure broke in. "That is too bad since he is dead." The Interpol detective motioned to Father Songoria.

"That is true. Brother Berthold's body was found hanging from a tree in the monastery cemetery. The Abbott believes he took his own life."

"Obviously you do not believe that." Maddox could tell by the man's comment that he did not think the priest took his own life.

"It is still under investigation. The Vatican takes the death of any priest seriously, especially a death so blasphemous and damning." Father Songoria crossed himself. "My short time at the monastery led me to believe Brother Berthold's death was somewhat suspicious." He spoke softly, as if apologizing for his belief.

Devlin continued. "Thomas Pantterdyck reported tasting some concoction just before collapsing. Ms. Redmont finished her drink. She was much more severely effected. The man who may have supplied the drink is now dead. That screams suspicion to me."

"I had the opportunity to speak with a very confused young woman in the infirmary at Academia de Santos Domingo de Silos. She recalled seeing writing on a headstone… in blood. Maria Pallermo was the girl's name. She also mentioned often seeing Brother Berthold meet someone under the tree where he was hanged. The Abbott was unhappy that I spoke with her without permission." Father Songoria shook his head solemnly.

"So where'd the blood come from if he hanged himself?

Did you view the body?" *Just Jack* sat up with interest.

"Brother Berthold was already interred when I arrived at the monastery. There was no autopsy. He was a priest who committed the most savage insult against God. He was buried in an unmarked grave on unhallowed ground." Again, Father Songoria crossed himself.

"The Policia Floral has no jurisdiction on the Monastic grounds. The Catholic Church has its own law." Francois Bonaventure motioned to the Vatican representative who stood against the sink.

Smythe was incensed. "You mean to tell me, the secret brotherhood can do whatever they want behind the walls of their little castle, and no one knows the better? Oh that's sweet."

"Sir, they are men of God in pursuit of a holy life. Granted, this unfortunate incident is puzzling, but I find your attitude insulting." Finally, Father Songoria rose to the occasion. "I assure you, the Pope has instructed me to get to the bottom of this, and that I will do. I have the same resources as every agent in this room. I shall find the truth in this situation. You will be informed of the results." He crossed his arms in resolute body language.

"Of course you will tell us what the Vatican wants us to know. We get that. But American kids have been hurt at your school. Kids from other countries too, if the records are correct." Smythe was congratulating himself on scheduling two cars. He would not have to ride to the airport in stony silence with the over-righteous priest.

"Well," Maddox interrupted the conversation, which was on the verge of dissolving into a wrestling match. "If the Policia Floral and Interpol have no jurisdiction, we have no options." The Colonel spoke slowly as if he were considering all of the facts very seriously. "This looks like a lengthy investigation, appropriately in the hands of the Vatican. We can do nothing but offer our support and help the Father, if it is needed." It was a clear statement. "If we find something new about this substance, we will let you know." The Colonel took the card Songoria offered and shoved it in his pocket. "You can reach us through Smythe, here."

Smythe was clearly angered. He slid his cup across the table.

Devlin caught the cup before it flew off onto the floor. "Not much help, but like Frank said, science takes time. We have two very good doctors working on the stuff and they are in contact with

Walter Reed. I'm sure they'll figure this out at some point."

It was a non-committal statement.

This was a non-committal kind of meeting.

Aunt Mandy appeared in the doorway. "Gentlemen, can I get you anything before you leave?" Obviously she and Roger were monitoring the conversation.

"Just the way out, ma'am." Smythe stood. "If you have no more to add, Colonel…"

It was the first time Smythe used the Colonel's title.

It was totally inappropriate.

And Smythe knew it.

So did everyone in the kitchen.

"Then, gentlemen, Father, thank you for visiting. My husband will show you the way out." Aunt Mandy was exerting her matriarchal authority in her kitchen. "Goodbye." She disappeared back into the living room, to be replaced by her husband.

"Rob, Frank, I'll escort these folks to their cars." He looked directly at Smythe.

One by one, lead by the fuming Smythe, the group filed out of the kitchen and back to their cars. Roger remained at the door to the barn until the two Suburbans disappeared around the corner. Security cameras in the command center would follow them to the main road a mile or so away.

"That was mostly worthless, Frank." Captain Devlin refilled his cup and returned to the table where a plate of cookies had mysteriously appeared. He selected one with nuts and M&Ms. "Thanks Mandy, for not sharing these little guys." Devlin chuckled as he picked an M&M out and popped it in his mouth.

"Not completely. We now know Brother Berthold, maker of the questionable health drink, has mysteriously died. We also know we are not welcome at the Monastery. Brother Berthold's body has been adequately disposed of, with no autopsy, and no record of the location of burial. Quite the nice coverup." Colonel Maddox joined Captain Devlin at the table with his own coffee. He eyed the cookies.

"Oh go ahead, Frank. An extra inch on your waistline won't hurt." Captain Devlin patted his own growing stomach. "It's not like some wise-ass lieutenant is counting our sit-ups anymore." He chuckled again and grabbed another cookie as Roger came through the door.

"I could do without ever seeing that State Department puke

again." He took the cup his wife offered and joined the group. "No wonder the Feds can't get anything right in this country."

Mandy stood near the sink unloading her armaments. As she slid the flowery skirt up to remove her knife, all three men whistled. The fifty-eight year old biathlete was in great shape and didn't mind showing it off on occasion. She often teased the two single officers, but everyone down-under knew the solid relationship between she and her husband, and took the teasing for what it was; simple good fun.

"Great looker. Well-armed woman. What else can a man ask for?" Roger pulled his disarmed wife onto his lap and fed her the rest of his cookie.

'That'll be an extra mile today, Mr. Burnside." She kissed his cheek and took a drink of his coffee. Mandy remained in top physical shape with a daily exercise routine, as well as working the farm. She could often be seen on the command center security cameras running through the fields and shooting targets strategically placed around the property. The woman loved to run and shoot. As of late, Susannah had been joining her on occassional night excursions.

Devlin added his own observations. "That priest is not likely to ask for our help. The locals will be useless. Their hands are tied by Vatican accord."

"And years of cultural acceptance. Challenging the Catholic Church in the Basque country is like challenging Superman on Earth. Useless and dangerous. Guess we just have to be sneaky and more dangerous. I think we have that covered." The Colonel set his cup in the sink. "And keep in mind, this group of robed men kept vampires captive for centuries. They know the score. We'll have to be extra careful."

Down-under, Sergeant Miller was in complete agreement with the Colonel. "Yes, very extra careful," he muttered to himself. In the few years he's been with the Vamp Squad, despite his fear of being bit, he'd become attached to the team. Both human and vamp, he valued each member. This was the first assignment in his military career where he actually fit in. He thought back to Jackie's statement. She felt the same way. In their own curious and separate way, they'd found a home.

"Hey, Miller." Jackie came through the door yawning. "I'll never get used to not having a school schedule, or even a sleep schedule. Weird, but I like it."

"You'll get used to sleeping when you're tired, eating when you're hungry and working when we have a mission. The rest of the time, we hang out. I thought you stayed up with the girls and watched some sappy movie." Miller was reviewing the travel plans to San Leyre.

"Well, you weren't available." She smacked the back of his head.

Miller got a little thrill from her words, and a big thrill from the smack. He hoped Jackie was coming around. But he was afraid to hope. His heart did a little flip inside his hairy chest. "Sit, I'll show you what I was up to."

Jackie pulled up a chair and Miller proceeded to run her through the plans he'd been working on since the previous night.

"I had no idea you were such an integral part of this...place. I'm impressed."

Jackie was impressed!

Milo was in heaven. Something else stirred in his body, but it wasn't his heart. In fact, it wasn't in his chest at all!

\* \* \* \* \* \*

Monique tossed and turned in her day-sleep. The nightmare of her turning played over and over in her dreams.

She woke in a cold, dark cavern. Stretched out beside Phillipe Le Glaute, Duc d'Orleans, she remembered the men, the torches, the accident... the...

Pain exploded within her mind. Her body became a fiery mass of burning ache. She tried to scream but her dry lips could only issue a weak mew. She tried to move, but every limb was a thousand pounds of hideous pressure.

She could not breathe!

*She could not breathe!*

"Shhh! Do not wake the Master. He will not be happy with you." A whisper in her ear came from...

She could not turn her head or move a finger to see who spoke the warning.

"Lie still and accept it, mouse. You cannot change what you are becoming. We all went through it just like you will."

Phillipe shifted a touch in his sleep.

"Shhhh! Go back to sleep."

She could not breathe.

191

She could not move.

She could not go back to sleep!

*Ahhhhhhhhhhhhh!* Her mind screamed.

Was she dead?

Were they all dead?

A hunger began in her belly. The thought of petite fleurs with heavy cream was revolting. But she loved them…

Phillipe shifted again. This time she heard his voice. "Ah, my baby awakens with the hunger. Shall I suckle you? Or shall I leave you wanting?"

Monique tried to open her eyes, but found them to be lead curtains. She tried to respond, but a slight hiss was all she could produce. Again she screamed in her mind. *Ahhhhhhhhh!*

"Master, make her stop. She is hurting my head." It was a feminine voice that begged. "It is not yet sunset, but she tortures us with her rantings."

"Calm, my petit jouet. Hush and sleep." She could feel him stroking her hair, pacifying the need in her. Soon, a blackness crept over mind and body. Cold enveloped her body and stilled her mind.

"No!" Monique woke with a start. She was not in the catacombs beneath the Count's summer estate. She was not a pampered sixteen year-old and a member of the elite French royalty.

She touched the warm walls of her quarters. Her wide screen TV showed a flickering fireplace and soft classical music played in time to the flickering flames. She slammed a fist into her pillow. "Why do I have to relive this nightmare? What is wrong with me?" It was an anguished plea to an empty room.

The clock on her nightstand showed four-thirty PM. Not even sundown!

"Pah. My mind bothers me. I shall find someone to bother." Monique rose and dressed in her usual multi-colored leggings and a sexy, low-cut satin blouse. She fluffed her hair, which fell into perfect place, and checked her face in the mirror. "Perfect… as usual." She sighed. Her perfect, sexy appearance took no time or effort, now that her humanhood was a thing of the past. It just was. She sighed again. She really missed the old days, the excitement and anticipation. Spending hours primping with the comradery of her maids and the household staff at her father's estate was a lifestyle made possible by her position of birth. Her *rebirth* stole that life from her. It stole life, period.

The rest of the vamps in the facility were still asleep, so she wandered toward the lounge. It was empty but the command center lights burned bright. Inside she found Dr. Seizemore and Sergeant Miller bent over a computer console, deep in conversation. She stood silently and listened.

"So here is the chemical formula for the drug Proctor Pharmaceuticals was testing. Here is the resulting substance after eliminating the live cells and precipitate. Notice anything?"

"Sure do Doc. They are almost identical. Except for those letters."

"Those letters stand for monocyanidiate anthibium, a very volatile chemical used to bind genes. Apparently it is required for the survival of the integrated cells. How, I have no idea, but it must be present for the original specimen to exist in its complete form."

"So, without the mono stuff, the live cells, kind of like a virus, can't live. Right?" Miller was catching on to molecular science rather quickly.

"Crysillus Extract is what Proctor called the solution." Doctor Seizemore commented from his notes. "Can you put this flow chart on a slide for me, Sergeant?"

Monique gasped giving away her position in the shadows.

"Good evening Ms. Merchant. You're a little early for the night briefing." Doctor Seizemore rose and offered his chair. "Have you heard of this drug before?"

"Oui, once. A long time ago. I do not remember much. How do you know this drug, Doctor?" Monique bit her tongue before the word *elf* slipped out.

"I did some initial testing for Proctor Pharmaceuticals on contract. I needed the money. The money was good, too. But the drug was not. It didn't do what they professed, and it never came to the FDA for approval. At least I haven't heard anything more about it."

"Oui, I see." Monique took the chair he offered and peered at the screen. "I do not know these letters and numbers."

"They represent chemical combinations. Each letter stands for…" Doctor Seizemore began a Chemistry 101 presentation.

"No, no, no, Doctor. I do not want to know these letters. I do not know science and that is fine with me." Monique waved her hand over the screen. "I much prefer the pursuit of amore over the pursuit of little letters and numbers." She giggled at the look the scientist gave her. "I do not have a head for such things."

"Everyone should know basic chemistry. It is all around you. Science is everything from simple cooking to nuclear bombs."

Again she cut the doctor off. "I do not cook. I do not like bombs. I much prefer a good manicure and shopping in the computer."

"…on the computer, Ms. Merchant." Sergeant Miller corrected Monique.

"On, in, what is the difference? I find what I want and then it comes. Right here. Voila, no?"

Percy could not argue with that. The Sergeant didn't want to.

"The slide, Sergeant?"

"Of course, Sir. No problem. I wasn't interested in dinner anyway." Miller swung around and began to develop the requested slide from Doctor Seizemore's notes. "Just great." He mumbled under his breath. "CE comes back to haunt us."

"Excuse me, Sergeant?" Doctor Seizemore had very good hearing.

"Nothing, Sir, just reading out loud." Miller shot Monique a meaningful glance.

She got the idea.

"Doctor Seizemore, would you like something to eat before our meeting?" She took his arm and steered him toward the mess hall. "Our kitchen is stocked with all kinds of hu…hungry people snacks and meals."

"I guess I haven't eaten all day. I could use a good tofu stir fry with soy and ginger."

Monique looked at the doctor. "Is that English? Or is it something the elves eat?"

This time they both knew she was teasing.

"Definitely elf food. Keeps my ears pointed." He reached up and felt his left ear. "Yep, its starting to round out again. I sure don't want to be confused with humans. They're so boring."

Monique giggled. "You have no idea."

She escorted him to the mess hall, known in the civilian world as *the kitchen*. "I am useless in this place, so I must leave you on your own. Just peck in the cupboards. Have what you want." She took a seat at one of the small tables. "I will wait."

"Peck? How about peek? What about you? Can I fix you something?" Percy thought he was being solicitous.

"No. merci. I have eaten. I must watch my figure." She patted her tummy. It was a lame excuse but she hoped he would accept it.

"Okay. But I have it on good authority, elf food has no calories." He was on a roll and wanted to stay that way. He realized he liked the voluptuous, but slightly intimidating woman. He'd never had the attention of such a gorgeous gal like Monique before. It was exhilarating and a little addictive. Actually, given his set of specific characteristics and his physiological responses every time he was in close proximity to the French operative, it was a little more than addictive!

"Ah. It is very filling so I must decline. But I shall have something to drink." Before Percy could offer to get her something, Monique jumped up and grabbed a bottle of blood wine and a small glass. "This is made specially for me." She'd almost said *my kind* but caught herself at the last minute. "It is very bitter and is skinny."

"You mean diet?"

"Oui, diet. You would not like it, I don't think." She hoped he did not want to try it!

"Only natural and organic go in this elf's body." He was definitely proud of his diet.

Doctor Anderson had ordered a selection of Vegan delights when Doctor Seizemore agreed to come to Olney Farm and help out with TPS. She knew his diet well and provided nicely so he wouldn't go snooping around.

Within a few minutes, Percy sat down with his plate of mixed veggies, tofu, spices and sauce. Monique thought the stinky mess... a stinky mess. "How do you eat this...food? It reminds me of the smell in the barn." Her nose wrinkled and she frowned.

"Well, this elf is not offended. But I am hungry." He stuffed a huge fork full of the mix into his mouth.

Monique sipped her wine, eyeing the new doctor. "You have no family? Oui?"

Percy munched, his mouth full, but nodded.

"Moi non plus. I have no one left."

Percy cleared his mouth with a gulp. "An accident?" He queried.

"No, they..." She paused. Her family died in the French Revolution but that little piece of information would not due in this situation. "They... died in the war." It was close to the truth.

"Which one?" Percy was curious. He knew Monique was French.

"Ah, it was a long time ago. Je ne veux pas en parler." She hoped he would not ask any more.

No such luck. "I don't know French. What did you say?" Percy paused and put down his fork.

"I do not like to say about it. I get sad." Monique made the sweetest sad face and made a little sub-sub noise. She wiped away invisible tears and sniffed. It was the perfect act.

"Oh, sorry." Percy picked up his fork and began stuffing food into his mouth. Talking around a large piece of broccoli, he proceeded to fill the silence with his own story. "I never knew my folks. My earliest memory was of a nun feeding me horrible gruel and lumpy milk. They had cows at the convent nearby and provided their own milk to the orphanage. I was thirteen before I knew milk was not supposed to be warm and lumpy."

"C'est terrible!"

"Yes, well, it was food and I was a growing boy. It's amazing what a kid will do to survive." He concentrated on his plate.

"Ah, the scars you have. I understand." She reached across the table and pressed her hand to his. "We have much in common, Dr. Elf."

Percy pulled away a little too fast, covering his discomfort with a reach for his glass of soymilk. "Yes, well... we seem to have both survived. So, it was what it was, and I decided at a very tender age, that I would never be at anyone's mercy ever again. That is why I became a doctor and top in my field. Education is the great equalizer. Being the best is a very nice moneymaker. Both afford independence and resources." Done with his meal and personal history, Percy rinsed his plate and placed the dishes in the dishwasher. "Does anyone clean up or do we do it ourselves?"

"We do most things ourselves. We are a small place. Aunt Mandy does the laundry if you ask her nicely and smile." Monique got up from the table. "I like to do my own. It makes me feel..." She was about to say *human* but paused, "like a girl again! I will see you at the briefing." She patted Percy on the back and headed towards the command center and Milo. She wanted to know about CE and how it played into their investigation. He would have time. The night briefing was still an hour away.

******

Percy was in the lab...drinking his usual cherry flavored energy drink and manipulating simulations on Helga's computer. He was frustrated and in need of sleep. Unfortunately he could not turn off the questions in his head. As usual.

"Percy, do take a break. You look like you are on your last legs." Doctor Anderson looked up from the microscope's computer screen. She'd been watching the cell energy transfer on a sample of TPS and recording frequencies.

"The brain won't settle down. It's after nine and I'm so frustrated I can't even sit still." He gulped the last of the energy drink and set the can along the wall behind his computer station. It joined the ten other empty ones stacked there.

"Maybe you should slow down on the Flyin'-Hi Cherry..." Helga picked up a can and read the label, "power-in-the-tower! Sheesh Percy, this is thirty-two ounces of pure sugar, caffeine and B12!"

Percy took the can from his mentor and carefully placed it on top of the pyramid he'd been building with the empties. "No lectures from the woman who lives on Double Stuffed Oreos and coffee. Did you see this?"

Helga took the printed sheet from his hand and skimmed the contents.

"Now, will you tell me what's going on around here? I'm working in a vacuum behind the emerald curtain on the left. Everyone is talking around..." He circled his hands around and around as if stirring a pot, "...*something*. Our little briefing was a bunch of double talk, only half of which I got. Not a mushroom, Helga." He referred to his previous conversation at the CDC which he had recounted for her.

Helga sat down and stared at the page Percy had just given her. She quickly realized he had their answers. He deserved an explanation. They had to get on with the investigation and it was becoming impossible to brief the others without transparency. "Stand by, Percy." She hit the intercom to summon Colonel Maddox. "I think I may need help with this."

Percy eyed the woman he'd come to respect and revere above all else, early in his career. Now he was questioning her motives and his manipulated part in this farce.

"Ah, Colonel Maddox. Do come into my lab." She handed

the Colonel, Percy's printout. "I think it's time to come clean. Percy has so much to offer but we...I...he needs to know, Frank."

Percy took a swipe at his pyramid and sent the cans flying. "Know what? For God's sake?" Frustration twisted his features.

"Sit, young man. Now." Maddox kicked a can out of his path and took the chair next to Doctor Anderson. "This may be difficult for you." The Colonel folded his hands and stared at the ground for a couple seconds. "We haven't exactly been completely... honest isn't the right word, but it'll do for now. You see..." Colonel Maddox had never had to explain his team to anyone but the Joint Chiefs before and found the words just wouldn't come.

"Let me, Frank." She sat up straight and looked directly at her cohort. "This team...the installation...it is a safe haven for a coven of government operatives. Complete with support folks, great resources and... well... vampires. We work for the government and do things human teams cannot. We also work with a kind of quasi-government organization of vampires that are dedicated to keeping the human race ignorant of the existence of vampires, as well as safe from some of their more extraordinary abilities." She paused, calculating the effect her words were having on the scientist whose entire life was based on facts and research.

"Right. Now how about the real story?" Percy wasn't swallowing it.

"No son, listen. This place..." Colonel Maddox lifted his arms to encompass the facility. "I built this place for my daughter, in the beginning."

"Come on, do you really think I'm going to accept this bullshit?" Percy kicked a can out of the way and stormed out of the lab.

"Well, that went nicely." Doctor Anderson patted Frank on the thigh and went after her friend.

Half way to the mess hall she caught up with Percy. "Wait! I know I sort of messed that up, but it's true. I had a hard time accepting it at first too.

Percy spun. "Show me your fangs then. Turn into a bat and fly around or something. Vampires... right."

Susannah, Elizabetta, Natalia and Yuri all sat in the mess hall sipping synth-blood for breakfast. They'd all been privy to the lab conversation, thanks to Maddox hitting the facility-wide intercom button before he began the tense discussion. Percy sped by, grabbed another Flyin'-Hi from the fridge and spun to face the group he'd been working with for the last two days.

Slowly, one by one, they smiled at the scientist, their fangs extended.

Slowly, inch-by-inch, Percy descended to the floor… in a dead faint.

At the edge of the dining room, Doctor Anderson stood with her hands on her hips. Out of breath after her dash from the lab, she slowly shook her head. "Did anyone, with incredible vamp-speed, think to catch the good doctor before he hit the floor?"

Four blank faces turned to stare at Doctor Anderson. All somewhat dumbfounded…

Chapter 16

Science and Right

Science can define almost anything,
Given enough facts.
But science in a vacuum,
Imparts only cracks,
In the view, the assumption, the deduction of right,
Just beyond, hidden, secured from sight.

However, like nature's desire and morning's light,
Sooner or later, facts become might.
And might is always right.
Right?

*Pamela Langston, PhD., MD, JD*
*Center for Disease Control, Director of Eccentric Projects*
*Department of Health and Human Services, Washington DC, 2013*

Percy awoke with a start. He lay on his bed in his own quarters. It had been a nightmare of a very original kind. Usually he had horrible dreams about the orphanage and the priests who beat him on a regular basis as the other kids watched and cheered them on. But vampires? Wow! He must have downed way too much energy drink!

The digital clock above his door displayed a seven, a three and a four. Seven thirty-four in the morning?

And when did he go to bed?

Last he remembered, he was in the lab with Helga and Colonel Maddox.

He'd found the key to TPS.

The triple helix genetic substance still boggled his mind, but…

He punched the intercom button. "Doctor Anderson?" She would probably be in the lab.

"Doctor Seizemore, Doctor Anderson is in a meeting at the moment. May I help you?" Percy recognized Miller's voice. Did

200

the man ever sleep? Or maybe he slept in his chair in the command center?

"Ah, no. I think I'll get some breakfast and then come your way. I have some new information on TPS I'd like to disseminate through your system, if that is alright?" When confused or agitated, Percy always resorted to work and science. It was concrete. It was real.

"Roger that. I'm here all day." Miller sounded a little disgusted.

"Right. Then I'll be over soon." Percy let go of the button. Food would do him good. Today he'd lay off the red go-juice and maybe his brain would quit playing tricks on him. That dream had been so real, so vivid.

Vampires!

Right.

Dressed and headed for the mess hall, Percy felt the stillness of the day.

Odd for a fully functioning military facility.

Vampires slept during the day.

Doctor Anderson was unavailable, in a meeting during the day.

Percy shook his head.

Ridiculous.

He heated a platter of veggie omelet and nine grain toast, then mixed a cup of hot chocolate. No Flyin'-Hi today. Looking for a can of whipped cream to top his cocoa, he opened the black fridge... and froze.

Stacks of small sacks of liquid lay organized with little labels like A+ and O-. The entire three shelves held row after row of the bags filled with a deep red liquid. Each bag had two little rubber nipples about an inch apart.

Percy slammed the door. "What the hell?"

"What the hell, what?"

Percy turned to face the biggest black man he'd ever seen in the flesh.

"I'm Ted. We haven't met yet." Ted smiled at the confused and frightened doctor. "Humans use the white fridge, Doc. The vamps have the black one. We don't mix our food. It makes the vamps kind of sick." He grabbed a Coke out of the white fridge. "Helga said y'all had *the talk* last night. So, you cool with the vamps and all?" Ted motioned to a small table surrounded by three chairs.

Percy set his plate on the table and stood starring at the big man. "Are you…"

Ted got it immediately. "Nah, I'm a human." Ted pointed to his Coke then to the white fridge. "Been on the down low before this place even started. I had a little trouble at first. The whole idea of vampires is a little hard to swallow for a good Southern Baptist boy… until you see one of them pop out those fangs, or move faster than lightning. In prison, I was one of the strongest guys around," Ted flexed his gigantic arms effectively displaying bulging pectoral muscles and a tight ripped set of abs beneath the stretched tee-shirt he wore. "Then I saw Fiona toss three bad guys with the flip of her hand. And she's the size of a peanut." He smiled to himself. "But I still got a warm spot for that little thing. She's so… well, a cute little thing"

Somewhere in the facility a little tinkling bell could be heard.

Ted chuckled. "You're welcome." he said.

"I'm welcome? For what?" Percy's mind was spinning at a high rate of speed. He couldn't get a handle on his thoughts as they whizzed by and turned the corner of reality. It made him a little dizzy.

"Nah…nothin'. Never you mind, Doc. So now that you got the flick on the triple helix thing, where do we go from here? Just curious, ya know."

"Ted, give Percy a few minutes. This is a lot for him to digest." Helga Anderson stood near the entrance to the command center.

Percy jumped and backed up against the white fridge, as if it could somehow protect him.

Helga bit her tongue to keep from giggling. "Percy, I wanted to…"

The good doctor interrupted his cohort. "Which fridge?"

Helga looked a little confused for a moment, then smiled. "White, of course."

Percy almost fainted into his chair, staring at the food on his plate. His appetite had fled with the dawning of double refrigerators. "Thank God. I thought for a minute, that…" he pointed at the black refrigerator, "was the reason you disappeared from the world a few years back. You're sure you're human, right?" He shot Helga a skeptical look.

"Of course I'm sure." She plucked a small package of Oreo cookies from a basket on the counter and took the third chair across from Percy. Popping one into her mouth, she chewed loudly then stuck out a black and white tongue covered with masticated Oreo goosh.

"See-food! Your daughter used to do that at dinner." Percy smiled, then sobered. "Sorry, Doc. I didn't mean to…"

"Another life, Percy. Not to worry. I assure you I am fully human and sound of mind. Now." She popped a couple more cookies in her mouth and grabbed a generic soft drink from the white fridge. Retaking her seat, she watched Percy stare at his food. "Not eating that omelet will not change you, this place, or the circumstances in which you find yourself. Eat your breakfast, young man." Helga sat back and sipped her drink.

Percy took a fork full of eggs and put it in his mouth.

"Chew, Percy." Helga recommended.

Ted let out a hoot and Percy about fell out of his chair.

"Sorry, man. I was just thinkin' about the first time I saw Susannah pop out of her coffin with those pearly whites hangin' down. I had a little trouble eatin' dinner that night. But I didn't freeze up like Colonel Maddox. Man, that guy just stood there." Ted shook his head with a huge grin on his face.

"Susannah is a…" Percy pointed to the black fridge.

"Yep. The entire reason this place exists." Ted opened his arms wide and looked at the ceiling just as Colonel Maddox had. "That's why we're underground. That's why Maddox put this whole Vamp Squad idea together. We keep adding people, vamps, toys, etc. as we go. You know… Black Budget. And do we have a Black Budget!" Ted downed the rest of the Coke and grabbed another one along with a hand full of snacks from the basket. He tossed the small package of Oreos to Doctor Anderson.

"Black Budget? I am not familiar with that term." He chewed around his second bite of breakfast.

"Remember I mentioned the "no limits" on resources. That's the Black Budget. Congress and the President have money that's ferreted away for all kinds of *special* projects and missions. We, luckily, financed our own black budget with a mission a couple years ago."

Ted interjected, "That's putting it mildly, Doc."

Helga continued. "No money problems, Percy. This place is a scientist's dream."

"More like a nightmare, which I had last night. Now I am questioning that nightmare. It wasn't a dream was it?" Percy took a sip of his cocoa. "Any chance there is some whipped cream around somewhere?"

"Hah! The man just found out about vampires and he's asking for whipped cream for his cocoa!" Ted rose and playfully punched Percy in the shoulder. "You'll do just fine, Doc. I gotta go Skype with my mama. Greaseman's daughter showed her how and gave her some kind of tablet. Now we got a standin' date. Every other day at nine sharp! Really cuts into my game time, but I only got one mama." He gave a lazy salute and sauntered off toward the command center.

"Well, you got Ted's approval." Helga patted Percy's arm. "And mine." She let the statement sink in. Percy would have a lot of questions, but right now he needed to come to terms with the information they provided... and his breakfast. "I'll meet you in the lab in about an hour. I need to see Captain Devlin about the planned *visit* to San Leyre. I'll fill you in on that latest scoop then." One more arm-pat and she was on her way, leaving Percy to finish his breakfast and muddle through his latest discovery that completely conflicted with his scientific brain. Conflict was too tame a word. His two worlds had colided in a mega explosion leaving his brain irradiated and throbbing!

He chewed slowly, almost afraid to swallow. Swallowing meant he was awake and aware. Shoveling another forkful into his mouth, the mound joined the previous one. His mouth was full but he couldn't bring himself to force it down.

Percy stared off toward the lab hallway.

A noise across the mess hall drew his attention.

He jumped.

His mouth emptied all on its own as half chewed egg omelet shot across the table.

Jackie rounded the corner dressed in running pants and a halter-top. Her iridescent tennis shoes matched the print on her pants. An AR-15 was casually slung over her back. "Morning, Doc. Helga told me she let you in on our special teammates. So much easier now that you know." She grabbed a granola bar off the counter and took an energy drink from the white refrigerator. "No idea why Helga thought you could come here and work without knowing."

Percy relaxed a bit. He took several napkins from the

holder and began scooping masticated omelet off the table. "You're Thomas Pantterdyck's sister, right? Is that..."He pointed at the rifle on her back. "... For the..." he pointed at the black refrigerator.

"Not sure I follow." Jackie shot him a quizzical look.

Percy scraped a fingernail against his canine tooth then pointed to the black fridge again. He couldn't bring himself to say the word *vampire* quite yet... but it was coming.

"Oh, sheesh! No. I'm going running with Aunt Mandy. She's a Biathlete. A really good one. So I decided to train with her. I'd never shoot one of the team. Wouldn't do any good anyway."

Percy shook his head. "How do you protect yourself from..." he pointed at the black fridge again.

"Protect myself? From the vamps? Why would I have too? We all sign a Pact of Cohabitation when we hire on. No fraternizing, well, no biting and no nookie back and forth. We all behave and get along just fine. It's cool. We actually don't see our team as *we* and *them*. We're just a team. With special abilities and..." she tapped the strap across her chest that secured her rifle, "good toys. It works. Gotta go."

Somehow in between conversation, Jackie had consumed her breakfast bar and drink. She headed toward the command center. "See ya at the briefing."

"What briefing?" Percy dumped his breakfast in the trash bin as Jackie trotted down the hall. Standing alone in the mess hall, he had to ask the qiestion; "Why am I always the last one to know about briefings?"

There was no one to answer his question. Human or otherwise.

******

"So how's your man handling Revelations, Chapter V?" Captain Devlin lounged in the command center with Doctor Anderson.

"Well, last I left him, in the mess hall, he was trying to swallow it all. Guess he thought our little discussion from yesterday was a bad dream. Reality dawned a little rough this morning. He'll be okay. He figured out the triple helix really fast. And the fact that it could not exist, given genetics as he knew them. His scientific mind and his human brain will reconcile the facts and accept the conclusion... eventually." Helga chuckled. "It was a stretch for me in the beginning. If Susannah hadn't lost her temper and popped out those canines... well, I got the point, so to speak."

"Ya know, that gal has come so far in such a short time." Devlin twirled the handle of his cane. He still used the cane when the weather changed or after a hard workout, despite the physical therapy he'd completed with flying colors.

"She has, and her father just beams with pride. Nice to see."

"So, Doc, tonight's briefing should be interesting. Turns out Monique isn't just another blonde vampire! She actually believes TPS is made by vamps. So my question remains; if the monks at San Leyre are dedicated to killing vamps, or chasing the Devil out of them, whatever they believe... how is it someone at the monastery is working with one?"

"Good question, Rob. And I'm glad it's your job to figure that one out. I wouldn't count on Monique's help. She is terrified of that place and the monks."

"Yeah. Susannah told me she is experiencing something like PTSD. Nightmares, can't sleep, crying jags. She's afraid of her own shadow. Apparently she was the only survivor of a group they held prisoner in the dungeon. One gal was her friend from when she was turned. Monique watched her being destroyed. Shame." Devlin rapped his cane on the floor. "Those monks should have been arrested. Vampires have rights too!"

Helga looked at Rob.

Rob looked at Helga.

Both broke into laughter.

"I can't believe I just said that." Devlin was the first to recover. "Here're the plans and a map. It'll be on your terminal as well. Miller is researching San Leyre. He is also looking into the major benefactor of the monastery, the owner of Le Glaute Industries. It's some high fa-lootin' make-up company in Europe. He says all the famous beautiful people use Francois Le Glaute!" Devlin effeminately swished his hand in the air.

"Oh my! Any chance I can get some samples? I've heard of the products, but no way can I afford them." Helga patted her face and chin.

"Ah come on Doc, you're not the foo-foo type. We plan to go live at five am tomorrow. The vamps can sleep on the way over and we'll have a command center set up before they rise. Miller should have more info on Le Glaute Industries by the briefing tonight."

"Sounds good. I'm going to go see if Percy made it to the lab, or if he's still chewing his breakfast." As Helga rose to depart, Colonel Maddox stuck his head out of his office.

"Doc, how's Doctor Seizemore handling life with the Vamp Squad?"

"Not sure yet, Colonel. I'll let you know when I find him."

The Colonel shot her a thumbs-up and ducked back into his office.

Helga found Percy in her lab scanning the genetic code derived from the sample of TPS. He didn't even look up at the whooshing of the lab door. "So vampires have a triple helix genetic code. It all makes sense now. Well, I mean, the genetics make sense. Vampires? Not so much, but I'm working on it."

"So anything new on the horizon?" Helga meant the research horizon.

"Sure. Everything I believed about human genetics is down the toilet. My sci-fi world has crashed into my scientific world. I'm closeted underground with vampires. I'm not sure who is human and who is not, and you're walking around like everything is just normal. I would say that is a new horizon. Actually, a new universe." He raised his eyes to Helga's face with a steely stare. "How the hell did you get hooked up with these…do you call them people?"

"Yes, Percy. We are all people. Humans are just that, human. Vampires are mutated humans. Our vamps live on synthetic blood products." Helga looked apologetically at her friend. "It's a lot to accept. When we figure out this newest threat, I'll show you all of the documentation."

"So how do I know who's who, or who's what? How am I supposed to keep working on this…?" His voice broke.

"The same way I did, Percy. Colonel Maddox's team found me in my depression at our old beach cabin. I was drinking myself into oblivion after the fire. He convinced me, he needed me more than the fish offshore. So I went with him instead of taking a walk into the ocean. I didn't care where, or what, or how… or anything." She looked at her hands. "He gave me the kind of puzzle I could not resist. His daughter. She's a vampire. It's a long story, but he built this place and the Vamp Squad to protect her. Miller, bless his black heart, found Elizabetta to teach Susannah how to live. Maddox couldn't kill his daughter when he found out what she had become. You think vampirism is hard for you to understand and accept. Try being a hard-as-nails Army Colonel!"

"I *cannot* imagine." It was a dry statement but Percy could see how Colonel Maddox might be a hard nut to crack. "So how'd his daughter get...become a vampire? I mean, don't you have to get bit by another... holy shit. How many of these things are there?"

"These *things* are mutated humans and can live successfully among us, given appropriate resources. And I have no idea how many vampires exist. Obviously more than you see here. Susannah's sire, the one who made her a vampire, was destroyed and so was most of the coven he came from. The others have vowed to live as Techno-Vamps. They don't live on human blood. Only naturist vamps live on warm blood from humans or animals. There is so much to tell you about vampire society. But that has to be a subject for later. Right now we have a serious threat to figure out."

"TPS. So...now I realize this drug is infused with vamp blood. Right?" Percy went back to his screen. "Do genetic samples for vampires..." He said the word and didn't choke. Step one. "...work the same way they do for humans, individual to the vampire. Right?"

"Yes. We know that much." Helga agreed. "Each vampire sire's genetic code is related to the progeny and the virus that creates the vampire is also related. It somehow recognizes its progeny." Helga put her hands up to stop the questions. "I know it sounds impossible for a virus to be sentient, but trust me, it is. It's called Vampticious Meticulosus Deliriotum, or VMD and it knows it's own."

"VMD huh? Knows its own, huh? Then this stuff must *know its own*. Right?" Percy's mind was spinning again, but much more productively this time. "If its owner is around, then it should know it. Right?"

"Well, therein lies a problem. It seems to react to every vampire. We don't know why, but it is like crack to an addict. We still don't know why a vampire would create something so dangerous to vampires and introduce it to humans. We don't know how it effects vampires if they touch it or ingest it because they are so out of control in its presence, we don't dare test it." Helga paced back and forth in front of Percy's computer. "And why would he or she, introduce it into the human system if it kills the human? All good questions. All unanswered at the moment."

Percy had grabbed Tommy's file and was scanning through the data. "This file is ridiculous. There is nothing here. How did you get the sample from Lucy?"

Helga stopped pacing. "Well... that's another one of those things you'll have to take on faith. Even I don't completely understand how Natalia did it. She has this talent."

Now it was Percy's turn to hold up his hands. "White or black?"

"Definitely black. She is Rasputin's daughter. When she killed him, she somehow assimilated his power and abilities. They magnified her own, that's kind of how it works." Helga realized she was revealing more than she wanted to about the team members. "Anyway, she is a super compeller. She somehow got inside Lucy's brain and destroyed TPS but got a sample. Jackie helped."

"Wait, Jackie's white, right?" Percy was a little confused. "Rasputin, the guy in Russian history?"

"Well, yes... and no. Jackie is human, but she has ESP... or something." Helga scrunched up her nose. "We're not certain. Natalia didn't even know until she needed to borrow some strength... oh God. I'm making this more complicated than it was. Jackie was there. She helped some way or another. Voila – TPS sample." She pointed to the silver containment box.

"Okay, on faith, the TPS sample came from Lucy. Got it. Too bad we don't have a sample from Tommy to compare the genetic code. Then we would know if there is only one creator or more." Percy pulled out a small notebook and scribbled something.

"Good point. There is another bit of information I've left out." She looked apologetic again. "The precipitate you came up with. We are very familiar with it. We actually have a sample here in the vault."

"What?" Percy jumped up. "We have both parts of the equation! Where is it?"

"Percy, wait. The chemical you described is called Crysillus Extract. It's a drug developed for vampires by Proctor Pharmaceutical. Long story short, it is as destructive and addictive to vampires as meth is to humans. We destroyed the source. Or so we thought. In light of this stuff, we may need to re-evaluate that intel."

"Why in the world would Proctor Pharmaceuticals develop a drug for vampires? I worked on contract for them. And how do they know about vampires? Oh please don't tell me…" Percy put his hands over his ears. "La la la la la…"

"Percy! Stop that. If you must know, Proctor, the owner of the company, was a vampire with his own naturist coven. He was trying to develop a drug to addict other vampires so he could control them. He had plans to control the entire US. But that's another story. We stopped it."

His brain was erupting in revolt. Percy stood up and began to twirl in a circle with his hands on his head. "I can't take any more of this. Is the whole world infected with vampires?"

Helga grabbed Percy and stopped his twirl. "Listen, you are getting Vampire 101, 201, and 301 in one fell swoop. It's not what you are thinking, and there is so much more to the entire picture. Right now, let's figure out TPS. Okay?" She kept ahold of him as he swerved dizzily.

"O-K-A-Y. Let go." Helga knew Percy did not like to be held in restraint, but he was swaying back and forth dangerously. His vertigo had set in with the twirling.

"Alright, but grab the chair first." She let go and shoved his office chair at him.

As Percy slid into his chair, still weaving back and forth, Doctor Anderson pulled up the chemical formula for Crysillus Extract on her monitor. "This is the original formula. Your version has this formula and another simple precipitate. Well, not so simple, but you get the picture."

"Right." The vertigo had fled in light of a new scientific challenge. He was back staring at the screen. "So how do we identify the vampire who belongs to the genetic material? Is there a catalog somewhere? Can I see more genetic codes? Like from one of the vampires here?"

"I guess that would be alright. I have genetic samples from all of our team members. Take your pick." Helga hit a series of keys and up popped thumbnails of the human and vampire team members' genetic pictures. "We keep all medical data on our team in case someone gets hurt on a mission."

"So these are obviously human." He pointed to the column on the left. "And these are triple so they are vampire, correct?" He pointed to the column on the right. "Hel-lo." Percy pointed to the third box in the column. "This is very similarr to the code from TPS. But not exactly the same."

"That sample belongs to Monique." Helga supplied the name for Percy.

"No, no, no, no! That gorgeous blonde is a black? The one who calls me an elf? Impossible!" Percy shook his head sadly. "I had dinner with her... no, I had dinner. She only drank..." Percy winced and shuddered.

Helga had a firm grasp on Percy's name for vampires. "Yes, she uses the back fridge. She is a vampire, Percy. You may want to be careful about the use of black in reference to vampires, we have a couple black humans around here. One very big human you met this morning."

"Oh, ah, yeah. Right. Monique is a vampire? Such a shame. I though we had something in common. I was starting to like her."

"Liking is not dependent on the species, Percy. Give it some time. All of this is so new to you. Monique is a lovely girl and very hurt by her background. She has issues with Monks. You probably figured that out, but that is her story to tell." Helga began pacing again. "The Colonel is sending part of the team to San Leyre, undercover, to see what they can turn up at the monastery. They head out in the morning. We have specific knowledge of this place. We liberated Monique from the Monks there a few years back. She was almost gone when we found her and brought her here." Helga paused.

She gave Percy a curious look then rushed to the computer. "You thinking what I'm thinking, Doctor Anderson?" Percy watched his cohort hectically searching for something... some connection.

"Monique came from San Leyre. The kids are getting TPS from somewhere at San Leyre. The genetic material is similar to Monique's genetic code. Could there be a link to another vampire from around there?"

Helga took a deep breath and exhaled rapidly. "How would we ever know?"

"Ask Monique." It was a simple answer, but impossible at the same time.

Percy had no idea how traumatized the pretty vampire was from her time with the torturous monks in the dungeons of San Leyre. Dragging up her history with all kinds of questions could be even more traumatic for the sweet blonde.

Helga wrinkled her brow. "It might be better to ask Susannah. She and Monique are like sisters, only closer." Helga laughed. "If that's possible."

"Well, where can I find Susannah?" Percy looked directly at Helga. "Oh, yeah. Black fridge."

"She'll be at the briefing tonight. She usually rises just before sundown. Even underground the solar cycle effects baby vamps. Susannah is only a few years old. I'll make sure you two find a quiet place to talk."

Percy shot his cohort a serious look. "Alone? With a baby vamp?"

"You'll be fine. Susannah only drinks synth-blood. And she is a dedicated operative." Helga gave a little huff. "And she will be your best source of information, short of Monique herself."

"Okay, but I am putting my blood in your hands!"

The intercom buzzer sounded. Helga depressed the button on her desk phone. "Yes, Miller?"

"I got some interesting intel about your favorite cosmetic company." There was a touch of excitement in the Sergeant's voice.

"On our way."

Chapter 17

Baggage

The past is only a memory of what was.
We carry its baggage through life because,
Without its foundation, a building will fall,
And without our history, there is no *all*.

We need roots, a semblance of family and self,
More than stories, and pictures on a shelf.
To be grounded and whole, an individual must know,
From whence they came, for all to show.

And in the twilight of times, we choose to leave,
Who we were, how we lived, the stories we did weave,
A picture of life, of family and such,
The truth for those, we love so much.

*Elizabetta Zoeltel, Coven Mistress*
*Olney Farm, Maine, 2013*


Colonel Maddox sat at the head of the table surveying his team. It was growing exponentially. He wasn't sure if that was a good thing, or a bad thing. Since he'd discovered the truth about vampires, his entire world had expanded...exponentially, as well.

"The spec ops plan was loaded into your computers this morning. New intel is up on the screen. Sergeant Miller, if you please."

"Yes, Sir." Miller motioned to the slide on the SmartBoard. "Le Glaute Industries, shown here, is the major source of financial support for San Leyre. It provides the monastery with the ability to remain independent of the Vatican's political and financial strings, much to the Vatican's dismay. Apparently there are significant differences in the philosophy and mission of the monastery and their parent organization, so to speak. What those differences are, is a closely guarded secret. However, we are aware of a very specific mission that provided us with one beautiful operative,

213

much to the dismay of the residents of the monastery." Miller clicked his handheld remote and nodded at Monique. "The Very Reverend Father Songoria has made it clear he represents the Vatican and is investigating the death of Brother Berthold, a monk who supposedly hanged himself at the monastery. The same Brother Berthold who, we now know, provided Thomas and Lucy with his newly developed energy drink." Pictures of the individuals under discussion appeared, as the Sergeant continued with his briefing. "The Abbott of San Leyre is a very venerated priest and has been in place for over 40 years. He controls his small community with a very tight hand. He claims to know nothing about Brother Berthold's suicide and feigns sorrow at the loss of a member of the priesthood, but has very efficiently seen to the disposal of the body without autopsy or governmental process. It seems the Church is the law in this case."

"That is putting it mildly, Sergeant." Doctor Seizemore commented quietly.

Sergeant Miller continued. "The school, Academia de Santos Domingo de Silos, was established in 1745 and only closed once during a Basque revolt. In the early 1900s, most of the royalty of Europe sent their children there for education. The standard of education provided is exemplary, and their sports program is famous for how many championships they have won."

"Now that's my kind of hoity-toity school!" Ted smacked the table causing Dr. Seizemore to jump in his seat. "Sorry Doc. I forgot you're a newbie." Ted smiled at the anxious doctor. Ted pointed to his chest with both index fingers and mouthed *white fridge*.

Percy already knew Ted was human and couldn't tell if the reference was a joke or reassurance.

"Le Glaute Industries is a family owned corporation. The current president is the fourth generation Le Glaute to run the company. The family name dates back to before the French Revolution. Needless to say, for the ladies in the audience, it is a very popular and highly rated cosmetics and beauty supply company. Headquartered in France, they have labs throughout Europe. Coincidently, one lab is located in Yesa, a stones throw from the monastery. Company assets exceed two point six trillion Euros a year. That's about two point eight six trillion American dollars." Miller smiled at Susannah's soft gasp. "It goes without saying, this family can well afford to support the entire monastery, and the school if they chose."

Monique sat quietly but blanched at the name Le Glaute.

Could it be?

Could all of this be related to him?

Her sire?

Impossible!

He was destroyed.

She saw it, as she and Mathilda escaped the mad crowd of revolutionaries who set fire to his estate and dragged him off. He was beheaded in front of the Committee for Public Safety!

A vampire beheaded was destroyed.

He could not have survived.

Monique shifted uneasily in her chair.

"So who is this family? Are they suspect in this mess we are investigating?" Captain Devlin adjusted his sore leg with a groan.

"That's the clincher, Captain." More pictures appeared. Houses, buildings, cosmetic samples and all manner of advertisements flashed across the screen. "There are no pictures of the family members available anywhere. Now that, in and of itself is suspicious in this day and age." Miller shook his head. "I could not find one clear picture of the patriarch, parents, kids, aunts, uncles, nada, nit, nothing."

"Now I am impressed. The Mill-man has been defeated!" Ted let out a whoop and once again Percy jumped. "Sorry, man."

Ted did the white fridge thing again with his thumbs.

Percy adjusted uncomfortably in his chair.

"It's pretty hard to stay off the Internet radar with every human being owning a phone with a camera, so I either have a great deal of respect for the guy who avoids all media, or a singularly deep suspicion."

"Are you thinking like a shell corporation? A shell family? Maybe the family doesn't really exist, but the story is for the press. Makes the product seem more personal and nurtured, like Este Lauder cosmetics. Only she was real." Susannah volunteered her opinion.

"Good point, Suze. But someone is signing paychecks and making deals in person. Here's an article about Monsieur Le Glaute's gala at The Four Seasons Hotel George V. It was built in 1928, just off the Champs-Elysées." Opulent pictures appeared, one after another.

Monique peered at the pictures. Some of the building was familiar from her human days, but the Champs-Elysées looked nothing like it did in her time. She sighed softly. Nothing was left of her human existence except the memories that haunted her dreams.

"Here're pictures of the affair. Not one shows its organizer or any of the family members." The last picture showed the back of a tall statuesque man in a tuxedo surrounded by obviously wealthy people hanging on his every word. The man's hair was mid-length and clearly styled in a sophisticated manner. The only identifiable parts of the man that could be seen were one ear and the tip of his nose. "The caption on this picture from The Guardian indicates this is the head of the Le Glaute dynasty. It's media. Who knows if it is fake news or someone captured a part of **Monsieur Le Glaute. I have nothing to compare it with.**"

"Ah heck, I'd recognize that guy anywhere." Captain Devlin snorted.

"Yes, Sir. And therein lies the problem. We know his company, his estates, his pant size, his favorite drink, his income, his everything… but his face."

"So, is that important, Sergeant?" Doctor Anderson was puzzled.

"Not unless he is part of this crazy mystery. It's pretty hard to tell right now. But maybe when we have boots on the ground, we can determine what role, if any, Le Glaute Industries or Monsieur Le Glaute himself, plays." Colonel Maddox's comment made sense. He stood, pointing to several of the operatives and support team members in the room. "Mr. and Mrs. M, Susannah, Elizabetta, the V Team, we bug out before dawn. Doctors," he bowed to the two doctors at the table. "Please continue your outstanding work here in the complex."

Monique almost took a breath, expecting his finger to point her way. What blood she did have in her face, drained to wherever it could drain to, and she paled even more than usual.

But the finger point never came.

"See you all on the flip side." The Colonel made his exit, shortly thereafter, followed by a nervous Monique Merchant.

"Sir?"

"Yes, Ms. Merchant?" He paused in his office doorway.

"What is my assignment, Sir?" Monique had to ask the question, despite fearing the answer.

"You'll be holding the fort down right here, Ma'am. Suze told me about the dreams." His voice was only loud enough for Monique to hear. Actually, Monique and the rest of the vampires in the facility, but no humans. "I will not put one of my team members at risk, even for this mission." He softly patted her arm. "Stay here. Stay safe. Help the doctors. Work on getting rid of those nasty dreams."

Monique was totally taken aback. She'd never seen the softer side of Susannah's father. And a physical touch? The Colonel was definitely getting used to vampires... and his softer side.

And he cared!

Monique was close to tears.

No one had cared about her like that since... since...

She couldn't remember.

"Come on, Frenchy. You can help me organize and pack." Susannah saved the day, dragging Monique down the hall towards the vamp quarters, before things became awkward. "And I promise not to wear mom's watch, Dad." Susannah commented to her father.

The Colonel waved them along. The watch Susannah referred to was a sore spot that had healed nicely since their last mission. Her lost watch caused a snafu that put Captain Devlin in the hospital and jeopardized the entire team. But since Susannah began taking her training seriously, and turned into quite the operative, her father no longer worried about his daughter's behavior. It was up to par and he was a proud boss and father.

"See you in a bit." Maddox retreated into his office and slid the glass door shut. Tears were never good with him. Human or vamp.

"Hey, didn't I tell you Dad would figure it out and keep you away from those monks? I must say, he has developed EI. Finally..." Susannah dragged Monique through the lounge toward her room at a trot.

"What is e-eye mean? And stop pulling me!" Monique jerked to a halt. "I will never return to San Leyre. Never." Her tears finally let loose. "I am so... he can not...Susannah!" Monique dissolved into Susannah's arms smearing red tears across her sister-vampire's t-shirt.

"It'll be okay, Frenchy. EI is an acronym, letters that stand for words. It means emotional intelligence. Like IQ stands for smarts. Never mind." Susannah pulled a tissue from the back pocket of her jeans. She'd taken to having tissue around since the whole San Leyre thing began. It saved on stain remover. "Here. Clean up those tears. We can talk while I pack."

Monique let Susannah drag her into Susannah's bedroom and close the door. Deposited on her sister vampire's bed, her eyes continued leaking their deep red tears. Soon a pile of tissues began to grow on the night stand. A large duffle bag flew toward Monique and landed on the floor before she was able to even consider catching it.

"So spill the beans. What's the worst that can happen? We'll be checking things out and you'll be here with Miller, monitoring the situation." Susannah began throwing clothing at Monique. She missed each toss. The duffle was on the floor and a disarrayed stack of clothing lay tangled on the bed in front of her.

"Susannah, J'ai tellement peur. Afraid. There. Here. If this Le Glaute is…" Monique burst into tears again, sobbing all over the pile of clothing.

"Whoa! What are you getting at?" Now Monique had Susannah's full attention. She felt herself pulled from the bed into a close chair. "If Le Glaute is what? Who?" Susannah tossed a box of tissues toward Monique.

"I never use his name. Not after…" More sobbing and red tissue. The stack on the bedside table was precariously leaning. "He cannot be alive, Susannah. I saw him... During Le Règne de la Terreur." Hiccup and more tears. "Il a été guillotine." Monique was so enveloped in fear she could feel her heart begin to beat erratically.

"You mean…" Susannah drew her hand across her neck in a slicing motion.

"Oui." Monique repeated the motion. "Détruit. He cannot have survived and he was the last of his line." She whispered his name, "Phillipe Le Glaute, Duc d'Orleans. He was more often called Phillipe, Comte d' LeEgalité during the Revolution."

"And you are sure you saw him… détruit?" Susannah stood motionless, her mind a flurry of activity. "Come on. We better go see Elizabetta."

More dragging of Monique and within seconds the two vampires sat before their coven mistress.

"Houston, we have a problem!" Susannah did not consider the fact that neither of her companions would know what she meant with that statement, but she continued on. "Monique's sire was a Le Glaute. She says he was guillotined in what?" She turned to Monique for help.

"Oui, in the fall. Eighteen ninety-three. Novembre septième, dix-huit-quatre-vingt-treize." Elizabetta handed Monique a box of tissues, patting her daughter on the hand.

"Then there is no worry, daughter. He is destroyed. I know of no vampire beheaded who has survived, or come back from destruction. Sergeant Miller's Le Glaute cannot be the man you fear so."

"But the DNA evidence? His home? The fact that there are no pictures of him? I am thinking shades of Dorian Gray. He faked his death and recreated himself every once in a while to survive in society. Could this Le Glaute be... what? A first? Maybe it was someone else on the guillotine? He was some relation of the French King and I would assume he had power back then." Susannah was weaving a conspiracy theory at warp speed. "Money at least. According to my high school world history class, money was almost as important as political beliefs during the French Revolution."

Monique began to shake. "But I saw his face. He had grown a beard in the Conciergerie. He was taken to the Place de la Révolution to be beheaded. I saw it all. With my own eyes." Her deep sobs punctuated each sentence. "At sunset. Mathilda and I hid in the sewers. But we saw. And we celebrated...quietly." Monique dabbed at her eyes and blew her nose.

"Possibly you should see Doctor Anderson and Doctor Seizemore about this idea. He had sons, this Phillipe Le Glaute, did he not? Before he was turned?"

"Oui, Elizabetta. One became King for a short time. But he had a very short life." She made the slicing motion across her throat again.

"Possibly this company, Le Glaute Industries, is from a nephew." Elizabetta volunteered.

Monique had not considered her sire's human relations. She began to calm down and the tears ceased to flow so profusely. "C'est peut-être possible. I shall go and find the doctors immediately."

With fresh insight and somewhat less fear, Monique rushed from the room.

"Well, that was interesting." Susannah shook her head with

a grin. "Guess I'll go finish preparations, now that we've stemmed the blood bath." Susannah pushed the stack of tear stained tissues into the small trashcan next to the table.

"And I shall begin. This investigation is becoming more and more interesting. It does give me pause to wonder. If Monique is sure her sire was beheaded, he must be destroyed. Possibly one of his relations had taken his place? Or like your Jordi, this Le Glaute turned his son? Interesting."

Susannah considered the idea for a moment, then took her leave. There would be time to find the connections once they could do a proper investigation on site. That would happen late tomorrow at the monastery. Monique would be safe, and somewhat sound, at Olney Farm while the team provided the necessary clandestine recon at San Leyre. They would find the answer to the mystery of TPS. They would stop whoever was poisoning the students. She pulled out her cell phone and hit the speed dial. The call went directly to voice mail. "Is this the new, super sexy Chief Research Officer at Proctor Pharmaceuticals? I heard he was easy, so I thought I'd call for a late hook-up." Susannah giggled seductively. "Miss you Jordi. We bug out to- morrow. Call you from France. Love you, babe."

******

It was close to three o'clock in the morning. Percy's eyes were burning but his mind was in full swing. He had spoken briefly with Susannah and gotten the CliffsNotes version of Monique's history. It was just one more stack of fuel that fired his hatred of Catholicism and the ancient, sick, secret society that manipulated so many people's devotion to belief in God and the words of the Bible. He sat in the dining area munching yogurt covered pistachios and thinking. Since coming to Olney Farm, he'd taken up munching instead of pulling on his ears when he was in deep thought. Habits weren't the only thing that were changing. His entire belief system was morphing into... something. Something not so concretely scientific any more. Something so different than it had been, just a few short days before. He tossed a handful of nuts into his mouth. Several missed, bouncing off his rumpled t-shirt to hit the table. Deep in thought, he ignored them.

"S'il vous plaît! Did those who raised you never teach you to clean yourself?" Monique had appeared behind Percy.

He jumped at the sound of her voice, dumping the bowl of nuts all over the table and floor.

"Merde! Regardez ce que vous avez fait." She moved with vamp speed to the closet and returned with a broom and dustpan. "Il n'y a pas de femmes de ménage dans cette maison."

"Whoa... Ms. Merchant, I do not speak French. Remember?" Percy was stunned by her split-second movement... and the fact that she wanted him to clean up after himself.

"I am aware of that." Her nose was in the air as she held the broom and pan out to him. "I must see Doctor Anderson. Do you know where she is?"

"She retired to bed hours ago. She will be up in time to see the rest of the team off on their mission." He eyed the broom and pan.

"Bien. I will see her then." Monique thrust the broom toward Percy.

He popped a couple nuts in his mouth from the tabletop and carefully took the broom and dustpan from the vampire. "Can't you just make them go poof and disappear, or something?"

"Do not be ridicule. Making go poof is not one of my gifts." She took a bag of synth-blood from the black refrigerator and slapped it to her fangs. Sucking the bag dry while an open-mouthed Percy watched, was tit-for-tat in her book. She tossed the bag in the trash and burped loudly, just like Jackie had taught her.

Percy paled.

Monique smiled sweetly as she turned with a flourish and headed back to the vamp quarters. Percy would learn not to make fun of Monique Alys Merchant! Make things go poof! Pah...

For the first time in a very long time, Percy's mind was blank. His brain ceased to work. He sat holding a broom and dustpan for quite some time, starring at the retreating beauty who had just polished off a pint of O-Positive and belched with satisfaction! When he finally came to, Monique was gone. Nuts still covered the table and floor and another very important thing in Percy's life was beginning to change. A dopey kind of grin plastered itself across his face as he bent to sweep the floor and collect the stray nuts. His mind settled on a short mantra that could not be ignored. God, she was beautiful!

God, she was beautiful...

God, she was... Percy dumped the dustpan into the trash and shook his head. God had very little to do with what she was.

That famous saying crept out of the trash and smacked him on the forehead; *A fish may love a bird, but where would they live?*

His dopey grin faded as he headed back to the lab. His fantasies had little to do with his reality. The woman, neh… female vampire, hated him. But he could still wish…

## Chapter 18

### Questions...

If love is the answer, what is the question?
From whom do we seek, that perfect affection?
Do we search for a mate so rare,
Or settle for a more simple fare?

You might as well ask great scientific minds,
Who created the universe or made atoms bind.
It is a mystery for the ages,
Remembered in tomes, from ancient pages.

*Bambi Sanders, Poet and Pole Dancer Extraordinaire*
*Madame Shiela's Respectable Establishment,*
*New Orleans, 2015*

Jackie leaned over Milo's shoulder watching the monitors above as the Vamp Squad headed out. "Nice transport, Milo. I kind of wish I was going too, but I have to finish setting up my classes for the last semester."

"Hey, no sweat. There'll be more missions down the line. You're kind of close to the problem. Not that I don't think you'd handle the situation appropriately, but if someone almost killed *my* brother, I might think seriously about returning the favor." He grinned up at his sorta-girlfriend.

"Well, don't get any ideas about how sweet I am all the time. I have a mean side there, buster." She poked him in a spot that always made other parts of him respond inappropriately. "But I'm so close to graduating, I need to get it done. I also promised the General I'd follow through. Not that *that* is my primary motivation. I want to do this for myself, and the Vamp Squad. I was serious when I said I feel like I belong here. I don't have to pretend to be normal around people who don't understand." Her arms slid around Milo's neck and she peered over his shoulder. "There they go."

He held up his hand for quiet, then spoke into the

microphone. "Tango five-niner-six, safe flight." Milo signed off. "I know exactly what you are talking about. Believe me. Not much to do for the next few hours. I'm going to hit the hay for some shut eye." He rubbed his scruffy face. He hadn't shaved in thirty-six hours with the hectic plans for this mission underway. "Later on, how about we go topside for lunch and some ice cream? I haven't been into town for a few days. I like to keep tabs on the locals, just in case something starts brewing. Maybe take Mandy and Roger with us?"

"I think that's a great idea. I should have my registration done and my final graduation review request in by then. Say, eleven hundred hours? I love this military talk!" Jackie trotted down the hall. At the secure door she turned, "Meet you back here."

"Roger that, Jacks." Milo smiled to himself. He was making progress. It certainly didn't hurt that Jackie was joining the ranks as a full-fledged team member. He was hoping, God willing and the creeks don't rise; she'd be joining his family, too. He sent a quick lunch invite to Mandy and Roger up top, then headed for his quarters and some much needed sleep.

******

After the team's noisy departure, Monique found Doctor Anderson in the lounge munching a bowl of Oreos and milk for breakfast. Actually it was more like slurping a black and white mushy mess, but breakfast, none-the-less. A hot cup of coffee steamed next to the bowl of Oreo goop.

"Doctor Anderson, I would like to have words with you." Monique took the chair across from Helga. She yawned and shook her head. Day sleep was calling and she was not immune to its draw.

"Of course, dear. What words would you like?" Doctor Anderson was used to Monique crucifying the English language.

"I was talking to Susannah… and Elizabetta. You know my background and my sire, but I am not sure you know his… I think you say… common name? He was called Phillipe Le Glaute." Monique paused to let the name settle in.

"As in Le Glaute Industries? Hmm… and?"

"I was very afraid that he… the DNA for TPS is close to mine. You and the elf doctor think it is infused with vampire

224

blood, no? So I thought maybe," Her voice dropped to a whisper. "Possibly he lives. My sire?"

Immediately Helga could feel Monique's fear. Was her proximity to vampires beginning to change her? Was she starting to feel their *feelings*? Interesting...

Monique continued. "I asked Elizabetta. She says she knows no vampire who was beheaded and survived. I saw him guillotined... but I am so afraid." Monique clasped her shaking hands together. "I have dreams... they began some time ago, but then... this mission... at that place." She did not even want to say its name out loud. Giving voice to your hideous fear was like saying Candyman three times. She'd seen that movie. It did not end in a good way.

"Well, I am not sure if there is a way to isolate the genetic strain that is his, from your blood. You are his only progeny left alive, correct?" Helga was intently contemplating her blackish goo.

"Oui, oui. Mathilda and I were the only two who escaped when the Revolutionaries came to burn the estate and arrest the Duc d'Orleans... Phillipe. We ran so deep into the grottes, they did not follow." Monique covered her face with both hands. "We could hear the screams and smell the burning... C'était horrible!"

"Shush now. Do not think about that time. You are here now, and we will figure this thing out. Together. It is unfortunate your friend did not survive. Between the two DNA samples, Percy could find the common elements and isolate your sire's DNA."

"Mathilda was a maid in the house of the infamous Mademoiselle Elliot. The Duc d'Orleans turned her so I would have a maid. C'était un tel bâtard! Bastard." Monique pounded the table. "All that is left to me is her placette d'enfance. A piece of her baby hair is inside. We hid it in the grottes. I went back later and took it."

"Monique, you continue to amaze me! You have a piece of Mathilda's hair?" Helga jumped up from her seat, setting the coffee mug to rattling.

"Oui. Mais à quoi ça sert? We cannot make her come back with a little piece of hair? Can we?"

Helga was quivering with excitement. Obviously Monique had no idea about *23 and ME*, or the process of basic genetic testing! "Unfortunately we cannot bring her back. However, I can decipher her genetic code from a hair cell. Then we can compare your genetic code and hers, rule out the non-matching alelles and have a good chance of figuring out TPS's genetic code and, voile! The vampire who contributed it!" Helga dumped the uneaten breakfast into the sink, emptied her cup and turned to Monique. "Or at least his or her genetic code. You get the hair and I'll get Percy. He'll be able to do this in half the time I can." And she was gone, off running down the hall, shouting for Doctor Seizemore.

Monique stood and watched Doctor Anderson disappear into the research wing of the facility. She still couldn't figure out how the doctors could get a code from hair since there was no blood in hair, but she was willing to try it. The locket was in her room, wrapped in tissue in a small wooden box, along with her grandmother's wedding ring. They were the only things left from her human life and she kept them safe and treasured. Locked away. Just like her human life.

Percy heard the commotion in the hallway before it registered in his dream soaked mind. He'd been on a sailboat with a beautiful blonde French woman who spoke no English. They were learning to communicate with their hands, and other things. The obvious bulge in his red flannel pajamas was a good indicator of the *other things* they'd been doing. He shook the sleep from his head.

Was that Helga's voice?

His intercom buzzed.

"Ah… Doctor Seizemore? Sorry to disturb your morning, but Doctor Anderson is hollering for you and waking the entire place up." Miller's sleepy voice came over the speaker.

He punched the red button. "I'll… look into it. Thanks… I think." Percy grabbed his well-worn robe, slipped into the overly generous arms, put a quick knot in the belt and headed for the voice. Why hadn't she just called him? Or used the intercom? What was wrong?

His bare feet slid on the polished cement as he sped for the lab, colliding with Monique as she rounded the corner. "What's wrong, Ms. Merchant? Where's Helga?"

Monique caught the sliding scientist before he hit the wall. She eyed the disheveled man in her arms. "There is nothing wrong, I think. Unless it is your fashion sense." Monique smirked as her eyes paused at the pajamas he wore and the obvious protrusion just below the waist band. She looked the scientist up and down. "Doctor Anderson is excited about hair." Monique stated as they both charged on down the hall toward the labs. Obviously the elf

226

doctor was excited about something else, Monique thought to herself.

"Hair?" Percy just about fainted.

Hair?

All that commotion over hair?

This had to be good.

He followed Monique into the lab, adjusting his pajamas.

Doctor Anderson was seated at her lab table concocting the liquid in which DNA samples would be processed. "Percy! Percy come look. Monique has Mathilda's DNA sample. We can deconstruct these two samples and see if there is a common link. Monique thinks…"

"Wait, wait, wait. I'm not awake yet, Helga. Who is Mathilda? What has Monique and Mathilda have to do with our research?"

Both women stood staring with open mouths at the frumpy scientist in baggy, red flannel pajamas and what looked like it used to be a robe of some sort. His wedge-wood colored hair was smashed against his head on one side and spiked straight up on the top. His robe lay open above the waist showing a pale, but well developed chest.

"This may be a breakthrough, Percy, but…" Helga covered her lips to disguise her unseemly giggle. "You could have taken time to dress. Is that the same robe…"

Percy looked at his toes then his robe. "Yes, it's the same robe Sarah gave me when I joined your team as a full-fledge researchist." He pulled the robe closed over his chest and tightened the belt. "And… the breakthrough?"

"Doctor Anderson, si vous plait…" Monique took a seat on the stool next to Helga's huge microscope. "Phillipe Le Glaute, the Duc d'Orleans, was my sire." She stumbled on her words but both doctors waited patiently for the story to unfold.

Helga knew what was coming and she watched Percy with a somewhat humorous eye.

"The vampire who made me a vampire. He is called my sire." Monique impatiently waved the statement away. "No matter. Phillipe Le Glaute, demon that he was, also made Mathilda a vampire." She looked up at Percy to see if he was following. "And… well… he did it for me. So I could have a maid, forever. See…" Monique's eyes began to glow a soft red.

Immediately Helga moved to Monique's side and slid a

comforting arm around the very emotional vampire. It was hard to watch, but Helga knew Monique needed to tell her story.

"I was a noblewoman, as a human. It was the French Revolution, a horrible violent time. My father was cousin to King Louis XVI. The revolutionaries came to our home…" Monique leaned her head against Helga's shoulder. "They killed everyone and burned the buildings, my house, the stables, everything."

Red rivulets marked Monique's cheeks as she continued. "The Duke was at dinner with my family when they came. He saved me and I escaped with him. Or at least I thought I escaped. But, how do you say? I jumped from the kettle to the pan."

"The frying pan into the fire, dear." Helga hugged the beautiful French vampire, then reached for a tissue to wipe the red tears from her face.

"But in the end, there was only Mathilda and me. After the Revolutionaries learned of his… affliction… they came for Phillipe and all of us, the ones he had made. He was guillotined. It was too painless an end for that monster. Mathilda and I watched from the shadows. It was a happy day for us but we were what we were, and had to survive on our own after that. Phillipe Le Glaute's entire coven was destroyed, all but the two of us. We ran and hid. In the caves." Monique blew her nose and snuffed.

Percy had no words. He mumbled, "I am so sorry."

"So was I… for a long time." Monique straightened. She did not want the elf doctor's pity. "But we survived. Until the treacherous devils from San Leyre captured us. Then I lived in hell. Mathilda and I held on to each other for many years, but the devils finally…"

Monique turned her face away and wept.

Helga held Monique as she mourned her friend. "Mathilda was destroyed in the dungeon at San Leyre. The monks there tortured her too much, then let her burn in the sun." Helga finished the story for Percy. "That is why Monique hates the Catholic monks and priests."

"Completely understandable." Percy shook his head. "And I thought I had a tough life. Just goes to show you, when you think your life is so bad, things can always be worse."

Recovering, Monique stared at the geeky scientist in the outrageous robe. "Oui, After Mathilda, I was the only one left. They were very determined to save my soul. Pah! Those devils enjoyed what they did to me. They should all burn in hell. Many times over!" Monique slammed her hand on the table. "Ow." It was a pitiful soft sound. Anger had taken the place of sorrow. Monique threw her wadded tissue toward the trashcan, missing by several feet.

Percy stooped, retrieved the bloody tissue and tossed it into the can. "I completely agree with you, Ms. Merchant. Completely."

"You do?" Monique was confused. On one hand this scientist challenged everything she was. On the other, he could be almost … charming. He'd picked up her tissue without a second thought. And agreed with her about the priests. Possibly, he wasn't so bad after all… for an elf. Like the jumbled, chaotic, incongruencies that made up the stunning French vampire, Monique's feelings about the good doctor just… changed. And just like that, the charm switch flipped from odium to affection, she smiled the only way she knew how, sweet and seductive.

Monique's radiant smile gave Percy a definite reason to tug at his tattered robe and move toward the table. He'd never seen such a smile in all his life. Not directed at him anyway…

In for a penny, in for a pound was Monique's trademark. And she was in for the pound. "That is so sweet for an elf." She batted her eyes at him… on purpose.

"Yes, well…" Percy was suddenly without words. The red began at the collar of his robe and proceeded upward at a rapid rate. "I…" Percy cleared his throat. "We should get to work then, and figure out this genetic puzzle." He turned toward his computer console. "Your friend's hair may be the missing piece we have been looking for." Percy rubbed his unshaven face and sat down, the early wake-up call catching up with him as the initial adrenaline surge began to wear off.

"Oui, how can I help?" Monique jiggled with excitement. "These science things are so much fun."

Doctor Anderson shook her head with a smile. "Dear, this will be a long process with very little you and I can do. Percy must concentrate and prepare the samples then process… never mind. There isn't much to do." She patted Monique's shoulder and rose.

Percy's fingers were flying over his keyboard, but his ears worked just fine… and he wanted to keep the object of his recent fantasy around, if he possibly could. He wasn't quite sure about Monique, but she stirred things in him like no other woman ever had. In fact, there had been no other women, period. This was totally new territory and Percy was ready to jump into the deep end. "I could use a hand." He kept his eyes on his monitor as he patted the chair next to him.

Monique giggled.

Helga's jaw hit the floor.

It took a few minutes for the good doctor to find the appropriate words...and they weren't really that appropriate. "Well then... I'll just... go get a cup...of Joe, I guess."

Again Monique giggled as she quickly moved to sit next to the elf doctor. "Absurdité Doctor Anderson, you do not bite humans. Not even a human named Joe, whoever that may be." She turned her brilliant smile toward Percy who audibly gulped.

"Monique, dear, a cup of... oh never mind." Helga sauntered toward the door with a quick glance at her cohort. "Percy, you'll be okay?"

Percy mumbled something Helga interpreted as *sure* just before the door swished open. "Okay then, I'll... um..." She exited her lab with a feeble wave toward the two individuals that sat close, peering at a single computer monitor.

Through the window she saw Percy point at something on his monitor as Monique bounced up and down in her chair... very close to Dr. Seizemore. The only thing that Helga could think was... Percy has no idea what he is getting himself into! And Monique has no idea how vulnerable Percy actually is. She strolled toward their kitchen facility deep in thought.

"Yo, Doc," Jackie sat at a table with her laptop computer open. "I have a kind of personal question. Do you have a minute?"

"I sure do and a little diversion may be exactly what I need right now." Helga smiled at the newest member of the Vamp Squad's human team.

"I just finished getting my classes all set up and I've been thinking." Jackie was obviously trying to get to some point so Helga sat quietly, listening. "You know when that little vamp, Fiona, popped in? And she shook my hand, then went kind of weird on me?"

"Yes?" Helga poured herself a cup of coffee then added a small shot of vanilla cream to the cup.

"Well, she called me something like brighten. I've been searching spellings of the word and finally I think I hit pay dirt." Jackie frowned at the doctor.

"And?" Helga waited patiently.

"And I found the word Braughtenin." She turned her laptop

around to face the doctor. "That was the word she called me. Braughtenin. Look." Jackie stood and leaned over the laptop to point to a graphic at the top of the screen.

Helga peered at a hideous picture of a creature with sharp pointed teeth, huge glowing eyes and long sharp claws. The thing had small lizard-like wings and a tail that ended in what could only be called a devil's spike. The creature had long brilliant red hair and a gossamer gown that flowed about its limbs as if the material were part of its body. A vicious fanged snake served as a waist belt for the garment, and the thing held a heavily bejeweled sword that gleamed with some kind of glowing light.

"I read the description and the history of the mythical creatures. They were small warriors that terrorized the cultures that inhabited Europe and the British Isles. They were pre-Druid, or there-abouts. According to the legends, the Braughtenin females had talents like vampires. They ate their enemies, Doctor Anderson!" Jackie sat down with a plop and pointed to the laptop. "Why does she think I am... that?"

"Good question." Helga scanned the text. "They disappeared before the Roman's set out to conquer the north. I don't know much about Fiona and where she came from, but I do know she is old Celtic and she was some kind of princess or royalty." Helga turned the laptop toward its owner. "It says here they were also seers. They would guide certain people or groups they liked."

"As in liked-like, or liked the taste of?" Jackie shuttered. "I don't even like rare meat."

At that comment, Helga had to laugh. "My world just gets stranger and stranger. A female vampire is in my lab, flirting with a virginal scientist, and you think you might be a descendant of some weird little cannibalistic creature from ancient times. I think I need another cup of Jo... coffee."

"I think I need to talk to this Fiona a little more."

"Good luck with that one, Jackie. She is an enigma in and of herself. She comes and goes as she pleases and is one of the most powerful vampires I have ever met. She dotes on the Librarian for the Council of Elders, who happens to be her husband, and has more information in her little finger than the Library of Congress."

"That's exactly what I need. Do you think she'll talk to me? Or maybe I can talk to this Librarian?" Jackie's enthusiasm was clearly not subdued by Fiona's position.

"Jackie, you don't understand vampire society at all. It's best you take this slow and talk to Elizabetta or Natalia first. The Council of Elders do not trifle with humans…much. We," Helga drew a circle around her head, "are kind of an exception. But still we do not ask them questions. We sorta speak when spoken to, as the case may be." Helga sipped her second cup of coffee. "Fiona, I don't know about."

"She curtsied to me, like I was something special. That doesn't exactly mesh with what I read about the Braughtenin." Jackie pointed to the image on the screen again.

"Well, in any event, you'll have to wait until this mess with TPS is resolved. Fiona cannot be allowed near the stuff, or any of the Council members. They are the most powerful vampires in our world and who knows what they would do."

"Right." Jackie shut her laptop. "The team should be on the ground around 7:30 their time. They are landing at Rhein-Main Air Base then direct to Pamplona. Then they will go on from there to Yesa and meet the Policia Floral representative. They've rented a chalet-type place near the monastery and are undercover as a group of eccentric tourists interested in historical architecture."

"Sergeant Miller is so imaginative. He never ceases to amaze me with his ingenuity." Doctor Anderson laughed, watching Jackie's reaction.

"He sure has become an important member of this team. It sort of amazes me. I was so angry, for so long, about our break-up. Now I see this place and how everyone works together and seems to mesh. Honestly I feel like I've come home, sort of." Jackie sighed wistfully. "I just hope I measure up. I've been training with Susannah and Aunt Mandy, but everything is so new… and boy do I mean everything." She pointed at the black fridge. "Me, Milo and Aunt Mandy and Uncle Roger are going for ice cream in town after noon. Wanna come?"

"I'd love to, but Percy and Monique are working on a genetic test and…"

"What? Sexpot and the pre-pubescent scientist are alone together? Working? Monique can hardly put a sentence together let alone a genetic code. She's French and Percy's Geekoid! How's that gonna work out?" Jackie was getting a great deal of humor out of the situation.

Helga was simply worried.

"I know. I'm a little concerned. I know Percy's background. His time in the orphanage and the impact it had on him. I worry about his fragile heart. Monique is such a…" Helga gave Jackie a kind of blank look.

"A sexual predator looking for willing participants? A nymphomaniac with a heart of gold? How about a Brigit Bardot look alike with fangs? I hope Percy isn't anemic. Her kind of love could kill him… accidently of course. She's actually funny and nice, but around men she seems to go into a divide and conquer mentality. She'd flirt with a box if it had a penis and balls." Jackie immediately noticed Helga's wince. "Oops. A little too much info, huh Doc? Enough said."

"Percy became part of my family… when I had one. I just don't want to see him get hurt."

Jackie rounded the table and slung an arm across the Doctor's shoulders. "He got a handful of degrees. He's what, thirty five-six? He'll survive a little tug on the heartstrings. It's about time he got his banana peeled anyway." Jackie gave the doc a little squeeze. "He'll be fine, mom."

Helga had to agree on one hand, but her protective tendencies were in full bloom. "He's just so innocent about life things. His science is rock solid, but…" She let her worries trail off with the unfinished sentence.

"Then there is nothing better than to throw him to the sexy French vampire and never look back." Jackie was still having fun with the whole situation, much to Helga's consternation. "And pray the banana doesn't get bruised." Jackie winked. "I'm outta here to go figure out if I should start eating my meat raw."

"That, my child, is enough! I'll never eat a banana again. That's it! I've got to go supervise weird science." Helga trotted off toward the lab with a chuckle.

"Good luck, mom." Jackie hollered as she headed in the opposite direction. She had time to shower and pretty up. Milo was taking her for ice cream.

\*\*\*\*\*\*

"Niner-niner-five-Victor-Sierra, long final for runway three seven. Permission to land. Order number four, six, seven, zero, zero, zero."

"Niner-niner-five-Victor-Sierra, Rhein-Main tower. Clear to land. Special message when ready to copy."

"Niner-niner-five-Victor-Sierra, roger. Ready to copy."

"Niner-niner-five-Victor-Sierra, refuel tanker ready. Taxi to holding, alpha five. Colonel Severin will meet your crew and passengers for briefing." The tower passed on the message.

"Five-Victor-Sierra, roger. Taxi to holding, alpha five. Receive and refuel." Casey Calhoun, the crack fighter pilot the Vamp Squad inherited from the US Air Force, pressed the intercom button. "Colonel Maddox, Colonel Severin will be coming aboard for a briefing when we refuel. You may want to chill some Moosehead. He's a Cannuck with a taste for home." Casey released the button and snickered. Colonel Severin was known throughout the European theater as a very astute officer of impeccable ethics, and a keen doctor with a taste for his Canadian brewed beer.

"Roger that Casey." Maddox responded. "Thanks for the heads up. I assume you stocked the bar?"

"Next to the Coors, Sir." Casey prided himself on pre-flighting everything he climbed into. In more ways than one.

Maddox woke his team as they prepared to land. All in civilian clothing with appropriate tourist essentials and architectural props scattered around the cabin of the Gulfstream Six-Fifty ER, he reminded the group to use only first names, and keep their comments to a minimum. Each member of the team had received a dossier on their character for this undercover op. They spent the first hour of the flight going over and memorizing their covers and quizzed each other to make sure each one had their story down pat.

Captain Devlin was the tour leader as his hobby was building all matter of replicas; buildings, furniture, toys, trains, etc. He could talk the talk, and draw the walk, literally. The Captain was an accomplished artist and designer, though he kept it quiet around his Army buds. Something about being in touch with his feminine side...

Colonel Maddox was the quiet, serious student who followed the leader. His extensive drawing pad held a variety of designs and notes on architecture, created with pleasure by Q2 back at the farm. He wore a pair of thick black-rimmed glasses and his pocket protector was bulging with mechanical pencils.

Tank wore tight jeans and let his hair hang loose like the exocentric architectural student he pretended to be. Bear played his overly muscular partner, along for the ride and some fun in the

European sun.

Elizabetta, dressed in her native Romanian style, carried a sling bag with camera equipment and a small notebook for taking notes. She would pretend to be an heiress, looking for realistic ideas for remodeling her ancient castle in Romania. She also carried a great deal of cash in the lining of her bag in the event bribes were required. Lieutenant Previn was still fuming about releasing the money without appropriate receipts and paperwork to match. In his opinion bribes were akin to governmental fraud. That was Previn.

Natalia and Yuri posed as exactly what they were, a married couple from Russia with a deep interest in world architecture. They were scouring Europe for examples of original Romanesque buildings. The Monastery of San Salvador de Leyre or San Leyre as it had become known in modern days, dated back to around the early eight hundreds, and was one of the most important historical monasteries in Spain.

Susannah had the least impressive cover story. She was simply the spoiled daughter of Frank Maddox, dragged along on her father's educational vacation, against her will. It was a part she could play with ease and true enjoyment.

As the jet taxied to its designated refueling area, Colonel Maddox dialed in the code for his briefcase and opened the latches. Withdrawing a manila folder with the words TOP SECRET plastered across the front in big red letters, he thumbed through the loose pages and removed an order document. It would allow his plane and crew to pass around the usual security checks and move on more quickly, no questions asked.

When the plane had come to a halt and Casey pronounced it clear to get up, Yuri popped the main door and waved to the driver of the rolling air stairs. Through the window Maddox could see Colonel Severin waiting patiently on the tarmac, a manila envelope in his hands.

As soon as the stairs to the plane's passenger door were secured, Colonel Severin bound up, two at a time.

Captain Devlin nudged Colonel Maddox. "This looks interesting, Frank."

Maddox stood to receive their visitor.

Severin moved to salute, then refrained. "Maddox, I'm Colonel Severin, Royal Canadian Air Force, Medical Services. I have new information for your...trip." The smug smile said he knew this was an undercover op and had been read in on the nature of the mission.

"Welcome aboard, Severin. We're an informal lot here." Maddox took the envelope offered by the Canadian officer. He peaked inside at the documents within, then handed the paperwork to Captain Devlin and motioned to Severin. "Have a seat. It will be a few minutes before we are refueled. I am given to believe you might enjoy a touch of home. Moosehead, correct?"

"If you have Moosehead onboard, this *is* a special mission." The smile on Severin's face was simply beautific.

Maddox handed him an uncapped bottle from the fridge.

"Not a usual habit for me during duty hours but… don't mind if I do." He took a long drink, closed his eyes and virtually purred. Opening his eyes and peering at the bottle, Severin spoke softly, "It's been a while, my dear."

Maddox felt Elizabetta's mental touch. *He is aware of our mission, TPS and vampires. We can talk freely. Apparently a child from his country was exposed… and died. He is the officer and doctor on the case.*

Maddox let out a long breath and sat down across from Colonel Severin. "So, you've dealt with the same issue we are investigating."

Severin looked up with deep sadness clearly displayed in his eyes. "It will take many more of these to explain what I have seen, Maddox." He took another long drink. "MaryEllen was my former CO's daughter. She was studying at the Academia de Santos Domingo de Silos." It took another swig to get the full story out. "She got sick. The school medevac'd her to the facilities here at Rhein-Main, but… she didn't make it." He studied the green bottle in his hand. "I did the autopsy. I have no words to describe what I saw." Looking up at Maddox, he sniffed loudly and wiped his eyes. "I just… this is beyond anything I know or understand."

Natalia moved to stand next to the Canadian Colonel. She placed a calming hand on his shoulder, exuding comfort. She closed her eyes and whispered, "Be comforted that this girl died painlessly. You could not have helped her, no matter what you did. This plague is an evil thing. We will find the source and exterminate it."

"If there is anything I can do…" Severin finished his beer and swung the bottle between his fingers. "I owe you one, Maddox. This has been a special treat."

Maddox took the bottle and Yuri replaced it with a six-pack. "No charge, Severin. We'll be in touch. Rest assured, we will find this threat and destroy it."

The Colonel stood to take his leave. "Nasty business, but a pure pleasure, Maddox." He lifted the carton of beer bottles. "Definitely pure pleasure." He spoke to the bottles. "Come on girls, we have a date."

Maddox chuckled and slapped the Canadian officer on the back as he started to descend the stairs. "Casey, how long before we lift off?"

From the open door of the cockpit a voice answered, "About five minutes, Sir. Secure the cabin and we should be off soon."

"Right. Thanks. And Casey," Maddox poked his head into the cockpit, "it's Maddox or Frank."

"Right, S…sure!." Casey pulled out an instrument flight chart and tapped buttons on the instrument panel. "Refueling complete, S…sweet. Ready to depart, if you will take your seats." He hollered through the doorway.

"About time. Dad tell me again why I have to come with you on this stupid trip." Susannah whined from her seat while she pushed her bag under the seat ahead of her and buckled up.

Maddox shot his daughter a confused look.

"Just practicing, Dad." She blew her father a kiss and settled in for the short flight to Pamplona.

Chuckles and giggles could be heard throughout the passenger cabin. "You go girl." Bear effected a feminine voice and tried to cross his muscular thighs… with absolutely no success.

"Don't go hurting yourself, sweetie." Tank patted his buddy's knee.

The entire team broke into laughter.

"Niner-niner-five-Victor-Sierra taking the active."

And they were off.

Chapter 19

Greens or Genes

We are what we eat, so say scientists and gurus,
But the question of genetics continually ensues.
Nature or nurture?
Greens or genes?

Life is such a jumble of confounding mysteries!

*Dr. Percy Seizemore, Research Scientist*
*Center for Disease Control*
*Washington D.C., 2016*

"Ooh, this is so very interesante, Doctor Seizemore. How do you know these pictures?" Monique squinted at the genetic patterns on the monitor.

"They are like a foot print or a finger print. Each set is specific to the individual, but the common ones are from the parent source." Percy pointed at six pairs highlighted by the computer. "You, Mathilda and our source have these six in common, so…"

"These come from the vampire who made us. I see! It is not so hard." Monique clapped her hands and planted a noisy kiss on Percy's cheek. "Especially if an elf can figure it out!"

Percy turned to see Monique's bright smile and mocking expression.

She pinched the tops of her ears and pulled them up to points. "Maybe I am part elf. Can you tell by those marks?" She giggled.

Percy relaxed. She was poking fun at him, he realized after a moment. But it was not mean spirited. And she was making fun of herself as well. He'd spent so much of his childhood being a target for other's mocking and abusive intentions, it was difficult for him to understand the difference between ridicule and humor. Being smarter than most of those around you, including the adults, at the tender age of ten, did not endear you to your peers or keepers.

Monique saw the shadows cross his face and felt the stabbing hurt as if it were her own. "I am sorry." She clasped her hands in her lap. "I did not mean to make remarques insultantes." She hung her head in repentance. This man covered his hurts with a false veneer that let no one in. She made up her mind, then and there to work on that. The elf doctor had many hurts that needed healing, just like she herself. They had that in common.

"It's okay. I'm used to it." He turned his face to the monitor. Computers were safe. They didn't insult, or hurt. They displayed facts and figures and only responded when commanded to. That was why he liked science more than people. He felt his morning's fantasy fading to dust in the back of his mind. *Remember Percy, old man, fish and birds.* He mentally reprimanded himself.

What was he thinking? Monique Merchant was a gorgeous, voluptuous woman who could have any man she wanted. What would she want with a skinny, scarred scientist who had the personality of a trigonometry equation? "This next part is difficult. If you don't mind…" He glanced toward the door.

"Oui. I shall leave you to your work." Monique had considerable empathic abilities and was reading this man correctly. He needed space and time. It was one of the things that allowed her to seduce men so quickly and easily. She need only reach out to a man, feel his excitement, understand his need and produce it. The pain she felt emanating from Doctor Seizemore broke her heart. "Of course. I can have things to do."

It was a lie. She had nothing to do. Nothing at all since most of the team was on the mission in Spain, Jackie was all tied up with Milo. Ted had his games. And she preferred not to bother Q2. He was always so dirty and greasy and making something she did not understand. He was confusion to her. He did not care for women. He did not care for men. He found excitment in his machines and gadgets. Q2 made her skin itch.

She placed a gentle hand on Percy's shoulder, "I am sorry for my joke."

Percy did not even acknowledge her comment, but continued to stare at his computer screen.

As Monique exited the lab, her vamp hearing allowed her to pick up his wistful comment as the doors swished shut.

"Damn. I'll be fine. I always am." It was a sad comment on his life.

She watched him for a few seconds, through the glass window of the lab. He slumped over the keyboard for a moment, then straightened. A futile shake of his head and he was obviously back at his work. His dejected posture tore at Monique's heartstrings. She promised herself - no more elf jokes. This man… this scientist had left his world to help them conquer a horrible threat to human, as well as vampire society. He had left everything behind to come to their rescue, her rescue. He was a real hero in her mind. Her hero. Her very innocent hero…

In her quarters, Monique realized it was almost noon and let the need for day sleep lull her away. Curled up on her bed, a pillow clutched to her chest, she drifted in her dreams.

******

"I'll have a double scoop of Moose Tracks. What would you like, babe?" Uncle Roger kissed his wife's head fondly. Their relationship was something Jackie envied. They were so tender and cute with each other, something she'd never seen with either her parents or her friend's parents.

"Oh, I think I'll have raspberry sherbet. No wait. One scoop of lemon and one of raspberry. In a waffle cone." Aunt Mandy smiled up at her husband of almost thirty years.

"I don't know if the budget can handle the waffle cone, sweet thing." At his comment, Mandy poked him in his ever-growing belly, with a laugh. "Spousal abuse. I have witnesses!"

Jackie ordered her ice cream. "Don't look at me. I support the sisterhood."

Roger turned to Milo, "Guess it's just you and me, Milo."

"You got my vote, Uncle Roger." Milo slurped his Rum Nut Crunchy cone.

While in town, they all maintained the designated covers that were established early on, when the Vamp Squad assumed the old safe house as their permanent headquarters. Olney Farm was a real working farm of about sixty-five acres that produced corn, hay and chestnuts. The previous family that farmed the place had planted chestnut trees as a windbreak, and for privacy, which worked out fine for the clandestine activity that went on around, and below the farmhouse. About ten miles out of town and a mile down a private road, no one was privy to what went on; the comings and goings of helicopters, or the unusual behavior of the farm hands. Roger and Mandy were personable, but private. Many of the folks in the town of Olney, Maine knew Mandy was a famous biathlete and ignored occasional VIP visitors or gunfire, if they were even aware of it in the first place. Miller pulled his alien stunt on kids who had ventured off the main road, but generally the community respected the Burnside's privacy. For all intents and purposes, they were model citizens, contributing to the high school sports program, and the food bank, when the crops were harvested.

Sitting in the sun on the little patio, the foursome chatted like the family members they were. "So, Jackie, honey, tell me how your school plans are coming along." Aunt Mandy had encouraged Jackie to get her classes early after she read an article about how students were spending a fifth year at some universities, just to get a basic degree.

"Actually, I finished my online registration this morning. I have three semesters to go to finish my Bachelor's degree in Financial Management. I registered for eighteen hours since I'm staying with you guys and I won't have much to do until the end of the summer. I'll actually have one extra month because I registered so early with the online program to finish. You do the classes at your own pace and get your degree when you have completed the required class curriculum." Jackie licked a dribble of chocolate ice cream off the side of her cone. "The only time requirement is that you don't complete the entire class in under thirty days, and you meet with your cohort, either in person or on the video conference system the university has set up. It's pretty cool."

"What if you have trouble with something?" Milo never earned a formal degree. His education was inherited from his family, or learned in the school of hard knocks.

"The instructor is available on the phone, online or you can set up a time to Skype with him or her. My PE units are actually being supervised by Aunt Mandy. We set up a program the university accepted as soon as they saw her name on the paperwork." Jackie took a big bite of the chunky chocolate ice cream. "Ahhh. Bwain frueez!" She fanned her mouth to add warmth.

"That's what you get for wolfing down frozen milk fat and sugar," Milo smirked.

Jackie wiped her lips and ran her tongue around the inside of her mouth. "Anyway, I have a lit class that will be a breeze, Biathelete Training 101 which will just be fun. I'm taking French using the Rosetta Stone program and I can practice with Monique. My other classes are Audit Theory and Practice, Economic Statistics, Business Management 301. Audit Theory and Practice will be the only challenge. Maybe I can get Previn to give me some advice."

"Ooooh, bad advice Jacks. That's all you'll get from him." Miller's serious tone made Jackie look up.

"If he's got a brain, I can pick it, can't I?" She hated it when Milo tried to be a control freak with her.

"Slim pickins, honey." Aunt Mandy lifted an eyebrow and glanced at the elderly couple sitting close enough to overhear their conversation.

Jackie shrugged, shot Miller a dirty look, and changed the subject. "After that, I have one semester of a six-hour internship the university assigns and ten hours of electives. I'm seriously thinking about taking ground school. I've been toying with the idea of learning to fly, like my cousin, Susannah."

Uncle Roger shot Jackie a surprised look. "That's a fantastic idea! Then Susannah will have someone to fly around with. You two can keep each other out of trouble." Roger poked his wife with a deep chuckle.

Milo mumbled into his cone.

"This weather is so nice. It's an unexpected pleasure to have sunshine and warm temperatures in April, don't you think, dear?" Mandy waved at a young couple across the street. They waved back before entering the hardware store. "Ralph, at the post office told me Timmy and Sandy eloped last month. They look so happy. Just like we did all those years ago, Roger." Mandy leaned her head on her husband's shoulder.

"Just like we still do, my lovely bride." He kissed his wife. "Guess we should head back to the farm, huh?"

The small group strolled to the parking lot, savoring the last of their sweet treats.

Jackie had never been more content in her life.

Milo had never been so envious.

※※※※※※

Across the pond, things were brewing. "You've got to be kidding, Dad!" Susannah posed like a spoiled teen. "Across from the Guardia Civil? Way to stay under the radar, Pops."

They stood next to the first of three silver Suburbans parked in front of the Hostal de la Renya de Yesa, their quarters for the duration of the mission. Across the street sat an ancient looking, three-story building with a small stable next to it. The fence around the stable connected to the building and opened at the far end. The building windows were slender and high. Probably in years past, the windows served as gun placements during the Basque area's tumultuous history. Wires were strung haphazardly across the street and slung low along the building below the windows. Susannah snapped a picture with her cell phone.

"Bet Milo could hack that network with one hand tied behind his back." Susannah smirked and grabbed her handbag from the back seat of the SUV. "We gonna stand here all day?" She started up the stairs.

The town of Yesa, nestled against the base of the Pyrenees mountains was in striking distance of NA-2113, the road to the Monastery of San Salvador de Leyre! The reservoir created by a large dam spread out miles beneath the mountains. The town was a multi-level jumble of ancient and contemporary styles often found in the mountainous areas of Spain. They'd arrived at the public airport in Pamplona as the sun was setting, now the tiny streets of Yesa glowed with soft yellow lamp light.

"Hold up there a minute, young lady. There are no porters or skycaps here." Maddox held out his daughter's huge suitcase with a grunt. What had she packed?

"Daaaaad," she drew the word out as she stood midway up the two flights of stairs leading to the entrance.

"Suuuuusannnnaaaah," Her father returned the sentiment. With a wide smile. They were both having fun playing their parts. Susannah finally retraced her steps and took the suitcase.

Elizabetta approached from the last car to lend a tone of calm. "We have rented this entire place for two weeks. There are eight bedrooms, each ensuite. I believe there is only one room with twin beds. I suggest Tank and Bear take that room." She glanced at the group disembarking. The pile of luggage grew with each individual who exited from the SUVs. "There is parking on the side street." She held a folder of rental information. "The staff and Manager have been given a paid vacation for the next couple weeks, so we have the place to ourselves, and…" She pointed to the entire group one by one. "We will behave and see some wonderful architecture." Her eyes moved toward the camera above the entryway of the Guardia Civil Puesto de Yesa.

Tank yelled, "Do I have an Amen!" For effect.

He was ignored as usual.

One by one, each member of the team trucked their luggage up the various sets of steps to their designated rooms, then met in the great room near the dining room. The Hostal de la Renya de Yesa had once been a sumptuous villa where royalty would spend hot Spanish summers hiking in the mountains, retiring to pray at the church on the grounds of the monastery, soaking in the spas fed by the many local hot springs or swimming in nearby Lake Argon. Placards littered the place detailing famous visitors and the many entertaining activities and religious holidays of Yesa and San Leyre. The house was in immaculate condition, the dark wood, characteristic of many mountain villas, was polished to a gleaming finish and the kitchen was up-to-date with modern amenities and appliances.

Built on a hill, the central courtyard of the villa sported an intricate Spanish tile fountain, and a small shrine with a stone bench and a statue of Mother Mary. The shrine stood in an alcove framed by flowering vines and potted plants, the perfect place for personal meditation, or reading a good book if you didn't buy into the whole Catholic praying thing. Across the stone courtyard, off of the kitchen, sat a huge stainless steel barbeque, big enough to feed a crowd, encircled with small tile tables and handworked leather chairs. With flowers and bubbling water, it was quaint and romantic. The great room of the villa opened onto the courtyard through wide french doors.

"Ah, hun, this is where we should tie the knot. Right?" Tank sidled up to Bear and rubbed against his muscular arm.

Bear made some kind of rude noise while Devlin finished sweeping the room for bugs. With the thumbs up from Devlin, Bear responded, "Fuck you, you faggot."

Tank threw an arm around his buddy, "You love me and you know it." He gently tapped Bear's nose.

"In public only. And you do that again, I'll tap your cute little nose on the intricately patterned tile floor, asswipe." He moved away from Tank with a growl.

Tank glanced at Bear's overly developed chest. "Got it, bro."

"Okay, you two. Cool it. We have work to do." Devlin began unpacking a large hardsided suitcase full of computer and communications gear. Sergeant Miller had condensed everything they would need to stay in touch, into one suitcase with a drawn schematic on top of the tangled wires. All Devlin had to do was look at the drawing and reassemble the spaghetti tangle of wires, boxes and screens.

Helpless when it came to technology, Tank scoured the built-in bar and grabbed two bottles that looked to contain beer. "Yo, pretty boy, catch." He threw the bottle in the general direction of his friend.

"Ugh. Tank!" Bear launched himself across the coffee table and caught the bottle mid-air before crashing onto the leather couch. "Bro, chill. Wasting beer is tantamount to original sin. Never chance losing a... a... a ZerB? What the hell is this?"

Tank peered at the label on his bottle, then popped the top. He first smelled the liquid, then shrugged and took a swig. "Beer." A loud burp confirmed his correct identification. "Yep."

Bear sprawled on the couch, reading the label. He was a little more concerned about what passed over his lips. "Says Basque Cerveza Extraordinario. Opener?" He stuck up his hand as Tank took aim. Catching the bottle opener, he popped the top and smelled the beer. "Ummmm. Hops and grain. Nice brew. Well blended, slightly fruity, blonde ale."

"Such a prima dona! Cheers. Captain, I mean... Rob?" Tank was definitely uncomfortable calling his superior officer by his first name. "ZerB?" He prounanced the name with aplomb.

"I want Miller. Damn," Devlin turned the drawing around and around in his hands. "this looks like some kind of modern art, not instructions to assemble a comm station."

Susannah giggled from the doorway. "Uncle Rob, let me. It's not that hard. You're just from the wrong generation, that's all. Have a beer with the guys and let the little lady do the heavy lifting." She bounced into the room and took the paper from Devlin. "Out, out, out!"

Plunking down on the couch next to Bear, she began assembling parts and wires. Within minutes, the comm center sat solidly on the coffee table and was complete. "Now all we need is electricity. Hope Milo included an international adapter." She rummaged around in the suitcase and came up with a large, unusual looking plug. "Voila!".

In moments the screen came to life and the little internet signal flashed blue. "Done and done." Susannah stood and did a little happy dance ala Colonel Sanders. "Anything else I can do for you?" She was back in snotty-teen character.

It went right over Devlin's head.

"Thanks, kiddo. Want a beer?" He grimaced. "Sorry, Suze."

'No problema, tio." She danced her way across the floor and planted a noisy kiss on Devlin's cheek. "I'm probably over twenty-one by now, but I never really liked beer. I went for the stuff that made you really stupid... hence." She smiled extending her fangs just a touch "Get the point? No pun intended."

Everyone in the room got the point.

"I'm gonna find Dad. He's probably trying to text, or something." She bounced on out of the room.

"That girl has grown up too fast." Devlin shook his head and took a gulp of beer.

A loud burp punctuated his statement. "Yep." Tank agreed.

******

Monique woke with a scream. She was back in the catacombs beneath San Leyre, running through the maze of tunnels, searching for a way out. Brittle corpses lined the walls reaching for her, tearing at her clothing and hair as she sped by. Out of breath, she struggled on as bony fingers scratched at her, their dry rough fingers pulling hunks of flesh from her arms and legs. The wounds burned and tortured her body, while fear encompassed her mind. Would this never cease? Would the pain never end? Would she forever live in this hell on earth?

Monique sat up, rubbing her arms and legs.

No wounds marred her flesh.

Not even a bruise could be found.

The tears began again, completely soaking her French lace nightgown. There was nothing to do but let them flow.

Monique curled into a ball and lay on her side, sobbing her heart out. There would be no comfort from her coven mates as they were all thousands of miles away. Her misery would be her own this day.

While Monique relived her worst nightmares in her room alone, Doctor Seizemore worked, alone, in his lab. Well, that wasn't quite accurate. He wasn't physically alone, just mentally cut off from everything and anything that disrupted his scientific focus.

Helga moved about the lab working on projects, testing different theories on her computer, running simulations… marking time and watching Percy. She was tired, however she was concerned about her friend and cohort.

"Damn…" That was strong language for a man raised in a Catholic orphanage by nuns and priests. "Double damn!" At some point, Percy had taken time to dress and comb his hair. Now he sat, bouncing on his chair, one leg vibrating against the console, the other stretched out beneath the desk. "I was sure I had the right combinate this time."

"I'm sorry, Percy. Not following." Helga came to stand behind him. "What are you trying to do?"

"I de-constructed the TPS sample. Now I need to develop an interferon process that will… never mind." He returned his attention to his computer. He'd added two more monitors and now symbols and formulas covered all of them, flashing numbers and molecules at warp speed.

"Percy…" Helga used her best mom voice, "I am a scientist and a doctor. I think I can understand your technical jargon." She'd worked long enough with the geeky doctor to not be offended by his lack of social and communication skills.

"Oh, yeah. Sorry." He didn't take his eyes off the activity on the screen. "I want to develop a counter-drug, an inoculation to TPS that will knock out the vampire DNA. Like the way some cancers are interrupted, removing the altering DNA strands that mutate the cells to become cancerous in the first place. I thought I had it." He wiped a hand across his eyes. "Not the first disappointment today." He glanced toward the lab door. "But I will get it. There are too many potential lives at stake."

"Percy, when was the last time you ate something?" He looked pale and drawn to Helga.

"Huh?" He continued to punch in combinations and watch their reactions. "Damn."

"Percy, stop!" She took hold of the arms of his office chair and spun him around. "Did you have breakfast? Lunch? Are you even aware it's four thirty in the afternoon?" She eyed the small pyramid of empty cans next to his computer station. "Is that it?" She pointed to the stack.

"Huh?" Percy stared at her with a blank look.

"Is that all you've had today? Sugar and caffeine?" She

scolded him like the mom he never had.

"Ah… I don't know. I can't stop right now." Percy tried to turn his chair and found he did not have the energy to counteract Helga's iron grip.

"Up. Now! We're going to get some food in you, and then we'll talk about this." She pointed to the computer. "And this." She pointed directly to the heart in his chest.

"Helga, I almost have it. You have to let me work." Percy wheedled. His eyes were bloodshot and the lines around his mouth had deepened.

"No I don't. What I do have to do, is keep you from dying of malnutrition in my lab! Now up, or so help me, I will pull the plug on your entire system." She stood with her hand on the surge protector's main plug. "You know I'll do it."

Percy stared her in the eye. "No wonder Sarah used to call you the Iron Maiden. Did you treat her like this too?" He was almost whining.

"Oh much worse. I would hide her charger cord if she didn't listen." Helga grinned at the rumpled and tired doctor. "Now march, Mister!"

Percy was defeated and knew it. He rose and grabbed for the table to stay the wave of dizziness that threatened to overwhelm him. Caffeine and sugar was not good for stability during quick movements.

"Do I have to say, I told you so?" Helga took his arm and held him up until he seemed stable enough to remain upright on his own.

"Nah, I think I got the point. What's for lunch? I mean dinner, I guess." They left the lab, strolling slowly down the hall to give Percy a chance to get his land legs under him.

"We'll cook up something. How about a wonderful feta, and broccoli quiche? With a double shot of Hot Buttered Rum-sure?"

"What is a Hot Buttered Rum-sure?" He'd never heard of that kind of drink before.

"It's my own concoction. Captain Morgan's Spiced rum, buttered rum batter and Ensure. All the spice of Captain Morgan's with all the protein and vitamins of Ensure. Add a little whipped cream and you even have dairy. What else could you want if you have to kill brain cells, and beef up your protein level at the same time?"

"You have an evil and sadistic mind, dear Helga." Percy had the energy to shudder at the thought of a Hot Buttered Rum-sure.

"Of course. Did you ever doubt it?" Helga eased Percy into a chair in the dining area. "You sit right there and I'll cook. Dinner in ten minutes."

"I didn't realize how hungry I was." Percy's stomach made a loud growling noise about the time Jackie and Milo wandered into the chow hall.

"No kidding. You have a monster in there who wants out." Jackie laughed as she joined Percy at the table. Milo pulled a frozen pizza out of the large freezer next to the white fridge, and set one of the small countertop ovens to the appropriate temperature.

"Hey, looks like the doc here is cooking for two. Want to add a couple slices of pizza to that empty hole?" Milo was ready to take another pizza out.

"Don't do meat, but thanks." Percy slumped. "Helga's making me some quiche. She is a fantastic cook, did you know that? I used to eat with her family all... sorry." Helga's back was turned to him, but he still noticed the slight bow of her head, the barely perceptible slump of her shoulders.

"It's okay, Percy." She whispered.

"Well, you both missed some great ice cream this after-noon. We went into town and splurged with Aunt Mandy and Uncle Roger. Checked out the town. It was a quick check." Jackie filled the pregnant silence with nanner as the chill faded.

"Percy has been glued to his computer all day. He forgot to eat. So quiche it is. A double helping" Helga noticed Monique wandering toward the small group. She was rather disheveled and red stains dotted the front of her rumpled t-shirt. "Good evening, my dear."

Monique schlepped past Helga, dragging her feet in fuzzy pink bunny slippers. "Nothing good about it." She took two bags of AB and slumped into a chair across from Jackie. "Sometimes I detest my own mind."

"Nightmares again?" Jackie slid her chair around the table and threw an arm across Monique's shoulders. "Just remember, we will always keep you safe. You're family." She kissed her new friend's cheek.

The tears began anew as Monique hid her face in Jackie's

shoulder.

"Ah, come on Frenchy. Chin up." She hugged Monique and just held the sobbing vampire. What more could she do? Besides, girls have to stick together.

Percy looked at Monique, then looked at Helga. His beseeching eyes told her, he empathized but did not know what to do or say. "I'll be right back." He stumbled toward the human quarters.

"Percy! Dinner in a few minutes. Don't make me come get you." Helga warned the retreating doctor in momma role again. All she got was a thin smile and a feeble wave in return.

"What's with him?" Milo shoved the frozen pizzas into the oven.

Helga pointed to her heart, then toward Monique, then the human quarters and the closing door.

"Oh-oh." Milo shook his head. "Big time."

Helga had to agree.

As the beep sounded and the pizzas were done, Percy rejoined them with halted steps and something in his hand.

He sat next to Monique and placed a small fuzzy thing in front of her on the table.

"My Trouble Tribble."

Monique looked up. "What is Trouble Tribble?" She poked a finger at the hairy thing. It made a weird noise and she started.

"Tribble? Like Star Trek Tribble?" Jackie touched the thing and it made a burbling noise, like a Tribble should. She giggled. "It is a Tribble!"

"What is Tribble? How do you know this thing?" Now Monique was engaged in the question instead of her horrible day-sleep nightmares.

"The TV program Star Trek. From the, oh heck, sixties or seventies. Then there was a bunch of movies after that. I'm a Trekkie." Jackie picked up the Tribble and shook it, giggling at the sound it made.

"I thought you are human. What is Trekkie? Is that why Fiona treats you so different?" Monique was confused.

"No! Ack, Monique. You missed the Star Trek genera-tion?" Then Jackie grimaced remembering how many years Monique had spent in the dungeon at San Leyre. "Sorry. Anyway, people who loved the TV program and then loved the movies and followed the different generations of Star Trek are called Trekkies.

We have special events and follow the cast members, etc. You know, William Shatner, Leonard Nimoy, Nichelle Nichols? She was my role model, the first women officer in a TV program that was truly independent and smart! And sexy! And…"

"Down girl." Milo served the pizza. "That thing," Milo indicated the Tribble on the table, "was in one program out of a bazillion and it stuck. I think the program was called The Bad Thing About Tribbles."

"Nope, The Trouble With Tribbles." Jackie corrected Milo.

Monique stared at the both of them. "This is from TV program long time ago?" She poked at it and smiled at the sound. "Why did you show me this?" She turned to Percy who was doing his best to stay awake.

"My Trouble Tribble. When I used to… be sad, or mad about what people did to me, I'd tell it to Trouble Tribble and…" He stopped and took the plate of quiche Helga offered. "It made it better. Maybe…" He shoved a huge fork full of fluffy quiche into his mouth, then spoke around the food, "Maybe if you tell it about your bad dreams, they will be better too." He smiled at the tear stained vampire next to him. Bits of broccoli, cheese and egg stuck to his teeth.

Monique was amazed. She didn't know what to say. She just sat there, staring at the Tribble, then at Percy's teeth, then at Jackie and Milo.

Helga dished up a big slice of quiche for herself and joined the group. "It beats an alcoholic daze and a truck load of Oreos." She smiled at Monique. "These dreams have always been part of your life, but they seem to have gotten worse when San Leyre came back into your life. It makes sense. Your experiences there were simply, well not simply, I don't mean to make light of your pain at all, but the dreams are your brain's way of revisiting your past, now that San Leyre has come back to haunt you, so to speak." She chewed thoughtfully. "When individuals suffer terrible things, our minds place those memories in a box and store them away because they are too painful to deal with. When the box opens, for whatever reason, the memories often surface in dreams. It's a kind of PTSD."

"PTSD? What is this PTSD that tortures me in sleep?" Monique was back on the verge of tears. She took the Tribble and held it to her like a teddy bear.

"Post traumatic stress disorder." Milo interjected. "Like

when soldiers come back from Afghanistan. They've seen so many horrible things, they just can't think right. Sometimes they commit suicide, they are so disturbed."

"Ah, thanks, Milo." Jackie frowned at the Sergeant.

"Oh, I can never take my own life. It is impossible for a vampire to end their own life, unless we go to the sun. And that would ruin my beautiful skin." She rubbed the Tribble against her cheek, then handed it back to Percy. "Thank you, doctor. I do feel better now."

"No, you keep it. I am done with it anyway. I am a scientist. What people say about me no longer matters, only my work and the science I believe in." Percy was gaining strength as he ate. "This quiche is fantastic, Helga. I didn't realize how hungry I was."

Monique rubbed the Tribble against her cheek again as it burbled softly to her. "It does seem to soothe." She smiled warmly at Percy who continued to shove large forkfuls of quiche into his mouth.

Milo kicked the scientist under the table. To no avail.

Percy continued to eat.

Monique continued to smile. Warmly.

Chapter 20

Sugar and...

What are little girls made of?
Sugar and spice and everything nice?
That's what little girls are made of.

What are little vampires made of?
Bites and terrors and bloody nightmares?
That's what little vampires are made of.

*Fiona Fabriacci, Wife*
*The Council of Elders*
*Unknown Location, 2016*

"You look lovely, honey," Colonel Maddox watched his daughter descend like an angel in white and gold. Maddox sniffed and wiped at his eyes. "You look so much like your mother, I..." He couldn't go on.

"Ah Dad, that's so sweet. But mom never had these." She smiled and let her fangs drop a touch.

It was the perfect thing to cool the mood. "You're right about that." He took her arm like the proud father he was. "We have a daddy-daughter date with our informant in forty-five minutes. He'll meet us at the La Cabra Feliz. It's a club about three blocks away. Apparently they specialize in cheeses and micro-brews. I think it means the Happy Cat.

"Goat, Dad. The Happy Goat." Susannah giggled and hugged her dad. "We never did the daddy-daughter thing when I was human. I'm glad I get a second chance." She kissed him on the cheek.

"Me too." The Colonel whispered just for his daughter's ears but knew the other vamps could hear everything. And he didn't care. Things had really changed in his life, and his relation-ship with his daughter. There were times he could hardly believe his own self anymore.

"We will be here with backup if you should get into trouble, Sir." Yuri sat near Devlin watching the comm screen.

"Thank you, Yuri. We will attempt to find only information. Apparently the Policia Flora, the local cops, are treating the suicide at San Leyre with kid gloves, since it involves the church and the monastery. Shall we, dear?"

"Of course, Pops." Susannah grinned as they headed for La Cabra Feliz and a date with their local informant.

It was close to midnight and the streets were bathed in amber light from old gas streetlights and aged glass globes. People strolled along the sidewalks and streets, moving slowly in the humid evening air. Several small cafés were filled with tourists spilling out onto the streets as they dined and chatted. It seemed everyone was eating and talking, despite the late hour. Typical in Europe.

"Dinner at midnight? Everyone is out. Look at this place." Maddox was not used to the culture of socializing around food.

"It's common all over Europe to eat out with friends late into the evening. This is Spain, not Olney, Maine. They don't roll the sidewalks up at six, Dad." Susannah walked comfortably on her father's arm. "It's a very different way of life, but I think I like it." Susannah peered across the outdoor tables and into a candlelit restaurant. People sat around small tables, munching, drinking and talking. Laughter was everywhere. Friends hugged and kissed each other on both cheeks. Wine was poured and finger food was shared. It was delightful. It was slow. It was friendly and inviting.

"Maybe if Americans slowed down a little and smelled the tortillas and cheese dip, we'd be nicer to each other. What do you think, Dad?"

"I think we need to take care of business. Our contact is Lt. Franco Etxebarria. Señor for our purposes. He was at the farm a while back. He's about yeah tall," Maddox lifted a hand to about six feet, "and looks like… a Spaniard. Dark, mustache and close cropped beard…"

"I saw him, Dad. Monique and I were coming back from a flight. We watched on the monitor."

They approached La Cabra Feliz and immediately amazing smells assaulted their senses.

"Oh yum. Smell those spices, honey." Maddox was in heaven. "What is that wonderful aroma?"

"I'm about to barf. Smells like toxic waste to me."

Susannah turned up her nose and frowned. "I do miss real food, but a good O negative is just as appealing."

"Ya know, that's too bad. I don't know what it is, but I do believe I could just about slobber like a dog." Maddox took a deep breath. "Shuuuu-weeee. Damn that's good."

Under her breath, Susannah muttered, "Good thing I don't have to breathe."

La Cabra Feliz took up the entire first floor of a somewhat new office building. The wide sliding doors, which were rolled completely back, opened to the street where tables spread across the sidewalk and halfway into the street. A long bar occupied the left side of the building and bottles lined the back wall at least ten feet high. A flamenco style band played on the opposite side, while patrons danced on the small floor in the middle. Waiters in traditional flamboyant Spanish costumes served drinks and piles of food on huge trays the men carried on their shoulders as they danced between the crammed tables. The back of the establishment opened onto a magnificent stone patio overlooking the valley below, and the ruins of some ancient castle. Huge rattan fans kept the air moving and a gentle breeze blew in through the open back doors.

Maddox scoured the restaurant for his contact while Susannah hung on her father's arm, surveying the establishment with teenage wonder. She'd been many places in her human life, before her father had become a spec ops soldier and the family was left in the care of Fort Bragg and the US Army. She was very young when their family had been stationed overseas. Besides Afghanistan, this was the first country she'd been to as an adult. There hadn't been much time for sightseeing in that desert shit-hole where they'd retrieved Yuri and taken down the right arm of the Taliban. No one was shooting at them now so she sauntered and inspected the place to her heart's content.

Susannah was intrigued by a massive mural of San Leyre's garden that covered a large portion of the north wall. "Dad, I'm gonna go look at that mural. Be right back." She let go of his arm and wandered toward the painted fresco wall. Close to the dance floor, a movement enveloped in greenish light caught her eye.

Vampires.

Naturist vampires!

Susannah ducked below the undulating crowd and concentrated on making her pale aura disappear. All vampires had

255

the ability to sense each other's auras and often recognized a coven's brand. Naturist vampires, ones who dined on live blood from humans, always glowed with a fierce bile green tint. Techno-modern vampires, the ones who drank synth-blood and used especially designed supplements to exist, exhibited pale auras, usually pink or light blue. Susannah, having only once tasted human blood, displayed a very soft, pale pink aura that she was learning to mask.

She sent a psyche-message to her sister vampire and coven mistress. *There be vampires here, people. Stay away.*

Quickly she searched for her father. Across the room, tucked into a dim corner at a small table, sat Maddox and his contact. Susannah recognized the handsome Spaniard from his visit to the farm. Carefully she made her way between dancing and dining customers, keeping an eye on the group of green auras seated near the band. Pressing against the stone wall, she slipped behind her father and took a seat.

"Ah, this is my daughter, Susannah. Susannah, Franco Etxebarria. Our new friend."

Susannah smiled and extended a hand low on the table. "Nice to meet you, Sir." Catching her father's eye, she made a V with her fingers as she scratched her nose.

Maddox sat up a little straighter raising his eyebrows.

Susannah got the message and whispered, "Next to the band. Left side. Two men, two women, and…Oh my God. Faith Morrison!"

Lt. Franco Etxebarria, a very adept detective, immediately picked up on the quiet communication between father and daughter. "Señorita Maddox, your father and I have been discussing El Festival de Luces tomorrow night at El Monestario de San Salvador de Leyre. Por favor sea mi invitado, be my guest." He slid a newspaper toward Maddox. "It is written in this news-paper. You can read it later."

Tucked between the folded newspaper pages was a file folder.

"Thanks, Franco. I will. It sounds like a wonderful evening, even my daughter might enjoy."

Susannah saw one of the vampires across the room turn their way. She ducked beneath the table. "I dropped my phone, Dad."

"Here, let me help." Maddox ducked beneath his table as

well.

Soon Etxebarria had joined them. "May I be of assistance?" His smile virtually glowed brilliant white in the dim light.

"Susannah recognized some of your town folk. We should leave. Do you know a back way out?"

"Of course. My cousin is the head cocinero here. We will go through the kitchen. I will show you the way. Who do we watch?" Etxebarria seemed happy to be a co-conspirator.

"Five vam... people left of the band. Two men, three women. The blonde one I know from another case." Susannah whispered beneath the tabletop. "Which direction is the kitchen?"

"Follow me. Our table is good. They will not see us." Etxebarria pointed toward the back wall where a waitress seemed to appear out nowhere. "Around the corner, there is a door. Stay low and the crowd will make us cover."

As they slumped their way toward the kitchen entrance, Susannah stayed next to the wall, her father and Etxebarria hopefully blocking view of her and her pale aura.

"If that bitch is here, then we know how CE got here." Susannah swore beneath her breath as they exited out onto the back alley, stepping through a pile of rotting vegetables and moldy bread that had been thrown out.

"Such language!" Maddox decried in fake distaste. "Things are beginning to fall into place, aren't they."

"You know I must ask... who is Faith and what is CE?" Etxebarria stood his ground, blocking the alley.

Colonel Maddox gave a few seconds thought then responded. "Faith Ford was part of Proctor Pharmaceuticals in the States. They were developing a specialized drug that would, well, I'm still not sure what it was supposed to do, but it failed. Miserably. And it was very dangerous for some... people."

"And...?" Etxebarria wanted it all.

This time it was Susannah's turn to stumble around the V problem. "And our CDC scientist believes CE is part of this new drug effecting the students at Academia de Santos Domingo de Silos. We were all under the impression that CE had been destroy-ed and the research terminated."

"Susannah's boyfriend is one of Proctor's managers. He saw to the cleanup and destruction. Faith must have somehow gotten away with some of the stuff when she disappeared during the raid. Bad news. Very bad news."

Susannah ducked behind a pile of boxes. "They're leaving."

Etxebarria glanced at the group and winked at Maddox. "I will follow them."

"Be careful, Franco. They are violent and will not consider killing you anything more than stepping on a bug." Susannah touched the Lieutenant's arm softly.

He smiled that brilliant smile as he kissed the back of Susannah's hand. Turning to her father , Franco commented, "She has a boyfriend, eh? Such a shame." And with that, he was off dodging down the alley and disappearing around the corner.

"Man, he doesn't know what he is getting into. Dad, can't we…"

"Nope. He knows." Maddox had opened the secreted file. He showed the first document to his daughter. It was a compilation of clippings about vampires in old Spain. The next sheet was a dossier on Le Glaute Industries and their sponsorship of the monastery. "Let's get back to the hotel and see what the other's think. Can you call Jordan? What time is it in Florida?" Maddox looked at his watch.

Susannah pulled out her phone. "Six hours difference. It's almost midnight, so it's almost six pm in Florida. It doesn't matter. He takes my call any time, night or day." Susannah hit the speed dial number for her boyfriend.

"I wonder why…" Maddox had become a little more comfortable with his daughter's relationship and considered Jordan almost part of the family, but like any dad, he hated the idea of losing his daughter to another man. Even though their own relationship had been rocky, he treasured his only child and was proud as punch at how she had buckled down to become a very valuable operative. What father wouldn't be proud of a child who decided to enter the family business? He chuckled to himself. Family business? Hmmm…

"Hey sleepyhead, you there?" Susannah giggled.

He *did* answer the phone so obviously he *was* there.

"Maybe… what's up? Are you okay?" His voice cleared on the phone along with his sleep soaked brain.

"Yeah. I'm good. But guess who just popped up on our radar?"

"I was just waking up looking at your picture on my nightstand, so I better hear some dirty-down talk, Su…zie." Jordan growled in his sexy, sleepy way.

"Nooo-oooh, goofball. Faith Morrison. She's here. And so is my dad, right next to me, by the way."

"No shit! Faith Morrison? In Spain? You think she's connected to this new stuff?" Susannah could hear Jordan smack his head over the phone. "Of course she is. Didn't you say TPS had CE in it? Man that crap just keeps haunting us."

"Yes it does. So... there are also vampires here. Naturist vampires. I saw the auras."

"Suze, be careful. You know how diabolical Proctor was. I'm coming over there. Let me talk to your father." Jordan was fully awake and full of fear.

"No, I'm not going to let you talk to my daddy. And no, you are not coming here. We have Yuri, Nat, Elizabetta and the rest of the team, minus Monique and Morningstar." Susannah stood in the alleyway, feet planted somewhat solidly in a pile of goop, with her right hand on her hip. "We will be fine. And we may need you to do some snooping around at the company, depending on how this thing rolls. Get it, bonehead? No v-porting, right? Anybody at the company know what happened to Faith? She just went missing after the raid, right?"

"If a human can disappear in a poof of smoke, she was the one who did. Along with Sal. But he's a vamp so he could be anywhere at any time. He was a v-porter."

"Ah, crap. The plot clots. Well, it was a long stretch anyway. Enjoy your evening, babe. And, Jordi, you show up here, no sex for a year. I mean that!"

Maddox watched his daughter and listened to her tone of voice. He felt for Jordan. The young vampire was head over heels in love with Susannah... and he was old fashioned, just like Maddox. That was a tough row to hoe with his daughter. He cringed at the last sentence.

"Okay, but Suze, be careful, baby. I love you so much. I don't want to spend eternity watching dumb movies without you."

"Back atchya, babe." She made a kissy noise before ending the call. "Jordan said nobody knows what happened to Faith. As we suspected, she disappeared right after the raid and change of power at Proctor. My guess is, she disappeared with some CE. What say you, father of mine?"

"Ah, Suze, please don't talk about sex in front of your father." Maddox was shaking his head with a lopsided grin. "It's hard enough to see you all grown up and in harm's way all the time. This old ticker might not be able to take much more Susie-Q."

Susannah burst into laughter as she dragged her father toward their hotel. "Gottcha, Pops."

\*\*\*\*\*\*

Back across the pond, it was almost sun down. Percy's eyes blurred as he stared at the chemical configurations. Thirty-six attempted. Thirty-six failures. Nine to go before he would have to abandon his theory. Abandon? Never! He would preserver. He would be triumphant. "What one man can invent, another can discover. Think, Percy." He was channeling Sherlock Holmes again.

"Nothing clears up a case so much as stating it to another person." Monique spoke quietly from behind the frustrated scientist. She held two huge sandwiches, one in each hand. They contained no meat, but thick hunks of cheese and humus spread. Tomatoes hung out of the wheat bread and lettuce leaves could be seen beneath the cheese. They smelled like ten-day-old garbage to her.

Percy jumped and spun in his chair. He caught the edge of Monique's left hand and the sandwich flew across the lab. "Sorry, I..."

She placed one sandwich on the table with vamp-speed and collected the pieces of the other as they fell toward the floor. In less than the blink of an eye, she once again stood before the scientist holding a hastily reconstructed sandwich.

"I... how did you do that?" Percy's mouth dropped wide open.

"Talent, Doctor Seizemore. Talent... and grace." She curtsied handing him the sandwich and gently tapped his chin closed with one delicate finger. "I am a vampire, you know."

"Yes, but... how, I mean... I don't know what I mean." He took the offering. "I'm starving. How did you know? Another vampire thing?"

"Oh no. I cannot read minds, but I feel... I feel émotions et sentiments, you know." She rubbed his tummy.

"Oh." He kept his eyes on his sandwich. Actually, he tried to keep his eyes on his sandwich, but failed. He looked up at

Monique's charms, both of them... and blushed. She was magnificient. And she had delivered a sandwich... no two sandwiches, to a starving man. Could there be anything more beautiful in the entire universe? He licked his lips self-consciously...

"You know Sherlock Holmes movies? I love the stories." She pulled an office chair around the table and sat down. "What do you work on now?"

With humus smeared across his chin, Percy pointed to his computer monitor with what was left of the first sandwich. "I am running compound simulations to see if I can find an antidote to TPS. I reverse engineered the formula, now all I have to do is figure out what will break the linked substances and make the stuff inert." He grabbed the second sandwich and bit into it with relish.

Monique giggled as a tomato covered in humus and mayonnaise slid from between the slices of bread, landing in the middle of his chest. It stuck just above the light sabre point wielded by Princess Leia. She reached over and peeled the tomato off the t-shirt and handed it to him. "What is this enearth?

"Inert. Unable to work." He smiled at her desecration of his language. "The least you could do is catch the tomato before it hit my favorite Star Wars t-shirt?" Percy pointed his sandwich at her. Remembering their last disastrous verbal intercourse, he added, "Just joking."

"I was not thinking. Your stomach was talking to me of its pure joy in being fed, once again." She pointed to his flat stomach with a delicate finger. "You, human, should eat more. I can see your ribs and I hear the screams of your stomach in my room." She laughed.

"You do?" At that statement, his analytical mind was immediately primed with a million questions about vampire powers.

"No." Again she giggled. "Doctor Anderson told me I should bring you food." The giggles continued. But they were happy giggles, enjoying just being with the doctor. A fleeting thought sped across her brain. She'd never really enjoyed just being in the company of a man without the sex factor. And a smart man, at that.

"You got me there." Percy laughed as well.

"Where do I have you?" Monique was immediately confused.

"No. I mean... It's a saying. Means you made me believe

you, and you were joking. It's an idiomatic expression." Percy tried to explain the saying. "English can be very tricky."

Monique frowned. "That is so true. I try so hard, but I still do not understand these idiot sayings."

"Idiomatic sayings, means… never mind." Percy finished the second sandwich. "I guess sometimes they are idiotic. Thank you for the food. Sometimes I forget to eat when I am on the trail of some problem."

The computer dinged and the screen showed a message.

*Compound failure.*

In big red letters.

"Damn! Only eight combinations left to test." He punched in a set of commands and the computer showed a short blue line that began to grow as they watched. "Cross your fingers."

"Why?" Monique looked blank.

"For good luck, of course." Percy held up his right hand and crossed his index and middle finger.

Monique did the same thing… with a little help from the doctor when her fingers would not cooperate. His touch was gentle and soft. She felt his internal excitement with the momentary touch. Why did her scientist feel such pleasure by crossing her fingers? Did this have some meaning he did not tell her?

Percy pointed to the screen crossing his fingers on both hands.

They watched the line grow.

And grow.

And grow.

Monique uncrossed her fingers. "I do not think twisting my fingers off will help, Doctor Seizemore"

"Call me Percy, please. Doctor Seizemore sounds so formal. We practically live together."

The computer dinged.

Another failure.

"Number seven. Here we go." Percy crossed his fingers one more time and Monique followed suit.

The blue line grew.

And grew.

And… buzz! The computer froze half way through its blue line's path. A message appeared in green letters.

*Compound successful.*

Percy jumped up with his arms in the air. "Success! At

last!" In between bouncing and twirling, he did an elbow pump.

Excited, Monique stood and hugged the scientist, totally happy for him.

He bounced her with him and twirled her around the lab table before the concept of 'awkward' slipped into his totally ecstatic mind.

Percy lowered Monique to the ground, but his body couldn't quite let go. "Ah, sorry."

She looked up at the doctor with a huge smile. "That is okay." Monique had no desire to move. She liked his arms around her, as bony as they were.

They stood there.

In each other's arms.

With silly smiles plastered across their faces.

"Ah, Monique…"

"Oui?"

"Maybe… we should…" Percy glanced at the computer monitor.

"In a minute." She hugged Percy close and placed her head on his chest. "Your heart beats so fast. It is dancing with happy."

"We should…" Monique raised a hand to his lips, ending any more conversation, without lifting her head and inch.

Percy's heart *was* dancing with happiness. For more reasons than one. And his heart was not the only thing in his body that was dancing at the moment. But his brain had shut down and he had no idea what to do next. That always happened around women. Give him a quadratic equation, or a string of seemingly unrelated symptoms, and he would find a relationship. Give him a woman, a pair of arms, and a gentle touch; he was lost. No brain. No analytical genus. Nothing but a silly smile and an empty mind… well, not totally empty. He stood in his lab, holding the most beautiful woman in the world, who held him back. And, she didn't want to let him go! So he stood there wearing that silly grin, hoping Monique could not sense what other parts of his body were doing.

"Doctor Seizemore, I have an incoming video conference. Colonel Maddox requests your presence." It had to be Milo. Of course.

"No." Percy whispered.

He disengaged himself from Monique's arms and punched the intercom button. "Now? Really?"

"In five minutes, Sir. Would Miss Merchant be with you, Sir?" The intrigue in the Sergeant's tone was unmistakable.

Monique moved to the counter and pushed the button. "Oui, Sergeant. We have found the…" she paused for the word.

Percy supplied it. "Antidote, Sergeant."

"I'm sure you did." They could hear Doctor Anderson's gasp as Miller commented. "Video conference in three, kids. My place."

Percy flew to his keyboard and typed in a string of commands then hit send. "Let's go."

Completely unconsciously, he grabbed Monique's hand and dragged her out of the lab toward the command center. She could have gotten them both there in a flash, but she was actually enjoying his physical contact and the pure joy she could feel emanating from him. It was the first time Monique realized a man could feel elation connected to something other than greed or sex. This man was so different, so… exceptional.

They entered the command center just as Sergeant Miller accepted the call on his console. "Sir, we are all here. And I believe Doctor Seizemore has some new information."

The vid-screen showed the V-team gathered in the great room of the hotel in Spain. "All onboard at this end." The Colonel's nose appeared on the screen, then he took a seat next to his daughter. "What's up on your end?"

Percy slid into a chair in front of the camera on the computer. "Sir, Ms. Merchant and I have found the antidote for TPS." He pulled Monique close, in front of the camera. "The first test simulation was just completed a few minutes ago. We will need time to retest and manufacture a carrying agent, but I believe we can eradicate this threat now."

Cheers were heard all around, along with a few surprised looks and a wink or two. "Good work, Doctor Seizemore, Ms. Merchant. My congratulations. Keep us posted. Susannah?"

Susannah sat up straight and looked into the camera above the monitor. "Interesting developments here. Earlier Dad and I went to a club to meet the Policia Floral detective that has been following Brother Berthold's suicide case. The club, La Cabra Feliz, was really big, and guess what I saw?" She did not wait for an answer, but continued on. "Vampires! Four naturist vampires and one human, namely Faith Ford. Remember the bitch from Proctor Pharmaceuticals? Sorry, I mean the blonde female board member…" Susannah paused to let the information soak in. "They were sitting right out in the open, chatting like best friends. Now if I were a mathematician and put two and two together, I'd come up with four. Put Faith, vampires and TPS together and I come up with a plot to… do something really bad. I firmly believe she's the one who provided the CE for TPS's development. My only questions are, why and who put all of this together."

"Pauolo de Navarre de Colasion prepared these documents for us. He's Lt. Franco Etxebarria's partner in Navarre Province. It has a lot of documentation on Le Glaute Industries, vampires in Spain and France, and the history of vampires in this region. Apparently vampires are a known quantity to the Policia Floral here in Yesa." Colonel Maddox withdrew some documents from a dirty manila envelope. "Interesting. But no real help. Apparently Le Glaute Industries has a factory just north of Yesa. The Le Glaute family residence is just east, on Yesa Reservoir. It has a fancy name; le something or other. According to these documents, the compound is heavily guarded and no one sees the patriarch or family members, except approved individuals who have business with the company."

"This gets more and more suspicious by the hour." Helga commented.

Her fear rose from out of nowhere. Monique gasped… and vampires did not do that often. "Oui! Le Coucher du Soleil was one of Phillipe's summer homes."

"That's the place!" The excitement in Colonel Maddox's voice was unmistakable.

Monique continued. "After the Revolution, what was left of his family lived there in disgrace." Monique moved closer to Percy and took his hand. "Like beneath San Leyre," Monique could only whisper the name, "there are many grottes beneath the estate. Mathilda and I tried to find a way in, but, alas, we did not, after many searches. It was a good place to hide. For a while."

Percy squeezed Monique's hand out of sight of the camera.

"Lt. Franco Etxebarria followed the vamps and Faith out of the club. We are waiting for his call. Tonight there is a festival at the monastery. We'll be going, to see the architecture and lights, of course. If we don't hear from Etxebarria before that, he'll meet us there." Colonel Maddox stood and approached the camera. "I think we're on to something. I want to follow this thing to the end. Keep us in the loop, Sergeant. Docs and Ms. Merchant, great work." His belt buckle flashed before the camera, then the screen went blank.

Helga turned to Percy and Monique without even raising an eyebrow at the two holding hands. "I must reiterate the Colonel's words. Congratulations. Great work. So now what?"

Miller stood behind the couple making lewd gestures and mouthing the baby carriage song.

Helga bit the side of her cheek to keep from breaking out in laughter.

Monique was a vampire.

Percy was a geekiod scientist. And a virgin…!

Sitting together holding hands, they looked like innocent teens on the path to puppy love. Unfortunately that path was strewn with gigantic boulders and a sheer drop-off at the end.

"I need to replicate the results in a second simulation to be sure. Then it's production and physical test. We can use some of the TPS sample in the containment chamber." He turned to Monique. "You'll need to be out of the lab when I do the test."

"Oui, I understand." Her look at the doctor was pure adoration.

Percy smiled back… like a child seeing a birthday present for the first time.

Milo shook his head as he returned to his console commenting quietly, "He's a goner."

"I'll help. I'm sure you can use another pair of hands since yours seem to be engaged." Helga was enjoying the entire situation.

Totally immersed in their own world, Percy and Monique wandered off toward the lab.

"I think you're right, Sergeant Miller." Helga's parting comment only verified what Milo already knew. Percy *was* a goner. But then, Milo wasn't in much better shape.

✶✶✶✶✶✶

It was way after daybreak in Yesa and half the V-team had hit the hay for day sleep. Tank and Bear decided to do a little recon at the local tourist spots. Devlin and Maddox wandered off to find a good American style breakfast while Casey settled himself on the couch, remaining behind as security detail. He bit into a hot Pop-tart and swore rather imaginatively.

"We can bring you back some real food there, buddy."

Devlin could not believe anyone really ate those things.

"Thanks, no thanks. Loved these guys since I was knee high to a tadpole. Got enough to last me two weeks. Just in case." He waved them off with the half-consumed Pop-tart. "Cinnamon and raisin. My favorite."

Devlin shuddered at the sight. "And he's our pilot?"

Frank chuckled as they headed for a café at the end of the block. "So you think we should take a quick walk around the monastery after breakfast? Might scope out the place before we go there tonight. It'd be handy to know the layout, in the event we need to exit in a hurry." He looked up into the Pyrenees mountains towering above the village. In the morning light, stark white limestone and granite formations could be seen sprinkled between deep green forests and cultivated pastures. The high peaks and steep valleys presented convoluted and sculpted mysteries. When the Iberian peninsula crashed into the southern part of France in the Lower Cretaceous Period, the layers of sedimentary rock from the expanded Bay of Biscay pinched and lifted, creating some of the most wondrous sights to behold. One hundred and fifty million years later, they were spectacular tourist attractions and no less wonderous.

"Not a bad idea, but we oughtta take our props and blend in. Shoot some stills to share with the group. Maybe see some interesting geological formation and such." Devlin took a seat with his back to the stonewall of the building and watched the pedestrians strolling by. It was training and habit, but in the morning sun, the wall projected a gentle heat that warmed his back. No one moved very fast in Yesa. It was a picturesque town of small, steep stone roads, stairways to everywhere with hanging gardens that decorated the landscape. Basque herders still drove their sheep through the tight streets. A light breeze brought a mixture of floral scents and tempt- ing smells of baking bread and frying sausage.

Frank's stomach growled at the waitress taking the order. "Better make that two..." He paused, trying to pronounce the name of the local spicy sausage. "Anyway... two of them." He held up two fingers.

The waitress giggled. "Si, Señor, dos chorizos picantes."

Rob added his order and the young woman was off to the cook. "Ya know, I could sit here in the sun all day, and just watch the people go by. Feels good. Maybe some day I'll dump this gig and find me a chair in the sun near some beach. Someplace where the gals don't wear much and the guys can look all they want." He adjusted his bad leg. "Maybe I'll find me a lady who wants to wait on an old broken man."

"You'd be bored out of your mind in three minutes. Once a warrior, always a warrior, Rob." Frank chuckled at his friend. They'd had this same conversation on a slow sunny day, twenty years ago. "Women don't wait on men anymore. Look at Suze and Jordi. She gives him hell and he loves it. Course, I don't want to think about what they do behind closed doors." Frank crossed himself even though he wasn't Catholic. "She's still my baby girl."

Rob's chuckle turned into a belly laugh. "That baby girl can run faster than a race car, tear the hatch off an armored tank and rip a guy in half, not to mention the..." He pointed to his eye-teeth. "And she can fly now. I remember when she couldn't stay upright on a bike. With training wheels!" Rob adjusted his leg again. "We're getting old, Frank. Have you thought about the future of the Vamp Squad? Suze and the rest? We started this gig. Eventually it'll end for us, but what about them?"

Their food arrived and both men ate as they silently contemplated the future. No one really knew how long a vampire would live, banning destruction by an outside force. How do you plan for a thousand years out? Would America, as a country even exist in five-hundred years, let alone a thousand? It was a sobering prospect.

Maddox mumbled around his food, "If I had the answer to that, I wouldn't have these gray hairs."

Devlin choked on a large piece of chorizo. "And I would never find that chair in the sun."

"We're screwed, Rob."

"Yep, Frank."

Both men finished their meal in companionable silence and headed back to their quarters to retrieve a car. The Monastery of San Leyre was about five kilometers away. It was too far to walk, for Rob. And way up in the mountains. It would take about seven minutes in their Suburban. Maddox drove and Devlin rode shotgun.

"Look at this place, Frank. You could hide an army in these hills, and no one would see a thing. How did the Nazis ever take this place?"

"I did a little research on the Pyrenees. The mountain range

268

is filled with caverns, hot springs, but not a lot of small lakes. The actual geography makes this place a real wonder and great place to conceal all kinds of things. Nice."

"You mean, not so nice." They rounded the tight corner with care and had the first glimpse of the monastery and the surrounding grounds. "How does the human race construct such magnificent structures with bare hands, sticks and stones? This place is amazing."

"Maybe they didn't, Rob."

"Didn't what?" Devlin wasn't following.

"Construct this place. Humans. Maybe they had some supernatural help. Did you ever consider, if there are vampires in our world, what else could exist without humans really knowing? Until my daughter ended up with fangs, I had no idea vampires were real. Not only real, but had an entire society with a governing body, so to speak. Before... I was just this Army grunt, jumpin' and dodgin', tryin' to keep our world safe and free. Now...I don't think I would be surprised at anything. You could tell me little green trolls lived under bridges and I'd be checking it out with enlistment papers in hand." Maddox sighed. "Some days I wish I were still pleasantly naïve. We'll park near the school and go from there. How's that sound?"

"Pleasantly naïve? Sounds better every day. Let's go."

Frank and Rob caught a tour shuttle that wound up precarious ancient stone roads dropping them off at the sculpted gardens near the Porta Speciosa, the famed entrance of the monastery's chapel. Solemn chants could be heard echoing through the old stone halls. Youth in blue and white uniforms bustled about the grounds, coming and going from classes. The academy sat apart from the actual monastery, across a playing field and on a small slope that perched over more gardens and what looked to be stables. Beyond that, the mountains dropped off into the reservoir below. Way below. The view was spectacular.

"Look at that, Frank. Those stables date back to the fourteen hundreds." He held a thick pamphlet in his hands. "That's Columbus days." Devlin was getting into the architecture of the place and truly enjoying the sight-seeing excursion. "This school has a great polo program. The team competes in England every year at the Euro-Games. Says here," Devlin pointed to a page in the pamphlet, "They have actually stolen several championships from the Brits and Italians! Wow. I'm impressed."

"Well, let's go take a look. How's the leg?" Frank noticed his friend leaned heavily on the cane he used more often these days.

"Leg's good, just stiff from the long flight. Walking'll be good for it." They wandered toward the grand stables, pausing every now and then to take a picture or make a quick sketch. The place was magnificently maintained and each cobbled path was bordered by blooming flowers and manicured shrubs. "I'll bet this stuff is wasted on the kids here." Devlin pointed toward a group of young girls who stood in a tight circle giggling as they passed around a cell phone. Their crisp uniforms identified them as students, but their behavior screamed tweeny-bopper.

Rounding a group of whimsically sculpted trees, the soccer field could be seen below them. Stone stairs wound down the hill to a small patio covered by tan awnings stretched in triangles. Two teams raced across the field kicking at the ball and each other. This was definitely not the A team! One lone, four-foot high kid stood in front of the goal, obviously terrified, as both teams charged toward him. He moved back and forth nervously, panting and watching for the kick. When the ball finally materialized out of the middle of the melee, the young boy tripped on his own feet, falling face first in the grass, missing the ball completely.

Definitely not the A team.

Frank let out a whoop as Devlin cracked up. Not exactly the schooled response expected from adults supporting and nurturing the physical education of today's youth.

A lean adult in gym shorts and a black shirt sporting a clerical collar ducked from beneath the awning, glowering at the tourists who watched the practice. He took the stairs two at a time and in a flash stood before the two Americans. "Ces enfants apprennent simplement, vous devriez avoir honte de vous moquer d'eux! Allez-y, touristes."

On the playing filed, three teammates had gone to help the goalie remove the grass clumps from his face and find his spectacles. Obviously, the coach instilled good sportsmanship in his young team members.

Frank stuck out his hand before the coach could get away. "Hey, Sorry man, I don't speak French, but we didn't mean anything. Dev's kid is the same age and you should see him play football." He pointed to the recovering youth, "Same thing."

"Then why you laugh for children learning?" The coach

responded in broken and heavily accented English. He turned, blowing his shrill whistle and waving his arms madly. The students ambled back to their starting places with appropriate pats on the back for the goalie. They began the scrimmage again.

"So you are their coach? Good job with the team sportsmanship. Looks like a great group of kids." Devlin layed on the praise, in French.

It got the response he wanted. "They just start. I just start. We learn…" The Coach made a circular motion with his arms, "Together."

Frank got the idea Devlin was warming the coach up for some pleasant interrogation. Obviously this priest had taken Brother Berthold's place recently. He ambled toward the stables. "Catch ya later Dev."

Devlin waved his friend on and accompanied the Coach down the stairs with an over exaggerated limp to slow their progress. "My son's fourteen and a heck of a football player. Not the high school star by any means, but good enough to make first string. But that's American football. Even your goalie would kick his ass in soccer."

Devlin made a new friend with that statement. "I am a new coach. But this is a good program. We make champions here. I hope I can be as good as…. as the last coach." The priest and coach crossed himself continuing in French.

"Got lured away by the big money, huh? This place has a fantastic reputation." Devlin began to dig, slowly and methodically… but gently.

"No. Our brother went to the arms of God. It was quite tragic." He crossed himself again. Obviously this priest was aware of the untimely death of Brother Berthold and it struck deeply. Devlin held out his hand. "I'm Rob Devlin. We're here on an architectural tour. I love this place." They had reached the awning and Devlin shook hands with the coach, then took a seat at the picnic table under the canvas, with a groan.

"I am Father Manuel Tibruce. The students call me Father Manuel. You are in pain." The coach pointed to Devlin's leg. "You are welcome to rest a while and watch practice, although it is almost over. I cannot run these children too hard. They are young and it is hot. We have just begun this year's practice." Obviously the priest was now in a talking mood, all insults forgotten.

"So what happened, if I may ask, to their previous coach?"

Devlin adjusted his seat and groaned again. "Or is that a bad question? Forgive me, I'm American and we just blunder on, ya know."

"Not a bad question, just a bad death. So they say. We were friends. For a long time." A buzzer somewhere sounded and the students ran for a building near the end of the field, probably the locker room. The priest bowed his head and spoke softly. "It is no secret around here." He crossed himself again. "He took his own life. He was troubled…" Father Manuel look up at Devlin. "But not that troubled. He was a good man. A good servant of God. I will never understand…" The priest sat next to Devlin with a plunk. "…never."

Devlin patted the priest on the shoulder companionably. "There never is understanding, Father Manuel. There is only the Lord and healing. And it comes, after a time."

"Your words carry solace. You speak from experience?" Devlin had the priest and he knew it.

"Unfortunately, yes. We, who are left must go on and do the best we can. I am sorry for your loss of a good friend."

"Thank you, Mr. Devlin." After an appropriate moment of silence, the priest pointed to Devlin's satchel. "You are looking at the buildings, no? This is a good place to do so."

Devlin removed his sketchpad and thumbed through the drawing of the monastery, Q2 painstakingly produced as part of Devlin's cover. He paused at the sketch of the monastery's famous entrance.

"Impressive. May I?" Father Manuel took the pad and continued through the sketches. "You are very talented Mr. Devlin, but the true beauty in this place is in the chapel of the Santísimo. It was built between fifteen-oh-one and fifteen-thirty six. There is an amazing altarpiece and sculptures by Juan de Berroeta. You must not miss it."

"Really? Is it open to tourists? I would love to see this chapel." Devlin's interest was not only borne of their mission, he really was curious to see the *amazing* altarpiece.

"No tour groups are allowed, but I can escort you there, possibly later? With your friend. After the school is out. I think you will find it… interesting. Maybe the dinner hour?"

Devlin chuckled. "Your dinner hour or the American Dinner hour?"

The Father smiled, understanding immediately. "We have a

festival tonight. It begins around six thirty pm. Why do we not meet at…say five? At the Porta Especiosa?"

"I am coming to the festival. That would be fantastic!" Devlin stood with a groan and creak.

"You will see how the setting sun casts such beautiful patterns on the old arches. It is truly a religious experience." Father Manuel rose, took Devlin's hand in a warm shake, and trotted off toward the locker room.

"Until later then." Devlin shouted after the retreating priest. This would be interesting, he thought. A personalized invitation to get inside the hallowed halls of the monastery.

Maybe he would see something more than stunning architecture and magical light.

Devlin ambled toward the stables and his partner in crime.

Frank met Devlin at the large barn doors. He was shooting pictures of the wood patterns and beautifully constructed stables. The place was as immaculate as the grounds and each stall housed a stately horse. Saddles and bridles hung in front of each stall with a carved wooden placard over each stall door notating the names and breed of each occupant. The horses ignored the tourists, used to viewers and students in their domain. One huge gray steed munched complacently as Frank and Rob strolled by.

"That's gotta be one of the biggest horses I've ever seen, short of the Budweiser team. Holy mackerel." Rob peered at the placard. "Hercules. Hmm. Wonder who rides this monster?"

"That would be myself. I am Father Sinclair, the horse master here at the Monastery." His hands lay calmly clasped before him as he bowed…slightly.

"Hi there, Father. I'm Rob Devlin and this is my pal, Frank. We're tourists." Rob displayed a silly American tourist smile.

"Of course. Feel free to walk about the stables but please do not enter a stall or try to pet our animals. They are working horses and some do not… socialize well." The huge gray Andalusian whinnied at its master's voice and rubbed against the stall door. "Ah, take Hercules here. He is a bit aggressive, but definitely a prime example of true Spanish horseflesh. We are somewhat attached to each other. However…" Father Sinclair rubbed the horse's finely sculptured head. "The students do not ride Hercules. Only I."

Devlin decided to play the dumb tourist. "You're a Brit, Father. How long have you been the horse guy around here? This place is fantastic." Devlin never let his smile fade. He looked at the rafters and walls with childish enthusiasm.

"I came here as an orphan and have never left. This place is my home and my life. I am devoted to horses... and the Lord, of course. Please enjoy my horsepitality." The priest kissed his horse on the nose and retreated.

"Did he really say, 'horsepitality', Frank?" Devlin's smile widened. "These guys do have a sense of humor."

"I am sure Monique was never exposed to any horse-pitality, Dev. Keep that in mind." Frank snapped picture after picture. Under his breath he noted, "See that metal plate. Wonder what it covers?" He motioned to a thick steel plate expertly fitted into the flat wide stones of the floor. It's sunken handle was almost invisible in the cool dim light of the barn. "That's not on our schematics." He snapped several pictures. "We'll see what Miller and Monique think."

"I got an invitation for a personalized tour of the inside of the monastery tonight, before the festival." Devlin pointed to himself with both thumbs. "We bonded. I get to see the chapel of Santísimo. We need to chat with the rest of the team. Oh, by the way, you're invited."

Frank grunted as he dropped to a knee and snapped more pictures while Devlin played lookout.

A group of noisy teens, dressed in riding attire, entered the barn and all opportunity to investigate anything was over. Frank and Rob pressed against the wall to watch the kids select, saddle and bridle their horses, then stand quietly before the door, awaiting inspection. Father Sinclair appeared at the head of the group to walk slowly down each side of the barn, inspecting the student's work. As he dismissed each student, they led their horses out the back of the barn to the corral and training area, chattering the entire time.

"Gentlemen, please excuse me. I have a class." Father Sinclair expertly saddled up and rode after his students.

"Out we go." Devlin shot Frank a look and a nod toward the entrance of the barn. "That horse could do some real damage if he got pissed off."

"Then we'd best not piss him off. Let's get back to the hotel and share some pictures."

With that, both men headed for their rental car and a windy trip down the mountains. It was almost noon in Spain.

✳✳✳✳✳✳

It was almost daybreak at Olney Farm. Monique sat so close to Percy, he could hardly think. "So if this test is… valid," Her vocabulary was improving with exposure to the scientific process they had been witness to in the previous ten hours, "It is the answer we seek, oui?"

""Yes, yes of course." Percy shifted around to look questioningly at this beautiful, smart, fantastic, gorgeous… he ran out of descriptors. "The last thing to try is a live experiment. You…" He stammered. "Cannot be here. Bien sûr."

"I understand TPS is dangerous to my kind."

Percy smiled sheepishly. "Oui."

Monique bounced in her chair. He said a French word! His vocabulary was improving as well. "Oui! Very good, Doctor of Humans and Elves."

Percy chuckled. He was over the elf thing and it had become a kind of teasey-easy way between them. She was just so… everything rolled into a Christmas package with the most lovely decorations. His heart was putting out the most incredibly uneven beat and he loved it. "Oui, very pretty little French girl."

The intercom buzzed interrupting the intimate moment, as was its habit lately. "Doc, Ms. Merchant, Colonel Maddox will be live with new intel in ten. Would you like to join the rest of us scoundrels in the command center for midnight Margaritas? Ba dum dum dum…" Milo's voice was a little slurred and he was beating the table surface like a drum.

"Ignore that, kids. Milo is a little under the weather." Jackie's voice held a good deal of barely disguised humor.

"On our way. Margaritas?" Percy had never seen Practical Magic back in the nineties.

"Never mind, just… never mind. Milo had a run in with a six-pack." Then Jackie did laugh as Milo could be heard protesting, in song, in the background.

"We're coming." Percy grasped Monique's hand. It was becoming a delightful habit. "Let's go my pretty little French girl."

Monique giggled. "I'm not that little." She tippy-toed out the door rising above her already high heels.

In the command center, Milo was flying high. He'd been watching a game with Ted earlier and they'd both imbibed a bit.

275

Well, more than a bit. Milo's team won and he celebrated with one too many. Ted was out, snoring like a logger in his chair in front of the TV, which now showed some QVC program.

"Milo, get it together. You don't want the Colonel to see you like this." Jackie admonished her ex with tongue in cheek. Milo was a happy drunk and funny as all get out. Things just kept flying out of his mouth. Unrelated, but hilarious, none-the-less.

"Come mere, Wonder Woman, spin me a tale of woe, you Amazon Princess." He grabbed for Jackie but missed, tipping out of his chair and landing on the floor. He lay there on his back with his eyes closed chuckling to himself.

"Oh this is ridiculous." Jackie stood over Milo.

Helga sat on the edge of the table in sweats and a pair of worn tennis shoes, laughing at the Sergeant and Jackie. Her hair was a mass of tangles and she wore no make-up. Apparently she'd been in her quarters asleep when the call came in for a face-to-face with the team in Spain. Her scrubbed face and tossled appearance combined with the rumpled sweats lent a youthful presence to her usually staid and proper self. She swung her legs back and forth to Miller's Ninety-nine Bottles of Beer on the Wall.

"Has the Sergeant hurt himself?" Monique stood at the entrance to the command center staring at the dopey man on the floor singing and chuckling.

"Just his brain cells. A few thousand less right now." Jackie nudged Miller with her foot. "He celebrated a little too much after the game." She didn't bother to disguise her disgusted, motherly tone. She hit the comm button, "Q2, please come to the command center and save us all."

"We should put him to bed with egg and milk. That is what I used to do with my papa." Monique giggled.

"Be my guest. I'd let him sleep it off on the cold metal floor. Serve him right." Jackie nudged him again only to be rewarded with renewed singing and more chuckles. "What's so funny, shit-for-brains?"

"Shush, shush. Allow me." Monique lifted the Sergeant like a mom would pick up a small child, cradling the man as if he weighed nothing more than a doll. "The door, please."

Sergeant Miller cuddled into the French vampire's arms and heaved a sigh. The next second, that same mouth issued a loud, obnoxious snore.

"The door, please?" Monique could feel the Sergeant's

buzzing against her chest and fought back the feeding impulse that began to surface.

"Of course." Jackie led the way, opening doors and moving furniture out of the way. Soon the good Sergeant was tucked into bed, rattling the walls with his snores.

"He's not going to like the morning, or the fact that you put him to bed." Jackie laughed her way back to the command center.

"Oh, oui. Neither did my papa. He would be furieux the next day. But always grateful I did not leave him to lay where he was in front of the servants. It would not have been proper. He was always proper. And pompeux how do you say in English, pompom?"

Colonel Maddox's voice could be heard as they came through the doorway. "We're late." Jackie breezed through and took a seat on the table next to Doctor Anderson. Q2 sat at the sergeant's console.

"So, it seems this Father Manuel does not believe Brother Berthold killed himself either. Which tells me there is a giant coverup going on at the monastery."

Devlin appeared on the monitor with a big smile. "I get a personalized tour before the light show tonight. Looking forward to it. Bonded with the coach. Nice enough for a priest... and a coach."

Elizabetta sat behind Devlin. "We shall all go and see if we can beg our way in, as close friends on the same tour. Since we now know there are vampires here, in the open, we will need to be very careful."

Susannah's bright face appeared on the monitor. "I've been working on disguising my aura. I can almost make it disappear if I want. That may be handy, but I really have to concentrate."

Monique stood next to Jackie. She broke into applause at her BFF's revelation. "I shall also work on that, Susannah." One sister was not to be outdone by another! "Possibly Doctor Seizemore can help. We have figured out how to kill TPS!"

"Whoa, pretty little French girl, we haven't actually succeeded at the final trial yet." Percy's mind was still in the lab and still immersed in the intimacy initiated earlier.

Monique moved to stand beside him and took his hand. "Oui, but we will."

She smiled at Percy and the world faded away. For him, there was only Monique, her incredible smile and his erratic heartbeat. He stood there feeling the warmth of love, possibly for the first time in his pitiful, deprived life.

He just stood there, gazing at Monique.

She just stood there, smiling up at Percy.

In front of everyone.

For God and all to see.

"Ah, Doc? Doctor Seizemore?" Colonel Maddox was trying hard to cover his amusement.

"Percy!" Helga had to end this craziness.

Jerked out of his daze, Percy finally responded. "Yes, yes of course. The test will be complete by this evening." He looked back at Monique and softly moved a curl of hair from her forehead. "But all vamps must remain in their quarters, away from the open sample while I do the test.

Everyone in the room and on the monitor was aware that his warning was for all of the team members, but clearly he spoke to one person, and one person alone.

It was charming.

It was a little scary, too.

"Okay, so then until tonight, our time. We will see how this all comes together. Out." Maddox's big hand crossed the screen before it went black.

Helga patted Q2 on the shoulder. "Thanks for the pinch hit. Miller wasn't in any shape to set this up."

"No problem, Ma'am." Still not totally awake, Q2 wandered back toward the human quarters in his Mickey and Minnie pjs.

"Back to bed then." The pronouncement had Percy eyeing Helga with a strangled look. "Me and you, kiddo. I don't care what the rest of Weird World does." She hopped down from the table and dragged Jackie out of the command center, leaving Percy and Monique, still holding hands.

"Percy, maybe you should wait on the final test until I am deep in day-sleep. It would be safer. Helga can help you." Monique spoke softly as she squeezed his hand slightly.

Percy could hear her words. And they registered somewhere in his brain, but his brain wasn't listening very well. At least not the one between his ears. His heart was beating too loudly. And other parts of him were beginning to take over. He couldn't believe this brave, strong, smart, gorgeous woman held his hand. But Little Percy certainly could.

"Please..." The desperation in Monique's voice broke the

spell. "I cannot control myself around TPS. It is une chose terrible, terrible thing."

He paused for a second, only to make his lips move to form words when all they wanted to do was crush the other pair a few inches away. "Alright, we wait. I wait. You sleep." Percy took a step back to clear his mind. "What shall we do in the mean time?" He was not ready to sleep. Not the way his body was reacting.

"I have this wonderful video Susannah left me to see all alone." She sent Percy a coy look. "But I do not like to see videos alone."

"Then, the only scientific answer to this problem... is to watch the movie not alone. Together." He felt quite smug at his logical deduction.

"Oui. I will fetch this movie and we can see it together, in the lounge. You can make popcorn. I can enjoy a good blood wine. That is an excellent idea." She clapped her hands in glee. Like the teen she used to be.

It was charming. Percy's heart leapt. So did another part of him. "Back here in fifteen minutes?" Hopefully that would give the scientist enough time to get his mind and body under control.

"Oui." Monique danced off toward the vamp quarters.

Percy watched her go. He should not have. It didn't help his control issue.

Chapter 21

Fate's Temptation

Why do we want what we can never have?
Is it fate's tempt or a soul's salve?
Especially when hearts collide,
Racing from the other side?

What is there to do,
But follow through?

*Unknown Poetry*
*Poems for the Public*
*Santiago, Cuba 2015*

Monique jumped at the loud explosions on the wide screen TV, and squeezed behind Percy's shoulder, deeper into the over-stuffed couch. Why did Susannah want to see this terrible movie? It was horrible to see children die in a helicopter while those who should have been on board, watched from the ground. In her mind there were no losers when it came to helping children.

"I knew that was going to happen. Damn. Sucks to be those kids." Percy pitched a handful of salted popcorn into his mouth, missing with half of the kernels. They flew into Monique's hair and lap.

"Percy, that is awful." She admonished the man next to… and in front of, her.

"It's just a movie, my pretty little French girl." He tossed another handful all over the both of them and laughed as he tried to catch the individual kernels with his tongue.

"Not the movie, the popcorn. And I am *not* little." She picked several pieces from her lap and threw them sideways at Percy. "It smells like moldy bread, or manteau funéraire. She stuck her tongue out.

"Really?" Percy took a small sniff of Monique's Blood Wine. "That smells like iron dipped in alcohol."

Monique sighed heavily. "Alas, we shall never dine on haut

cuisine together like when I was human. My papa would invite the entire royalty to sup, and Cook would prepare the most delicious and tender specialties. She could bake a pastry to make your mouth sing with delight. Your mouth, not mine now. Puh. Now I cannot swallow a bit of such luscious treats. My stomach will revolt and I will…" She paused. "Sorry. I complain too much." She hung her head.

"Hey, don't worry about complaints. I promise to listen and not judge. The stories I could tell you. You may have been dining with royalty, but I was starving in a locked closet, learning to eat dust balls to keep my stomach from attacking my ribs." He slid around to face the French vampire. "I once fell asleep leaning against the wall. The blood from my beating stuck me to the wall. When the priests came to get me out for farm work, it darn near peeled the flesh right off my back. Later they beat me some more because I was an inconvenience." He wiggled a little with a wince. "Not everyone has lived the horrors we have. Yet here we sit, watching a shoot-em-up movie and eating popcorn and…" He looked at the bottle from which Monique sipped, "and drinking vamp booze. Not so bad."

Monique tucked her chin over his shoulder with a tender sigh…and stuffed a handful of the errant popcorn down the front of his t-shirt with an outrageous giggle.

"Hey, not fair!" Percy grabbed her bottle of Blood Wine and jumped off the couch. "No more for the pretty tittle French girl now." He held out the bottle just beyond her reach with a huge grin.

Monique had never really played as a child. Royalty was proper, staid and polite. They did not romp around or chase each other. The women dressed in elegant attire. They practiced impeccable manners. They married well, produced the required son and daughter, and retired from society to live out their lives in the solar, embroidering little nothings, gossiping about the current court intrigue, planning meals and doting on their grandchildren. That ended with her humanity. Then she was the sexual play thing for a masochistic predator who took her life and her innocence.

Monique did not know what to do. She'd never really play-flirted.

She sat there looking at Percy.

He stood there holding her wine out swinging it back and forth in a teasing manner.

She reached for the bottle.

He took a step back, his grin widening.

Something exploded on the television. Percy turned and before he knew it, the bottle was gone.

Monique sat on the couch as if she had never moved, but holding her wine.

"Guess I have to work on my form. How'd you do that?" Percy sat back down with his bowl of popcorn. "Teasing a vampire doesn't work very well, does it?"

"You tease me? Ah..." She cuddled behind his shoulder again. "Look, they set the building on fire. I do not like fire. Sex is much better in satin sheets and soft pillows. No broken glass and fire!"

Percy choked on his popcorn.

Monique patted his back carefully. She knew her strength and could feel his bones beneath her hand.

"You speak so..." He didn't have a word for her forthright way of talking about private things. Nothing was off limits and she was rarely embarrassed by anything. Especially sex stuff. He blushed. Maybe it was his Catholic upbringing. Maybe it was the fact that she was the most beautiful, spectacular woman he'd ever met.

"Freely? Oh, oui. It is often a problem. But I am French. I do not understand why Americans are so... what is the word... tightened up?"

"Up tight. And all American's aren't up tight, just the ones raised in the Catholic Church. You know. Sex is for making babies and serving your husband. That kind of bull." Percy tossed more popcorn into his mouth without choking this time. "Actually, that's not all true. I'm a little prejudiced. Recovering Catholic, ya know."

More explosions and fire on the television had Monique sliding farther behind her cover.

"It all started with the Judeo-Christian basis for this country. The Pilgrims were a very uptight bunch. Move forward six hundred years and about five hundred miles south, nothing has changed. Baptists, Penticostals, Methodists, you name the religion, I'll show you an uptight doctrine designed to control the body and subjugate the mind, not to mention empty the checkbook. I prefer science. Molecules don't care who you sleep with, or what the color of your skin is."

Monique was stunned. "You do not believe in the Lord?"

He gave her a quizzical stare. "That, from a vampire?"

Some man on an elevator was changing clothes and singing. What *was* this movie?

"But Percy, if there is no God, then there is no hope for mankind… and my kind, or sciencekind." She was making a very serious statement and Percy hit the pause button on the channel surfer.

"Am I really sitting here eating popcorn, watching the Losers save the world while having a theistic discussion with a vampire?" The fun had dribbled out of his popcorn bowl. Percy sat back and watched the frozen picture on the screen. "I am a scientist. I believe in the mechanics of the universe, the proof of real things. Discipline and knowledge, not fables and beatings. How can you sit there, with what you've been through at the hands of the monks, being what you are… and believe in a loving God who watches after his people?" It just came rolling out. Maybe it was the frustration of research and testing over the last few days. Maybe it was the fact that he was becoming seriously attached to… another species… for which there was no hope of a relationship, despite his growing feelings. Maybe it was the alignment of the planets. His mouth just spewed… "How do you balance the horrors of the world, the wars, the killing? If God was up there somewhere," he pointed toward the ceiling. "Why didn't he stop that asshole from making you a…" He clamped his mouth shut just before his Hollywood conditioning let the word *monster* fly out into the space between them.

"I am not so smart to know these answers. But I know there is a God. If not, there would be no love in this world." She whispered the last sentence with her head bowed. When she looked up at Percy, a red tear hung on her lower lashes. "And I do believe in love."

With that quiet statement, Monique rose. "I must sleep now. You can do your tests." She walked out of the lounge with her blood wine and a heavy heart.

Percy hit the play button and slid down in the couch. Tests-smests. If he couldn't save the world, at least the Losers could. He tossed a handful of cold popcorn toward his mouth.

One piece made it.

\*\*\*\*\*\*

It was close to four in the afternoon when Devlin's alarm woke him from his afternoon siesta. He was to meet Father Manuel in about an hour. It only took fifteen minutes to get to the Monastery from their hotel in Yesa. He had time. His eyes drooped as he slid back into a comfortable doze.

It didn't last long.

"Captain, time to rise and shine." Casey stood at the bottom of the bed munching a Pop-tart. "You said not to let you sleep past the alarm." Casey's Texas drawl made him sound slow and a little dull, but the man was a virtual ace behind the yoke and one hell of a concierge. He just seemed to know everyone's preferences and made them appear. Even though his job was flying, you felt like you just settled in at his ranch for a little dinner party every time you climbed aboard Casey Air. His cowboy good looks made the gals swoon. And that was before he opened his mouth with some sort of Texan-ism like, *ah shucks, ma'am.*

"Right. Why did I do that?" Devlin sat up and rubbed his leg.

"How would I know, Ma'am? I'm just the driver." He toasted Devlin with his pastry and exited with a flourish.

"Yee ha." Devlin picked up his cane and headed for a quick shower and shave, before attending the tour and festival.

In the great room, the team was slowly assembling. Elizabetta sat at the dining table in her native Romanian best. Natalia and Yuri opted for comfortable tourist garb, while Susannah was all teen flash and shine. Her gold studded heels clicked as she twirled in a Zara Aztec Gold mini and a peasant blouse with billowing sleeves. Lengths of strung beads wound around her neck accenting the low cut of her blouse.

"Whoa there missy, where's the rest of that skirt?" Her father came down the stairs.

The cover stories fell into place. "I'll have you know, Daddy Dearest, this is a Zara designer number I got for half-off. It was only one hundred and ninety-five dollars. A steal." Susannah continued to twirl.

"You didn't get your money's worth, young lady." He winked as he strode by, collecting keys, phones and camera gear. "How you gonna carry my lens bag in those spiky things. You'll break your ankle."

"Not a Sherpa, Daddy." Susannah winked back, grabbed her strappy little purse and did one more spin before heading for the car. "I call shotgun."

Elizabetta shook her head with a smile. "Who developed these cover stories, Frank?" She took his arm and led him toward the door.

"I have a sneaking suspicion it was that young lady in the really tiny skirt that just flew by." He chuckled.

Devlin joined the entourage at the curb and they set out for the monastery, and a date with Father Manuel. The steep drive had Susannah bouncing across the seat while Yuri had a good excuse to hold his new wife close. Occasional bleached white expanses of limestone showed up between grass and trees as they climbed the steep road to the monastery. A-21's new construction was complete, but the remnants of the expressway renovation across the Iberian Peninsula, still littered the sides of the road and massive machinery sat, still and unused in a roadside quarry.

As San Leyre came into view, Frank quietly reminded the team to stay in character. It was unnecessary, but he still retained some of his military command style, all the while, perfectly aware that the team knew their jobs inside and out. They also knew the critical nature of this mission, and were now very aware of the fact that vampires roamed openly, at least in the town of Yesa.

The towering walls of the monastery appeared in short order. "What is that funeral dirge? It's horrible!" Susannah hung out the window, cocking an ear to the wind. A Gregorian chant echoed across the parking lot, bouncing off the hills and buildings lending an eerie sound to the otherwise dead calm of the evening. The air hung heavy with moisture, spilling its sticky dampness across the vehicle and Susannah's arms. "Jeeze, Dad, what a downer. I might as well be listening to country western." Susannah plugged her ears and pulled a face.

"You could be back in private school listening to Mozart, or some other dead musician." Her father's retort was actually funny.

"Like Prince? At least it wouldn't make me want to down a bottle of Captain Morgan's and shoot myself in the head. Really…"

"Okay, children, enough. We're here and I think I see our tour guide." Devlin hopped out of the car and limped toward Father Manuel. He vigorously shook hands, then waved toward the car and the waiting *friends* who just happened to accompany him. Father Manuel's gregarious gesture had the entire team moving to join the priest quickly, before he changed his mind.

Their private tour began with the magnificent entrance called the Porta Especiosa. Father Manuel explained, it dated from the twelfth century and contained a likeness of the Devil himself, searching for lost souls, as well as the Archangel who will announce Judgment Day.

As Father Manuel lead them into the nave of the chapel of the Santísimo, Susannah let out a squeak as her strappy heels slid on wet stones. Not only wet, but slimy, slippery wet stones. Red, slimy, slippery wet stones that beat a path directly to the wall between two alcoves, one of which held a large ornate wooden box. There, in place of the granite sculpture of Jesus on the cross, hung Lt. Franco Etxebarria. His hands were nailed to rough hewn boards hastily attached to the wall. His feet were fastened tightly with an old rope. Great gashes rent his neck and belly. They no longer bled in rivulets, seeping across the floor. He'd been there too long. There was nothing left to flow from his cold, gray body.

Susannah pressed her face in her father's chest with a sob. It would not due to let Father Manuel see her eyes glow red and fangs descend with the smell of fresh human blood.

Frank held his daughter close, immediately understanding the need to not only hide her face, but control her blood lust.

"Holy shit, Father. Who the hell is that? What's going on here?" Devlin moved closer to the dead officer. "Should we call nine-one-one or something?"

Maddox escorted his sobbing daughter out of the church into the heavy air of the night. Elizabetta followed with an arm around Susannah. People were beginning to gather for the Festival of Lights, completely unaware of the drama behind the ornately carved entryway. Immediately Susannah ceased her fake sobs and wiped her face. Away from the blood she was fine.

"My God, I do not know. I must…" Father Manuel was overcome with emotions. "I must find the Abbott. He will know what to do. This is terrible." More to himself than to the others near by, he mumbled, "First Brother Berthold, now this…" Father Manuel herded his guests outside after Maddox and Susannah. "I am so very sorry. I do not know what to say. This is…" He flapped his hands as if to fly away from the tragedy, the obvious murder, within. "I must find…" Father Manuel turned and ran for the administrative building, leaving his guests standing, looking after the retreating priest.

"We have but moments before the Abbott and the authorities descend upon this scene. Might we make the best of our time?" Yuri held the huge wooden door for the others to re-enter the nave.

Immediately, Devlin and Maddox began snapping pictures to record evidence for later. Natalia cautiously approached the body of the officer, looking and listening. "His soul has fled, but, possibly, I can sense his end. She placed a hand on Etxebarria's face, closed her eyes and concentrated.

Elizabetta joined Natalia, placing a gentle palm on the compeller's shoulder. "Quickly, my dear. I can hear others. They come rapidly."

"There is nothing." Natalia shook her head. "He was unaware of his ending through someone's design." She turned his head exposing the right side of the dead man's neck. "This is the work of a vampire."

Just above the gash across his throat sat two puncture marks. Difficult to notice if one were not looking for the marks, but not completely disguised by the hideous slash.

"Back here." Susannah stood behind the cross, in the shadows of the first alcove. "There is a passage behind this bookcase." Susannah swung the bookcase outward to reveal a small arch with steep stairs descending into the darkness below.

Footsteps could now be heard on the steps just outside the entrance. Their time was up.

"Quickly, Susannah. Put it back." Elizabetta instructed. "We will return later and see where this goes."

A man in ornate prelate dress, obviously the Abbott, strode into the nave, his robes billowing. Behind him trotted another priest in somewhat less ornate, but very formal dress. "You must remove yourselves from this place immediately. There has been a terrible… accident. Please leave. Now." The Abbott motioned for the priest behind him to assist. "Please go with Father Sebastian."

The Abbott seemed more interested in getting the tourists out of his church, than worrying about a dead man hanging from a cross where a statue of Jesus should have been.

"Of course, Father." Frank slid his arm around his daughter, helping her to the door. "This is just awful. My daughter…"

On cue, Susannah sobbed and snuffed loudly.

Yuri and Natalia had already moved outside, quietly

287

standing together, trying to look shocked. Elizabetta helped Devlin limp behind Frank and Susannah. She looked appropriately disturbed and supportive of her friend, who tried for total disbelief. Father Sebastian fluttered behind the group, speaking priestly words of condolence and comfort.

Frank paused on the steps, handing his daughter off to Elizabetta's competent care. "Should we wait for the police, or something, Father? We just came to look at the Porta Especiosa. Father Manuel was so nice to meet us and... where is Father Manuel? Where'd he go? Is he okay?"

"I deeply apologize for this horrible experience, Sir. You understand, we must be discreet." He brought a finger to his lips as if to shush the man who had just witnessed a murder scene. "It is El Festival de Luces and there are many visitors here tonight. They must not..." Father Sebastian choosing his words carefully, "be disturbed by such as this." He motioned toward the exit. "Such a nasty business. Please leave your contact information with the Abbott's office and do not speak of this to anyone. The Policia Floral will contact you when they are ready and need information. Again, please accept our apologies for this terrible incident in our home." With that, Father Sebastian disappeared back through the entryway, shutting the door tightly behind him. Even without vamp hearing, Frank could detect the lock falling into place.

"Well, isn't that just peachy." Devlin leaned against the railing next to Susannah. "Please do not speak of this until the Policia Floral contact us? Really."

"You okay, Suze?" Her father placed a warm arm around her shoulders, then tipped her chin up for a quick peck. "You did meet Lt. Franco Etxebarria just yesterday and today, he's..." Frank waved toward the Porta Especiosa.

"I'm okay, Dad. I just feel bad for him. He left us to follow the vamps and Faith, now we find him here. Nat, are you sure he didn't know what happened to him?"

Natalia moved to hug her sister vampire. "He did not, little one. He was bitten, then most probably compelled. There was no pain in his mind at the end. Of that I am sure."

Music drifted across the field below the monastery. The festival was beginning. "We should find an out-of-the-way place to observe. If there are vampires in attendance, they may detect our coven." Elizabetta pointed toward people gathering in the field.

"There is a tool shed near the end of the field down there.

Frank and I explored it earlier. We could watch from there and stay partly behind the doors." Devlin pointed in the general direction of the shed.

"Let's move, people. I do believe the Monastery's mysterious benefactor has arrived." Frank indicated a string of large black vans with the Le Glaute company logo emblazoned on the side in fancy French gold script.

"Oh crap. Dad the second car is glowing neon green. Those are naturist vampires in that van. Yuri, get us out of here." Susannah grabbed her father's hand. "Grab on, Uncle Rob."

As instructed, the two humans connected and everyone disappeared, only to reappear, less than a second later inside the dim tool shed.

Devlin stumbled over an up-turned rake and sat down hard on top of a bale of hay. "Give a guy a warning, would ya, Yuri."

The Russian officer bowed slightly with a bit of a smirk.

"Hey, my cane..." It appeared next to him on the hay. "Thanks." Devlin stood and moved to the small dirty window facing the field. "Will ya look at that. Right into the church as if they'd been called on their own private nine-one-one line." Devlin tapped on the window with the handle of his cane. Dust mites drifted from the rafters above, disturbed by the vibration of the rap. "This doesn't make any sense. These monks are supposed to hate vampires. They held Monique and her friend captive and spent years trying to drive the devil out of them with torture. Now they have vampires right under their noses. I don't get it."

"Obviously, this mysterious benefactor, Monsieur Le Glaute is connected to vamps, Faith and CE somehow. Tank and Bear are doing recon tonight at Le Glaute's estate." Maddox opened the door to the shed to gain a better view of the light show, and the more important show across the field.

The music changed and more lights slid across the sky and walls of the monastery. The team crowded behind the Colonel and watched the clouds of heaven part as angels descended into nothingness, only to be replaced with more celestial beings and stars. The tempo of the music grew as the light show became more intricate and brilliant. Characters from various bible stories paraded across the high stone walls. The heavens appeared, disappeared and reappeared with lightning and thunder. Noah rode the helm of the Arc while every kind of animal imaginable held on in fear. Moses led his people out of the boiling sands of Egypt into the land of milk and honey, which grew into a starry night over a manger with kings and wise men kneeling in homage. On another part of the wall, Jesus dragged a cross up the hill to Golgotha, while a version of Michelangelo's all powerful-father watched and wept.

It was impressive. But not half as impressive as the Le Glaute presentation of money and power. Behind the beautiful light show, with its incredible stories and amazing art in light, a ghastly murder was being covered up. An innocent man was dead, and vampires strolled the grounds of the monastery at will.

"Can you tell which one is Le Glaute?" Susannah stood on an up-side-down bucket behind her father.

"I think he's the one who went into the church first, but I can't see the way you do, kiddo." He pulled a small pair of field glasses from his cargo pants. "They all went inside and haven't come out. I'm wondering when the cops will show up. Yuri, can you v-port us to the car so we can get out of here without being noticed?"

"Sure thing, Colonel." Yuri puled his wife close. "Say the word."

"I'd like to get a look at that secret passage, but I have a feeling the area will be off limits for a while. I wonder when they'll decide to call the cops, or *if* they'll decide to call the local constabulary. I think that ginger from the Vatican made it clear, Cannon Law presides over monasteries, not the regular law for you and I." There was a certain amount of disgust in the Colonel's tone.

"Wait, here they come." Susannah pointed over her father's head as she balanced on his shoulders with one hand. "You think he's that guy in the tux. The one strutting?" She handed the field glasses to her Dad.

"That'd be him, sweetie."

Susannah stepped off the bucket. "Then Le Glaute is definitely not a vampire." She let out a pent up sigh. "No aura. Not even a twinge of color around the guy. Check him out Nat. Maybe you can see something I can't." She joined her uncle on his bale of hay. "I was hoping he'd be Monique's maker, just so I could kick him in the balls for what he did to my buddy."

Devlin patted her on the knee. "You're a good friend, honey."

Susannah couldn't tell if he really meant what he said, or if he was being sarcastic.

"I doubt the Abbott will be calling the authorities, Frank." It was Elizabetta's turn with the field glasses. "There goes the body."

Chapter 22

I learned that courage was not the absence of fear,
but the triumph over it.
The brave man is not he who does not feel afraid,
but he who conquers that fear.

*Nelson Mandela, President, Activist*
*Johannesburg, South Africa, 2004*

"Yes! Success. Finally" Percy congratulated himself with a huge gulp of Flyin'-Hi Cherry. The last test came back positive. He'd found it, the antidote to the Pink Stuff! He could save the kids. He could counteract the affects of the drug and exterminate the triple helix DNA's programming that took over the neuro-net and turned humans into…what? That part he still did not know.

Percy carefully replaced what was left of the specimen procured from Lucy Redmont's brain. Locking the hazmat container, he buzzed Helga. "Doctor Anderson, could I have a moment of your time. In the lab if you please."

The loudspeaker chimed. "Sure. On my way."

It was close to sundown. He'd been working on the antidote since early morning when Monique had retired for her day-sleep. He couldn't wait to show her the results.

Doctor Anderson came through the door with two large plates of veggie lasagna and two Bud Lights. She must have read his mind, He was ravenous and ready to celebrate.

The hard part was over.

His brain was tired.

He was tired.

Soon he would be returning to his daily routine… that part stuck in his ribs a little.

Did he want to return to his daily routine?

"Here's sustenance for the hard working scientist. And alcohol to make it more fun." Helga slid the tray onto the counter and pulled up a chair next to Percy. "So what requires my presence, Percy?"

His grinned like the cat that ate the rat. "I did it, Helga. I created an antidote!" He twirled a small test tube of purple liquid in his left hand.

"Oh Percy, that's wonderful." She hugged the scientist and felt more bones than the last time. "Eat and talk." She took the tube and carefully set it in a wire holder, then shoved the lasagna in front of the starving man and pulled her hand back quickly, less she lose it. "Does Monique know?"

"No. She's still sleeping. This is fantastic." He gulped the food in front of him, following each bite with a beer chaser.

"Slow down, you'll make yourself sick! So how did you do it?" Helga figured if he had to talk about his discovery, he'd eat a bit slower. He looked like he'd been in the same rumpled jeans and t-shirt for a week.

"Well, after reverse engineering the formula, all I had to do was figure out what would break the link and cause the stuff to become inert. Cracking the DNA sequence was a little harder but, everything in time." He finished his can of beer and squeezed the aluminum can until it crumpled. "That's the power of science, Doctor Anderson." He tossed the can in the recycle bin.

"So what breaks the link?" He had her curious now.

"Exactly what made it in the first place, only more. It's like the right balance of ingredient in Spiced Koboacha Soup. The right combination in the right amounts makes it perfect and delectable. The wrong amounts ruins it and you get guck."

"Guck?"

"Yuck in the gut. Guck." Percy chuckled with his mouth full. "This is simply fantastic."

"So how soon will you have enough to send to our team? Is it hard to create?" Helga was on to the next step.

"Not hard at all, however, it cannot be prepared in large quantities without the industrial equipment of a pharmaceutical company, and then it would take time to calibrate the machinery, order supplies, develop packaging, apply for patents, etc."

"Right now all we need is enough to counteract exposure in case more kids have been drugged or our team is subjected to TPS. Could you do that here?" Helga was almost bouncing in her chair.

"I suppose so. Especially if I had a couple extra hands." Helga knew exactly what he was getting at. Those extra hands would belong to the resident French blonde. He wanted Monique in his lab.

Helga decided to make his request painless. "Would it be

safe for a vampire to work with you? You don't need any of the active TPS to make the antidote, do you?"

"No. In fact, I was thinking about asking Ms. Merchant to assist me. She has this unique ability to move faster than the eye can follow. It should cut our time in half or…"

"I think that's a great idea. I'll go find her and we can get started." Helga danced out of the lab before Percy could think. Monique could be helpful, and Helga could keep an eye on the two. Her motherly instinct was in full bloom.

Helga found Monique schlepping around the command center in her fake fur slippers and a rumpled pair of sweats. Obviously she'd had a horrible day-sleep. Her eyes were puffy and she stumbled a tiny bit as she crossed the room. Red stains dotted the front of her pink sparkly sweatshirt.

This was not good.

"Monique, dear, what is wrong?" Helga figured she knew exactly what was wrong, but it gave the French vampire an opening to talk.

"Doctor, I cannot sleep. I cannot eat. I cannot think. What is wrong with me? I have dreams… of those days." She melted into the waiting arms of the doctor. Tears began again. Through her sobs she mumbled, "I am so désolé. I do not know what to do. I should be with the team, but I can't…"

"Now, now, dear. You are indispensible here. If not for your help, Doctor Seizemore would never have found the antidote." Helga stroked Monique's back like she would comfort a small child.

"Antidote? He has found the antidote?" Immediately Monique pulled away and wiped the tears from her face with the back of her hand. "Then we have the answer!" Monique clapped her hands and bounced up and down in place. "I must go and congratulate our elf doctor!"

"Ah, Monique?" Ted leaned back in his chair, taking his attention away from the latest game on the huge monitor. "Might wanna do a little spit bath there." He nodded at her hands.

Red smears covered the back of both hands and blood spatters dulled the sparkles on her shirt.

"Oui, oui! This is to be a celebration. I must be beautiful so the elf doctor will be happy." Monique dashed off.

"But… oh what the heck." Helga shook her head. "Percy wanted her help, not her fashion sense. I wonder how long it will take to pretty up?"

Ted was intrigued. "He wants her help? What? Really...?" Ted actually got up and moved away from his game. At Helga's comment, even Sergeant Miller turned around with a surprised look on his face.

Helga shrugged. There wasn't much more she could do. "Apparently our lovely French vampire has learned some science."

"Who'd a thunk it?" Ted returned to his chair and game.

As incredulous as it seemed, Monique had picked up quite a lot of science. She hummed happily as she sped through her ablutions. They were close to the end of this mission. Maybe it would mark the end of her bad dreams and fears. The children would be safe. She did not have to return to the place of her terrors and the ghastly priests who tortured her, almost to destruction. One quick look in the mirror and she was on her way to the lab. Percy needed her. She would come through for him.

Monique actually beat Helga back to the lab. Rushing through the automatic door, Monique caught her mohair sweater on the latch and did a little spin to release herself before the sweater tore. "I am here, elf. How can I be of help?"

"Twirl on over here, my pretty little French girl, and I will show you." Percy thought her little twirl was just for him and Monique was not telling him any different.

Her five-inch heels clicked smartly as she crossed the room. Her heart was light and she was focused... on both the scientist and concluding this traumatic mission. "Oui. Oui."

Percy pulled a chair toward him and patted the seat.

"What do we do first?" She looked right into the face of what she thought might be the most wonderful man in the human world.

"Ah..." Percy was not given to stuttering but there was something about Monique that took his speech away. She made his mind spin and other parts jump with joy...which made his mind just simply shut off. "We... ah..."

Monique giggled. "Doctor, we must work. There are many lives depending on us." He was so cute, all discombobulated and sweet.

Percy shook his head. "Yes, work. We must work." He still sat there gazing at Monique like a little puppy eying a new chew toy for the first time.

Her heart was so light, she just couldn't keep the giggles

down. They bubbled up along with the incredible happiness that seemed to have invaded her entire body. She took Percy's hand and placed it on his keyboard and gently turned his face toward the monitor. "Oui, work."

The lab door whooshed open and Helga entered with somewhat loud steps. Not because she was in a hurry, or because she was angry, but she thought the two might need a little warning of her arrival. "So, where do we begin and what can I do to help?"

Within a few hours they were able to complete the last of the antidote for TPS. Twelve vials of vibrant purple liquid lay in a padded box ready for transport. Monique carefully placed the lid on the small box and secured the latches. "It is done." She let out a long breath and softly patted the lid. "Oui."

It was after midnight but 'down under' had no time schedule for humans or vampires. People worked when they had to, and slept when they were tired. Twice during their production of the antidote, Ted had appeared in the lab with food, drink, and more Flyin'-Hi Cherry. Doctor Seizemore was wired. Monique was in seventh heaven, and Helga slouched in her office chair in a state of contentment she hadn't known in years.

******

While the scientific side of the Vamp Squad was creating miracles in their lab across the ocean, the rest of the team was prowling the bushes to the west of the monastery, looking for the old well that would lead back to the catacombs beneath San Leyre. They'd liberated Monique just four years earlier using the well as an exit, but now it did not seem to be in the same place.

"Colonel, I do believe someone has covered your well. We've been searching for two hours. Even with GPS coordinates, we should have found it by now." Yuri loved scrounging around in the hills. It made him homesick for his own country and the stunted forests of his beloved steppes.

"It wouldn't surprise me, Yuri. After all, we stole their last vampire right out from under their noses. They probably figured out how we did it." Frank sat down on a large rock. "Too bad MorningStar is not here. She'd just talk to the dirt or something." Frank shrugged. "Where's the right vampire when you need her?" He looked up at the team. "Did I just say that out loud?"

Susannah laughed outright then clapped a hand over her

mouth. Natalia and Yuri grinned silently and Elizabetta chuckled softly. "I just have to tell Uncle Rob that one."

Devlin had stayed at the tool shed to keep an eye on the comings and goings at the church. He would not have done well climbing around in the bushes with his cane and sore leg.

The sound of dirt and rocks moving alerted the team to the fact that they were not alone. "Down, everybody".

As each member of the team took cover, a string of American curse words issued forth from a tangle of bushes below them. The sound of a mini rockslide broke the evening silence, just before a soft baritone voice could be heard. "Get the fuck off my shoulders. And watch the ears this time. I like my hearing."

Frank motioned the group to take cover.

"There's thorns on this stuff. Hold on." Tank's voice filtered up through the brush. "Yikes. Ouch."

Bear's baritone was also recognizable. "Pussy. Climb up."

Susannah snickered as she snuck through the bushes to the location of the voices. As Tank's head poked through an enlarging hole beneath some brambles, she pulled a few branches out of the way. "Hey guys."

"Bear, don't..." Tank disappeared beneath the ground with a string of grumbled foul words. "...don't drop me, idiot!" His voice echoed.

A deep chuckle rose from the hole. "Suze, that you kid?" The top of Bear's close shaved head appeared in the brush. "How about a vamp hand here."

Susannah quickly cleared the brush as Frank and Yuri pulled Tank and Bear to the surface. "Where'd you guys come from? I thought you were supposed to be doing recon at the Le Glaute estate."

"We were." Tank was brushing stickers and dust from his clothing and picking brambles out of his hair. "Followed a passageway from the guy's garage and ended up in a maze down there. We came out in the chamber where we originally found Monique, then crawled out through what used to be the well." He looked back at the disguised hole. "Used to be, being the primary description." He pulled a sticker from his shirt. "Le Glaute has himself quite the place. Le Coucher du Soleil, his estate, has a lab, house..."

"Mansion," interrupted Bear.

"...garage for about thirty cars, spa and really big gardens.

Apparently he runs his business out of the estate where they develop all the new stuff." Tank straightened.

"These caves and caverns are all over under the entire area. His estate connects to the Monastery and the school. This whole mess gets more interesting by the minute. And guess who I saw on her way to the cosmetics lab?"

"The notorious Faith Morrison?" Susannah sneered. "Of course."

Frank shook his head. "It gets more and more curiouser, doesn't it? I think we can put the facts together and come up with a scenario here."

Elizabetta approached silently. "I would surmise there is a connection between Le Glaute, Miss Morrison, sick children and TPS. And I believe the connection is down there." She pointed to the hole from which Tank and Bear had appeared.

"If the church is connected through a passageway, it would explain how the cop got killed and strung up in there without anyone seeing anything. I wonder…" Susannah squinted at her father.

"Whoa, whoa wait. What cop? Strung up where?" Tank looked toward the east. "We need to get our team back to the hotel. It's almost sunrise. You can fill us in on the way."

"I will gather the Captain and meet you at the car." Yuri kissed his wife and bolted for the tool shed and Devlin.

"Let's bug out. Thirty-six minutes till sunrise." Frank waved the team toward the parking lot and their ride down the hill. "We can regroup when everyone is safe undercover."

As the team scrambled toward their car, Yuri found Devlin in the shed, his face glued to a crack in the door facing the church. "So far, the only thing of note was the removal of Etxebarria's body. Otherwise, it's quiet as a graveyard."

"Captain, we need to exit. We meet the team at the car." Yuri handed Devlin his cane. "We must go. Soon it will be daylight."

Devlin opened the shed door and gazed at the lightening sky. "Yep, let's get out of here."

"Bear and Tank came out of a hole. They go to the car." Yuri pointed at the small group quickly climbing the hill to the church parking lot.

"Really? Hmm. That should be an interesting story. Was it the well?" They walked as fast as Devlin could accommodate with his cane.

"I do not know. Hole in the ground from a cave I think." Yuri took Devlin's arm and v-ported them to the back of the Suburban. He smiled at the startled Captain. "Faster. Easier." Yuri pointed at Devlin's leg.

"That it is, but how about a warning! I'm still getting used to beaming around."

"No beam. V-port." Yuri welcomed his wife as the team piled into the car. "We go."

As the Suburban wound down the mountain road, Tank and Bear described the Le Glaute estate and more of what they'd seen.

The estate covered about five hundred acres and maintained its own water source and solar power system. It seemed to work totally off the grid and was guarded by a private security force. Stone or cement walls surrounded the estate with ornate wrought iron spikes crowning the walls. Cameras had been installed at the gates and around the main house, but most of the grounds were not under surveillance. Which was how Bear and Tank infiltrated the property. The detached garage was more like a warehouse of elite and expensive cars. Beautifully sculpted gardens extended down the mountain in tiered levels, one of which contained an infinity pool and copula. To the west of the main house on the other side of the huge garage, stood two guesthouses. Tucked against a brilliant white granite outcropping was the Le Glaute Cosmetics lab where their newest products became reality.

"We took cover in the garage and caught some guy coming out of a stairwell. He pushed a button and the floor closed over the stairs. That's not exactly normal so we thought we'd take a look. Eight and a half hours later, voile! I stuck my head out of the bushes." Tank still picked at his shirt, finding more little stickers in the material. "Like I said before, the maze below the estate leads all different ways. We took a reading and picked the one we though would take us towards the monastery. Good choice."

Bear grunted. "We could have been down there forever, let alone eight hours. There were several minor tunnels that looked like they were man-made, but we followed the one with the most footprints. I don't ever need to go back there." He visibly shivered. "One of the grottos was full of stone shelves and dead priests all wrapped up in cheese cloth. There must have been a hundred or more. Brrrrrrr."

"Cool!" Susannah loved scary movies, mummies and

zombies. "I would love to see that place!"

"No can do, kiddo. It's obvious the tunnel we traversed is often used for travel between the estate and the monastery." Tank patted Susannah's knee. "Too dangerous."

"I do not understand this new revelation. If the priests of San Leyre were so dedicated to eradicating vampires, that they would hold and torture Monique for years, why would they now be in league with vampires?" Elizabetta was puzzled.

"We do not know they are in league with vamps. If there are vampires involved in this conspiracy, this new drug, the priests may not be aware. We need more information. We need to get our hands on Faith Morrison." Devlin smacked his own knee, then winced.

"Possibly Yuri can take her." Natalia's quiet comment got the Colonel thinking.

Faith had been at the club the night before. If they could find her alone and grab her…

"But if she hangs out with vamps, will Yuri be able to get away with her? Can they not follow?" Devlin was planning in his head. Faith had never seen Devlin or Yuri. They'd always stayed off video conference and out of view during the Proctor mission. "Vamps can recognize vamps, right?"

Elizabetta was the one to respond. "If Natalia can compel vampires, we may be able to pull this off without anyone knowing what is happening. Nat?"

"Of course. I can compel most vampires. I have never tried with a very old or very strong vampire though. If Yuri can be fast, it might work." She snuggled close to her husband. "But how do we know who is involved and who is not?"

"Faith. She'll know. She never gets involved without knowing who, what, why, where, and personal benefit to her!" Susannah stamped her feet on the floorboards. "And I'd love to get my hands on that bitch."

"Language, daughter." Elizabetta smiled indulgently at her surrogate daughter.

\*\*\*\*\*\*

The sun was up, above ground, but Monique was too excited to sleep. She lay on her bed with Trouble Tribble clutched to her chest. At every wiggle, it purred its strange noise and she giggled. She'd never been a part of anything as important as saving children before. The feeling of satisfaction was new and invigorating. Miller had sent a coded message to the team in Spain, a few hours before, letting them know the antidote was developed and twelve doses produced. Now they only need make arrangements to deliver the purple vials and all would be well. It was a simple way to think, but Monique was completely at peace. Now, maybe the dreams would stop torturing her. She cuddled Trouble Tribble and closed her eyes.

Percy lay atop his bed counting sheep, reciting the periodic table, anything to keep his mind off the gorgeous vamp he'd spent the evening with, over a computer keyboard and test tubes. The antidote was now a reality. But the bigger question remained to trouble his overactive brain; why had TPS been developed in the first place? Who created such a diabolical drug, or... he really couldn't call it a drug since a good portion of the substance was actually alive.

His entire world had morphed in the last five days. It'd been a mind-blowing experience, challenging every scientific norm he believed in. A couple of weeks ago, if someone had mentioned vampires and conspiracy theories, he would have laughed and planned to go see the movie. Now, he questioned even the human existence. If vampires are real, what other childhood horror was out there, lurking in the shadows? Or simply living underground, protected by his own government? He'd stopped sleeping without a soft blue nightlight to illuminate the corners of his small room. He'd just about stopped sleeping completely, as his mind wound around the new reality that had come in the shape of an old friend and cohort.

Helga sat in the command center with Sergeant Miller, sipping a decaf latte and waiting for the Colonel's call to catch up on what was happening in Spain. The six hours difference in time was inconvenient to say the least. It would be close to noon there.

The computer chimed.

Miller hit the keys and Colonel Maddox's face appeared on the screen. "Good afternoon, or morning, whichever." He looked hungry and tired. "Got your message when we returned last night, or this morning. Then things went to hell in a hand basket. Been on the run since. Here's the scoop." He rubbed his face and took a deep gulp of coffee. "Tank and Bear did recon at the estate and found a series of tunnels that connect the Le Glaute estate to the monastery and the academy, so now we have the how. How the drug got to the school." Again he gulped coffee. "Etxebarria is dead. Poor fellow. We know there is some kind of cover-up at San Leyre. His body was removed with no contact with the police. We passed an ambulance on the way down the mountain so I did a little checking at the hospital, tourista ya know." Frank rubbed his tummy with a tired grin. "Two more kids from the school are sick. One is from Belgium. Her parents are not available so the school infirmary finally called the hospital in Yesa. It's small but well staffed. She was immediately transferred to their sister hospital in Pamplona. She's in a coma." Frank paused.

"You think it's TPS?" Helga was fairly certain, even without an answer to her question.

"Oh yeah. They found the girl near the cemetery, unconscious. The other kid made it to the school infirmary before he passed out. Medevaced to Rhein-Main. He's Canadian. I've been in touch with Colonel Severin there. He's almost despondent. The kid's his nephew. Now the EDCD has been alerted and the entire place is blowing up. The EDCD is talking quarantine. "

"Have you seen Le Glaute? Any pictures?" Miller was immediately putting two and two together and coming up with the same ideas as Susannah. "Monique could confirm or deny the guy, if he's the vamp we're looking for."

"We think he went into the church after we discovered Etxebarria's body, but we were too far away. He didn't glow so he's not a vamp, according to Susannah." Maddox sat back in his chair. "He might be working for, or with the vamp we're looking for though. We need the antidote. A soon as Yuri gets a little rest, I'm sending him back for it. How much did you make?"

"We have enough for twelve doses. The amount is sketchy but I think we've got the dosage correct. It would be nice to know how much the children ingested. Can you figure out who gave it to them?"

"We'll do our best on this end. We have a line on Faith's usual dinner arrangements. We'll try to grab her tonight at La Cabra Feliz and feed her to Natalia."

Sergeant Miller blanched.

"In a manner of speaking, Sergeant." The Colonel chuckled at his sergeant's response. "Nat will get the info we need in short order. I'll notify you when Yuri is ready to come for the antidote. The sooner the better. Out." The screen went blue.

Helga sighed heavily. "The threat continues. And so do we." She stood. "I'm off to bed. Will you let me know when Yuri pops in? He needs to know how to administer the antidote. It should be administered slowly with an IV push." Helga leaned against the console, clearly bone tired.

"Roger that, Doc. Get some rest." Sergeant Miller returned his attention to the monitor in front of him. His fingers were already flying across the keyboard.

Helga fleetingly wondered what he was chasing this time. It was always something. She was too tired to contemplate. She checked her watch. Was it really only seven thirty in the morning?

Chapter 23

I don't run away from a challenge because I am afraid.
Instead, I run towards it because the only way to escape fear is to
trample it beneath your foot.

*Nadia Elena Comăneci-Connor*
*Olympic Gold Medalist, Sports Enthusiast and International Fund Raiser*
*United States, 2016*

Casey stood in the shadow of the curtain with a very large lens on a very small camera. He watched as one after another entered the police station across the street. He counted, photographed and identified via the facial recognition software Sergeant Miller had installed on his laptop just before their departure. When a tall ginger priest strode up the steps, he did not need the software. The Very Rev. Father Disjagio von Songoria was easily recognized by his stature, flaming red hair and confident stride. In Casey's opinion, the man was insufferable. He'd watched the tapes of the conversation in the Burnside's kitchen and knew the Vatican's detective could be a junkyard dog when it came to conspiracies... and even when it did not. The priest saw the world as one big conspiracy against all that was Catholic.

A snore from the couch alerted Casey to the fact that the Colonel had finally crashed. Casey recorded the time and Songoria's name in his little notebook. It was two forty-five in the afternoon and he was curious. Why was Songoria at the police station? Already two ECDC agents from the European Centre for Disease Prevention and Control, had arrived and not yet departed.

If curiosity killed the cat, what would it do to Casey? He quietly left the hotel and crossed the street. His camera, now sporting a normal sized lens, hung around his neck and he held a handful of tourist pamphlets. Taking the entry steps by twos, he burst through the front door with a bang.

"Oops. Sorry." A man at the front desk jumped. "I'm totally lost. Do you speak English? This is the police station, right?"

The officer looked Casey up and down. "Si, momento, Señor." He picked up the phone and spoke in rapid fire Spanish. Within a minute, another officer came down the hall.

"Hola. I am Officer Velasquez. How can I help you?"

Loud voices could be heard from behind a glass door that read, Jefe in capital letters.

"Wow, somebody's pissed." Casey commented as he took the Officer's hand and shook it vigorously. "I'm Casey Smith and I'm totally lost." He held up his handful of pamphlets. I want to find the…" He pulled one particular pamphlet from the group. "… Fountain of San Virila. I want to climb up to the top of Mount Escalar. There's supposed to be a spectacular view of the reservoir and the Pyrenees." He pointed to his camera. "Photographer."

More loud voices and scraping chairs caused Officer Velasquez to take Casey's arm and steer him to one side of the reception area. Which was a good thing, since the door immediately flew open discharging one obviously furious Father Disjagio von Songoria. Left behind were several whispering officers, one of which had more medals on his chest than General MacArthur. Casey didn't recognize the ECDC representatives standing at the back.

"Holy cow." Casey exclaimed as Songoria stomped out of the station. "That's one mad priest fella." His Texan accent was thick and slow.

Velasquez shrugged. "Religion and law often do not mix. Come with me. I will show you a topographical map. Your way will be clear. I have made this hike many times myself with my son. He attends the Academia de Santos Domingo de Silos at San Leyre."

"Your kid's gonna be a priest?" Casey laid on more Texan accent and the 'dumb American' attitude.

"No. No, of course not. He will be an officer, like his father. It is simply a very good private school. Although lately, I have my conerns…" Officer Velasquez paused, looking after Songoria. "Never mind. Come this way. You are a photographer? You will like this walk."

After touring the entire province via topo map, Casey thanked the officer and made his escape. Officer Velasquez was definitely a proud father with a studious son who enjoyed hiking and rock climbing. While chatting amicably, the officer did mention the hope that his son not be afflicted by the strange 'flu' going around at the monastery school.

Casey strolled on down the street and ducked into a quiet bar to quench his thirst and watch the people passing by. He loved watching people. He could spend hours relaxing in some quiet hole, studying the social interaction around him. He was fascinated by behavior and people's preferences, or their body language. Unfortunately, half way through his beer, he spied none other than the illustrious Faith Morrison entering a salon across the street. The salon was very small and she seemed to be alone.

Casey paid for his beer and bolted for the back of his hotel. This was exactly what they needed.

Faith Morrison.

Alone.

******

Yuri finished his third bag of synth blood and concentrated. In a blink, he disappeared.

"That still amazes me." Devlin shook his head. "I wonder what it feels like. It always happens when I least expect it... then woosh. I'm wherever."

"Ask him to take you sometime." Frank chuckled.

"Nah. I think I'll pass on that one." Devlin munched on a small pastry. "Not that curious, Frank. How about you? Then you can tell me what it's like." The easy teasing was built on years of working together, and surviving some very tough spots.

Casey burst through the hallway and slid across the polished tiles. "Guys, I just saw the Morrison woman go into a beauty salon. She's all alone." He was breathing heavily from his run in the heat of the afternoon. "And that priest detective just stormed out of the cop shop across the street." He took the camera from around his neck. "And he was pissed, to say the least."

"Shit, Yuri just left." Devlin was slumped in a lounge chair near the french doors to the patio. A gentle breeze sent warm air across his legs. It actually helped the stiffness.

"We can do this. Just us humans. She's only a woman. And did I mention, she's alone?" Casey was hyped and ready for some action. He'd been holding the boredom fort down too long. "There has to be a back door to the place, right?"

"Yeah, but she could cause a ruckus and then we'd have the cops, or worse yet, vamps all over us in a heart beat." Frank pointed in the general direction of the police station across the street from their hotel.

"They're already buzzing around like a bunch of mad hornets. Now Songoria shows up and more kids are sick." Devlin sat up. "This place is going to hell in a handbasket."

"How about I just use the ol' Casey magic on her? It's always worked for me before." Casey struck a pose and smiled enticingly. He raised his eyebrows in a 'come hither' manner.

"*That* has always worked for you? Imagine." Devlin got up stiffly. "We can surely give it a try, but she knows what Frank and I look like, if she remembers. And she probably will, since we were instrumental in toppling her little scheme with Proctor."

"You guys take the car and find the back side of the salon. It's just a block and a half down. On the right side. The sign said Salón de Cabello Fino. I'm on my way." Casey checked out his nails then messed up his mop of thick wavy blonde hair. Out the door he went.

Frank looked at Devlin. "Can't hurt. Maybe this'll work." He grabbed the keys to one of the Suburbans parked on the side street next to the hotel. "What is it about that boy that reminds me of Redford in Butch Cassidy and the Sundance Kid?"

"It's the hair." Devlin climbed into the passenger side of the Suburban. "And the attitude. He doesn't lack for self confidence with the ladies."

They cruised down the main street through town, watching for the salon. There were few people on the streets in the early afternoon. As the sun went down and temperatures cooled, the streets would be impassable, with people strolling, eating, and drinking into the late hours of the night. But right now? Right now was perfect. If Casey could come through…

"There it is, Frank." Devlin pointed to the sign. "It's small. Maybe this will work. Turn down there. That street looks like it goes around back."

Sure enough, the alley wound around the back of the shops. It was a tight fit for the large SUV, but Frank skinnied the car through and parked next to a dumpster at what he though would be the back of the salon. Then they waited.

And waited.

As the minutes passed by, the SUV heated up. "He better show pretty soon. That big garbage can stinks." Devlin had rolled his window down for air.

Two doors down, Casey appeared, waving madly at the two in the car, with one hand. The other hand was placed prudently on the derriere of the woman slumped over his shoulder.

As they helped Casey load an unconscious Faith into the back seat, Devlin casually mentioned. "So that's the ol' Casey magic, huh?"

Casey gave one last grunt as he hefted the woman onto the seat, pushing her down and out of sight. "Plan B. Let's get out of here." He crawled in around Faith's inert body and flopped down out of sight. "Please don't take your time, gentlemen."

A little faster than the initial ride, the SUV was soon parked close to the back patio gate of the hotel as the three men unloaded a still unconscious Faith. A lovely, large purple bruise was beginning to show on her left cheek. Carefully checking for on-lookers, the men carried the woman through the gate without anyone the smarter.

Yuri was sitting at the bar, sipping a shot of blood-vodka on ice. "Where you go?" He pointed to a small plastic box. "I get the antidote. It make my skin itch." He rubbed his arms and moved away from the box.

"Does it move to you like TPS? Do you crave it?" Immediately Frank was on the alert. He'd seen what TPS did to his nonhuman team members.

"No. But I do not like it. This is the Morrison woman?" Yuri had never met Faith in person.

"Oh yeah. Casey worked his ol' magic on her and she came quietly." Devlin snickered.

"Just for the record, I didn't have enough time for my magic touch so I opted for quick, as opposed to slick. Just for the record." Casey was a little insulted. He really didn't approve of men hitting women who hadn't lodged a first strike.

"Plan B." Devlin was enjoying himself watching Casey defend his womanizing ability.

Faith moaned and raised a hand to her cheek. "Ow. What the fuck?" She tried to sit up but gave up without opening her eyes.

Casey, almost always the gentleman, got a small bag of frozen peas from the kitchen. "Try this." He handed it to Faith.

The good eye opened. So did the mouth.

But not before Casey clamped a hand across Faith's deep red lips.

The struggle that ensued had Devlin running for duct tape.

It was a short struggle, and very effective duct tape.

Casey gently placed the bag of frozen peas across the bound woman's cheek and eye. "Sorry about the punch, Ms. Morrison. I don't usually hit women I don't know. Actually, you're the first…"

"Casey, shut it." Frank was in no mood for pleasantries. "Morrison, we know who you are and that you're somehow mixed up in this drug business. We now have you, and we need information. We can do this the easy way, or the vamp way. Your choice."

Anyone in the room could read the pure hatred emanating from Faith's one uncovered eye.

"You cooperate and you go free. No harm done. Well, except for Casey's little shiner. And he did apologize." Frank shrugged. "Clam up, and our specialist will glean the information from you anyway. Again, your choice." He pulled the duct tape from her mouth.

Greasy red lipstick smeared across her mouth and chin. "You have no idea who you are dealing with. You thought Proctor was a maniac? Just wait until you meet my new boss. Release me now and he'll just kill you quickly." She pressed her lips together stubbornly.

Her threat fell on deaf ears.

"Yuri, I know it's early, but could you wake your charming wife?" Frank slapped another piece of tape across Faith's mouth, not so gently. "I don't have time for games. Then, can you v-port three vials of this antidote to Rhein-Main to Doctor Severin?" He'd opened the box and was reading the directions and dosage Doctor Anderson included. The Colonel carefully placed three vials in a ziploc bag. "Casey, make a copy of these, would you." He handed the file to his pilot.

"I get Natalia." Yuri left the room.

Faith continued to watch the movement, but it was clear she knew what was coming. As involved as she'd been with the Proctor coven, she had to know about vampires and at least some of their more unique powers. And she probably would recognize Natalia.

In minutes, Yuri returned with a sleep-tossled Natalia. The sun was still not down, but the room was protected by shuttered windows. "Colonel, I don't think Yuri can make it to the base in Germany without a better idea of the location. He told me about the antidote, but he generally has to know where he is v-porting to. He's only been to the base once and didn't get off the plane. I fear for this idea." She took her husband's hand and lovingly kissed his cheek.

"I try." Yuri's blunt answer did not sit well with his wife.

"We cannot risk the antidote. And I can not risk you, moya lyubov'.

Casey came in with a couple sets of the documents he'd reproduced in the hotel office. "I can fly the stuff up there. It'd be a couple hours at most. There's a little out-of-the-way spot in Frankfurt that serves amazing garlic steak with mushrooms. The waitresses wear these little German outf…"

"I take him." Yuri pointed to Casey. "And the antidote."

"Whoa, hang on there, little doggie. I'm not so sure about flyin' without wings." Casey held out the papers to Frank and stepped back.

"That will work. Casey, you've been to Rhein-Main many times. The place is well set in your mind. All you have to do is think about it and Yuri will take you there. Do you know the hospital well?" Natalia smiled at the pilot with confidence. She snuggled beneath Yuri's muscular arm. "My husband is a transporting machine."

Yuri's grin was brilliant in the wake of his wife's compliment. "I am a machine. Da!"

"Settled. Before you two go, Natalia could you see what Faith has on her mind, please?" Frank joined Casey at the bar and poured himself a drink. "I'll send a quick message to Severin telling him to expect the antidote, my pilot and a Russian transporting machine." He toasted a still smiling Yuri with his drink.

Natalia knelt next to Faith. "This will not hurt, but it is better if you relax."

Faith began to struggle against her tape restraints. She tried to mumble, or scream, or something, but the duct tape did its job admirably well.

Natalia placed one palm on the woman's forehead and the struggles ceased. Faith's eye closed and her body relaxed. Her breathing slowed as Natalia concentrated.

In a quiet voice Natalia began. "Faith works for Le Glaute Industries now. She removed several samples of CE from the Proctor labs in the States and offered them on the vamp web, like the dark web, but for vampire communities. Interesting. I did not know something like that existed." Natalia paused then began again. "She was paid for the sample and offered a job, here in Yesa at the lab on the estate." Natalia gasped. "And promised turning, if her contribution to their project worked out." She stared at the bound woman on the couch. "You want to become a vampire?"

The hate in Faith's eye was searing. She mumbled something through the tape.

Natalia went back to work. "The company is run by a very powerful vampire with a human familiar as a front. They are developing a drug... to make vampire blood infuse human blood. In hopes of creating a food source that will allow a vampire to..." Natalia looked up at Maddox. "...reproduce...?"

Susannah had entered the room quietly, but now made her location apparent. "What? That's impossible. The virus makes us sterile. We create our progeny, not produce them, right?"

Natalia bent her head and focused again. "They are testing the versions of the drug on the children at the school. There are also some children at the estate who... are being kept in a secret lab in one of the caverns. They are experimenting on them. Oh Frank, we have to rescue them!" Natalia rose and melted into the arms of her husband.

"How can this bitch know about this, and let it happen? Course, she knew about the stables at the Proctor estate and did nothing, too!"

Now Faith lay still as the dead.

"We will. We will. Natalia what else can you find out? Who is the vampire that is doing this? Who is he or she working with at the school?"

Natalia went back to work. "Faith does not know the identity of the vampire behind this conspiracy, but the human familiar is a descendant of the Le Glaute family of old France. But he is not the brains, nor does he work for himself. He is...compelled." Natalia gasped. "The master hides in the catacombs beneath the estate. His contact at the monastery is a man called François d'Gaton. She has never met this man. He...is a..." Natalia was struggling to stay in Faith's mind. "...he is..."

Natalia fell backwards holding both hands to her head.

"My love!" Yuri was at her side immediately.

"There was a... trap." Yuri pulled her into a chair. "This vampire we deal with is very smart. And very strong. He planted a snare in her mind that almost caught me." She continued to rub her temples. "Almost...he knows we have Faith... but not where."

Faith choked then lay still. Again, as still as the dead, but this time...

"Frank, she's not breathing." Devlin rushed to begin rescue breathing, but was stilled by Natalia's vamp strength.

"To touch this woman is to die yourself. I do not know how this can be, but I know it here." Natalia touched her heart.

Devlin took a step back.

Silently, Faith Morrison slipped into the hereafter, without even a tiny whimper, as the small group looked on helplessly.

"A fitting end." Susannah spoke up. "For a despicable person. Can this big bad vampire track her body to us?" Susannah pulled a large throw rug from the hallway.

"No. Not now." Natalia leaned against her husband. "She is gone. There is no mind's path to follow. He did not touch me while I was with her."

"You are fine, my love?" Yuri was worried, but saw Natalia recovering rapidly.

"Da, da. You must take the medicine to the child in Germany." She stood and hugged Yuri fiercely. "Go, moi dorogaya."

"We go." He disengaged her arms and retrieved the small plastic bag of vials with the instructions tucked inside, then motioned to Casey. "Come."

"Hey, hold on a minute! I'm not sure I want..." Casey backed away from the big Russian.

"Just think about the hospital, some quiet corner, or maybe the back loading dock. Yuri will take you there. No problem." Natalia took Casey's hand pulling him toward Yuri. "He's done this a million times. Not to worry."

"Will it hur...?" Yuri grabbed Casey's hand and they both disappeared.

The space where the two men stood was empty.

"Okay then..." Susannah tucked the rug around Faith's body. "Time to get rid of the evidence."

"What will you do with her?" Elizabetta had joined the group in the great room, waking from her day-sleep due to the commotion.

"Her boss is the one who caused her end. He knows she's dead. If we go up the road by the reservoir, we can burry her at sea." Susannah made a tossing motion with her hands. "Man overboard." Susannah snickered. "Or rather, woman overboard!"

"Such a sensitive child." Elizabetta chuckled. "I will assist."

There was little sympathy for the woman who had complicated their lives during the Proctor mission and had secertly stolen CE from the Proctor Lab. But mostly the idea of using innocent children to test a new vampire drug stuck in everyone's craw. For the promise of being turned herself? Truly perverted.

While she and Susannah rolled Faith's body in the rug, Frank answered the call on his computer. It was Colonel Severin.

"Colonel Maddox, your delivery has arrived. Rather large fellow indeed." He moved to one side and part of Yuri's muscular leg could be seen behind the Canadian Colonel. "Got the directions as well. I will be administering the antidote myself, as soon as possible. I don't know how to thank you."

"No need Severin. It's our job. Go get that kid well." Frank shot the man a thumbs-up. "Out." He clicked off the video conference-call and peeked out the shuttered window. "Almost sundown. Might want to wait a few more minutes."

Frank noticed several people getting out of a large black van across the street. They entered the police station in quite a hurry. "Something's up over yonder."

Several more sets of eyes took to the shutters. "Oh yeah. That's Le Glaute's limo. And I think the short stocky fellow is his," Tank made quote marks with his fingers, "so called security expert, aka little person thug."

Bear joined Tank. "Yeah boy. That little fucker was beatin' down some poor little house guard when we were sneaking around in the garage. Guess the guy didn't wash the boss' Bentley right."

"So there is something rotten in Denmark. Hmm. I think we need to listen in. Which one of you is up for a little recon?" Maddox held out a small round bug he'd taken from a package in Miller's shipment.

Tank punched Bear in the shoulder. "How abouts we go see if we can procure a wedding license, honey?" His voice was squeaky and effeminate.

"Right, baby." Bear punched back, but it wasn't a love tap. Tank flew halfway across the room landing on his backside on the couch that had, moments before, been occupied by a dead woman.

"That's just not right. We're not even married and already

313

you're beating me. I might have to reconsider our pending nuptials, hon." Tank pulled himself off the couch, brushing non-existent dirt from his arms and legs. "I'm not taking you out in public, if you can't behave, sweetheart." Tank swished across the floor and flipped his fiancé off.

Bear grumbled and followed Tank with a scathing glare. "Tone it down, T."

They skipped down the front steps of the hotel and crossed the street, skirting the limo parked in front of the police station. As they approached the entrance, loud voices could be heard. Through the glass doors, several people stood milling and shoving. As Tank and Bear entered, a junior officer flew toward the doors. Bear caught him and set him back on his feet. "There ya are, fella." He brushed the officer's uniform coat off.

"Gracias, Señor." With a quick look over his shoulder, the officer excused himself and exited through the front doors.

Bear deflected two more officers and one man in a black suit before they managed to get past the rhubarb in the foyer. Tank leaned on the counter and rang the bell. Every officer in the building seemed to be surrounding the ruckus. One female officer disengaged herself and stepped behind the counter.

"Como puedo ayudarte?" She continued to glance at the melee.

"Do you speak English?" Tank turned on his charm.

"Yes, Sir. What can I do for you?" Her accent was British.

"My fiancé and I were wondering what it would take to get married in this province. Can we get a license here?"

"Of course. Same sex marriage has been legal in Spain since the Socialists took over in two thousand and four. We are much more progressive than the States." She was very proud of her adopted country.

Bear casually moved to one side, fielding another officer. Although he was big enough to walk through the group with ease and plant his bug on the Chief's nose, he let the next flying body knock him down the hall and into the Chief's doorway. One slight of hand later, the bug was well hidden and functioning.

"Ah, here ya go, buddy." He peeled the prostrate officer off his chest and set him on his feet with a flourish, then hollered at Tank. "Honey, let's come back when things aren't so... violent. I'm afraid you might get hurt baby." Bear threw an arm around Tank and dragged him out of the station.

"Oh look." Tank held up his phone. "I accidently snapped pictures of all the players in that mess!"

Bear smacked Tank's butt.

"Oh my God! Did you actually spank my patootie? Shame on you." Tank lisped through his comment and wiggled exaggeratedly as he walked.

"Please stop that. I'm gonna fuckin' puke on your shoes." Bear took the steps two at a time.

"You're no fun at all, babe." Tank followed, dropping the wiggle and lisp as he went through the door.

"Mission accomplished, Sir." Bear reported.

"Already monitoring. Good job. They're looking for Ms. Morrison and reporting her missing."

Tank responded with a famous country western song. "And that's one body that'll never be found. See little sister don't miss when she... aims her... toss." He laughed at his own attempt to make a new ending for Reba's hit song.

"That's enough, Sergeant." Maddox had a plug in one ear. "They're talking about Faith's husband who smacked her a good one, then carted her out of the salon. Disagreement about money, so said the hair dresser."

"So that was the Casey magic, huh? Good man. Responsible husband. In my mind." Tank grabbed a beer and flopped down on the couch. "I got photos, if anyone is interested."

That got Frank's attention. He pointed to the computer on the coffee table. "Run the FR program and send them to Miller. See if he can identify anyone. Ask him to have Monique take a look. I want to know who this powerful vampire is, and if they are related."

"Right on. I mean, yes, Sir." Tank set his beer down and hooked his phone into the computer with one of the cables Miller included in his box of spaghetti and directions. In a few seconds the pictures were on their way to Miller, halfway across the world. "It's after midnight there. I wonder if he'll be up?"

"Doesn't matter with Miller. He is biologically connected to his machines. Anything comes in, he's on it." Frank sat back, pulled the plug on his earphone and the room filled with angry Spanish and French.

"We need a translator." Tank slurped his beer.

"And so we are back." Devlin escorted Elizabetta into the room on his arm with Susannah behind him. "Your translator is here." Devlin settled Elizabetta on a lounge chair, grabbed a beer for himself, took a gulp and sat down next Frank. "So Faith is missed. That's encouraging." He toasted Susannah. "And apparently, her boss, Arthur Glaute is concerned enough to parade his butt into the police station and demand answers. Nice." Devlin listened for a couple minutes. "The salon owner is insisting Faith got into a fight with her husband. Then he carted her off after smacking her in the face. Guess that's not unusual here." He shrugged. "The boss is not going for it. He is telling the cops, rather loudly, again...she is not married."

"They won't find her until the water level drops significantly. I think I put a hundred pounds of rock in that body bag with her." Susannah smiled and slapped a bag of synth blood to her fangs.

"Young lady, you are getting way to much satisfaction from Faith Morrison's sorry end. Remember, she is a victim of this hideous master's plan, as much as the children he experiments on." Elizabetta commented quietly. "She may not have been in control of her behavior."

"She was in control of her greed, Elizabetta. That'll get you every time." At that statement, Yuri and Casey appeared in the hallway with a whoop.

Casey's Whoop.

"Ye hah! Ride em' Ruskie!" Casey flew down the steps and slid up to the bar. "What a ride! I gotta go again. Can I, please?" He grabbed the last beer in the small fridge under the bar.

"Shhhhh!" Devlin cocked an ear toward Frank's computer. "The bad guys are departing. The Chief has promised to look into Faith's disappearance, with a little less enthusiasm than Glaute would have liked. He's not a happy millionaire bad guy right now. Did we bug the car?"

"No, too many eyes. But we did plant a little listening device in the Chief's office so whatever they learn, we will as well." Frank stood and stretched. "Elizabetta, any vamps in that group?"

The coven mistress peek between the slats of the shutters. "No auras that I can see, Frank. No vamps."

"Shhh." Devlin shushed everyone again. "The Chief is well aware that he was just entertaining a messenger boy. He knows there is something fishy at the Le Glaute estate, but he is not welcome there. Some kind of nasty history between them." Devlin paused and listened. "He's telling his detective that there is some connection between Glaute and a missing Detective."

Susannah snorted. "No kidding. That would be our Etxebarria, I assume."

"They have some idea he may be dead, but there is no evidence yet. The officer missed his check-in time. Wonder what the glugs did with the body?"

Natalia snuggled on the couch with her husband, holding Yuri's second bag of synth-blood. "Glug? I do not know this word."

"That's because I made it up. Glaute and thug; glug."

"Good one, Uncle Rob." Susannah clapped.

"The question is; how do we get to the root of this evil. How do we find the Master?" Frank was thinking out loud.

"Finding him in the maze under the estate is definitely out." Bear shook his head and took a gulp of beer. "We spent a bunch of time just making it from the estate to the Monastery, and the way was marked and lighted." Bear shook his head again. "Not going to happen without a company of foot soldiers."

"Follow the money. We find this man named François d'Gaton. Maybe Father Manuel will know this man." Devlin shrugged. "He seemed to be a straight guy. If he'll talk to me again after what happened."

"How about bait?" Casey piped up.

"Bait Father Manuel? How so?"

"Not the priestly coach, the head glug. Vampire boy." Casey was reading the label on his beer. He looked directly at Elizabetta. "If head glug is a vampire and related to the Le Glaute family, he's at least a cousin of our lovely Monique. VMD knows its own, right?" In Casey's mind it was fairly clear; dangle Monique on a string and wait for the shark to bite.

"Not only no, but hell NO!" Susannah spoke up before Elizabetta could squelch the idea. "Frenchy won't come near this place. And we shouldn't even consider asking her to."

"Casey, Monique is out of the question." Frank was resolute. "Let's see if we can find this François d'Gaton. Dev and I'll go back to the monastery and see if we can talk with Father Manuel. Tank and Bear, take Susannah and see if the well still goes to stairs in the chapel. My daughter can watch for vampire sign as you move. Natalia and Yuri, you two can scope out the monastery grounds for any sign of vampires. Elizabetta and Casey,

317

man the comm and keep us all networked." Frank glanced out the french doors. "Sun's down. Let's move."

******

It was close to one in the afternoon at Olney farm and Miller was deep in his research. His screens flashed pictures at a mind boggling rate, comparing the photos from Spain with just about everyone who ever had their picture taken for just about any reason. Three of the men had already been identified. They were security employees of Le Glaute Industries. All legal. None had records. Not even parking tickets.

One fellow's picture contained notations from Interpol about a couple domestic disturbance investigations, but no convictions. Still, there was no Le Glaute. Nothing to identify the owner of the mega company in question.

Miller paged Monique. He had a burning question. Within a few minutes, Monique and Percy entered the command center.

"You wished to speak to me, Sergeant Miller?" The couple stood holding hands. Beauty and the skinny Beast. It struck Miller's funny bone.

"Oui! I have a weird question for you." Miller paused trying to put his question into words that would not offend Monique, but still get his point across. "If there is a vampire, like you... say, in a picture... could another vampire... like... see you? As a vampire? Is there something like a look, or a mark? I know you all can see each other somehow, but what about a photo?"

One screen paused and a bell chimed. The flashing photos stilled and red text reported MATCH. The last man in the picture was identified. The software recognized him as Regeridid Plasovitch, an Albanian citizen and a doctor expelled by his medical community. An Albanian newspaper article chronicled his expulsion and subsequent criminal charges. Seems the good doctor became a multi-millionaire providing organs to the European black markets. A very lucrative and specialized career field, to say the least.

"Who is this man, Sergeant?" Monique was curious.

"This," Sergeant Miller pointed to the doctor's mug shot, "Is a diabolical devil. He steals people's body parts and sells them on the black market. He also works for Le Glaute Industries. Wanna guess what he does for them?"

"Non!" Monique turned away from the computer. "In answer to your question, there is no way that I know to tell a vampire from a human in a photograph." She faced the hallway, tugging on Percy's hand. "I do not wish to see this man's face. He is horrible."

"Yes, he is." Miller agreed with the French vamp. "And he is connected to TPS, Le Glaute and the sick kids at the academy. The Colonel needs to know this." Miller was typing as he spoke. He turned to face Monique and Percy after hitting the send button. "Done." The doctor's image disappeared from his screen. "I know this is difficult for you, but is there anything you remember about the priests at San Leyre that could help the team figure out who is behind this nightmare?"

"Non! No, Sergeant!" Monique tugged harder on Percy's hand.

Percy winced but pulled Monique into his arms. "I promise, I will always protect you, my pretty little French girl," he whispered against her silky hair.

Monique melted.

The tears began.

"I'm sorry, Monique. I didn't mean..." The Sergeant was not comfortable with female tears, human or vampire. "I'm..." He turned around to face his monitors once again. "...just sorry... I guess." Sergeant Milo Miller was stuttering.

Percy pulled an office chair over and gently sat Monique down. He handed her a box of tissues and tugged the first one out. He perched on the edge of the table, still cuddling his beautiful woman, and he had to admit, in his mind, she was now *his* beautiful woman. He had no idea what she was to him in her mind, but he could hope. "You are safe here, with me... I mean us. Your family, or coven, I guess." He hooked another chair with his foot and rolled it over. "I'm serious, Monique Merchant. I will never let anything hurt you, ever again. I've seen these... people..." His voice caught on the word. "They are not some organized military unit I thought I was coming to work with. They are family. Your family. And I mean it when I say, I will protect you."

At that statement, Monique almost laughed, utterly without hope. "How can you say such a thing?" She began wiping the tears away. "You are human. I am a vampire." It was such a sad statement that spoke volumes.

Percy shifted to the chair and faced Monique. He tenderly

placed his hands on both sides of her face, looking into her eyes. "We just saved the world! We can do anything. No doubts." He almost added, *I love you and together we can conquer anything*, but held his tongue. He was human. And she was a vampire. No matter what his heart wanted, his brain screamed NO! Reality didn't need to scream. It slunk up his leg and killed what should have been a great hard-on.

Monique smiled with a sniff. "You are so..." She had no words. He was a wonderful man. So smart. So sweet. So...Percy. And he thought she was smart! He was the first man who recognized the fact that she had a brain and actually valued her for it. She'd been a virgin when the Duc d'Orleans made her a vampire, then took her body, again and again. She could not fight him. He was her Master. She was his plaything. Later, when he was gone, destroyed, she survived using what he'd taught her. What he'd made her. She always thought her vampiric gift was her body and the ability to seduce any man or woman, but lately something had changed. "Percy, I can't..."

"Yes! Yes you can. We can." Percy gently kissed her forehead. "We can, my pretty little French Girl. Trust me."

Monique half laughed, half snorted. "I'm not little," she whispered.

Miller cleared his throat. "Ah, Ma'am, Doctor? Colonel Maddox has responded." Miller was a little uncomfortable witnessing such a tender moment. "The team is investigating new information. Faith Morrison is dead. Some kind of vampire voo-doo, with all due respect," he nodded toward Monique. "She gave up the name of François d'Gaton. He's the contact for whoever is testing TPS."

Monique gasped. "Father François d'Gaton? The Abbott's favorite puppy. I know him well." She sneered the last sentence. "He is the worst devil!"

"He's a priest? The Colonel did not mention that." His fingers flew over the keyboard. "Let's see if he knows the dude he's looking for is a priest."

Percy took Monique's hands. "Tell me about him." It was a request, a suggestion, a demand, all wrapped in a warm, snuggly Percy tenderness. Percy safety.

"He was... the one who ended Mathilda's existence. He sentenced her to..." Monique's voice broke. The pain in her eyes was palatable.

"Burn?" Percy supplied the word for Monique's traumatic memory. He pulled her into his lap and held her close.

"He hated us with such a passion. He always had new ways to make us feel the hate." Monique hid her face and spoke in muffled words. "He would preach loud and long, then the beatings... the burning... the..." the last word was but a tenuous whisper, "... the rape."

Sergeant Miller's computer chimed. "Message. Hmm..." Miller quietly read the message from Maddox, as Percy softly rocked his pretty little French *vampire*.

"Maddox got the message. He's at the monastery talking to a Father Manuel." He turned to Monique. "Did you know this Father?"

"Non." It was a tiny squeak.

"Right. Guess we wait for more information." Miller's comfort level had hit rock bottom and was drilling into the bedrock of raw nerves.

"Well, I for one, could use some fresh air and a peak at the new litter of kittens. Maggs had her babies a week ago. What say you, my pretty little French girl? Wanna take a walk on the farm side and cuddle a kitten?" Percy was trying his best to lighten the mood.

Monique's response was a weak, "Oui." But she did not want to get up. She did not want to move an inch. Percy held her so close, so tight. She wanted to stay in his arms forever. She wanted to feel safe and cherished and... Dare she even think it? The word love had not been a part of her life for over two hundred years.

"One of us has to get up," Monique could tell Percy was feeling the same vibes. "Since you're on top..." Percy smiled indulgently.

"Oui, oh oui." Monique stood, straightened her long pink sweater and dabbed at her eyes. "Then we shall go." She turned to Miller. "Sergeant Miller, s'il vous plaît, send a message to Colonel Maddox for me? Tell him not to trust the bastard devil. Oh..." Monique turned before leaving the comm center, "...and hello to Susannah. I miss her so." Monique waved girlish-style and followed Percy out.

"Shall we take the elevator or steps?" Percy was as accommodating as he could be. The tear stains on his shirt looked dark brown now.

Monique peered down at her shoes; four inch glittering heels. She giggled. "I think the elevator would be best for you and a change of shoes would be good for me."

Monique disappeared in a flash and reappeared in another second with hot pink Nikes and puffy, glittery socks on her feet. She was about five inches shorter and stood looking up at Percy.

"What... ah... that was quick!" Percy startled.

"Oui. I never keep a gentleman waiting." She winked. "Unless there is a good reason."

Percy pushed the elevator button and they headed for the surface, some time with sweet cuddly animals and the beginnings of a crisp spring twilight. It occurred to the scientist that he rode in a very small cube with a very strong, smart and dangerous being. At the same time, it blew his mind that this smart and fantastically beautiful woman would even look twice at him, let alone take a romantic walk with the socially awkward boy who was never loved by anyone. A cast off. An orphan who never knew his mother or father. The whipping boy of the orphanage.

He had the scars to prove it.

He also had the brains to remove himself from it.

He chanced a glance at Monique. She smiled shyly and took his hand as the bell dinged and the doors opened into a dim barn. Only one 'farm hand' sat on a barrel next to a high stack of baled hay. His lazy salute indicated he had guard duty for the evening.

The new batch of kittens were nestled behind a stack of hay bales with their mother, Maggs. They were easy to locate by their soft mewing. Monique knelt in the hay next to Maggs, watching in awe, as the momma cat tended to her kittens. "She is so good with them, Percy. Look." Monique pulled him down next to her on the hay.

One tiny kitten crawled toward Percy, investigating the new smells. It toddled clumsily toward the scientist who gently picked up the fuzzy baby and handed it to Monique.

The French vamp took the tiny animal and held it close, cooing and stroking the kitten's ears. "It is so cute. Look, it has tiny claws!" She held a paw on her finger. "Oh so mignonne! Cute." She held the kitten close to her chest, smiling like a young girl in love.

Percy was a little jealous of the darn kitten. He wanted to be the one she held close to her chest. He reached out and stroked the kitten's back. It mewed softly and snuggled closer to Monique's chin. "Guess he, or she, knows where the love is."

"She is very happy. I feel her contentment." She gazed at Percy with an angelic smile. "Feel this." She took Percy's hand and placed it between the kitten's chest and hers.

"I think I feel something." Percy blushed about as red as his deep wedgewood colored hair.

Monique giggled. "And I feel more than the kitten's contentment, Percy." She winked and smiled sweetly. It was a different kind of feeling than she'd ever experienced before with a man. Not the hot, sexual thoughts framed in pure lust, but a warm desire that held promise of love, safety and something akin to adoration.

Percy quickly pulled his hand away. This was dangerous territory for him and he did not know what to do. He'd been teased by women who thought his awkwardness was something to make fun of and joke about, but he'd never felt special in anyone's eyes before. It was amazing, and confounding… and paralyzing! He just sat there, grinning like the geek he was.

Maggs broke the spell.

She climbed onto Monique's lap, searching for her missing child with a loud meow. "It is alright momma. Here you go." Monique lowered the kitten to its mother.

Maggs took the kitten in her mouth and returned it to her little family and settled down to feed the brood.

"Wow." Percy shook his head. "She's a great mother. Look at that." They sat there, watching the kittens nurse noisily. "My mother just left me in a basket on the steps of the church and walked away."

Monique felt the deep hurt and sadness Percy was feeling. His emotions were raw and true. There was no subtrafuge about this man. No falseness. Everything about Percy was clear and real… and perfect. "The sun has gone down. Shall we walk?"

They strolled out into the starry night. Percy breathed deeply. "Smell that spring breeze."

Monique sniffed just enough to sense the elements in the air.

Percy sneezed. "Yep, spring alright." He tucked Monique's arm in his as they walked toward the small stream across the plowed field behind the barn. "This is a really pretty place to live… under." He chuckled at the thought of living underground, beneath such a beautiful and quaint farm. "The Burnsides are lucky folks. And nice."

"Oui. Aunt Mandy has been like a real aunt to me. She tried to show me how to make cookies, but I do not eat them, so I have no idea if they turned out good...or bad." Monique laughed and turned to Percy, tucking her other hand into his arm. "But Sergeant Miller and Captain Devlin ate them all up! So they couldn't have been so bad."

She was so young, but so old. So sweet yet, so deadly. She was everything desired and everything feared in his world. Yet... he felt his heart move with a thump. His brain told him to stay away. His heart said jump in with both feet. What to do? Which path to take?

The slow running creek babbled in front of them. Roger Burnside had cleared an area on the bank and placed a varnished bench close to the water. Percy sat down next to Monique.

For a time, both simply enjoyed the soft song of the water and the chirping of crickets in the brush... and the quiet company of each other.

After a while, Percy shifted uncomfortably. He'd never been in a situation like this; never been with a woman alone in a romantic place before. He wasn't sure what to do. His teen awkwardness surfaced and he squirmed.

"Maybe we should get back?" His voice cracked a little. Just like in junior high school. Damn.

"Non. The night is lovely. The sky is so clear." She pointed through the budding tree limbs. "That is the north star. See it? It was the only star in the sky I could see through the tiny hole in my cell. If I pressed my face to the stones."

Percy's nervousness began to sprout wings. Monique was sharing intimate details of her incarceration. Instead of fidgeting, he sat deathly still.

"It was my only comfort that all was not lost, after Mathilda..." her voice dropped to a bare whisper,"...was destroyed." She smiled softly. "That star was my savior. One night I could only lay against the cold stones, healing the many gashes on my legs and arms. I felt Tank's frustration first. I heard the V-Team trying to find an entrance... to find a female vampire they suspected was being held." She turned to Percy. Her smile was as bright as the star she pointed to. "They looked for me!"

"And they found you." Percy finally moved. He patted

Monique's hand. It was an ackward little gesture.

"Oui, but not until the next night. I tried to call to them, but I had no voice. I was close to being destroyed myself." She lifted her voluminous hair to uncover a small scar at the back of her neck. "Vampires heal with no signs left of injury. Unless they are close to destruction. Then it takes much longer and sometimes scars appear."

Percy peered at the tiny mark on her neck. He had an irresistible desire to kiss the minute blemish. He leaned closer.

"You can touch it. It no longer hurts." Percy realized she was teasing him, but had no idea how to respond. He poked her neck with a clumsy finger, a little harder than he should have.

Monique giggled. "No silly scientist, not with your finger."

"What? I mean with what?" His voice cracked again and he shook his head. Dang, he was such a geek, such a dope when it came to women.

Monique let her hair fall and turned to face Percy.

Her face glowed like a silvery angel sent from heaven. Percy swallowed hard. He was mesmerized by her lips. They twinkled like starlight.

"With these." She tenderly leaned close and touched her soft lips to his. It was a gentle, fleeting moment but Percy thought his body would explode all on its own. His blood was on fire and electrical shocks ran through ever neuron, zinging back and forth from head to toe. He tried to breathe, but his lungs would not function. He tried to move but his muscles only quivered with the charged energy that ignited every cell. So he sat there, frozen in time. Enduring the most incredible, fantastically beautiful moment of his entire life.

"Oh my!" Monique's hand flew to her chest as her heart beat several times.

Her heart moved?

Impossible!

She took a deep breath.

Her lungs worked?

Vampire lungs did not breathe!

Mistaking her reaction for distress, Percy came out of his momentary paralysis. "Are you alright?" He reached to take her pulse and felt a slight beat. A beat? He'd been told vamp hearts did not beat. The virus that mutated a human also created a vampire support system without the need for a heart beat.

"Oh oui, I am…" Monique pulled him to her and placed her lips on his once again.

Percy's mind spun. The feelings raging in his body were miraculous. He'd never experienced anything close to what he was feeling as Monique's tongue searched for an opening. It was more than he could handle. As his lips parted and he felt his first deep kiss, the world tilted.

And he fainted.

Dead away.

Chapter 24

The Details

The Devil is in the details,
So say those who search for grails.
And, of course, the truth will set you free!
But in the truth, do you always see,
The best way, the answer, the future path,
Or what is ordained by the power he hath?

*Receida Malkovitch, Poet*
*Pamplona, Spain, 2015*

"Father Manuel has taken a vow of silence until he feels his mind is clear and he can return to his position at the Academia de Santos Domingo de Silos. I am sorry, but you will have to wait to speak with him. He is in seclusion." The Abbott rose behind his desk, indicating the audience was over.

"Well, if we can't talk to Father Manuel, maybe you can answer our question." Maddox bowed slightly. "Do you know a man called François d'Gaton? I understand he has a connection to this monastery." Frank looked past the Abbott to the many pictures on the mantle behind the priest.

"And why, pray tell, do you wish to find this François d'Gaton?" The Abbott casually clasped his hands before his ample stomach.

"He is a friend of ours, from the old days, and we understand he may be around here. I'd love to get together with him and share some old memories over a beer. Catch up, maybe." Devlin chuckled. "None of us are getting any younger, and I hate to lose track of folks from my past."

A slight twitch of the Abbott's upper lip was the only recognition reflex indicating there was more to this d'Gaton fellow than the Abbott was willing to reveal. "I am not aware of this man you seek. Here we only have priests dedicated to the service of the Almighty God." The Abbott moved from behind his desk motioning the two men toward his office door. "If you leave your information with my assistant, I will contact you when Father Manuel leaves his seclusion."

There had to be a reason why the Abbott would not acknowledge 'François d'Gaton, priest or no. Was the Abbott in on the diabolical goings on? Why was he protecting a possible vampire familiar? How deep did the TPS conspiracy go?

On their way to the parking lot, Devlin noticed two men in frocks escorting another into the administration office of the monastery. The escorted priest did not appear to walk voluntarily. "Frank, I'd swear that's Father Manuel."

Frank pressed the unlocking button for their car. "I wouldn't be surprised. This place reeks of conspiracy. Can't you smell it?" He started the car and headed down the mountain.

"I'd say it stinks to high heaven."

Devlin crossed himself.

The wrong way.

Just about the time Frank and Rob were leaving the monastery grounds, Tank, Bear and Susannah were deep beneath the monastery, hiding behind a pile of corpses, playing dead. A group of men ambled down the passage way that lead into the main burial chambers under the monastery. One man wore a lab coat and carried a container of deep pink liquid. They spoke in French.

Susannah was never more glad she'd been studying with Monique and sharing language skills, the vamp way. She understood enough to know these men were escorting the latest version of TPS and the hope for a perfectly effective trial run. As the last man passed her position, she peeked from behind a dry mummy and almost gasped. He glowed bile green.

A naturist vampire!

She concentrated on dampening her own aura and remained still as the dead she hid behind. She blinked at Tank and moved her eyes toward the last man, mouthing *vamp*. He got the idea and blinked back. Too bad humans couldn't psyche speak, she thought.

When the group had passed and they heard the metal door at the end of the passage clang closed, Susannah wiggled out from beneath her cover, and brushed the dust from her shirt.

Tank tossed the three corpses that covered him across the passageway and jumped up. "Dang, I never thought I'd be cozying up to some dried up priestly type. I've slept with some weird dates before, but never... ick." A visable shiver went through his entire body.

Bear calmly picked up the wrapped bodies and replaced them in the exact position they'd occupied prior to the uninvited guests sharing their resting places. "Have a little respect for the dead, man."

"The dead belong six feet under, not piled three high on top of this guy. What's next? Let's get goin'." Tank was all for beating feet. Anything to get him far away from the dead priests of yester year.

"I think we can track where these guys came from. I can see the vamp sign." Susannah studied the dirt walkway. "The last guy in line was a naturist vampire. His steps glow light green. Hurry before they fade." Susannah took off at a run following the signs only she could see.

"Hey, slow down kiddo. We're just human, ya know." Tank ran after her. "Let one of us up front in case…"

Susannah stopped unexpectedly. "In case of what?" She struck a teenage smart-ass pose. "What can I not handle guys? I'm faster than you, stronger and I can track the course."

Bear punched Tank's shoulder. "She has a point, buddy." His smirk was priceless.

"Yeah, but…"

"Try to keep up, team." Susannah set off again, at a little slower pace this time. She may not have been alive during the Woman's Rights movement of the eighties, but she was fully aware of her skills. There was no way her modern little mind would let the oppsoite sex tread on her superwoman cape.

"Just watch for traps and alarms, Susannah." Tank called after her. "They have to have some kind of security down here."

After about forty-five minutes of chasing Susannah, Bear called a halt, to catch his breath. "I need a minute here. I haven't run a marathon in a while, Suze." Bear was panting. Tank was dripping sweat and, for once, unable to speak.

The dusty floor stirred in tiny clouds of pale dirt to cover the pant legs and damp arms of the runners. The walls showed mechanical marks from their modern day excavation. This section of the tunnel was obviously man-made.

"Sorry guys. I just want to find this lab. We need to shut this operation down." Susannah paced back and forth. She wasn't even breathing, let alone breathing hard. "Those assholes back there are set to poison more kids. We have to stop them."

"We will. We will, kiddo. But not if we're dead." Bear

tapped his chest. "Ticker needs to keep ticking in us humans." Bear wasn't used to being the underdog. "Mine's on max right now."

"You guys take ten and I'll scout ahead." Susannah left them behind and trotted down the corridor. About half a mile farther, or what she thought might be half a mile, the vamp sign began to fade. Susannah paused. The passage way split into three separate tunnels. Single light bulbs hung on strung wire lighting in all three directions. There was no vamp sign to be seen.

"Shit! Double shit!" Susannah sniffed the air.

No help.

She studied the rock and dirt floor.

Nothing.

She trained her ears on one tunnel after another.

There was no sound that could be distinguished from any other.

Except Bear's panting and Tank's heavy footsteps coming from behind her.

She turned and whispered, "Hold up guys. We hit a dead end, or more like three dead ends."

Both men pulled up short and stopped behind Susannah. Their faces showed such disappointment. Susannah completely understood. She stood there looking down one passage after the other. "Don't know which one… which way to go. The Vamp sign just faded." It was her best apology.

"We did not come this way from the estate last time. I've never seen this junction." Bear pointed down the tunnels. He pulled out a compass and tried to take a reading. "Too much iron ore in these mountains. Can't get this thing to stop spinning." He tapped the compass a couple times.

"So do we split up and spelunk on our own?" Tank leaned against the carved wall of the tunnel. "Or do we turn around and let the rest of the team know there is going to be another round of tests. At least we've got an antidote."

Bear was the first to weigh in. "No splitting up. We're a team. We stay together."

"I need to find this damn lab, guys. I'll go ahead and search all three tunnels. You guys wait here. It won't take a minute." Susannah was back to pacing.

"I vote no. Once a team, always a team. Kinda like being a Marine." Tank was shaking his head. He knew he couldn't stop

Susannah if she was set on her plan. He was hoping her new commitment to the Vamp Squad and emphasis on her training would come to the surface, and she'd make a level-headed decision to remain with the team.

"But we've come so far..." It was an almost-whine.

"Suze, how do we know how far we've come? Or how far we have to go? Or, even if we're on the right track?" Tank supplied the voice of reason. "I should have worn my FitBit. Damn!"

"Right. You're right, of course." She bowed to Tank's experience and common sense. "And I can't see anything more in any of these passages. How did they get all that way without leaving a trail I can see?" She was talking more to herself than to the team.

"We could wander around down here until the end of time, or the end of us. Man I miss MorningStar." Tank slammed his hand against the rock wall. "Head back then?"

Susannah's head hung. "I guess. We need to tell Dad about the new trial going down. And get the antidote into whoever is exposed. Regroup and figure this lab's location out." She trudged back the way they'd come.

Tank and Bear followed, grateful for the trudging pace.

While the underground team wound their way back to the subterranean exit through the well, Yuri and Natalia crept around the grounds of San Leyre, keeping to the shadows and vegetation. Well aware that their aura could be detected by other vampires, they did their best to remain in stealth mode.

"These grounds are truly beautiful, my love." Natalia gazed around the manicured gardens and impeccably tended lawns. "There is much love for nature here. I can feel it."

"I prefer much love for children. Here, obviously there is little." Yuri thought back to his childhood friend, Sergi who now had three children of his own. "I loath those who hurt the innocent." He pointed to part of the academy, the part the plans they studied had shown as the infirmary. "They work late in that place."

Natalia looked up to the high windows of the infirmary. The ornate stained glass glowed with warm golden light... until bile green changed that glow to something hideous, and vampiric. "Look, Yuri. Look at the glow!"

"Vampire sign. Do you think..."

"They are poisoning more children? We must see. Come,

331

my love. Let us be very careful. If there is trouble, you can v-port us back to the hotel immediately." Natalia kissed her husband's cheek.

"Then do not let go of my hand, moy temnyy angel. Let us see." Yuri held his wife close. "I shall never let go of you!"

Natalia smiled up at the man who was her husband, and the vampire who was her soul mate. "Never. My love. Never."

They snuck around the edge of the garden that bordered the field below the second floor of the Academy dorm. The infirmary occupied the north end of the dormitory building. It was late, past curfew, and most of the students were already in bed, or in their rooms finishing some assignment that would be due the next day. Quietly, they moved down the hallway from the stairwell. The big white letters on the door spelled out Infirmerie Estudiante, Student Infirmiry. Natalia could hear voices behind the doors speaking angrily. A crack between the doors glowed bile green.

Natalia psyche-spoke to Yuri. *They argue about a new trial. Someone has a new version of the drug that must be started before... tomorrow!*

Yuri squeezed Natalia's arm. *Do not worry. We have the antidote. We must return to the hotel and Colonel Maddox. He must know this. I will take us.*

In a blink of an eye, Yuri and Natalia appeared in the courtyard outside the french doors of the great room at their hotel. The doors stood wide open and they could see the rest of the team inside.

Susannah sat on a bar stool talking with great gestures and animation. Bear and Tank loafed on the couch. Devlin sat in his usual place in the recliner near the doors, and Colonel Maddox perched on the corner of the dining table.

"That place is a maze of unparalleled size and breath. We can't possibly find the lab and this vampire's lair without a miracle or MorningStar." She slammed her bag of synth-blood on the counter. "Or a company of soldiers. Which we don't have."

Elizabetta leaned against the hallway entrance, her arms crossed lightly. "This becomes many dead ends. And we will have more dead children, I fear."

Yuri entered, still holding hands with his wife. "There is a new test beginning very soon. We heard through the door of the infirmary. There is a vampire there now."

"And he has TPS." Tank added. "They passed us in the catacombs. They had it with them. One was a naturist vampire. Suze said he glowed like The Hulk."

"They must begin the trial before tomorrow. We have to do something to stop them." Natalia added quickly.

"All right, all right. Everybody take a step back and breathe, or whatever it is you do to calm down." Colonel Maddox stood and crossed the room indicating Yuri and Natalia join the group. "Let's take a critical look at this whole mess. We have an antidote so, other than being sick for a while, the kids will be okay." He scratched his face, then continued, "We got nothing from the Abbott. We can't find this François d'Gaton. There is no way to track Le Glaute's men back to their lab. And we have no way to find the master vampire involved in this mess." Maddox looked at his feet for a moment, then looked inquiringly at each of his operatives for comment. "This has become a comedy of dead ends."

None of the operatives had anything to add.

But Casey sure did.

"Bait. That's all I'm sayin'."

Susannah jumped up. "No! Dad, no. We can't force Monique to come here. That's like torture and she had enough of that."

"Calm down, Suze. You know your father won't make Monique do anything she doesn't want to. But we can pose the question, can't we?" Devlin posed a question of his own.

"We can, but I know what the answer will be." Susannah was shaking her blonde mane.

"Anyone see another way? Given the current circumstances." Maddox needed ideas from his team.

His team was fresh out of ideas.

"Why can't we just storm the estate and grab that little three-piece suiter and squeeze him until he cries uncle... or vampire?" Susannah was grasping at straws. Anything to keep Monique safe and away from the monastery. "He was at the cop-shop so you know he's out and about in the daylight. He's no vampire, Dad."

Elizabetta weighed in on that idea. "Then we would surely have another dead body to..." She pantomimed the heave-ho motion.

"That's fine with me. They're killing kids, Elizabetta. Kids!

333

That's so many kinds of wrong."

"Down girl." Tank wiggled his finger at Susannah. "He'd be gone before we could squeeze anything. This Master is onto us. He won't let us do a Faith Morrison snatch and grab again. The pipsqueak will die for nothing and the vamp will go so far underground it'll take another Journey to the Center of the Earth to dig him out."

"Well, do you have any more ideas?" She rounded on Tank.

He held his hands up. "Not I, kiddo." He then pointed to the pilot lounging at the bar. "But…"

"Daaaad!" Susannah was becoming despondent.

"Susannah, listen. We can ask and she can say no, but I think at this point, we may be out of options. Anybody we grab to interrogate will just die on us. " Maddox paced back and forth in front of his computer screen. "We could search those catacombs forever and still find nothing. If we don't nip this in the bud, here and now, before these tests become successful and spread like a virus, we may not be able to contain the drug, or whatever it is."

"I say we let Monique decide. She may surprise all of us." Devlin put in his two cents worth. "And who knows, she may want a shot at this whole thing. After all, if San Leyre is harboring a vampire, after what they did to her? They have alot to atone for. She may want to be the atoner."

The very pregnant silence ended with a pensive Elizabetta's voluntary duty. "I'll talk to my daughter. I will know if she can do this without more… damage to her psyche." Elizabetta moved to the computer and punched in a series of commands.

The screen lit up with Miller's happy face. He was counting money. "Good morning all. Or good evening…whatever it is in your neck of the woods."

"Sergeant Miller, you have earned another bet from our favorite linebacker?" Elizabetta smirked and shook her head. The bets between Milo and Ted were well known in the Vamp Squad compound. And it was apparent that at the end of the day, neither won or lost much at all. The fun for the two men was in the winning and one-upsmenship.

"Yes sir-ee Ma'am. What can I do for you?" Miller was in high spirits.

"It is…" Elizabetta paused and checked the time on the menu bar of the computer. "… seven thirty in the morning where you are. Is there any chance Monique is still awake?"

"Yes, Ma'am. Beauty and the Geek are breakfasting in the mess hall. Want me to page her?"

"That would be wonderful, Sergeant. And congratulations on the win. I shall console Mr. Vanderloss when I return."

"Ah, he'll be needing it by then. The exhibition playoffs are this week. I'm up forty-two dollars and thirty-six cents." Miller punched the intercom button. "Ms. Merchant, please come to the comm center."

"Nice! Well, the best of luck to both of you." Elizabetta's mild statement adequately demonstrated her indifference to American commercial sports. "The team is here and we have a problem that possibly Monique can help solve." Elizabetta moved back from the screen so the camera could project everyone in the room.

Across the ocean, Monique and Percy entered the comm center, hand in hand. Monique's smile spoke volumes. Percy's face was calm and closed.

"Elizabetta! Did the antidote get to the child in time?" Monique slipped her arm around Percy, snuggling close.

"Yes, but Colonel Maddox has not had an update yet. We've been very busy trying to figure out this entire mess. We are not having a lot of success. The Abbott at the monastery will not budge. He will not identify this François d'Gaton. Susannah, Bear and Tank tried to find the underground lab, but the labyrinth below the Le Glaute estate and the monastery is endless. Yuri and Natalia discovered another drug trial will begin as soon as today. We are floundering." Elizabetta paused and look expectantly at her French operative and coven daughter.

Monique blanched and moved behind Percy, as if he could shield her from this devastating information. "What will you do?" Her voice was but a whisper.

"Well, we are out of obvious ideas, that is why I called. I would like to know if you or Doctor Seizemore can think of anything we have not."

"The monks at San Leyre hate vampires. They believe we are minions of the Devil, and they can exorcise the evil from us and save our souls. I cannot think they would willingly conspire with a vampire. I do not understand this. Not at all." Monique peeked out from behind the slender scientist who afforded little physical cover.

Percy wound an arm around behind his back to hold Monique close to him. The tender move was sweet and so telling. "Perhaps things have changed significantly since Monique's rescue, what... five, six years ago?"

"I saw a vampire in the school infirmary... with TPS. They talked of another trial beginning soon, if not now." Natalia sat next to her husband who nodded in agreement.

"There is a human who represents Le Glaute Industries, but Faith said, before she died, that he is only a front. The real power and direction comes from a very strong vampire who has a lair in the catacombs beneath the estate. But it's a maze." Devlin provided the appropriate segway for Elizabetta's request. "We'll never find him. We need some way to draw him out."

There was silence.

On both sides of the ocean.

Percy broke the silence. "Obviously you believe the monastery and monks are somehow connected to this mysterious vampire and the testing of TPS. It is clear. So let's confront the elephant in the room. Do you think Monique can help if she were there? With you all?"

"Well, that was diplomatic." Sergeant Miller snorted under his breath.

Elizabetta looked directly into the camera at the top of the screen. "Yes, Doctor Seizemore, I believe Monique could be helpful. But, dear, it is your decision. I will not command you." Elizabetta's heart was in her throat. She knew intimately, how much Monique had suffered and how she agonized over her dreams and fears. Her coven daughter projected her emotions uncontrollably, like a child in the grip of horrendous nightmares, screaming while still asleep.

"I cannot... I cannot. You do not understand." Monique was projecting palatable fear. Even Sergeant Miller cringed.

But not Percy.

He turned to Monique. "Yes... yes you can. Yes, we can." He pulled the quaking vampire into his arms. "You have to confront your fears to heal. To make these horrible memories finally find their place in the past. And we..." He motioned to all of the people in the comm center and to the computer screen, "...will be there to protect you and keep you safe." He continued his pep talk, tipping Monique's chin so he could look directly into her eyes. "You are smart and strong. You can do this. We can do this… together. I know it here." He pointed at his head. "And here." He pointed to her heart.

"No, Percy I…"

Before she could continue, Percy said, "Can. I can. Say that."

"But I…" Percy placed his fingers over her lips before she could utter the *cannot* word…

"I will go with you." He nodded in the affirmative, and continued to nod until Monique finally nodded along with him.

Again she felt her heart beat and took a deep breath. "You are sure?" she whispered to the doctor.

"I am more sure of this, than I have been of anything in my life." He squeezed her shoulders with renewed vigor. "Say it again: yes we can." He stared into Monique's eyes and nodded as he spoke.

"Yes… yes we can." She whispered as she nodded back. "Yes, we can." The second time was a little louder.

It took a moment before Monique moved around Percy to stand in front of the camera on Sergeant Miller's computer. She actually took a deep breath before pronouncing, "We will come."

Chapter 25

Bait

Dangle candy in front of a child,
And you can twist, turn or set the mind wild.
But to bait a maniacal animal,
Is the worst mistake of all.
So it is said.
So it is done.
Yet who doth pay the price?
The animal?
The bait?
Either way, an all-encompassing fate.

*Father Manuel Tibruce, Educator and Priest*
*Academia de Santos Domingo de Silos,*
*Monastery of San Salvador de Leyre, Spain, 2015*

Yuri, Monique and a dizzy Percy appeared in the great room of the team's hotel in Yesa, Spain less than an hour after the video conference. Monique held tight to Percy's arm as he gained his land legs after v-porting from Olney Farm. They carried another small plastic case filled with vials of the antidote.

Susannah jumped up and hugged her sister vampire fiercely. "You are my hero, Frenchy! Did I ever tell you that?" She kissed Monique's cheeks, both sides. "And you too, Dr. Seizemore." Then she kissed him on one cheek only.

Percy wavered but stood his ground. "Thank you, Susannah. We are here. With more antidote, in case it is needed."

Elizabetta also hugged her coven daughter, mentally sending her a warm message of love and strength. "I am glad you are willing to face your fear and find a way through."

"Oui, but not yet, Elizabetta. But I will try."

Percy squeezed her hand. He was very proud of the decision she'd made, and now they would face the enemy, together. He was almost bursting with affection and pride. It was a new experience for him. "Do we have a plan?"

Maddox wiped a hand across his eyes. "Yes and no." He was obviously tired and had been burning the candle at both ends. "But I think Monique needs to direct this one."

Monique stood, holding Percy's hand. "Colonel Maddox, I do not know. The devil who runs that place must know about the demon d'Gaton. I cannot think he is innocent. As much as I hate that man, he is the one you need to get information from, oui? He is the one."

Casey had been quiet enough. He was bursting with strategies and plans. "What if you confront him? With all of the team behind you? Tell him what is at stake. If he doesn't want to cooperate, Natalia can pick his brains, right?" He had jumped off his stool and now stood in front of Monique and Percy. "You will know immediately, if he is in on this drug business. If not, he's a mushroom. In the dark and full of shit."

"I will know his heart, but I cannot compel him like Natalia." Monique clung to Percy's arm now. "I am sure he will not receive me."

"What makes you think we'll ask?" Casey's smile was a touch on the vicious side. "We'll purloin the good Abbott, drag him off to a quiet place, and do our worst... I mean best. To solve this crime. It's a crime to drug and kill kids, even in Spain, isn't it?"

"He'll have to give up d'Gaton, if the priest is still in the monastery. D'Gaton will lead us to the master vamp, and voila! Mission complete." Susannah was rushing through a whole bunch of critical steps, each one frought with danger and possible failure.

"Whoa, kiddo." Devlin was looking more critically at the process. "We have to assume the big bad vampire in charge will know everything we find out. We need to move carefully and quickly, but not lose sight of the goal. Getting the boss... and the minions as we go, but the boss is the one we need to take out, or it's all for naught."

"This Master, do you have any idea who he is? Where he came from?" Monique leaned against Percy who slipped an arm around the beauty's waist.

"Ms. Morrison died before she could divulge the identity of the master. She said he was much stronger and much worse than Proctor. That says something." Natalia raised an eyebrow. "I wonder if the Council of Elders knows about this vampire?"

Maddox interrupted, "Let's keep the Council in the dark for

right now. I don't need the little crazy child-thing storming the monastery with her blood-thirsty knights-in-black-armor, eating innocents."

At that statement, Monique giggled. "Fiona could bring soldiers to find the master vampire. But you are correct, Colonel, many humans would suffer, possibly children at the school. And vampires out of control! That would not be acceptable. Or pretty. They often leave left-overs."

At that statement, Bear growled. "I like the little faerie gal. She's so cute." As an after thought, he added, "And strong as an ox. But cute."

Somewhere a little bell chimed.

"Bear grinned. "You're welcome."

"Possibly, the Abbott is compelled?" Monique looked to Natalia for an answer.

"I do not believe so. I did not feel a compelling force at the infirmary or around the grounds. It would take a very strong compeller, stronger than I, to control so many men. Especially men who have devoted their lives to a religious belief. I felt…" She paused and thought for a moment, "…a compliance. A means to an end the humans wanted. Either money, or to be turned. That was Faith's main motivation. She believed she would become a vampire as a reward for her part in this. And wealth, of course."

"Then we must find Father d'Gaton. The Abbott will know where he is. And I will see to finding out." Monique stamped her foot. With a resolute look, she crossed her arms over her chest and attempted a glare. She was half successful and way too pretty for a truly angry glare.

"We! *We* will find out." Percy peered out the open french doors, then checked his watch. "We have about three hours until sun-up. Shall we storm the Bastille?"

Monique looked curiously at her scientist. "This is not the Bastille, Percy. And we shall not storm it. I was there. Once was enough for me."

"I guess that saying has a different meaning for you, my pretty little French girl." Percy had to chuckle at himself, realizing Monique really was there, at the real thing.

"Oui. We shall v-port. No storming. Walking very quietly." Monique finally left Percy's embrace, but dragged him toward the computer by the hand. "How do I talk to Sergeant Miller? He has plans of the monastery. We can see where the Abbott sleeps."

340

Soon, the team had a copy of the architectural drawings of the monastery in hand. Casey had printed the copies Sergeant Miller sent and taped them together to show the entire floor plan of the residential wing where the priests slept in the priory. The Abbott's cell and reception was at one end of a dormitory style hallway in one wing, not far from his office and the connecting cloister walk. His room was the largest one in the priory.

The team grouped around the plans. "Here, this is the cloister walk." Devlin pointed at what looked to be a long corridor. It connects to the dormitory where the priests stay. It can be accessed by the gardens, here." Again he pointed to the drawing. "I took pictures when I was wandering around."

"So the vamps v-port to the cloister walk and the humans climb?" Maddox was looking at a way to get the team up onto the second floor cloister walk.

"Nyet. I v-port from ground." Yuri volunteered. "No rope. No fall."

"I can fly Bear or Tank, but not both. And Natalia could fly the other." Elizabetta chimed in.

"I'll stay with Percy, and Yuri can v-port us both when we are on the grounds." Monique pulled him closer to her with a smile.

"I v-port the rest. It takes only one second." Yuri flexed his muscles. "I am machine."

Natalia tossled her husband's hair. "Da, lyubov' moya."

"Translation here?" Casey always wanted to hear the sweet talk.

Yuri gave him a dirty look. "Nyet. Personal." Then he smiled at his wife.

Elizabetta whispered, "Means my love. You need to learn Russian."

"Alright then; Casey, you hold down the fort. Yuri, if you please?" Maddox pointed to the Russian transporting machine.

Devlin and Maddox were the first to disappear and reappear at the base of the wall supporting the cloister walk. There was only a sliver of a moon and the place was awash in dark shadows. Soon Bear, Tank, and Susannah appeared to join the team. Overhead, Elizabetta and Natalia soared in gentle circles. Monique had not relinquished Percy's hand and the scientist's eyes were as big as saucers when they arrived. His free hand clamped tightly over his mouth. They alighted silently on the cloister walk above, as Yuri quickly transported the rest of the team up to the walkway.

As soon as Percy's stomach settled in his abdomen, they sneaked toward the connecting door. There were no lights on in the monastery above the ground level. The security lights shone only on the entrance and the chapel, at three in the morning.

Well practiced hand signals served the team well and soon the heavy wooden door to the domiciliary stood open in the dark night, allowing unimpeded entrance.

Maddox pointed to the door which led to the Abbott's room. As the team moved on silent foot steps, Bear worked the handle. It was not locked.

Of course. Why would a monk lock his door? There should be nothing to steal. And anyone ripping off a head monk would surely be struck by lightning and immediately go straight to hell!

From within, a soft voice responded to the open door. "Is that you d'Gaton?" The Abbott sat in a high-backed chair next to a low burning fire, behind an ornate grate covering a fireplace in the ancient stone wall. Tall bookcases lined one wall of the cell filled with ancient books bound in old leather. As he spoke, he closed the Bible he'd been studying and turned to receive his visitor. Unfortunately for the Abbott, it was not who he was expecting.

"And I though you had no idea who François d'Gaton was?" Devlin moved to the Abbott's side with menacing speed.

"What are you doing here? Who are you? You do not belong in my private chambers. Get out now!" The Abbott tried to stand.

Bear closed the heavy door. "Not so fast, priest." The Abbott felt the heavy hand of a bear of a man push him back into his seat. The Bible fell to the floor.

The Abbot bent to retrieve the book that ruled his monastic life, only to be stilled by Bear. "Don't!"

The Abbott froze at Bear's growl. "Who are you? What do you want?" As Percy and Monique moved into the light, a deep rasp of fear issued forth from the old priest's mouth. "You!"

"Oui. It is I, priest." From somewhere, Monique's courage rose to the surface. Her fangs extended and she smiled sweetly. "You remember me, non?"

"Remove from my sight, abomination! Lord take this filthy beast from my presence." The priest crossed himself and fell to his knees, grasping the sacred Bible to his chest.

"Hold on there a minute, chubs. She's not an abomination, or a filthy beast." Susannah bent and smiled. Her fangs glistened in the firelight. "She's here to save your school kids, idiot. And maybe your overly large ass."

The Abbott fell prostrate on the floor covering his face and head with the Bible he held. "Take these evil minions from this holy place. Mother Mary, do not allow them to steal my soul, I beg you."

"No one named Mary is here, so sit up and pay attention." Tank yanked the priest back into his chair by the neck of his dark cassock, and pulled the Bible from his hands. Devlin efficiently duct-taped his hands to the arms of the chair while Bear kept the man's lips from making a lot of noise. Duct tape replaced Bear's hand and the priest was adequately restrained. Then it was Colonel Maddox's turn.

"I need information. Now."

The priest's eyes did not move from Monique's figure. He vigorously shook his head.

"Refusal's not an option. I need to know if you have any idea what is going on right here under your nose, Abbott." Maddox pulled up a stark wooden chair and sat opposite the priest. "If I remove the tape, will you answer my questions?"

Again the priest shook his head vigorously… in the negative.

"Okay then, we do it the hard way. Natalia…"

Natalia moved into the light, her fangs glittering in a wide smile. "My pleasure, Sir."

At that point the Abbott began bouncing his heavy chair up and down away from the advancing vampire as he attempted to scream through the duct tape. Of course, all that came out was a kind of mumble vibration. But perspiration covered his bald-head and his eyes teared.

"We can do this the easy way, or the vampire way. Your choice, baldy." Susannah smiled down at the bound priest.

The Abbott almost broke his neck pointing to the Colonel with jerky movements of his head. His fingers beseeched in obvious sign language.

"So if I remove the tape, you cooperate?" This time the priest nodded in the positive, but more resigned than vigorous. "You scream, holler, burp, fart, or anything but answer my questions, I'll give you to your ex-tenant here. She can figure out what

343

to do with you." Maddox motioned to Monique, who just happened to smile a little wider for the priest's benefit.

Percy was so proud he could have popped all of the buttons on his lab coat, if he'd been wearing a lab coat. "You go, my pretty little French girl." He whispered and squeezed her hand. She squeezed back and he winced.

Maddox ripped the tape from the priest's mouth.

"I demand to know..." the Abbott began.

"Ah,ah, ahhh. I ask. You answer or..." Maddox pointed to Monique.

The priest's jaw clamped shut.

"Where is François d'Gaton? Are you expecting him now?"

"I do not know where Father d'Gaton is. I am not expecting him, but he is the only one who enters my room freely. Now tell me..."

Maddox cut him off. "Nope. No talking when not answering *my* questions." The Colonel shook a finger at the priest. "You are, of course, aware that kids are getting sick at the academy, right? But are you aware that this Father d'Gaton is up to his cassock in it? And in league with a very dangerous vampire?"

"No! This is impossible. Father d'Gaton would never hurt a child! He is a man of God, a true priest of the cloth. He would never consort with... with the Devil's own. Ask this one." One finger pointed toward Monique. "D'Gaton was most courageous in the fight to save her soul. Unfortunately, the beast escaped before he could chase the devil from her body."

Monique had had enough. She released Percy's hand and moved to stand before the priest who'd not only ordered her torture, but sent the most foul, violent, hateful individual to fulfill the task. "D'Gaton is the monster. He loved what he did to me. You do not even know the extent of what was done. He is worse than an animal. He is the Devil's hand."

The priest turned his head away from her words, but Bear managed to grasp the man's head and forcibly turn it back. "You will listen to her words. You harbor a fiend and yet you call him holy. That makes you much the same."

"I harbor no one. There are only priests here. I swear before God...on the Holy Bible." The Abbott nodded toward his Bible.

"Natalia, Monique, does he speak the truth?" Maddox was convinced the Abbott was telling the truth, but needed proof.

Natalia closed her eyes and concentrated. "I feel no

344

subterfuge. He speaks his truth."

"His emotion is true. He does not know. Still he hates me." Monique backed away into Percy's embrace.

"So here's the scoop. Listen and believe. Your Father d'Gaton is mixed up in a nasty business with a very strong vampire who has created a drug that blends human and vampire DNA. He's been testing it on the children at the academy." Maddox laid out the story in no uncertain terms. "The drug is being transported using the catacombs and tunnels beneath the monastery grounds that connect to a hidden lab at the Le Glaute estate."

"Monsieur Le Glaute is our benefactor. He would never do something so foul! He would not consort with monsters." The Abbott was more incensed than shocked.

"Stop calling us monsters." Susannah moved closer and pointed her finger at the Abbott's nose. "We are simply mutated humans. A virus changed us, not the Devil and I am beginning to take offense at your attitude, priest."

"Do not speak to me, child of Satan. Go back to the hell from which you sprang." The Abbott was not getting the picture in the least.

"Enough. She is not the daughter of Satan, she is my daughter, and an effective operative on this team, which happens to be in the process of busting a dangerous drug ring right under your nose, and saving the lives of children." Maddox was in the process of dressing down the pompous priest in a stern, but quiet voice when several sets of footsteps could be heard outside the Abbott's chamber.

The team faded into the shadows, except for Colonel Maddox as frantic knocking began on the wooden door. Maddox threw a blanket over the priest to hide the duct tape and cautioned the Abbott with a slicing motion. He then took the seat across from the Abbott, opened the Bible to no place in particular and began to read out loud. He whispered, "Tell them to come in. Do not give my team away or there will be more than hell to pay, Abbott,"

"Come." The priest's voice was shaky, but clear.

The door flew open and two priests rushed in. "Father Christobal, there are three new cases of this mysterious disease that has been plaguing the academy. The children have been taken to the infirmary. One girl is unconscious, Bella Chantosiose. She is the daughter of the mayor of Catalonia. She must be taken to a hospital immediately." The priest was out of breath and panting between words.

The Abbott's eyes moved between his two priests and Maddox sitting close, then back again.

Maddox took the situation in hand and improvised on the spot. He rose, closed the Bible with solemn aplomb and addressed the two priests. "I am Doctor Maddox. I am here at the request of the Abbott to investigate this disease. Please continue to keep the students warm and as comfortable as possible. I will come to the infirmary with my nurse, as soon as I can fetch my instruments."

"Father Marcus, do you know where Father d'Gaton is?" The Abbott asked as he squirmed beneath the blanket.

"I last saw him by the gym, Father. That was about seven o'clock last evening. The soccer team was in late practice. Surely he is in his chamber sleeping. I must return to the infirmary. Doctor, please hurry. I fear for these children. This curse is so strange. The disease must be spreading." Father Marcus wrung his hands as he spoke, shifting his weight from one foot to the other."

"Go then, Father. I shall come with the doctor." The Abbott dismissed the two frenzied priests as Maddox closed the door after their departure. "Are you truly a doctor? Can you help? This is terrible for the children... and the school's reputation. They are the newest in a string of..." The Abbott's voice trailed off.

"A string of tests. And no, I am not a doctor. But he is." Maddox turned to Percy who emerged from the shadows, once again holding Monique's hand.

"We have developed an antidote for this thing we call TPS. Never mind how or where. It works and can save the children." Monique spoke very directly. "No matter what you believe, I am not a monster, and we are here to help. To put an end to this horrible drug. I have hated you, this place, the priests here for so long. I do not want to help you. You are dangerous animals to me, just as you say I am a monster to you. I have come here to help the children. They are the ones who suffer and pay the price for d'Gaton's mechanicians. Do not be so self-serving that you with-hold medical help for these ones who have been trusted to your care, priest."

Percy held out the plastic box of vials. "This is the antidote. It has been tested and proven to work."

"How do I know this?" The Abbott was still skeptical.

"Tommy Pantterdyck and Lucy Redmont. Healthy and whole. With their families in the States. Thanks to this." Percy pointed to the case. "And her." He pointed to Monique. "She figured this thing out and set me on the right track. Abbott, we must hurry. Make a decision. Do the kids live or die? Because that is what they will do if they don't get the antidote. TPS only kills."

"Alright, yes, yes, yes. Do release me. I will go with you to the infirmary, then we shall find Father d'Gaton and set this straight. I cannot believe he is somehow involved." The last comment was more of a self-assurance than a statement of the truth. Monique could feel anger building in the Abbott. She could also feel a sense of betrayal. How close was this priest to d'Gaton?

Tank and Bear released the Abbott with words of caution, which the Abbott took to heart as he led Doctor Seizemore and the team toward the infirmary in the student dorms. Halfway across the garden between the buildings, Elizabetta hissed and froze.

The windows of the infirmary glowed a hideous bile green in her view. "There are vampires there." She pointed to the windows. The nonhuman members of the team could see the color glow clearly but the humans were unable to detect anything amiss.

"What? Elizabetta, what do you see?" Maddox was beside his coven mistress immediately.

"Frank, there are either several naturist vampires in that room, or one very strong and powerful vamp. We should proceed very carefully." She warned the team.

"Vampires stay here. Take cover so they can't see you. Dev, Doc, Abbott, you're with me. Tank and Bear, hang out here with the vamps." Maddox took the Abbott's arm and dragged him toward the building.

"Who are you people?" The Abbott stumbled.

Percy couldn't help it. He just had to add, "If we tell ya, we have to kill you. Best not to know."

The Abbott swallowed with a gulp and tried a little harder to keep up with Maddox.

Halfway across the courtyard that bordered the gardens, Maddox did a comm check as they moved. Everyone's unit was broadcasting in case there was trouble.

"Entering the building now. Stay alert." Maddox opened the door and shoved the Abbott ahead. "Play nice and you won't get hurt."

The Abbott nodded and started up the stairs that lead to the infirmary. Voices above drifted down. The Abbott paused and placed a finger to his lips. He was beginning to accept that something strange was going on at his monastery.

"No more. No more tests after this one. If this doesn't do what you want, we can't do anything else for you." Someone was arguing with another very angry person. Their voices were loud and threatening

The Abbott mouthed *d'Gaton* and pointed up.

"We cannot have students falling by the wayside like this. It is bad for the school... and the children. I cannot allow it to continue." A light appeared at the top of the stairs. It became a little brighter as the second voice was heard.

"You will do as I say, priest, or I will see that all funds and support are withdrawn from San Leyre. Then where will your precious monastery be? Huh? Without the wealth and influence of the Le Glaute family? Under the thumb of the Vatican once again. That is where you will be. Do you understand d'Gaton?" The dim light passed the stairwell and disappeared as the voices faded down the upstairs hallway. "I will come again tomorrow night. With Doctor Plasovitch. He will take samples. We will be successful this time. I can feel it."

Then the voices faded and were gone.

And so was Father d'Gaton.

And the vampire.

The Abbott climbed the stairs rather rapidly for a very large man. "Hurry." He ushered the Doctor toward the infirmary. "Before it is too late."

The attending priests in the infirmary, calmly went about their work, tending patients with artless care. Their faces reflected blank indifference. Their bodies moved as if controlled remotely. They did not even notice or react to the new comers.

Five students now lay lethargic, covered with sterile white sheets. Their pale faces looked devoid of blood and their hands showed a blue tint to their fingernails. IV tubes fed them liquid and oxygen masks covered their noses and mouths. "Help me set these up." Percy pointed to the antidote vials as he rummaged through the white supply cabinet. Quickly finding what he needed, he passed out empty syringes. "Draw all of the fluid into the syringe. Like this." He took a vial and demonstrated. Then pointed at the IV line of the first student. "See this access port? Inject the antidote like this." Again he demonstrated. "Press the plunger slowly. Do a ten-count as you inject. It works rapidly so we will need to stay for a while. Just to make sure the kids don't develop any issues while the antidote begins to fight the TPS. It will take about two hours. Be sure to keep your waste when we leave, then no one will be the smarter. Especially these guys." He pointed to the automatons moving between beds, straightening sheets and puffing pillows, oblivious to what was happening around them.

As the Abbott, Devlin, Maddox and Doctor Seizemore administered the antidote, the rest of the team remained under cover, as best they could. As Father d'Gaton and the vampire emerged from the student dormitory building, Monique gasped and grabbed Susannah's arm. She psyche-spoke to her sister vampire and her coven mistress. *It is he. My sire. I cannot believe this*!

As they watched, Phillipe Le Glaute, Duc d'Orleans, or Phillipe, Comte d' LeEgalité, cousin to King Louis XVI, paused and sniffed the air. He peered into the shadows of first the garden, then the cops of trees to the south, cocking an ear to listen.

"What is it, Le Glaute?" Father d'Gaton looked around the grounds of the only true home he'd ever known. The home that was now at risk if he did not do as Le Glaute demanded.

Le Glaute stood stock-still, but after a moment, the vampire shook his head. "Nothing. Old cobwebs, I fear." He continued down the stone path that wound around to the back of the monastery. "Memories of another time, priest. Tomorrow then. I will come for the tests."

Father d'Gaton quickly entered the monastery's small side door and disappeared from sight. Le Glaute simply disappeared.

Elizabetta held Monique's arm and Susannah propped her sister vampire from the other side. Monique was close to fainting. Tears streamed down her face and shirt. "I saw him destroyed. I swear I saw him destroyed." She buried her face in Elizabetta's shoulder. "I am lost." She whispered.

The way was clear now, so Elizabetta motioned to Yuri. "Can you take her to Doctor Seizemore?"

"Da." A man of little words, Yuri took Monique in his arms and disappeared. The two reappeared just outside the infirmary doors and Yuri carried a quietly sobbing Monique to her scientist. "She is upset."

Yuri's words were not necessary in the least. Monique's face and blouse were covered with red vampire tears and she seemed oblivious to her surroundings. Percy took Monique into his arms, bending under the weight of the beautiful and very upset vampire.

"Shush now. What is wrong? Tell me, my pretty little French girl." The endearment worked.

Monique hiccupped between words. "I am not so little, Percy." She wiggled to stand, knowing his strength was giving out. "He is here. I am doomed."

"He who? Who is here?" He placed a tender fingertip beneath her chin and lifted her face as he dabbed at her tears. "Who?"

"My sire. The one who made me. He was in this room. He will find me and I will be lost." The tears began anew and she dissolved into Percy's arms.

His arms were ready and willing. He held her close, whispering words of support and... love.

As Percy held his distraught vampire, Yuri returned to the team to bring them to the infirmary v-style... and the Abbott tried for his escape. Appearing and disappearing vampires, bloody tears and the Vamp Squad's newest turtledoves-in-love were more than he could take.

"Hold on there, priest." Devlin stayed the escaping Abbott before he reached the doors of the infirmary. "Where do you think you're going?"

"Away from this debauchery. I must find Father d'Gaton. He can tell me what is going on. This..." He motioned to the team and the students. "This is... I must find d'Gaton. He will set me straight." The Abbott was wringing his hands and shuffling from one foot to the other.

Natalia placed her hand upon the Abbott's shoulder. He winced slightly at her touch but immediately relaxed. His face went blank and the deep lines on his forehead and mouth smoothed a bit. "This man is not who he seems." Natalia spoke softly. "He serves as Abbott here, but in reality, this Father d'Gaton influences him greatly. They have been close for many years. This priest relies on d'Gaton for strength and rigorously values his counsel." She turned to Maddox. "Colonel, the Abbott will be of little help. The true strength and direction of this monastery is in the hands of d'Gaton."

Elizabetta added, "And d'Gaton is in the hands of a very strong vampire, this Le Glaute."

Monique wiped a paper towel across her face. "He must be destroyed. He will take me. I know this. I cannot live through more of his..." She could not go on.

Percy hugged her tightly to him. "I will not allow him to take you. Believe me when I say that."

It was Maddox's turn. "*We* will not allow him to take you anywhere. Believe that!"

"You are strong. You are one of us, Frenchy. Dad won't let anything happen to you." Susannah bounced over to the couple and did a three-way hug. "We all love you." She kissed the nasty, messy face of her sister vampire.

At that point Tank decided a little humor was needed. He swished his way across the tile floor and threw his arms around the group. "And I love you all." Before anyone could resist, he planted a noisy kiss on each of the heads of the huddle-hugging group, then swished away just as quickly. "Now, can we *please* get back to work?"

"As I live and breathe…" Devlin held onto the Abbott as Natalia withdrew her psychic touch. "What shall we do with him?"

Maddox had an idea. "Natalia, can you show His Eminence here, what TPS does? Can you take him in…" Maddox motioned to the closest student's head. "…there?"

Natalia smiled. "I think that would be a good idea, Colonel. I will try." As she approached, the Abbot cringed. Had it not been for Devlin's restraining grip, the Abbott would have bolted out of the room.

"Do not touch me, Devil child. Stay away from me. I am a man of God!" He struggled until Natalia once again placed a hand on his shoulder. Then his struggles ceased and he visibly relaxed.

Natalia guided the compliant Abbott to the student and placed her free hand upon the child's head. Concentrating, focusing her energy on both the child and the Abbott, she dove deep into the child's brain, guiding the Abbott through the diseased neural pathways sheathed in the pulsing pink intruder. She continued moving, pointing out the already apparent effect the antidote was having. *This Le Glaute, your monastery's saving grace, is the root of this evil. See how it grows and destroys these innocents. And yet you do not believe. See Le Glaute's work.* She had reached the seething pink monster's center. It seemed to be panting, fighting off the slowly approaching purple antidote. As purple touched pink, it sizzled and crackled, sputtering, before dissolving into nothingness. *We bring life back to these children. He brings only death. And your Father d' Gaton is his servant.*

Natalia withdrew from the child, taking a stunned and

confused Abbott with her. As she removed her hand from his shoulder, the Abbott stumbled, catching himself on the edge of the bed. "I had no idea. I thought there was only something going around. Father d'Gaton said…" The Abbott paused. He did not know how to go on.

"Definitely not something going around, Abbott." Percy was checking vital signs. "Responding well, Colonel."

Susannah clapped her hands and smiled. Monique stood close to Elizabetta who held an arm around her coven daughter. "Now we must deal with this Le Glaute. He will surely have a coven of his own to protect him." Elizabetta was thinking out loud. "And be well hidden."

"No finding the guy the human way." Tank and Bear both shook their heads. "The catacombs never end. We were lucky to find the well exit when we liberated Percy's pretty little French girl." Tank had a twinkle in his eye.

"Hey, that's not for public consumption. She's only *my* pretty little French girl." Clearly Percy was claiming possession for all to note.

"I stand corrected." Tank did a little bow in the doctor's direction.

"You! You are the ones who removed our charge before she was healed of the evil within her!"

"Charge?" Elizabetta took on the angry Abbott. "Victim! No one charged you with her. Kidnapping is a crime. Torture is a crime. Rape is a crime. You," she pointed a finger directly to the Abbott's nose, "are a criminal. Of the worst kind."

The Abbott's indignation departed but he was still up for a fight. "It," he pointed to Monique, "Is not a person. There is no crime against a soulless monster, only exorcism and atonement."

The students were doing fine and Percy had enough of the pompous priest. He'd experienced exorcism and atonement at the hands of arrogant, self-righteous priests, all of his childhood. Enough was enough. And he was a scientist. Monique was not some evil, Satanic being. She was a mutated human. A very beautiful, sweet, smart, brave, loving… mutated human being. He crossed the room in several quick steps and held a fist to the priests face. "Stop. Now. You know nothing of what you speak. Your mind is petrified in the Catholic rhetoric of manipulation and control. You live to pronounce good and evil by some long ago scribbled book, and the dictates of a man who lives in a gilded palace, while others starve and die." He was shaking with anger for the hideous torture of the one he loved. And for all the years he spent living in his own hell on earth, in an orphanage manned by priests of the same cloth. "You think you can chase the devil from some evil vampire? You don't even recognize the human evil beneath your nose, you God damn bastard!"

Monique hid her smile. Percy, the gentle scientist who wouldn't say shit if he had a mouthful? Was defending her! Her face washed and blouse dabbed, she watched her hero take on the nemesis before him. He was fighting for her and standing up to the priest that had ordered her torture and confinement! She wanted to kiss every inch of his scientific body. She wanted to rush to him and hold him forever. Her heart did a little flip in her chest.

Her heart moved? Again?

Wow!

"Percy..." She took a step toward the man she loved. "He will never understand. Talk is lost on this one." He reached for her and they met halfway. She hugged him fiercely. A little too fiercely.

Percy squeaked. "A little less enthusiasm, my pretty little French girl." He kissed her lips lightly, with a slight wince.

"Oui." She couldn't take her eyes off of him.

He couldn't take his eyes off of her.

Until one student began to cough.

"Go." She released Percy with a nudge.

TPS was dying and the students were beginning to heal. They no longer needed the oxygen that fed them through the masks covering their noses. "Help me remove their $O_2$." He pulled Monique along with him.

Devlin leaned toward Maddox, "How cute," nodding toward the couple who worked in unison.

"Right." Maddox snorted. "Now what?"

Elizabetta and the Abbott stood on the other side of one child's bed, but close enough to hear. "This man will find d'Gaton and bring him to us, here. It is the least he can do." She looked at the Abbott. "If not voluntarily, then the vampire way. Natalia?"

The Abbott tried to move away, but puny human strength was no match for Elizabetta's staying hand. "No! He is my friend... of many years. I will not let you hurt him. I am sure he is only misguided in this..." He pointed to the student in the bed in front of him.

"Misguided? No. Bring him back to us, or our Natalia will compel you to do what we ask." Colonel Maddox gave the command and was not about to be ignored.

"Dad, we can't trust him. He'll just rabbit, and we'll never find d'Gaton." Susannah spoke what everyone already knew.

"I know. That is why Bear and Tank will go with the fine Abbott." Bear and Tank both stepped up as the Colonel made his pronouncement.

"Yes, Sir." They both responded in military precision.

"Who are you people?" The Abbott shook his head in resignation.

Susannah, always ready with a joke, leaned in, "Wanna die?" She drew a finger across her throat in a slicing motion. "I could tell ya."

Her extended fangs glistened, just a touch.

## Chapter 26

### Revenge

Revenge is mine, sayeth the Lord,
But he never walked a mile in my shoes.
What goes around, comes around, says the Karma Club.
But mine seemed to come around, before I ever got a chance to go around.
Personally I prefer the saying of Heinrich Heine:
We should forgive our enemies, but not before they are hanged.

*Journal of Commander Alana Maitrice, Prisoner 23445*
*Naval Consolidated Brig*
*Miramar California, 1998*

They found Father d'Gaton in the first place they looked, his chamber. He answered the Abbott's knock and request to enter immediately. Apparently, he had arrived shortly before their visit. He was out of breath and nervous. When he saw the Abbott, flanked by two large and imposing men dressed in black, bearing arms, the priest fell to his knees and began to beg forgiveness.

"François, do stand up. You look shameful there on your knees." After everything the Abbott had heard and seen this night, Father d'Gaton's behavior seemed a stark admission of guilt. But what was he guilty of? That remained to be discovered, in the Abbott's mind.

"Please, Father Christobal, I only meant the best for our home." Father d'Gaton began to wail.

"Hush, François. Do stop this blathering and get up." He hoisted his fellow priest to his feet and brushed the dust from the front of d'Gaton's cassock. "Sit and tell me everything."

The distressed priest fell into his desk chair as the Abbott pulled a small wooden stool from the corner and sat directly in front of d'Gaton. "Now speak. These men will do you no harm. The truth, François."

Tank thought the Abbott looked stern, like a father asking a son about the dents in the family car, already knowing the details of the accident. It was a complete change of direction and attitude on the part of the monastery's leader. Possibly he was beginning to believe everything he'd been told.

"Christobal, I have only worked to keep this place above the water and solvent. For you and the brothers here, our brothers. I did not mean to hurt anyone. I have not sinned in the eyes of God! I swear! I have only…" The priest's eyes began to water. He could not go on. "I do not know how this has…"

"Take your strength from the Lord and do go on." The Abbott leaned in closer. He sat lower than d'Gaton and could clearly see his friend's face. What he saw was anguish… and fear.

"I do not understand how this simple…" d'Gaton bowed his head. "I have…"

"Speak, François. Now." The Abbott stood to command one of his own.

The priest fell to his knees, babbling on, making no sense at all. When d'Gaton hid his face in the hem of the Abbott's robe and sobbed, Father Christobal finally knew that what he'd been told was true. His friend of many years was involved in something horrendous and despicable. He also realized he would get nothing that made any sense from the prostrate priest, at the moment.

The Abbott pulled his garment from the hands of the groveling priest. "Do not sully my robe." He was totally disgusted. "Bring him. We shall return to the infirmary to see if someone can translate this blathering fool's babblings."

It was a command, but Tank and Bear did not mind. They pulled the priest from the floor and half dragged, half carried him, after the departing Abbott. Tank whispered, "This should be good."

Bear's almost imperceptible nod indicated complete agreement. He spoke through the comm. "On our way, Colonel. We have d'Gaton."

Father d'Gaton continued to mumble and moan through the entire trip across the field and garden to the infirmary. His wild irrational assertions were unintelligible at best, as he slobbered and wiped snot from his face. As they ascended the stairway to the infirmary, the Abbott paused their progress. He turned to the priest whom he had trusted with the life and sanctity of the monastery for more years than he wanted to reveal. "One last chance, François. Will you not explain this to me?"

"I will die. He will kill me. Or worse! He will make me one

of the damned." The priest shook with fear.

Tank stood below d'Gaton on a lower step in the confining stairwell. Always ready on the spot with some comment, he said, "Okay." He pointed up. "Move. Now." The last word came out as a growl and the party moved.

The infirmary was a flurry of activity. The attending priests still moved silently about the place, adjusting bedding and checking IVs, oblivious to the recovering students. Percy went from one child to the next, checking vital signs and listening to heartbeats. Monique followed, cleaning perspiration from foreheads and gently touching each, monitoring their emotional condition and soothing their healing process.

Percy took a clipboard from the foot of one young man's bed. "This one has been here the longest. Monique, can you tell me how he is feeling?" He had come to depend on Monique's ability to sense how each student felt, mentally and physically.

"His mind is trapped in fear. He is aware of the fight within his body, but is too weak to help himself." Monique frowned. "The battle rages but TPS has been with him for so long…"

"Can you help? Is there something you can do to…soothe his…" He turned to Monique. "I don't even know what I am talking about."

Monique smiled. She'd never *soothed* a child before. Her empathetic abilities had only been consciously applied to men in terms of seduction. It was a new concept, but she was willing to try. "Possibly… I do not know, but I will try. This child will not die!" The determination on her pretty face was a new expression Percy had never seen before. She was so brave!

Natalia came to stand with her vampire sister. "I will assist, if need be." She quickly hugged Monique. "Go ahead."

Monique placed a hand upon the forehead of the young boy. She closed her eyes and focused on the root of the child's fear. The healthy, remaining consciousness of the boy fired erratically through his neural network in great red flashes. His mind was on fire with fear and Monique could tell he was hysterical, but trapped in his own brain. She caressed a neural path and it slowed, changing color to a warm orange. Again she touched his erratic thoughts with a calming influence. She pictured herself holding a fresh kitten, rocking the kitty to sleep with a sweet song and tender cuddles.

Slowly the boy's face began to ease and he took a deep,

cleansing breath. Although still unconscious, Monique could tell he was relaxing. She could feel the tempo of his heart rate return to a pleasant rhythm and the speed of healing increase. She withdrew her touch.

"I have vanquished his demons. He will heal well now."

As she spoke, the Abbott, followed by a sniveling Father d'Gaton and the guys, came through the doorway. Actually, followed was probably a bad descriptor. Tank and Bear dragged a sniveling, struggling and sobbing Father d'Gaton after the Abbott. As Father d'Gaton looked up and realized who spoke, his struggles became an intense attempt to escape. He kicked and screamed, scratching and twisting.

Tank clamped a meaty hand over the priest's mouth and Bear did what his name implied. He held the man in a tight bear hug. Still d'Gaton managed a viscious kick to the shin before Natalia was able to still the priest with her compelling skills.

"Thanks, Mrs. M." Bear released the stilled d'Gaton. "He's a wiry little guy under that dress."

The Abbott cautiously approached his previous *charge*. "You have helped this child?" He was astonished at the progress of the healing around him.

"Ya know, if we had vamps that could do what Monique just did, in all the hospitals, we wouldn't need half the machines or drugs. Imagine that!" Percy was jazzed at what he'd just seen. But to tell the truth, his comment was more for Monique, rather than the Abbott.

"But every vampire has a different gift. I can't do what Frenchy does." Susannah peered at the visibly healing boy in the bed next to Percy. "But I think I'll be a good compeller. And Yuri is a transporting machine!"

Yuri repeated, "I am machine." He flexed toward his wife who smiled indulgently.

It was cute.

The Abbott looked startled. "Gift?"

"Long story, Father. For later. Right now we've got a mission to complete." Devlin motioned to Natalia. "Madame, if you please."

Natalia crossed the room and placed a tentative hand on d'Gaton's shoulder. He stood there immobile. "I must be careful of traps like the one planted in Faith Morrison."

"Traps?" The Abbott was way out of his league and had

begun to realize it.

"This man is Le Glaute's minion." Natalia began. "They have been working together since we rescued Monique from this place." Natalia closed her eyes. "The Le Glaute family has supported this monastery since..." Natalia jerked and removed her hand. "It is as I thought. There is a trap. The Master knows..."

Natalia did not have time to finish her sentence when François d'Gaton, Keeper of the Archives and Assistant to the Abbott of the Monastery of San Salvador de Leyre, ceased to live. His heart stopped and he slid to the floor, cold and very dead.

"François!" The Abbott rushed to his friend's side. "Help him! This is an infirmary. Do something."

"Do not touch him!" Natalia pulled the Abbott away. "He is nothing but a vessel of death now. There is nothing to be done. To touch him, is to die."

"No! He is a good man. We must do something." The Abbott was despondent. He'd just watched his old friend collapse and die right in front of him.

Susannah calmly pulled an automated external defibrillator from the wall and handed it to the shaking Abbott. "Here ya go, buddy."

Devlin smirked, which wasn't exactly appropriate, but he truly enjoyed Susannah's developing sense of sarcasm in a pinch.

The Abbott looked at the machine, then at Susannah who stood there calmly. "I do not know..."

"There's directions. Read 'em." She pushed the machine toward the Abbott.

He took the box from Susannah and bent to save his friend. The closer he moved, the more shallow his breathing became. As he touched the throat of 'd Gaton, his own heart lurched, sending surging pain throughout his body. The Abbott fell backwards, dropping the AED machine.

Susannah took the box and replaced it on its bracket on the wall. "No can do, huh?" She turned and pinned the Abbott with her sternest stare. "Nat tried to tell ya. That guy's an IED waiting to happen." She made an explosion sound with a closed fist, then opened her hand, fingers splayed. "Boom. All gone...except for the leftovers."

"Ick." Percy's comment ended the conversation as Bear helped the plump Abbott from the floor.

"Obviously the master vampire of this debacle must know

359

something has happened. How do we prepare for him?" Maddox addressed his coven mistress.

"You die." Phillipe Le Glaute, Duc d'Orleans, Comte d' LeEgalité, cousin to King Louie the XV, and now Master Vampire, stepped from the shadows to stand in front of the door. He smiled wickedly at his progeny. "I have missed you, my wonderous child. But now you are restored to me at a most prodigious time."

Monique screamed.

The Abbott fainted.

The entire Vamp Squad moved to stand their ground between this interloper and Monique, one of their own.

"You will have to go through us to get to her." Susannah expressed what everyone was feeling. "And that's not gonna happen." Though she was the youngest vamp in the squad, she stood resolute, feet spread, hands on her hips.

Yuri immediately appeared next to Monique and Percy. The three disappeared just as quickly.

"No! I will have her…" At that point, the female student in Bed 3 woke with a mumbled curse. "What have you done? You have ruined everything!" Le Glaute screamed as he appeared next to the girl. Noting her healthy appearance and gaining strength, he too disappeared from the scene, but not before his hideous bellow woke the entire monastery.

The chaos that ensued was somehow muted by a revived and quick thinking Abbott. He eloquently claimed the bellow as his heartache upon finding his friend dead of an apparent massive heart attack. The story explained their presence in the infirmary as two concerned men of God praying for the souls of the children in their care. Natalia planted that same memory in the minds of the attending priests who'd not been even aware of their presence and the activity under their noses, prior to Le Glaute's appearance and immediate disappearance.

After having left Monique in the care, and arms, of her scientist, Yuri returned and deftly transported the vamps and V-team back to their hotel.

Elizabetta was the first to speak when the group had assembled in the great room. "He knows we are here. VMD knows it's own, and he will come looking for Monique."

Percy held Monique on his lap in a big, overstuffed chair at the end of the couch. "Over my dead body."

"Do not wish for those things you could easily have. This

vampire is incredibly strong. I could feel his power." Elizabetta was pensive.

"Possibly he has the same gift as I." Natalia sat cuddled up to her husband. "Possibly he takes from other vampires, da?"

"He is only a few human years older than I. How is it he has become so strong? I felt his command but was able to resist with all of you between us." The last few words were not much more than a whisper as Monique snuggled beneath Percy's encircling arms.

"Two possibilities." Elizabetta continued, "You now live on synth-blood as we all do." She held up one finger. As the second finger popped up she explained, "And you belong to a coven, my coven. And I do not let go of my people so easily." Her eyes took on a soft red glow. "Never forget that, daughter. You belong now. We are family, and family protects its own."

Susannah added, "Even the humans belong. Call it a diversity move. Like Angelina Jolle's kids. The family of mampe… man and vamp."

Casey had heard the entire story by proxy and was concerned but reassured. "Where do ya come up with these crazy acronyms, kiddo? If I didn't know better, I'd say you been hittin' the ZerB."

"Alright. I defer to my coven mistress." Maddox was out of his league and knew it, so the next best thing was to enlist the appropriate league.

"Any of Le Glaute's minions or coven members will be traps, set just as Father d'Gaton was. We cannot gain information from them. The police, human police, will be nothing but collateral damage, which we should avoid at all costs." Elizabetta drained the last of the blood wine in her glass. "At this time, we cannot storm the estate, more collateral damage and Le Glaute is probably making plans to move as we speak."

"So?" Devlin was getting the idea their current situation was hopeless.

After a few moments, Casey broke the silence. "Bait."

Nine sets of eyes turned on him.

Monique buried her face in Percy's shoulder. "Oui." She whispered.

Chapter 27

Alone we can do so little.
Together we can do so much.

*Helen Keller, Author, Inspirational Speaker, American Icon*
*Huntsville, Alabama 1954*

Monique stood alone near the well entrance where she'd found freedom on the shoulder of a human, just a few years before. Nearby, her team hid amongst the thick trees and boulders. She set her mind free and called to him, adding as much sensuality and need as she could gather.

VMD knows its own, Elizabetta had said. He would know her and come. What would happen after that was anyone's guess.

How had Le Glaute managed to survive his beheading? How strong was Phillipe now? There were so many questions. She had to get as much information as she could from him, before he took her. At least then the squad, and Percy would know what to do. They could end this thing once and for all. She may not survive, but they would. Her family would. Percy would.

Monique cast her desire to the wind.

Phillipe Le Glaute appeared scanning the landscape. Monique could feel the suspicion in his posture and mind. "My child. You called?" He kept his distance, still cautious and filled with mistrust.

"Oui, Master." Monique had practiced what to say, and how to garner his trust. "I thought you destroyed. You abandoned me." She threw in just enough pathetic whine as she cast her emotions in a flurry of waves.

He smiled and took a step forward. Her ploy was working. Monique cleared her mind of all but want. Want for a home. Need for love. Desire for her Master.

"Nay, child. My son, my human son, arranged for a servant to take my place before the guillotine. His family was adequately compensated." Monique knew Phillipe had not changed a bit. He had no value for anyone but himself. He still considered manipulation an acceptable strategy, no matter the consequences to the innocent.

She'd been innocent... once. But no more...

"I would have come for all of you. All of my children. But I saw you all destroyed in fire as they took me. My son told me the estate was burned to the ground. Nothing was left. I mourned for all of you in the filthy hole they kept me in." He took another step forward.

Monique stepped back one pace, matching Le Glaute's advance.

"You fear me, child? Did I not save you? Give you life eternal?" His beautiful smile glowed in the dark of the predawn, despite the fangs.

"Oui. You must have known I was here. Yet you let them," she pointed in the general direction of the monastery, "have me. Torture me. For many years." She manufactured a small tear and held it on the edge of her lashes, quivering slightly. Years of survival alone with Mathilda had taught her many skills.

"My poor child. I had no idea. I have only these few years past, come to work with Father d'Gaton. I found him despondent in the cemetery. The monks were about to lose their decrepit hovel." Le Glaute shook his head. "I gave him a way to save his ugly pile of stones..." He shrugged. "...and he took it. Of his own free will." He took another step. "You see, I have discovered a way to reproduce. You could be the first of our kind to give birth. The mother of a new civilization! A vampire civilization that is free to subjugate the puny humans and live as we were meant to live, worshiped as Gods." His enthusiasm was disgusting.

"That is not possible, Phillipe. You know that." Monique took a slight step back. Just a half step with the hope of drawing him in. "Where is your coven? Surely you have other females."

"Where is your adopted coven, child? Are they not missing you?" He was a sly one.

"They do not know I am here." Emotion was her strong suit. She projected as much deceit in her mind as possible. "They consort with humans, Phillipe. I am not so... liberal."

"Ah, then you wish to come home." He moved again.

Monique raised her hands to halt his advancement. Again she called on her gift and plunged hideous loneliness and abandonment into her communication, both verbal and mental. "You left me once. Forgive me if I do not follow like the blind virgin I once was. I was almost destroyed once, delivered into the hands of these devils by one so deceitful I cannot describe. I will not allow anyone that close again, until I am sure…" She let the hanging tear slide down her cheek. It was a practiced art she'd mastered over the years. It worked very well.

"I am so filled with regret, my heart aches for you. Come home with me and I will treasure you always. As I did before…" He held out a hand.

"Where is home, Phillipe?" Monique produced another small tear from the other eye.

"Safe with me. That is your home. It is where you belong." Monique could feel the draw. Phillipe was trying his best to pull her in. She allowed herself to lean in as if it were working.

"But I will have to share you and you will leave me." She wavered on purpose. "You are so strong."

It was Phillipe's turn to be manipulated and Monique poured need and longing into her thoughts. "There is none but you, Monique, my love. I have spent a hundred years hunting vampires. With each conquest, I take what I need to survive. You understand. But my palace is now a thousand miles of secure stone and you shall rule as Queen by my side, mother of my children."

"You destroy your own kind? Our own kind? Phillipe! How do I know you will not destroy me?" Monique controlled the three steps she backed away in feigned fright. "How can I be sure?" She placed a delicate hand to her throat. "My team has ended your experiment. The children are healing. You must hate me. How can I trust you?" He'd made her a vampire, but along with the VMD virus came a gift. She'd learned well to control and manipulate that gift. Now it was time to control and manipulate her maker. Now it was her turn…and paybacks could be such a bitch!

"I am your maker and you will be the mother of my children." He thought he held the carrott that every woman desired; family, children. "I know this trial, had it progressed to its conclusion, it would have been successful. The mixed blood would have allowed any vampire female feeding from it, to be fertile. Think of it Monique! Motherhood? Is that not something every woman cherishes?" Le Glaute was wrapped up in his sales pitch and immersed in convincing Monique of his desires, not particularly paying attention to the individuals who moved silently around him. The backup team remained undercover and unnoticed.

Monique reacted just as Phillipe wanted. She clapped her hands and smiled with pure pleasure. "Oh Phillipe, I had thought it never a possibility for me. Are you sure?" She took a springy step toward the vampire, as if to rush into his arms at any minute.

"Yes. Lady Monique. Your child, wrapped in your arms. Our child. You are the only one of my progeny left and I had thought you long ago lost. Now all is new again, and here you are! You will be my royalty. A new line in our own world. A new beginning. I will have children again."

He was lost in his own planning. It turned Monique's stomach. He had not changed one bit.

"Then I shall go with you, Phillipe. We will be together always." Monique held out a tentative hand staying her revulsion at his touch.

Le Glaute grasped the hand and the two disappeared.

The last thing Percy could see in the coming dawn was the slight twinkle of the high-tech transmitter disguised as a sequin on the back of Monique's fancy jeans.

"She will be fine, Doctor Seizemore. Do not worry." Elizabetta patted the doctor's arm.

"I hope so." He spoke through gritted teeth.

******

Phillipe Le Glaute's underground *palace* was sumptuous to say the least. Monique gazed around his huge cavern, decorated in the style of pre-revolutionary France. At first glance, it could have been mistaken for her home of many years ago.

She continued the game. "Oh, Phillipe! It is just like home. How did you do this?" She danced circles with her arms out, really feeling the ambiance.

Obviously pleased with her reaction, Phillipe pulled her into his arms and covered her lips with his. It was all Monique could do to not vomit in his mouth. She focused on emitting waves of desire and sexual excitation. It was the first time she'd really felt dirty in a man's arms.

Phillipe pulled away. "You have cooled in these passing years."

Monique danced away but continued to smile. "I am over two hundred years old, Phillipe. Things do change, even for a vampire." She giggled enticingly. "But I have learned a lot as well. You will see." She tried to add enticement to her smile. "But first I should like to see my new home. Please? Am I truly the only one?"

"Yes. I have lived a solitary life, planning this," He waved his arms around the huge room, "and planning for the family I shall have. Now that you are here." He took her hand as he had done all those years ago, and kissed the back tenderly.

He was a good actor, but Monique was better. She slid her hand from his grasp and seductively licked the back where he had kissed. It had the effect she desired. Phillipe growled and moved to take her in his arms again. But before he could do so, she danced away toward a connecting tunnel. "Our new home, Daddy?"

"Of course. Forgive me. I am too eager."

He led her down the tunnel she had selected. Gilded sconces provided light and the floor was tiled with lavender and cream squares in delicate patterns. Every few feet, a soft throw rug of complimentary colors softened the echoing footsteps as they moved into a sumptuous bedroom. Monique mentally smacked herself for choosing the tunnel that lead to the bedroom, right off the bat. That was her luck!

The placed dripped of old romanticism. Peach, lavender, old rose and periwinkle fabrics gave her the impression she had just entered her mother's private chambers. Ornately scalloped tables sat, carefully placed around the edges of the room and a large roll-top desk occupied a curtained alcove. The mammoth four-poster bed sported a blue, tan and white comforter with about a dozen pillows crowning the piece. A crystal and white satin chandelier hung directly over the center of the bed. Tall slender faux windows provided soft light from behind frosted glass, illuminating the family crest of the Duc d'Orleans, which had also been intricately carved into the headboard of the bed.

"Oh, Phillipe! This is just like home!" She moved about the room, touching each piece of furniture with loving remembrance. Phillipe was enjoying his tour as much as Monique. She could feel his satisfaction in her comments.

For a few moments, she was transported back to her humanhood, to a sweeter, simpler time, a time when the privilege and wealth of the royalty created a revolution of the masses. "But how do we come and go? I must feed at night."

"Do not worry. I can take us anywhere at any time. I have one more thing to show you." Monique was afraid of this very answer. She was a prisoner here. She could not v-port like Yuri and there was no way out! "Come this way, my love."

Phillipe lead her to an ornate metal door. Withdrawing an

ancient skeleton key from his pocket, he inserted it and turned. A loud clang preceded the opening of the door and Monique squinted at the brilliant sterile light in the rooms beyond. Three people in white lab coats worked at tables upon which sat large monitors and several computer towers. Through a glass partition she could see several rows of beds. Only four were occupied with small bodies connected to IV bags and oxygen masks. All looked to be emaciated and grayish. These were the orphaned kids Faith Morrison had mentioned just before she died!

"Who are they, Phillipe?" Monique peered through the glass at the children.

"No one. Orphans. They will provide what we need. Won't they Doctor Plasovitch? I'd like you to meet Lady Monique. She will be the mother of my future children."

The doctor looked up from his monitor, lowered his glasses to sit on the tip of his nose and peered suspiciously at Monique. "I am Doctor Plasovitch, head of Le Glaute Research and Development. Nice to meet you." He did not smile or extend a hand. He simply replaced his glasses and returned to his work. Apparently he was not impressed with the future mother of Le Glaute's brood.

"That woman is Vanessa VonRatten, nurse. And here we have Stepanovich Luglottsov, statistician and project manager." He pointed to an empty computer station. "We recently lost one of our researchists. I believe you knew her. Faith Morrison?" He did not dwell on the missing Faith whom he, himself had destroyed.

"No. I do not recall a woman by that name." The subterfuge had been practiced. Monique let an emotional confusion accompany her statement.

"Ah, well. Her work was done well, but she was not... indispensible." Monique already knew no one was indispensible in Le Glaute's world. They moved on.

Down another brightly lit hallway was another door. This one was not ancient and locked with a key. A white pad beside the door held numbered keys. Above the door, red glowing letters spelled *exit* in French and Spanish. "And this is something you will never need to use." He pointed to the letters. "But in the event you are here, in this lab and must escape, the code is one-seven-eight-eight. Seventeen eighty-eight. The year I became immortal."

Of course. It had always been about him. Monique smiled. "Can I try it?"

"Yes, yes of course. This is your home now. I want you to

be comfortable."

Monique pressed the buttons and heard a resounding click. The door opened automatically swinging outward. She peered down the black tunnel. "Where does it go?"

"Out. Into the maze that eventually connects to the monastery. But you will not need to go that way. As I said before, I can take you where you need to go." His tone held a, not so well disguised, threat. "You would not want to get lost in the tunnels. They extend for miles. Some go as far as the underground lake. Others end in nothing. The way is not marked. For security reasons, you understand. Our research is a precious commodity. There are many who covet it." He pulled the door closed.

"Does your staff live here then?" Now she was really curious. Why would he allow humans so close? And how would they survive, always underground?

"They have their own way," was all Le Glaute would say. "Come, it is sun-up above. We must rest." His leering smile told Monique what was truly on his mind. "You will share my bed to-night and every night thereafter. I will have no one but you, My Lady." He kissed her hand once again and pulled her through the lab. Monique could not help but notice the angry and disturbed looks of the staff who remained at their computer stations.

"They hate me." She whispered to Phillipe as he closed and locked the door to his palace-beneath the-ground.

"Nonsense, my love. They envy you. That is all." He tried to pull her into his arms once again, but she wiggled free.

"This is our first night together since… well in a long time. I want it to be perfect." She smiled teasingly. "Where can I freshen up?"

"You are a vampire, Monique. You are perfect all of the time." Phillipe was impatient to get her into bed. He remembered the fun he'd had with the females in his coven. And then the delectable morsel, Monique had come along and put all of the others to shame. Just the memory of their first night together made him hard as the rocks he lived within.

Monique had to get out of there. She knew there was no bathroom and Phillipe, being a man, had not built a dressing room. She took his face in both her hands, planting a noisy rough kiss on his lips. "I am also a woman. Give me that at least, Phillipe." She stared into his eyes and focused the strongest desire she could manage. "I want to be with you, as your mate. I want to have your children." She paused, watching for his reaction. "I want to be perfect."

Le Glaute actually sighed. Resigned to allow Monique her primping, he relented. "I will take you to the guest room at the estate. It has everything you need."

She kissed him again. More gently this time. "I won't disappoint you, Your Grace." She threw that little title in as an enhancer… and it worked perfectly. His smile was back and he was putty in her hand. Putty wrapped around some very dangerous other stuff.

He placed his hands over hers. In the blink of an eye they appeared in the guest suite of the estate above Le Glaute's lair. "Do not be long, my love. I am anxious that we reacquaint ourselves in the most intimate of ways. I will be downstairs, speaking with my great-great-great…" He waved a hand. "Great-whatever grandson. He occupies this house now. He also thinks he runs the family business." He kissed her hand. The heavy drapes of the bedroom window had been closed to shut out any sunlight. Had they been expecting her?

As soon as the door closed, Monique depressed the tiny button on the transmitter on her jeans. It signaled the rest of her team that the coast was clear and Yuri could bring them to her.

Soon they were assembled in the guestroom of the Le Glaute estate and Monique was filling them in on what she had learned. That is after soundly kissing Percy and hugging him tightly.

"Somehow the humans can come and go through an exit other than the one that leads to the tunnels. I did not see it, but I spent little time in the lab. Percy, there are four children there. Do we have enough antidote to save them?"

"Yes, we have six vials left. That should be enough." He had yet to let go of his precious vampire. "Are you okay, love? Did he hurt you?"

"No, no of course not. He wants me to have *his* children." Monique looked sideways at Percy.

"He didn't…" Percy wasn't quite sure how to ask if she'd been sexually molested.

Monique squirmed out of his arms. "You want to know if we had sex?" She asked a bit incredulously. "You're jealous, my genius scientist!"

Percy snorted.

Colonel Maddox broke in. "We don't have time for this. You guys can have a green monster dance later. We need to find the exit the staff uses."

Monique gave Percy one last look of amazement and continued on. "It has to be some kind of hidden elevator. That one guy couldn't climb three flights of stairs every day. Maybe Phillipe transports them."

"Phillipe? Now you call him Phillipe?" Percy shook his head.

"Hush, Percy." Susannah moved to stand next to the scientist. "Really. Just leave it for later."

"Where is Le Glaute now?" Devlin had an ear up to the door. "Do you know how many people are in this building?"

"Phillipe is downstairs with the latest grandson in his line. He is human. And as for the rest of the place? Unknown."

Percy whispered to Susannah. "There she goes again. Phillipe, Phillipe, Phillipe. I hate that name."

Natalia and Yuri stood in front of the drapes covering the window. "Ah, Percy, vamp hearing…" Natalia pointed to her ear. "Remember?"

Percy had the decency to blush over his own jealousy. "Right."

A knock sounded at the door. "Lady Monique, the Master has sent me with necessities. May I come in?"

Yuri and Natalia tucked into the closet, shutting the door quietly. Tank dove under the bed. Bear, Percy, Elizabetta, Devlin and Maddox moved into the spacious bathroom. Susannah shimmied herself into the empty wardrobe. Monique unbuttoned the front of her blouse allowing full view of her voluptuous figure.

When Monique answered the door, no one was visible except herself and one other vampire; the man who carried his Master's tray of pampering tools, soaps and lotions. She wasn't sure if the male vampire's eyes ever got to her face, but she didn't care. Her open blouse was the distractor she counted on.

"Ooh la la! This is exactly what I need. Merci beaucoup!" She closed the door slowly as the vampire backed up, eyes still glued to her bodice. "Au revoir."

Monique dropped the tray on the first table available, paying no real attention to its contents. As the other members of the team emerged from their hiding places, Monique queried, "What do we do now. There is at least one vampire servant here in the house. Maybe more. There are humans around. I could hear them when the door was open."

"We need to isolate Le Glaute. Can you bring him back up here?" Maddox asked.

"I believe he will respond to my call. Then what? He is so strong." Monique was wringing her hands.

Percy was inspecting a coat of arms and an ancient broadsword that hung beneath it. He was trying his best to ignore the fact that his girlfriend had been in the company of her sire for less than an hour and already she was calling him by his first name and he was sending her special little trays of goodies.

"Then we work together to dispatch him." Susannah made another heave-ho motion. "Find the entrance to the lab. Cure the kids, then destroy everything in sight." She struck a model pose. "Easy peasy."

"And what will the other people and vamps do around here while we're stepping on Superman's cape and feeding him kryptonite?" Devlin sat on the edge of the gorgeous four-poster bed.

"Good point, Uncle Rob." Susannah joined her Uncle on the bed. She smoothed her hand across the painted silk. "This is nice."

"Good ques…" The guest bedroom door flew off its hinges, splintering wood everywhere.

"You betrayed me, you little slut."

"Oh, hello Phil-li-pe." Percy's drew out the man's first name. His sneer was ugly. His lips curled over his teeth and he actually growled a touch. It came out more like a kitten's mew, but Monique thought it was a lion's roar. He *was* jealous! She'd never belonged to anyone before, and this feeling was so wonderful. Her heart was full to exploding, which would just be fine with her, since it would grow back.

On the other hand, Phillipe had only eyes for Monique, the one who betrayed him. The woman who had lied so convincingly. The woman he loved and had built a home for?

No… wait… he didn't really love her. He didn't even know she'd escaped the fire in the seventeen hundreds. The fire that, he thought, destroyed everything including his coven. If he truly thought about it, he could have any woman he wanted for the mother of his precious children. He didn't even care for Monique that much. But she was convenient. She was his by right! A growl issued from deep in his gut.

"Phillipe, stay where you are. Do not come any closer or I will…" The malevolence in his eyes halted her speech. Tank and Bear moved to interviene.

"I will kill you, you heartless bitch. I will tear that beautiful body from limb to limb and lay the pieces in the sun to turn to ash." He moved toward her in slow paced steps, totally unaware, or uncaring, that others watched and could possibly stop him.

He should have v-ported.

It would have worked out better for him…

Percy grabbed for the broadsword that hung on the wall. Had he not been so hyped on adrenaline, he could never have even lifted the sword, let alone swing it. But swing it he did. The weight of the sword added a momentum of its own to Percy's anger and jealousy. It slipped through Le Glaute's neck like a hot knife through butter, draging the slight scientist with it.

Phillipe Le Glaute, Duc d'Orleans, Comte d' LeEgalité and Master Vampire, added another title to his string of such. It was Dead Man. His head landed in the middle of the tray he'd sent up to Monique, with a dull thud. Soaps and lotions scattered. His body fell to the ground in a heap that soon turned to a large pile of ash on the ornate rug.

"I now join the ranks of Bill Cosby and other notable comedians." Susannah smirked, "Who's gonna clean up that mess?"

Percy still held one end of the massive sword. It was almost as long as he was tall and carried the Le Glaute crest as well. Now it was all he could do to support the thing. It dripped with the vampire's blood and the point stuck in the carpet where it landed. He looked helplessly at Susannah. "Cosby said that?"

"Yep! He was Noah, talking to God about the Arc. Zuppa, zuppa, zuppa, ding! Noah…" Her comedic recitation was interrupted by footsteps in the hall. *Many* foot steps in the hall.

"Here they come. Are we ready?" Everyone pulled guns from beneath clothing and took what cover they could for a somewhat large group in one rather small bedroom.

Percy stood alone in the middle of the doorway. "Ah people? A little help here?" His back was to the wall and he had no room to drop the sword without some part of it landing on him.

First a human appeared in the doorway. His facial features were patrician all the way, like Le Glaute's. But he was short and

372

stout. One hand still held the pen he'd been writing with. "What the hell?" He almost stepped in his ancestor's ashes. How anyone could do that was beyond Monique. Phillipe was not a small man, headless or not, and his pile of ashes was thick. She stepped forward as people piled up behind the current head of the Le Glaute family.

"Phillipe Le Glaute is destroyed." She stood in full view, feet apart and hands on her hips. She looked like a fabulously beautiful GI Joe, only in sparkly jeans and a satin blouse… with make-up… and a great manicure… and heels to die for! "My team terminated his evil plans."

The rotund man in the doorway stopped, glanced around the room at various barrels aimed his way and huffed. "Oh thank God. That devil finally got his due. Which one of you do I thank?"

Yuri v-ported to Percy's side, took the sword and replaced it in the rack on the wall. Blood and all. Then he nudged the scientist forward.

"You?"

"Ah I guess. But it was a team effort." He really didn't want to cop to killing this dandy's relative, vampire or not.

"Then let me shake your hand. My name is Arthur Le Glaute, I am embarrassed to say. This monster has been running the family business for as long as I can remember. Running it into the ground I might add. Now I am free and can actually fix some of the harm he has done in the last few years. Thank you from the bottom of my heart." He continued to shake Percy's hand.

"Yeah, sure. I guess." It was not the reception Percy thought the team's handiwork would get. "What about those folks?" Percy pointed around Arthur at the group gathered behind him.

"There is another vampire among you." Natalia hissed.

"Yes, yes. I know. He was head of his…" Arthur pointed to the ash pile, "security, but he will not be a problem. We came to an agreement when this hideous drug development began. Who are you people anyway?"

"We seem to get that question a lot these days." Devlin stepped forward, careful to avoid the remains on the floor. "We're a counter-terrorist team from the States. Your… what was he to you again?"

"Times-five, great grandfather. Doesn't matter." Arthur shook his head. "All that matters to me is that he is permanently dead. He is, isn't he?" Arthur pointed to the ashes. "He can't, like, come back or anything."

"Your times-five, great grandfather will not be coming back to haunt you. He is destroyed, like the woman said." Devlin shook hands with Arthur, but ended the shaking quickly as opposed to standing there holding the slightly effeminate hand.

Monique broke in, "There are children below who need medical attention. If you are not part of this problem, be part of the solution. Show us how to get to the lab."

"I'll have Bernie show you. They know him. If Regeridid is there, you will have a fight on your hands."

"Regeridid? I did not meet him." Monique thought she'd met all of the lab rats.

"Doctor Plasovitch. That's what he calls himself. He's a despicable human being. At least I think he's still human. He worked to curry favor to be turned into…" Arthur pointed to the remains. "I haven't seen him in a month. I don't go down there. Can't stand to see the things they do."

"Ah yes, the doctor with glasses." Monique had met the man after all."

"Well, let's go take out the trash. Arthur, if you please…" Devlin offered Arthur Le Glaute the lead.

"My pleasure." He headed down the stairs. "It's in the kitchen cellar. An elevator at the back of the commercial freezer. No one would look inside a freezer. I saw it only by chance when workmen were installing a new heating coil."

As the team filed into the elevator, Colonel Maddox surveyed the keypad. "We'll need Miller to figure this out."

"Let me." Monique moved in front of the Colonel. "Seventeen eighty-eight. The year the Duke was turned. He told me so I would have a reference to remember."

The doors closed and the elevator lurched into motion. Within minutes, a bell rang and the doors slid open to reveal a view of the lab and three heads that swiveled in sync. Monique exited the elevator first.

"Where is…" Doctor Plasovitch was on his feet immediately, reaching for a gun stashed beneath his desk.

"I wouldn't do that if I were you." Maddox aimed his nineteen-eleven at the doctor. "I'm probably a better shot. But if somehow you get me first, my team here has instructions to eat all of you."

The woman at the far table sat up, her eyes were as large as saucers. Doctor Plasovitch sat back in his chair. "What do you want? Where is Le Glaute? Why is this bitch with you?"

"TPS. Destroyed and she," Percy motioned to Monique, "is not a bitch."

Natalia, Elizabetta and Yuri took care of rounding up the humans and securing them. Devlin, Tank and Bear went in search of the drug, preferring the human touch to the out-of-control vampire craziness. That left Percy, Monique and Susannah to care for the children and administer the antidote.

Luckily, Devlin found the hazmat furnace as well, and the remaining TPS was disposed of very efficiently via fire.

"So what will we do with the good doctor and his nasty little staff? If they leave here, they can always make more TPS. Susannah was whispering to her sister vampire."

"I do not know. Possibly Natalia can pull this information from their heads…" Monique inserted a syringe into the free port and began inserting the antidote. "How long have these children been here?"

Susannah picked up a clipboard that hung from the foot of the beds. "This one says two weeks! Oh my God. No wonder they look like death warmed over."

Percy took the clipboard from the bed of the child he was treating. "Two weeks, four days. He should be dead. We need Natalia!"

Monique queried her coven mistress through psyche-speech. Before Percy knew what had happened, Natalia came through the door.

"Mrs. M., these kids are really bad off. Can you do that thing you do, and see if the antidote is even having any effect?"

"Of course." Natalia moved to stand next to the child whose record he'd just read. She placed a hand on the child's forehead. "This one is almost completely infected and too weak to fight. The antidote is moving, but it is not enough." She withdrew her hand. "The TPS test has failed and the child is dying."

"More antidote. We need more antidote!"

Natalia stayed the doctor's hands. "This one will die, Doctor. Let it be. There are times when you must let go." She looked sadly at the shrunken child who barely breathed. "He is no longer human. He is not vampire. We cannot change what the drug has done to him." She bent and placed a chaste kiss on the boy's forehead as he took his last shallow, rattling breath. "You have three others to look after." She turned the doctor away. "They may live, if we are in time."

Percy set to work, more strongly committed than before to saving the three remaining patients.

Susannah sat next to a young girl. Her dark hair lay limply about her shoulders and face. Her lips showed a bluish tinge. Susannah took her hand and focused, trying to reach the little girl's mind to lend support and strength. The TPS was there, but slowly loosing its battle and not the least interested in challenging Susannah's presence. It fought for its life. Susannah fought for the life of Simza. She'd found the name on her chart and now she called to the girl, using that name. "Come on Simza, fight! You can do this. I am here. I am calling you, telling you to reach out to me. I will lend you strength and together we can conquer this thing in you." Susannah rocked back and forth, holding Simza's hand and whispering to the child.

It seemed like an entire day, but in reality it was only about two hours when Percy pulled Susannah away. "Her vitals are improving by leaps and bounds. I believe she is out of trouble."

Susannah startled at the doctor's touch. "Did I fall asleep?" She felt groggy and bone tired.

"No. You've been talking for over two hours. Whatever you did, saved this girl's life." He patted her on the back. "Look." He pointed to the bed by the wall. "Monique follows your example. She is somehow healing that little one." Percy was proud to busting, watching his pretty little French girl rocking and whispering. Her eyes were squeezed tightly shut and frown lines had appeared above her nose between her eyes.

"Percy, I've never seen Monique concentrate so hard on anything." Susannah was astonished. Natalia sat next to the last child, two beds down. She too held the boy's hand and spoke quietly to him.

Percy shook his head in wonderment. "We definitely need people like you in hospitals. Imagine what modern medicine and vampire healing could do together!" Percy's stomach growled loudly. It was close to noon now, and the long, exciting night was taking it toll on the human. "Sorry." He patted his stomach. "I'm only human."

Susannah took a close look at the doctor for the first time since he'd arrived. Deep lines showed around his mouth and the crows feet behind his glasses had become canyons, emptying into dry bloodshot eyes. "When was the last time you ate something?"

Percy was looking at the vital sign machine above Simza's bed. "Huh?"

"Food Percy. When was the last time you had some?" Susannah didn't pay much attention to human food anymore, since she didn't eat.

"I don't know." He sat down on Simza's bed and wiped a hand across his face. "I don't even know what day it is. Or what time."

"Well, you better start paying a little attention to that. Humans don't run on empty. You're going to dry up and blow away. Then what will we do with Monique?" Susannah chuckled. "She'll de despondent. Cry a river and ruin all of her clothes! Be right back."

Susannah ran into the adjoining lab where a small refrigerator stood on a table in one corner. "Please God, let there be real food in here." Her prayers were answered. Inside the fridge were three carefully wrapped sandwiches. One ham, one beef and one tuna. She opted for the tuna. It was the closest to vegetarian she could get in a pinch.

"Here," she held the sandwich out to Percy. "Eat."

He took what was offered and proceeded to stuff half of the thing in his mouth, hardly chewing before he swallowed in a gulp. "I hate tuna."

"Eat. You need food and if it has to be in the form of stinky fish surrounded by bread, then so be it."

Monique roused from her healing bond and sat against the back of her chair watching the exchange between her vampire sister and her man. She'd had no idea she could heal until she tried it. But now her efforts, though successful, had tired her to the point that her eyelids drooped and she slumped in her chair. The little boy who lay in the bed beside her, breathed normally and his color had returned to a rosy pink, normal for a human.

Natalia was still deep in the third child's mind speaking tender words in some foreign tongue. These were Gypsy children. How did they end up here, in Spain, in a test lab? Susannah knew the human slave market was a concrete thing but... children for experimentation? That was horrendous and evil. But then so was this Doctor Plasovitch, and Phillipe Le Glaute. She yawned, finally realizing how her own body and mind were. "Tell ya what, Doc.

Why don't you and Frenchy hit the sack for some shut eye and I'll hold down the fort until everyone gets back."

She pulled Percy up by his arm and guided him to the bed next to where Monique sat, her head almost hanging in her lap. He'd finished the tuna sandwich, much to his own disgust, but much to the delight of his empty stomach. "Down you go, buddy." She lifted his feet up on to the bed and lowered him down onto the pillow."

Then Susannah turned to Monique. "Your turn, Frenchy." She pointed to the empty space next to Percy. It would be big enough for both of them. She helped her sister vamp into bed and covered the couple with a blanket. "Nighty-night." She then turned the lights down in the lab and went to join Natalia. "Need any help?"

"No, but it is a kind thought. This one will make it. She was very weak, like them all, but lacked the will to live." Natalia sat up straight and stretched. "I hope that is changed. She has no family and was raised in a terrible place. Little food. No care. What will become of these children, Susannah?"

A commotion in the lab drew their attention. It was Arthur and three other humans. Susannah ducked around the glass wall to see what they needed. "Mr. Le Glaute, what can I do for you?"

"This is ended? I feared to come here, but my wife…" He pointed to the estate above, "she heard there were children here that were… ill." It was obvious who wore the Le Glaute pants in the family.

"That is true, Sir, but they are healing nicely. We have administered an antidote to the drug they were given. Unfortunately, one did not make it. A youth. I am sorry, but he was too far gone." Susannah shifted uneasily.

"My wife… she cannot have children and has ever been a force in the community for helping the young. This news will be devastating." He began to wring his hands. "To be a part of this debacle, this killing of innocent children. It will break her heart. She will blame me, of course." He looked beseechingly at Susannah. "I could do naught but what Phillipe said. I was not strong enough…"

An idea just popped into Susannah's head from out of the blue. Arthur's wife could not have children. They had three kids the team did not know what to do with. Three that needed a good home and a loving family. "Sir, if I may be so bold, would your wife be interested in making up for…" she didn't want to lay more guilt on the poor man, but it might work out to everyone's benefit! "…all of this? Possibly taking on the responsibility of the kids who were made sick?" She gave it a minute to sink in. "There are two boys and one very frightened girl. Cute as the dickens."

"Really? You would give them to us after what my family has done?" His face lit with joy. Obviously his wife was not the only one missing children in her life. "How… I mean can this be possible?"

Susannah patted the gentleman on the back. "We can do just about everything. Wait and see."

"These men are here to cleanse this place before I have the elevator removed and this place shut forever. I will go above now and broach the subject. I believe it will not take much broaching." There was a definite spring in his step and a twinkle in his eye.

"You just made that man very happy, pumpkin." Susannah's father whispered in her ear.

She jumped. "Where'd you come from? Holy cow, Dad, don't sneak up on me like that." Susannah hugged her father. "Not in here, anyway." She held him just a little longer than normal.

He let her.

"Report, kiddo. How are they doing?" He nodded toward the dimmed room through the glass.

"Good. We, ah, lost one but the other three are responding well and all are out of trouble. I think I may have found a home for them." She smiled up at her dad. "A really nice home, as a matter of fact."

"I see our love birds are nesting." Maddox chuckled. "About time Percy passed out and got some rest. Best to do it snuggled up to his lady."

"What about the TPS and CE? Did we get it all this time? No little vials sneaking off in the hands of some scheming woman?"

"Ya know, the amazing thing about the doctor? He kept impeccable records. So yes, we got it all, and it is now so much ash and some smoke. Harmless. Gone. Done. We also burned the records and hard drives." He held out a skeleton key. "Last thing to do before we bug out, is clean up Le Glaute's lair and play some mind games."

"The doc and his staff? Natalia?" Susannah had already figured that out.

"Yep. Almost done." Now it was Maddox's turn to yawn. "Long day, and night… and day." He tossled Susannah's hair, like he did when she was a child. "Come on, kiddo." They headed for Le Glaute's lair to see what they could find.

Chapter 28

Somehow, destiny comes into play.
These children end up with you and you end up with them.
It's something quite magical.

*Nicole Kidman, Australian Actress, Mother*
*Sydney, Australia 1998*

Monique and Percy stood on the tarmac in Pamplona, hand in hand. The plane was ready to leave but they waited for some special promised surprise. No one had any idea what it might be, but they remained, waiting patiently.

Their equipment, baggage and personal items were already stowed on board and Casey was busy pre-flighting the Gulfstream.

"What do you think this can be? Arthur said he would be here at seven thirty." Percy wan't patient. He was antsy to be on his way and nervous about the flight. Would he have days of illness, or would Monique be able to still the motion sickness he always suffered from? That could be one more perk of their budding relationship!

A limousine entered the private airport parking area and five people burst from the car, three children and two adults. The children each ran with a sheet of paper clutched in their hands. Monique recognized Arthur attempting to keep up and his wife laughing at the circus.

Simza tore across the pavement and hurled herself into Monique's arms. "I have it, Monique. I have it!" She opened the crumpled page for all to see. "I am family! I have a mother and father!"

Monique hugged her close. "I am so happy for you, Simza. I will always remember your smile and the happiness in your heart."

Simza gave her a strange look. "Of course you will. Because I will write to you every day. When I learn to write! Which will be soon, because mother..." The little girl giggled at the use of the word. "... says I must go to school."

Arthur had finally caught up to his three children and was

panting. "This is an ecstatic event for us, but challenging as well." He tried to catch his breath before his wife joined them.

"I understand." Maddox shook the man's hand. "I raised an energetic one myself." The two men chuckled; one at memories, the other at what was to come.

"We only wanted the children to show you they have officially become part of our family." Allegra, Arthur's wife, smiled enthusiastically, as she took Simza from Monique's arms. "It will be a full family and lots of work, but our hearts are in the right place." She kissed Simza who returned the kiss just as readily.

Elizabetta and Susannah congratulated their small patients with hugs and encouraging words. As the new family returned to their car, the Vamp Squad boarded their transportation.

Monique paused at the base of the stairway. "Colonel? May I have a moment."

"Sure. What's up?" He was ready to be gone and headed home.

Elizabetta silently joined them. "What is it, my daughter?"

"When we return I will need to leave." There was an aching sadness in her eyes. "I must leave the coven and the Vamp Squad." She bowed her head and spoke softly.

"For heaven sakes, why, dear?" Elizabetta took her daughter into her arms. "Whatever has happened?"

"I broke the pact. I have consorted with a human and now must leave. I will go with Percy. Back to his city. He will take up his work again, and I will… survive."

"You're kidding, right?" Susannah flew down the steps. Thank God for vamp hearing! "You can't just up and leave. You're family! Daaaad?"

"I must Susannah. I agreed to the rules and now I have broken my word. I cannot stay." Monique's sadness flowed across both the humans and vampires.

Elizabetta looked at Maddox over Monique's head as she comforted her daughter. "Frank?"

"What? Frank what, Elizabetta? Why is it always, Frank? Like I have all the answers to the world's problems." He shifted from one foot to another.

Casey shouted out the door above them. "Flight plan's filed. Let's move it!"

Susannah stood in the way, blocking the steps. "Daaaad?"

She put a little mental nudge into the word. It wasn't fair, but nothing ever is, when it comes to family and love.

Elizabetta released Monique. "Fraaaaannnnk?" It was a playful mockery of her youngest coven daughter, but obviously Monique needed closure right then and there. She could not allow this overwhelming sadness to torture Monique any longer. "We will figure this out, my dear. Do not worry your head over the choice between love and family." She smoothed Monique's hair.

"Oh for heaven sakes! First Natalia and Yuri. Then Jackie and Miller? Now Monique and her doctor? What am I commanding? The Love Boat? How am I going to justify adding a family wing to the facility?"

"You'll think of something. You always do!" Susannah pulled Monique up the stairs. "Last one in's a rotten egg."

Elizabetta mounted the stairs with a motherly smile.

Frank stood at the bottom.

Alone.

"Guess that'd be me." He took the stairs two at a time and pulled the hatch closed behind him. "Home we go." He yelled to Casey through the open cockpit door.

Home was beginning to take on a new meaning all of its own.

Frank chuckled to himself. It wasn't such a bad thing.

He buckled in and closed his eyes.

Home.

He didn't have to count heads or check seats. He knew Mr. and Mrs. M would be holding hands and making kissy faces at each other. His daughter would already be surfing the Internet, quacking or tweeting. Devlin would have his leg up and already be snoring. Tank and Bear would have the chess set out and starting a game that would last all the way across the pond. Elizabetta would be wrapped in a comforter relaxing into one of the overstuffed seats for the long ride back.

And Monique… she would be actively breaking the pact she was so worried about, cuddled up to her geeky scientist who had saved the children with his brilliant research. He could already feel Monique's happiness radiating throughout the cabin.

Maddox picked up the cabin phone. "Casey, second star to the left and on until morning."

Casey chuckled. "Right, Frank. And that's second star to the right."

"That's Colonel to you, Captain." Maddox replaced the phone in the cradle and smiled as he closed his eyes. A family wing at Olney Farm? Hummm...

# Connect with
# Miriam Matthews

Each of the first five books in this series are about the Squad's vampires and how they came to be part of Colonel Maddox's group of top-secret, anti-terrorist operatives for the US government. Each book is also a romance! Book 1 has been out since 2015 and is all about Natalia and the first VS mission. Book 4 is in development and due out in 2018. It is story of how MorningStar became a Skinwalker (Native American word for vampire), and what happens when she returns to her tribe to investigate a string of murders. Book 5 will tell the story of the Coven's Mistress, Elizabetta Zoeltel who is a very unusual vampire… and daughter of the notorious Dracula!

<u>The Vamp Squad Series</u>

Book 1: Strange Beginnings
Book 2: The Death of Innocence
Book 3: The Secrets of San Leyre
Book 4: A Dark Deception
Book 5: The Roots of Betrayal

You can always catch up with Miriam, or send your comments to:
miriamthewriter@gmail.com.

See what's new in Miriam's life on her website at:
www.miriammatthews.com

You can also follow Miriam on Facebook and keep up with her news, new books and trivia questions at:
www.facebook.com/miriam.matthews.773